S0-ACO-996

ACKNOWLEDGMENTS

My gratitude to my reading committee: Al McMillan, Alex Thorliefson, Roger Harris, & Marilyn Pitts.

Many thinks to the wonderful members of South Coast Writer's, past and present, for all your help and nurturing.

Many thanks to my children—Debra, Michael and Kimberly, who have never failed to encourage me.

A special thanks to my agent, Mike Hamilburg for keeping the faith.

"It can be said that all vile acts are done to satisfy hunger."

Maxim Gorky, 1906

Prologue

The crisp October weather turned damp. Bone-chilling damp.

He stood in the shadows outside the beach house unconscious of the cold. All he felt was the hot agony that had begun to overwhelm him. He had no business getting involved so close to home, but the torment was more than he could bear. He had to find relief. At first he'd only been nauseated, which wasn't so bad, but then he'd turned feverish—every fiber of his body throbbing with a searing pain.

It was after midnight and the party going on in the beach house was loud, the music pulsing and erotic. He stood in the shadows. Listening. Waiting. Knowing it wouldn't be long before someone wandered out, heading for home. Aromas drifting from the house tortured his senses. A half-dozen brands of beer. Cigarettes. Marijuana. Perfumes. Pizza. Cookies. He breathed in the scents and waited, fighting down the agony.

He smelled the two young women before he saw them—a ripe sweet scent to their young flesh—mineral rich blood pulsing through their veins. Dos Exis beer steamed on their breath. Both wore Estee Lauder's Knowing perfume.

The first of the two girls to come out of the beach house was tall and fair-skinned with thick blond hair that hung down her back like shimmering metallic threads. She was eighteen or nineteen and walked gracefully, heading down the beach toward the peninsula. He moved to follow, but before he did, the second girl, a year or so younger than the first, came jogging out of the house, calling after the first one to wait for her. He could smell her plastic earrings, the gold heart at her throat, and her canvas tennis shoes. Sisters! He could tell by the aroma of their skin. A sameness. If he were clever, he could have them both! As he watched the two of them, the throbbing ache in his body grew stronger, the agony so intense that in some perverse way it became a sensation of pleasure.

A bank of fog hung just offshore, like a smear of white paste. Slowly, it moved inland, obliterating the stars. Good, he thought, nature had contrived to conceal him. He slipped out of the shadows and moved silently along the beach behind the girls. He would have the older of the two first. From his shirt pocket he took a thin sharp blade and felt its edge— honed to a whisper. He sucked in his breath sharply, anticipating the sweet scent of the girl's flesh and the coppery spice of her blood.

He could smell her close by now, perhaps lost in the fog which had grown so dense it seemed impenetrable. He sucked in the aroma of her, an exotic perfume that made his ears roar and his heart flail like a wild animal inside his chest.

When the girl turned and saw him her deer-brown eyes went wide, her delicate mouth open in astonishment. Then her astonishment turned to fear. He could smell it—hot and sweet and sharply sour, like a mixture of vinegar and honey—the scent streaming from her pores like steam.

"I'm sorry," he said, blinking back hot tears as he reached toward her. "Please, forgive me."

DOROTHY McMILLAN

VILE ACTS

PINNACLE BOOKS
WINDSOR PUBLISHING CORP.

Dedicated to Alray—for a million reasons.

PINNACLE BOOKS are published by

Windsor Publishing Corp.
850 Third Ave
New York, NY 10022

The P logo Reg U.S. Pat & TM off. Pinnacle is a trademark of Windsor Publishing Corp.

First Printing: February, 1995

Printed in the United States of America

Chapter One

Detective Ted Bearbower stood in the aisle of the Williams-Sonoma, deeply engrossed in reading a new pasta recipe. When his pager beeped he jumped, startled by its intensity.

"Damn," he muttered and replaced the cookbook on the shelf. He started to make his way out of the store, stopped for a second to inspect a bottle of spaghetti sauce, then picked up a small earthenware pot containing pasta spices. His stomach grumbled. He was hungry. He was always hungry. He woke up hungry and went to bed hungry. When he slept he dreamt about food.

Ted Bearbower, affectionately dubbed Teddy Bear by his coworkers—a name that made him cringe—was a gourmand. A hundred years ago they would have called him a glutton. He liked the word gourmand better. A person who delights in eating well and heartily. Ted looked like a gourmand. Although, at six-feet five-inches, his two-hundred-sixty-pounds were evenly distributed so that he appeared more immense than obese. When his wife,

Sylvia, was alive he had managed to keep his weight around two-thirty. Two years ago, after twenty years of marriage, she had left him to fend for himself, and he found it hard to forgive her. She had been the one who ate sensibly, didn't smoke, jogged every morning, took vitamins, and had a regular checkup at least once a year. She was supposed to outlive him, but one morning she had a massive stroke and never woke up. He missed her terribly. The pain of it never went away, no matter how much he ate.

He put down the pot of pasta spices and made his way out of the store. On the way to the telephone, his pager beeped again. It sounded impatient. He fumbled in his pocket for two dimes.

"Bearbower here," he growled into the phone when someone answered.

"Yes sir," the man on the other end said. "Just a minute."

Ted drummed his fingers against the phone, waiting for the dispatcher to put through his call.

"Ted?" It was the voice of his new partner, Steve Locke. Locke, although still wet behind the ears, was going to be one hell of a detective someday. He'd bet on that. Having a partner only twenty-six years old had seemed like a mountain of trouble at first. But Locke turned out to be remarkably intuitive, and dedicated. Besides, being around someone so young kept his own juices flowing. He had to keep moving just to keep up.

"That girl—the one they found in the ocean— she's finally conscious."

"Will they let us talk to her?" Ted asked.

"Yeah. But for only a few minutes. She's in pretty bad shape."

"Is she going to make it?"

"The doctors are guarded, but optimistic."

"Glad to hear that," Ted said, genuinely pleased.

"Shall I meet you there?"

Ted looked at his watch. The damn thing had stopped again. "Shit!" He hissed, shaking his wrist.

"What's that?"

"Seiko. My Seiko is having fits again. What the hell time is it?" Ted was one of those people who couldn't wear any kind of watch. It would run for a month or so and then stop and start until it drove him crazy and he went out and bought another, only to have it do the same thing. It had been that way since he was a kid. His mother had told him he had too much static electricity in his body. Or was it magnetism? Anyway, the result was a drawer full of watches—cheap ones, expensive, it made no difference.

"It's six-thirty," Locke told him.

"Okay, fifteen minutes. I'm at South Coast Plaza."

"I'll wait outside the girl's room."

"Locke?"

"Yeah?"

"You had dinner yet?"

"No."

"When we're through with the girl, I'll treat you to some poretti crepes over at Gianni's in Crystal Court," Ted offered. As much as he loved to eat, he hated eating alone.

"Teddy Bear," Locke chuckled. *"To watch you eat is a terrible experience!"*

"Fifteen minutes," Ted said and hung up.

The girl, eighteen-year-old Megg Duff, looked as white as the hospital sheet that was pulled up around her shoulders. Her throat had been bandaged with a puffy pad of gauze. Her dark brown eyes had an odd glaze to them and her cheeks glowed with fever. Her left wrist was attached to a needle and tube that led to a plastic bag of blood plasma, a bottle of Ringer's solution and an antibiotic, all hanging on a metal pole.

Ted pulled a straight-backed hospital chair beside the bed and sat down. "Megg, I'm Detective Bearbower. We need to find out who did this to you. Do you remember anything that happened last night?" he asked gently.

The girl nodded. "Some."

"Is it difficult to talk?"

The girl nodded again and grimaced.

"I'm sorry," Ted said, feeling her pain. "But we need to find out everything we can. We want to stop whoever did this from doing it again." He started to say that they wanted to help find her sister, Lucy, but he didn't know if she'd been told yet, about her being missing. "You were in the ocean. Do you remember that part?"

She shook her head no.

"You're lucky," his partner, Locke, chimed in. "An off-duty fireman was out fishing in all that fog. When he pulled in his gear, he snagged you on his line. His paramedic training saved your life."

The girl gave a weak smile. "I'll have to thank him."

"Do you remember where you'd gone that evening?" Ted asked.

"Party. At Linda's house." The girl's voice was raspy. "I was mad 'cause my baby sister had to tag along."

"That would be Linda Harmon's house?" The girl's mother had already given them as many details as she could, considering her hysterical state.

The girl nodded.

"And you were on your way home from the party when you were attacked?"

The girl nodded again.

"Was it a man?"

"Yes."

"What did he look like?"

"Dark."

"Dark hair?" Ted asked. "Or skin,"

"No, his eyes," the girl whispered. "Dark blue eyes. I couldn't see too well . . . the fog and all. At first I thought I knew him . . . but then, well . . . he looked . . . acted so strange."

"What do you mean by strange?" Locke asked.

"I don't know. His face. . . . he . . . was crying." The girl sighed and closed her eyes.

"Megg . . . do you remember what he did to you?" Ted knew from the medical report that the girl had not been raped. Her throat had been neatly cut, across the carotid artery on the left side. She'd almost bled to death.

She opened her eyes and gave a puzzled look, then shook her head no.

"Nothing?" he asked gently. She's blocking it out, he thought. Things too painful to remember were stored away in the attic portion of the brain. Good for the victim, bad for the investigation.

"Besides my throat . . . the doctor said . . . he did this." She pulled the sheet down revealing her hospital gown and slid the gown off her right shoulder to reveal another bandage. "The doctor said he took a big bite out of me." She closed her eyes again. "It hurts." Then her breathing became slow and rhythmic. She had drifted off to sleep. It was obvious they weren't going to get anything more from her, at least until she was over the worst of the trauma—if ever. All they had was the information forensics came up with.

Ted felt a surge of relief as soon as they were outside. He hated hospitals—the smell of them, the unfamiliar sounds. They stood beside the hospital's tinted glass doors where Locke lit up a cigarette and took a deep drag. The sea breeze swirled the smoke away in little curls. It was colder than usual for Southern California in October. Quite often October was the hottest month of the year. Ted snugged his collar around his neck, wishing he had his windbreaker instead of his suit jacket.

"Christ! This guy's the big bad wolf!" Locke said. "I mean, shit! He took a *bite* out of her." Locke's eyes, the color of rainwater, darted, blinked, closed, opened again. He took another drag and held the smoke in his lungs for a moment before exhaling. He looked like the typical young Newport Beach guy with sun-bleached hair and freckled nose. His teeth were slightly crooked in front.

"No sign of the younger sister?" Ted finally asked.

"Nothing."

"She'll probably come up as a floater before long. That is, if he dumped her in the ocean the way he did the older girl."

Locke fiddled with his cigarette and narrowed his eyes. Ted thought he saw questions forming behind the eyes. He turned away, toward the glass doors, and was startled to see his own oversized form reflected in them. Because of his weight and his fifty-two years, Ted was always taken by surprise when women openly flirted with him, as they often did. His thick blond hair was streaked with silver, and his eyes were a penetrating blue that seemed to deepen over the years rather than fade. He'd been with the Newport Beach Police Department twenty-six years. He'd refused to apply for the rank of Captain. He liked being a regular detective, even if he was the oldest one on the force. He liked solving mysteries. He was pretty much a loner, except for his partner, and the department let him have his way when it came to working on a case. They trusted him. He liked that. The captain, however, nagged him continually about his weight and gave him an ultimatum that if he went over two-seventy, they'd fire him. Once a week he stepped on the bathroom scales, holding his breath, praying he was still under the line. He quickly looked away from his reflection. He felt roaring hungry, as usual. And, as usual, he would not restrain his pleasure of eating. How could you cope with life's pain if you didn't indulge in life's delectations?

Ted forced his mind back on the case. "Let's get back to the office and run this through the computer. See if there's been anything else like it in the county lately."

Locke took another drag on the cigarette and blew the smoke out through his nose. "Teddy Bear?" He said, using the nickname he knew Ted hated. He dropped his cigarette on the cement and crushed it with the heel of his shoe. "What do you think he did with it?"

"Did with what?" Ted asked, cringing as usual at the sound of his nickname.

"With the chunk of flesh he tore out with his teeth."

Ted looked at Locke—a bright-eyed guy just beginning to see the horrors of the job. "You don't want to know," he said. "You really don't want to know."

A sharp sea breeze curled around the edges of the house like the salty breath of an old sailor. Beyond the house stretched the green of the Pacific Ocean, its sandy beach glittered with golden strands of kelp. A low tide swept a foaming serpentine of emerald water against the seaweed.

Elizabeth Rosemond stood in the alley behind the house, peering up at the two-story structure, wondering what it was about the place that made her feel so strange. It was old, but rather beautiful, its weathered siding gone blue-gray from so many years of sun and brine—Cape Cod in California—a quaintly feminine style of architecture, much larger than its New England predecessor. Its window-eyes seemed to shine with a peculiar intelligence as it peered back at her.

Elizabeth gripped her husband's hand. "Andy, it's like that Winslow Homer painting, isn't it?" she said. " 'Houses on a Hill' I think it's called."

Andy shrugged. "Leave it to an artist to look at it that way. To me, it's just an old beat-up beach house. But then, I'm only a writer."

"And a writer should be thinking of better ways to describe it," she teased him. Sobering, she said, "I still can't grasp it. The idea that Aunt Mary left this place to me. I hadn't seen her in ages. Why do you suppose she left it to me?"

"Honey, for crying out loud, don't look a gift horse in the—"

"Come on Andy . . . another cliche?"

"Look, Lizzy, we should be grateful for the windfall. Even if the inheritance taxes did take most of our savings. This place is worth a fortune."

"Sure, after about fifty thousand in repairs." The wind ruffled Elizabeth's long ashen hair and sent a chill down her back. "An old house, and a defunct pharmaceutical company. No cash. Wouldn't you know." She shivered. "And it's damp here," she said.

"It's always damp at the beach."

"And the house . . . I'd swear it's looking at us." She looked up at the windows again.

"Sure. It's wondering what kind of people are going to inhabit its rooms."

"What kind of people, indeed." She shook her head. "The perfect examples of how not to succeed." She sighed and tugged on her bangs. She'd cut the damn things crooked again. For some reason she could never get them straight. They always meandered in the wrong direction, just like her life. She and Andy were bickering again. About nothing of real importance. That seemed to happen more and more lately. She loved him dearly, but he could be a real pain in the ass at times. Or, maybe, it was the other way around. She didn't know any more, what with both their careers in the toilet.

Andy put his arm around her and pulled her close. She looked up at him and saw him smiling. His round boyish eyes were such a nice chocolate brown, she thought. He needed a haircut. His hair fell like a dark fan across his forehead. And he looked cold. But then he always looked cold, his arms and legs so thin, like a delicate five-year-old's. The two of them were so different—Andy tall and slender while she was barely five feet with full hips and breasts. He had a warm olive complexion while she always looked pale. Even her hair was pale. Andy used to tell her all the time that she was beautiful, but no matter how many times she looked in the mirror, she never saw it. All she ever saw were things like the crooked bangs, or her unusually full mouth that, although she was only twenty-six, had already developed minute cracks at the corners. It seemed evident to her that she would be one of those people who would show the ravages of age early in life, the same way her mother had.

"Look, Lizzy . . . this could be terrific for us," he said. "Just be thankful we're out of that cramped little apartment with my computer and books stuffed in the corner of the living room and your painting gear jammed into the bedroom." He stopped and looked grim for a moment, then the smile reappeared. "Here, I have space. I can breathe. I think maybe I can get my career on the right track again."

His career! What about *her* career? Damn him! Why did his work always have to come first? It hadn't always been that way. In the beginning of their five-year-old marriage he took as much pride in her work as his. But when things got bad—when the paintings didn't sell and when his books didn't do well, or he had writer's block, the way he did now—he drew away from her. But then she didn't suppose it was all his fault. She wasn't any saint. Whenever she was turned down by a gallery, she became as moody as an old owl, feeling sorry for herself, and enjoyed the sulking. She certainly wasn't much fun to be around these days either. Maybe he was right. Maybe the change, the new house, more room, even the sea air, would help them both.

Andy gave a scolding look. "Come on honey, stop fretting. This is the new start we've been praying for."

"It *would* be a good place to start our family." Elizabeth said, bringing up a touchy subject. After all, they hadn't made love in several months. It seemed impossible to feel passion, after all the rejections she'd encountered in her work. She supposed that was the problem with Andy, too. Writer's block was a type of rejection. Almost as if he were rejecting his own talent.

Andy gave her a frown, then shrugged. "We'll see."

Elizabeth looked around at the house and garage. "You realize, I'll never be able to see Judy again," she complained, referring to Judy Bird, her closest friend from childhood who lived in the San Fernando Valley.

"Don't be silly. You two are joined at the brain. Besides, Judy loves the beach. She'll be down here like a shot."

"In all that traffic?"

"Nothing will keep her away. Wait and see."

"I hope you're right."

A rumbling at the far end of the alley caught Elizabeth's attention. "Shoot! The movers are here and we haven't even opened the house yet. With our finances in such a sorry state, we can't afford to keep them any longer than necessary." She gave the house one more glance, then managed to shake off the odd feeling that had engulfed her and rummaged through her purse for the keys.

The two of them made their way through the small backyard that looked bleak except for a clutter of rose bushes blooming along the fence in great bursts of red and yellow. A pile of unraked leaves sat by the back door, and despite the sea breeze, a string of tarnished metal wind chimes hung motionless from the eaves of the house.

Inside, a bevy of shutters had been pulled across the kitchen windows. They gave the air a deep gloom. The kitchen was done in faded French Country, with a copper hood over the stove, blue and lemon-yellow hand-painted tile on the counters, a brick floor, and an antique butcher block set in the middle of the room. In one corner, near the sink, a spider had spun a large silver web where a papery dead fly hung tangled.

Elizabeth opened the shutters over the kitchen sink and a cloud of dust puffed out. "I knew we should have done some cleaning before we moved in."

"Don't worry about it." Andy coughed from the dust. He leaned across the sink and scooped up the spider web with the palm of his hand. "We can do it as we go along. Besides, it was either move in right away or sign another year's lease on that dreary apartment."

In the dining room, Elizabeth pulled open the heavy drapes, letting in a stream of dusty yellow sunlight. Aunt Mary's dining room table sat in the middle of the room like a regal monarch—a Regency table of faded rosewood, six William IV chairs, and a matching break-front.

"Christ!" Andy said. "We only took a quick look at the place. I'd forgotten about the damn wallpaper. This room looks like a pharoah's tomb!" He glanced around at the walls papered with drawings of Egyptian scarab beetles and pyramids.

"This all has to go," Elizabeth said, wrinkling her nose with distaste. "Right away."

Andy nodded agreement. "As soon as we get the money."

They moved on into the living room that was as long as it was wide, with high open-beamed ceilings and an elephantine fireplace of old brick. Deep-blue Persian rugs covered polished wood floors. The windows were draped with deep blue velvet—a fabric much too heavy for the style of the house—and the wallpaper design resembled the one in the dining room. Scarabs and pharaoh heads. A row of beige dust-bunnies stood at attention under a glass-topped wicker coffee-table.

"What a hodgepodge," Elizabeth said, pivoting about in the center of the room. "But not all bad." A tangle of white wicker furniture, yellowing around the edges, filled the room. Sofas, rockers, chairs, tables, a desk and several chests. The sofas and chairs were heaped with lopsided cushions in faded blue cotton. The one good piece in the room was a tall John Brooker Germantown clock that stood against the north wall. The case was walnut with a scrolled top and a moon-phase calendar face. The works had stopped, which gave her an eerie feeling, almost as if time had stopped in the room. She wanted to wind it but didn't—too many other things to get done.

"Anybody here?" boomed a voice from the kitchen.

"It's the movers," Andy said.

"We're in here," he called. "Straight through the kitchen and dining room."

A tall, heavyset man with a graying mustache walked in carrying a clipboard. "You'll have to tell us where ya want the stuff." He looked around the room and gave a low whistle. "Heyeee, it looks as if you already got a ton of furniture."

"Yes, well, we . . . I inherited this place from my aunt, furniture and all. But two of the bedrooms upstairs are empty, and also, the little room just off the kitchen. That one's going to be my husband's office. You can put our old sofa and chairs in there, along with the big desk and bookshelves."

"Nice place," the mover said, scratching at his mustache. "Right on the beach. Must be worth a bundle. Especially way out here on the Peninsula. Newport Beach is pretty much a money place, ya know. Nothing like the San Fernando Valley where you've been living." The man nodded his head as he looked around the room. "That sliding door look out on the sand?"

"Yes it does," Elizabeth said as she pulled open the drapes on the glass door. Outside, a long redwood deck stretched across the back of the house. On the far side of the deck, a sidewalk edged the sand. A gleaming sweep of deep-green ocean tumbled in along the beach, the tide now turning.

"Nice," the man said, looking around and nodding. "Well, we'd better get started. Gonna need some extra care what with all these wood floors. Don't want to scratch 'em. Be a real shame."

It took a long time for the movers to do their job. Elizabeth stood in the kitchen, worrying about how much the moving bill would come to. They probably thought she and Andy were rich, moving in here on the Gold Coast of Newport Beach. Little did they know how penniless they were. Actually, they shouldn't be moving in at all. They should be selling the house. But the market was off. Real estate wasn't moving. The place needed a lot of fixing. If they sold it now, they would lose a great deal of money. Besides, Andy was right. They needed the space. Needed a fresh start. Andy had sold two novels which made him neither rich nor famous. He didn't even get a decent literary review. After that, he couldn't write—not a word, for almost a year now. And no one but a few decorators seemed to care for her paintings. In the beginning, right out of college, it seemed so easy. All they had to do was work hard and the right things would happen, or so they'd thought. But that wasn't the way it worked. She'd watched while other people with less talent had succeeded with less effort, while she and Andy struggled continuously.

Elizabeth heard a loud crash. She rushed into the living room to find one of the movers had managed to drop the large and very expensive mirror her mother and father had given them as a wedding gift. It had shattered into a million shimmering shards. She looked down at the mess. In one of the jagged pieces she caught a glimpse of her face looking white and pinched. Damn it! What a way to start their new life! It was a good thing she wasn't terribly superstitious. Such a beautiful mirror. She had planned to use it over the fireplace, but now she would have to hang one of her paintings instead. At least they were good for something. The movers looked sheepish and quietly swept up the pieces.

To Elizabeth's surprise, the house developed a cozy sense of style as their own belongings were moved in and mixed with all the things Aunt Mary had left. She opened all the windows to air out the dank odor that permeated the place. The rooms smelled like wet newspapers, but the briny air quickly cleared it away. She had the moving men put her canvases, easels, sketchbooks, boxes of paints and brushes in the first bedroom at the top of the stairs. It had a skylight that faced north, which made it perfect for a studio. Next to the studio was a huge square bathroom, overwhelmed by a fat white porcelain tub, an ancient toilet, and a slightly cracked sink. Pale-red Egyptian beetles on lime-green paper covered the walls. The paper had curled away from the wall in places and she had to curb the urge to peel it off.

The second bedroom was large and empty. She told the movers to put the old bedroom furniture in there, since she planned to use Aunt Mary's antique bed in the third bedroom for their own, and make this room into a guest room.

While they moved the bed inside and set it up, she peered around at the wallpaper—pharoah heads in gold gild surrounded by packs of wild dogs with long teeth. What an eccentric old lady her great-aunt Mary had been. It had been years since she'd seen the woman. Elizabeth had been only ten or twelve when she'd last been to the beach house. She wasn't sure why her visits had stopped as she always enjoyed them. What she remembered most about

Mary were her flowing silk caftans, and her arms laden with gold bracelets. The caftans trailed swirls of bright color like the wings of a butterfly and the bracelets had chimed in harmony as she walked. None of those severe navy blue or black career suits for Aunt Mary. A bright, beautiful woman, Mary had owned and run Warren Pharmaceuticals with considerable success until she was almost eighty. Then she'd quietly closed it, retired and lived her last few years alone in the beach house.

Elizabeth wondered if she had been lonely, living alone those last years. She'd had a son. What was his name? She couldn't remember. Her mother had mentioned him now and then, although Elizabeth had never met him. He'd been off to boarding school every time she'd visited. Mary had had him late in life, the year before she turned 50, the same year her husband died. The whole family was aghast, certain the child would be retarded or something worse. Despite not having a father to help raise him, and the late age at which his mother had given birth to him, he turned into a quiet, well-behaved and extraordinarily brilliant young man. He finished high school at fourteen, went on to college and earned his Ph.D. in biochemistry before his twenty-second birthday. Mary had set up an R & D division of her company, just for him. But then he'd become ill. Mary refused to talk about it, even to the family. After a shockingly short time, he died, leaving Mary by herself. If he'd lived, he would have inherited the house. Still and all, Mary was never one to let things get her down, although she stopped giving her lavish parties and seldom invited family members to visit.

It was too bad, Elizabeth thought, that Mary hadn't kept the company going somehow. Or hadn't sold off all the patents. Inheriting a little cash flow along with the house, sure wouldn't have hurt. Their finances were such a disaster. With a deep sigh, she pushed the guest bedroom window open wide and looked out, taking in a deep breath of salty air. The window overlooked the garage and the alley in back of the house. Something in the shadows moved, stopped, moved again. She squinted, trying to make out what it might be. When it moved once more, she saw the dim form of a man looking up at her. It must be Andy, she thought, and gave a wave. But as she did, the form jumped back into the shadows.

"Andy?" she called, only to be startled when he answered from the doorway of the bedroom.

"What?"

"Oh!" She quickly backed away from the window. A sudden shiver struck her. "Someone was looking up at me from the alley. I thought it was *you!*"

"Where?" Andy asked, moving to the window.

"Right over there. Between those two houses in back of us." But the shadows were empty. Whoever it was had gone.

"Just a neighbor," Andy assured her.

"Sneaking a peek at the new people, I suppose."

"Maybe he doesn't like the look of our old patched-up Toyota."

Elizabeth sighed. "We'd better keep the garage door down. Everyone around this neighborhood seems to own a BMW, a Mercedes, or a Lexus. Everyone but us, that is."

"So, we'll start a new trend."

She looked down at her oil-paint-stained jeans with ragged holes that let her knees escape. "Think this kind of garb will catch on?"

"Actually," Andy said. "I think that's the *in* look right now."

She gave him a forced smile. "It's going to be tough, keeping this place. We probably should have sold it, even at a discount. It will be ages before either one of us can buy new clothes, or a new car."

"Look," Andy said. "We've always dreamed of living at the beach, haven't we? Right now our work is stalled, that's all. It's temporary. Things will start moving now. We've worked hard. Paid our dues, as they say. Come on, don't be a Doomsday Dolly."

"Okay." She forced the smile again. "If you say so. And in that case, we'd better get this damn move finished. Come on, I need a hand putting some clean sheets on the bed in Aunt Mary's old bedroom."

The wallpaper in the master bedroom looked just as god-awful as the rest in the house. Elizabeth surveyed the room. Pretty dreadful. But given a little time and eventually some money, they could put it to right. The room was huge, with a cedar-lined walk-in closet, a black marble fireplace, Aunt Mary's baroque cherrywood bed, and a matching bureau with the mirror missing. Next to the bureau stood a long chest or box of some kind painted with lapis blue and metallic gold symbols that matched the wallpaper.

Andy gave her a hand putting on the clean sheets, which smelled like sweet lemons. He gave the mattress a push with his hand. "Not bad," he said. "Feels pretty springy. Do you think we'll be able to sleep in here with all this terrible wallpaper staring at us?"

"I'm so tired I could sleep in the middle of the freeway." She walked over to the low chest next to the bureau. "Do you suppose this is some kind of a hope chest? It looks rather odd." It was longer than Andy, and about three feet wide. It had a door on top with a ceramic handle. It appeared to be made out of deep blue fiberglass that had been hand painted with Egyptian scenes. She gave the handle a tug, and the lid sprung up, causing her to jump slightly.

Andy came over and looked inside. "Well, in here it looks like a shower, tipped over." he said. A strong scent of brine wafted out.

The inside was fairly dark, but Elizabeth saw what looked like a thick crust of crystals along the sides of the box. She cautiously touched them with her fingertips. "Salt?" She lifted a few of the crystals to her nose. "Yep, salt."

"Maybe Mary kept some of the ocean in her bedroom," Andy chuckled.

"There's nothing in here," she said, fingering the salty crust, "but this." She brushed the salt from her fingers and felt around on the bottom of the box. Her hand suddenly touched on something in one of the far corners. It turned out to be some sort of packet that was small, slick and cool. She lifted it out and held it between two fingers. "Look, a plastic bag filled with some kind of powder. What do you suppose it is?"

Andy squinted, inspecting the bag. "Cocaine?"

Elizabeth chuckled. "No, seriously."

"Beats me. Maybe it's some kind of roach powder."

"Ugg!" She dropped the pouch back into the chest. "Oh, Andy, don't tell me the place has *roaches!* I couldn't stand that!"

"I'm only kidding. Haven't seen any of those little buggers around. Which is unusual in a house this old."

"Well, thank God!" She wiped her fingers on her jeans and stood up.

Andy continued to inspect the box. "This is really strange. It's got some sort of motor or something here on the outside, and there's an electrical plug. And right here," he pointed inside, "is what looks like speakers."

"You mean audio speakers?"

"Yep. And here on the outside is a built-in tape player." He pulled open a cartridge slot. "See, you can just slip a tape in there and press play."

"What do you suppose it's for?" Elizabeth asked. "Some sort of sauna, or a small hot tub?"

"With a door on top?"

"I don't know. Aunt Mary always was a little eccentric. Marched to her own drummer most of the time."

Andy pushed the top down on the box, stood up and looked the thing over. "Mighty odd."

"Come on, Andy. The movers should be finished. Let's go pay them before they charge us for another hour. We can figure this thing out later."

The two of them stood in the alley watching the moving van as it reached the end of the street and disappeared around the corner.

"Well, that's that," Andy said.

"I feel a thousand years old," Elizabeth groaned. "My legs are screaming at me for going up and down those stairs so many times."

"It's good for you."

"Yeah, if I survive." Elizabeth leaned her head against Andy's shoulder. She looked up at the outside of the house again. This time it looked friendlier. The window-eyes appeared softer with all the drapes and shutters open. Perhaps it would be all right after all. The way Andy said.

"Lizzy?" Andy looked at his watch.

"Yes?"

"It's after five. Are you hungry?"

"I don't know. I'm so tired I can't tell."

"Let's get the boxes unpacked, and then I'll go out and pick up some fast food."

"Could you chew and swallow for me, too?"

"If you like."

A gust of sea wind made Elizabeth shiver. Andy took her arm and led her toward the house. Something in the alley crackled. They both turned.

"Someone's there," Elizabeth whispered.

"Where?"

"Over there between the houses. *Someone's looking at us.*"

"I don't see anyone."

"He's there, I tell you."

"Then it's just a snoopy neighbor, like I said before."

"I'm cold," she said as a shiver rippled over her.

"Come on," Andy said. "Let's get finished so we can rest."

Elizabeth took one more glance toward the alley before allowing Andy to lead her into the house. Just a neighbor, she assured herself. Only a snoopy neighbor lurking about in the deep-blue shadows of the early night.

HE stood in the alley and watched the young couple as they made their way back into Mary's old house. Why were they there? he wondered. They didn't belong there. Someone should tell them to get the hell away before something terrible happened to them.

Such an unsullied-looking couple, he thought. The man, tall and thin, was mostly skin and bones, yet had an air of dignity about him. The woman looked ripe and bursting with the robust health of youth. He guessed her to be about twenty-five or so. She seemed familiar, although he wasn't sure why. The man smelled of aftershave—a blend of spices and musk. He also smelled of paper, ink and books. His sweater had the essence of lamb's wool. The

woman had bathed with Ivory soap early that
morning, and the scent of her body lotion still lingered—lemon with lanolin. Over the lotion he discovered the odor of oil paint and linseed oil. A
painter perhaps? An artist?

As soon as they disappeared into the house and
shut the door behind them, he pushed the thought
of them out of his mind. He fished in his shirt
pocket, found a thin gold chain and tugged it out.
The gold heart at the end of the chain glowed in the
semidarkness—a talisman from the night before.
The gathering of such items was a despicable habit,
but one he'd found impossible to break.

As he swung the tiny heart he mentally retraced
his actions of last night. The scene sharpened in his
mind, the way it always did after the agony left him.
The details replayed themselves in a peculiar swirling fashion, as if he were viewing them through a
child's kaleidoscope. He had no business getting
involved so close to home again, but the agony had
been more than he could bear. He'd gone out for a
walk, hoping to quell the first symptoms. But the
party going on in one of the beach-front homes had
tempted him, escalating the agony. When the two
young girls came out of the house, the fever in him
rose to such heat, he no longer had control.

He closed his eyes and let the memory wash over
him. That night he had stepped out of shadows and
made his way along the beach behind them. An icy
sea mist cloaked him from their view. He had increased his speed, silently making his way around in
front of the first girl. With one swift move he
reached for her and pulled her close to him, his face

against the skin of her throat, and breathed in the bouquet of her body. She would relieve his agony and make him whole. She would be his savior. He felt hot, salty tears sting his cheeks. He hated what he was. What he had to do.

"Hey! Let me go!" she said, her voice barely a whisper, as if she could not understand what was happening. "I have to get home!" She flailed her fists at him, but her strength was of little value. He quickly pressed his hands against the sides of her face and broke the surface of her skin with his fingernails, and rubbed the wound with his fingers. It only took a moment before she stopped struggling.

With his blade—gleaming, thin, sharp—he slashed the carotid artery on the right side of her neck. Not his favorite way, but fast. The incision was neat, less than an inch long. Having felt no pain, she let out only a breathy gasp. The metallic scent of warm rich blood overrode the smell of fear. Even in the darkness he could see the deep red fluid as it streamed down the white curve of her throat. It looked luminous, as if it had a life force of its own, apart from the body in which it had been born. While her blood flowed, the girl made little mewing sounds, her hands fluttering about like the wings of a tiny bird.

He leaned down against her throat and let the warm substance gush into his mouth. It tasted like liquid copper. As he closed his eyes and drank, bright flashes of gleaming colored lights played against his eyelids.

He wasn't half through before he heard the other girl calling. He pulled away, still thirsty, but knew there wasn't time to finish. He took a moment longer to tug a small opal ring from the first girl's finger and put it in his pocket. After that, he pulled open her blouse, slipped it off one shoulder and placed his lips against her skin—so soft, so sweet. Then he sank his teeth into her and neatly tore away a small slice of flesh, held it in his mouth to savor the delicate flavor, then carefully chewed and swallowed it. He craved more, but he knew there was little time.

Regret washed over him. He had chosen someone so young. Just beginning life, really. But the agony had hit with such fury. And, it still railed at him. He closed his eyes and fought back the tears. Then he lifted the girl and carried her into the churning surf. The turning tide would take her out. He didn't have time to transport her to the end of the breakwater. The second girl was only a few yards away. He remembered the gold heart glowing at her throat, and despite his regret, knew he would have her too.

The second girl struggled even less. With her, he used his teeth instead of the blade, tearing at the skin that sheathed her artery, the scent of blood and flesh so delicious to him he could not have stopped had he wanted to. He drained her slowly, savoring the warm vitality of her lifeblood. Only once, when he lifted his head and paused, did she open her eyes and look at him. Her whole body trembled in his arms as if she were dreaming and trying to awaken herself.

The thrill that shot through him was electric. He loved her at that moment—adored her for the purity of the pleasure she gave him, and for the release from the agony. He took every last drop from her, not wanting to waste any of her precious gift. When he'd emptied her, he pressed his teeth against the skin on her arm and quickly tore off a piece of flesh. The taste of it electrified him. So sweet and tender. He pulled her blouse open, revealing her soft white breasts, ran his tongue over the pale skin, smelling the delicious odor, then let his teeth tear loose a large, soft morsel. He still craved more, but knew he was pressing his luck. Then he reached down and snapped the gold heart and chain from her neck and slipped it into his pocket. His lucky charm. A foolish obsession, he knew, but somehow he believed it might keep him from harm's way.

Now, as he stood in the dark shadows of the alley behind the beach houses, the tiny gold heart swinging from its chain, he felt a stabbing sense of guilt. The agony had ebbed, for now. But at what price? His body felt rich and full, his life force overflowing. He should have no regrets, for he wanted to survive. But the reprehension of what he'd done threatened to overwhelm him.

He frowned, thinking about the young man and woman who had moved into Mary's house, and wondered why the woman was so familiar. They had never met, as far as he knew. But he loved the smell of her. The delicious scent tempted him far too much. When the agony returned, would he be able to resist her? He thought not. His hunger for her grew, even, as he thought about it. The scent of Ivory soap and oil paint still lingered in the alley— and beyond that, the deep, musky aroma of her body permeated the air. He sniffed at it delicately, gave a deep sigh, then turned and disappeared into the night.

Detective Ted "Teddy Bear" Bearbower had two favorite types of food. Pasta and desserts. He craved all kinds of pasta—spaghetti, linguini, fettuccine, macaroni, and egg noodles. He liked his pasta with cream sauce, pesto, clam, marinara, tomato, prosciutto, alfredo, cheese and, best of all, with a simple mixture of butter, basil and fresh garlic.

His appetite for desserts was enormous. Custardfilled chocolate eclairs were his passion. But he would settle for almost anything chocolate—especially chocolate mousse. Some days, he didn't eat regular meals. He just brewed a pot of dark coffee and sat down to a platter of eclairs, or cream puffs, or a bowl of chocolate rum pudding. He never drank alcohol, since he existed on a sugar high.

He enjoyed the two-bedroom, two-story condominium where he lived. Situated in Newport Beach, overlooking Pacific Coast Highway, it gave him a splendid view of the ocean from his living room window. The kitchen was a gourmet's dream, with every kind of cooking gadget and machine ever invented. Gadgets cluttered the cupboards, counter tops, and lapped over onto the small pine kitchen table. The room held a permanent aroma of spices. The rest of the place was decorated with treasures he and his late wife had collected together throughout their marriage—a tavern table with Windsor chairs in the dining area, a parson's bench, an old sea chest, a hickory bentwood chair, and a cupboard filled with painted tin toleware in the living room. The bedroom held an antique white iron bed, covered with a Rosepath quilt and a wonderful old walnut armoire. For a while after Sylvia's death, he'd considered getting rid of everything and selling the place, then he realized that despite the pain, he cherished his memories. So he'd stayed and was glad of it.

It was after eight in the evening and Ted had heated some leftovers for his dinner, something he rarely did since there seldom were any leftovers. His stomach grumbled impatiently as he scooped a plateful of macaroni and cheese from the pan, tore off a chunk of fresh French bread, poured a cup of coffee, and took them all upstairs into the small bedroom he used for a study. Not wanting to disturb the papers on his desk, he set up a TV tray next to his chair for the food. He took several bites of the macaroni and cheese and a swallow of coffee. The cheese had the sharp edge to it he loved. He took another bite and savored the tangy flavor.

His wife had spent thirty-five years watching him eat, an expression of continual amazement on her face. She'd had little appetite, seldom thought about food, and didn't really like much of it. She had eaten only out of necessity most of the time. She never really understood the ecstasy it gave him.

The only other passion in his life was his work. He'd been in homicide for twenty years. The murder rate in Newport Beach was extremely low, which meant he had the luxury of time. Once he was on a case it never left his mind. Bits and pieces of it filtered into his head even during sleep. Sometimes, when a case appeared unsolvable, the tiniest clue would suddenly come traipsing through his dreams, and by morning he *knew*—absolutely knew whatever it was he needed to know in order to solve it. It was a process he didn't understand, but respected.

He shuffled through the computer printouts he'd picked up at the department. He and Locke had spent the better part of the day searching for cases similar to the Duff girl's. He hadn't looked through them closely, but he didn't like the thick stack of papers in his hands. It meant there were an awful lot of matching cases. And these were only the ones from the local county.

He picked up the phone and dialed Locke's home number.

"What now?" Locke answered.

"How did you know it was me?" Ted asked.

"Who else?"

"I was just about to go through these cases. Did you get anything on our check of similar M.O.'s outside Orange County."

"Not yet. Pretty early. Probably tomorrow."

"Have you looked at these? How many fucking matches are there? I've got a big stack here."

"I took a quick look. It's kind of scary. In the past five years there have been twelve similar deaths. That is, if you count everyone that's even close."

"Are all of them listed as unsolved homicides?"

"Yes."

"Mostly male or female?"

"Even-steven."

"Okay. I'm going to check them over. Carefully. All of them." Ted sighed, knowing the tough job ahead.

"You got any ideas?" Locke asked.

"Maybe. Maybe not."

"It wasn't sexual," Locke said. "She wasn't raped."

"That doesn't mean it wasn't sexual."

"Yeah, but—"

"He might have masturbated. Not at the scene, but after he got home. Sometimes they get off thinking about what they've done. Remembering it—not doing it. They keep getting off on it until the memory fades. Then go for a fresh kill."

"Christ!"

"Ummmm."

"Okay Ted, what is it you're not saying?"

Ted hesitated, hating to say the word. "Serial," he finally managed.

"Oh, shit! You really think so?"

"I hope not."

"Yeah, me too."

"All I can do is check through all these tonight. You peruse them again tomorrow. See what we come up with."

He hung up the phone, picked up his coffee and sipped it. Then he took a few bites of his dinner as he scanned one of the computer printouts. It was a case of a woman, who was found dead behind a convenience store in Anaheim, just a mile from Disneyland. The only signs of trauma to her body were some rather deep scratches, a few bruises around her wrists, a chunk of flesh missing from her right breast, and the cut that had severed her carotid artery. There were no obvious signs of ritual murder, rape, or vaginal mutilations that might indicate a lesbian affair. The cause of death was an extreme loss of blood—although, they had found only a small amount of blood at the scene. Forensics found no evidence she was killed elsewhere and dumped there. No drag marks, blood trail, car tracks, or footprints. No traces of sand or soil from another geographical area. Nothing. The alley was clean. More important was the placement of lividity stains, stains that appear on the skin after death where the blood—pooling to the lowest part of the body—forms blue or reddish-violet marks. If the body was moved after death, the stains would have been different from what they were. Of course, with so much blood missing in this case, the lividity might not tell the whole story.

The wound analysis on the dead woman—a process whereby a paste of barium sulfate was squeezed into the wounds so they could be x-rayed—showed that the instrument used to cut the jugular was twenty-five millimeters in width, approximately one millimeter thick, and precision-sharp on at least one edge, with a pointed tip. Possibly some type of surgeon's scalpel. It also showed that the piece of missing flesh had been removed by human teeth. The barium sulfate had clearly revealed the impression of two upper central incisors, one lateral incisor, one upper cuspid, better known as a canine tooth, two lower central incisors and two lateral incisors.

Ted checked the results of the antigen test done from traces of saliva found at the bite area. It was remarkable, he thought, how far forensic science had advanced during the twenty years he'd been with homicide. From even a minute amount of saliva, urine, semen, or sweat, a person's blood type and sex could be determined. The person who took the bite out of the Anaheim lady was AB negative—a rare blood type—and had the XY chromosomes which meant the killer was probably a male. Although a small number of women had them, too.

He set the printout on his desk. Remarkable forensics, he thought. The blood type and sex narrowed it down to less than one percent of the population. And they could take it even further. They could send some of the saliva out to be genetically fingerprinted. But without a suspect, none of that was much good. No one in the area had seen or heard anything unusual. No sign of the weapon. No fingerprints.

He didn't at all like the similarities to the Duff case. The trauma to the carotid artery, the bite made by human teeth. But you couldn't do an accurate forensic workup on someone who was alive. Any trace of saliva at the bite site on the surviving Duff girl had been quickly cleaned away by paramedics or a nurse. The severed carotid artery was already healing. As for the younger Duff sister, he was certain it was only a matter of time before her body was found. Her parents still held out hope that she had been kidnapped and was alive. His gut instinct told him, she was not.

He sighed. At least, he thought, if they *do* find her body they might have more to go on than they had now. He sat back in his desk chair and scooped up some of his macaroni and cheese. His coffee wasn't piping hot, but he didn't mind. He took large sips to wash down his food.

If the missing girl had been dumped in the ocean the way her older sister had, her body would show up in a day or two, maybe a week, depending upon the currents and tides and where she'd been dumped. If they found the body and it matched the case of the Anaheim lady, as well as, that of the older Duff girl, they probably had a serial killer on their hands. The idea of that sent a jolt over his body, as sharp as an electric shock.

He could handle crimes of sudden passion, as horrible as they were. But serial killings were generally done by sociopaths. Sociopaths didn't think like other people. It was close to impossible to second-guess them. They lacked any internal control or moral code. And most of them were bright and cunning. They understood they had committed a criminal act, but found it thrilling and were impervious to the anguish of their prey. Many of them enjoyed it.

He picked up another case, glanced through it, put it down and picked up another. Before long, he had them narrowed down to seven that were remarkably like the Duff girl and the Anaheim case. None except the Duff case were his. They were all still open, but inactive, even though some of them had occurred as long as five years ago. Not one of them had any more physical evidence than those two. If related, there had to be something more he wasn't seeing. Some hook on which everything hung. He would go over each case again one by one, microscopically, no matter how long it took. He'd find that hook, if it was there, and something told him it was. And, he had to find it before the public got hold of the fact that a serial killer might be out there. It was a tough line to keep—that of the public's right to know, and help protect themselves, verses the need to avoid public panic.

He wolfed down the rest of his food and drank the lukewarm remains of his coffee. Then, he took his plate and cup back into the kitchen and rummaged in the refrigerator. He hoped he had at least one or two of the cream puffs left from the dozen he'd bought yesterday. He was going to need them. It was going to be one hell of a long night.

It was after eight PM by the time Andy and Elizabeth had unpacked the last of the moving boxes, flattened them, and stored them in the garage. They toddled into the house like two very elderly people, their muscles screaming from all the unaccustomed exercise, and stood in the middle of the living room really looking around for the first time that day.

"It smells a whole lot better." Elizabeth rubbed at a deep ache in her back.

"It's really not so bad. Even the wallpaper looks better at night." Andy walked over to the sliding glass door and pulled it open. The sea breeze was light and smelled of kelp. The rumble and hiss of the surf echoed through the room.

"We're actually living on the beach," Elizabeth said, hearing a touch of disbelief in her voice. "It's hard to believe."

"We're going to love this place. You'll see. It's exactly what we needed. A new start. A new place to live."

"Well, I'm not going to live much longer, unless I rest and have something to eat."

Andy took their little beat-up Toyota and went out to pick up barbecued chicken at a little restaurant they'd spotted a few blocks away. While he was gone, Elizabeth looked over the Germantown grandfather clock in the corner of the living room. She found the key taped to the back of the pendulum, but didn't wind the clock. She never wore a watch. Didn't want to be tied to a timetable. She'd have to check with Andy's watch to make certain she set the works to the right time. When Andy got back, she was so hungry, she forgot all about it. Using some dry driftwood, they found in the garage, they lit a roaring fire in the fireplace, spread out an old quilt and had a picnic on the floor, listening to Paul Simon's *Graceland,* and Joemy Wilson's hammered dulcimer on their tape player.

The minute Elizabeth finished eating an overwhelming drowsiness hit her. Thank God, they'd had the foresight to put clean sheets on Aunt Mary's old baroque bed while the movers were at work. Now, if she could only manage to get herself up the stairs, she'd be even more thankful.

"Listen! Someone's having a party," Andy said, getting up from the floor. "When the surf quiets, you can hear people talking. Sounds close by." He walked to the sliding door and peered out.

"Oh great!" Elizabeth unkinked her legs, stretched and got up. "Don't tell me we've got neighbors who throw loud parties in the middle of the week!"

"Come here, Lizzy. Take a look." Andy pushed the sliding door open farther and stepped out onto the deck. "It's right next door."

Elizabeth shook off her drowsiness and went to look. At the house next door, on a long narrow patio that looked out over the ocean, a group of people were sitting around on stark-white Brown-Jordan furniture. Now and then during a lull between waves she caught the tinkle of ice in a glass, or a bit of laughter.

Elizabeth picked up Andy's arm and looked at his watch. "It's kind of late for a weeknight, isn't it? It's after ten." Fatigue gnawed at her bones.

"Hello!" came a voice out of nowhere. "Hello there! Why don't you join us?"

Elizabeth looked around trying to locate the voice.

"Over here! Oh, wait a minute!"

Elizabeth heard the soft ruffle of someone padding down the narrow sidewalk that ran along the edge of the sand, and saw a blur of white.

"Hi," said a barefoot woman in a flowing white dress, all out of breath from her dash. "I'm sorry. I didn't mean to startle you all. I'm Tyree Rattigan and I live in that big old white elephant next door." She was tall, thin, and ivory-skinned, with a deep peach bloom to her cheeks, eyes the color of blue-glass marbles, and the brightest, longest red hair Elizabeth had ever seen. It was hard to tell her age. Somewhere in her thirties, perhaps. Her hair, blowing about in the sea breeze and caught by the lights from the house, looked like long curls of flame.

"Hello," Andy said. "I'm Andy Rosemond, and this is my wife, Elizabeth. Lizzy's Aunt Mary used to own the house. Did you happen to know her?"

The woman stepped up on the deck, tossed back her head and laughed. "Know Mary? Why, *everyone* knew Mary. She was such an old reprobate. Didn't know when to lie down and give it up. But we all loved her. In fact, she was the center of all our gatherings, right up to the end."

"Then she didn't suffer, or anything?" Elizabeth asked.

"Oh, no!" Tyree said. "She was sitting on my porch the day she died. Sipping a Bloody Mary, telling the raunchiest jokes you've ever heard. The next thing we knew, she was gone."

"She died on your patio?" Andy looked a little ashen.

"No. No. On the way to the hospital. Everything just stopped, I guess. Wore out. Nice way to go, don't you think? Still clutching a Bloody Mary in the ambulance." Tyree gave a chuckle. "Those poor paramedics didn't know how to cope with her."

"Well, I'm glad to hear she didn't suffer," Elizabeth said.

"Not a bit. Look, why don't you two come on over and join us?" Tyree asked. "Just a few neighbors. And my husband, Boo."

"Boo?" Andy said.

Tyree laughed again. "Isn't that awful? But his real name is worse—Beauregard Rattigan. Disgustingly Southern, isn't it? Come on, we're just sitting around chatting over there. Not a party actually. We've got some music, and a few dips if you like. It's a nice way to meet some of your new neighbors."

Elizabeth unsuccessfully tried to stifle a yawn, then looked embarrassed. "I'm sorry. It's been an awfully long day. Could you please give us a raincheck?" Tyree nodded and smiled, giving Elizabeth a glimpse of what looked like a tiny diamond embedded in one of her front teeth. Elizabeth tried not to stare, but didn't quite manage.

"Why, of course," Tyree said. "In fact, that's much better. I'll give a special little bash just for the two of you. That way *everyone* on the block will come, and you can meet them all in one swoop. Would you like that?"

"Well, I guess—"

"Let's see, how about a week from tonight?" Tyree went on. "That gives you plenty of time to get settled. Let me know, if there's anything I can do for you in the meantime."

"Well, thank you," Elizabeth said. "That's very nice."

"I know it's none of my business," Tyree said, in a rather conspiratorial voice. "But, are you planning on refurbishing Mary's place and selling it? Or are you going to stay?"

"I think we're here to stay. That is, if we can get our finances straightened out." Elizabeth said, a little taken back by the personal question.

Tyree gave her a rather odd smile that looked almost forced. "Then, you're not planning to sell or rent it out?"

"No. I don't think so. At least, not for a long time. The market is terrible." Elizabeth said, wondering if this woman was always this curious. And, a bit rude. Then again, perhaps she knew someone who might be interested in the place.

"Did Mary leave you any of her business?"

Elizabeth pursed her lips, getting quite annoyed at all the personal questions. "She closed the business. Years ago. Probably had a rough time of it in later years. No money left from the sale. Except for a worthless patent, the house is all that's left."

"My goodness. I had no idea Mary was in such straights. Of course, she did stop throwing those wonderful parties of hers. But, I thought that was because of her age. Come to think of it though, she always came over to mine and had the time of her life." Tyree paused. "She was a great old lady. Everyone in the neighborhood was fond of her."

"I used to love visiting her. But I hadn't seen her for a long time, before she died." Elizabeth felt a pang of regret. She really should have come to visit, even without an invitation. But, she'd been so busy with her schooling and career, such as it was, that there never seemed to be time.

Tyree appeared to consider something for a moment, then she shook her head, as if she'd made some sort of decision. "Well, now, we're going to be great friends, honeybunch. I just know it." This time the smile was genuine. "It'll be such fun showing you all the nifty little places around here to shop."

Elizabeth winced. She hated to say that it would be centuries before she would have any spare money. Perhaps, after they got to know each other, Tyree would understand the term 'starving artists.'

"Listen," Elizabeth said. "Why don't you come over for coffee in the morning. Andy's a writer. Hopefully, he'll disappear into his office first thing and try to get his new novel going. I don't have my studio set up yet, so I won't be working on my painting for a few days."

"Oh, honeybunch, I'm afraid I'm one of those late, late sleepers." Tyree raked her hand through her flowing red hair and pulled it to one side to keep it from blowing about so wildly in the wind. "I got my hours all mixed up when I worked in the theater. But I'll see you later in the day. And listen—" She let go of her hair and it went into a frenzied dance around her face. "Don't you worry about dinner tomorrow night. I'll bring over something. Just a casserole, nothing fancy. I know you'll be busy getting settled."

"Well, I . . . that's thoughtful of you," Elizabeth said, wanting to say no, but also not wanting to offend their new neighbor right off the bat, even, if she was too nosey.

"You know," Tyree said, squinting at her in an odd manner. "You remind me a bit of your Aunt Mary. She was such a pretty thing."

"Thank you." Elizabeth said, catching another gleam from the diamond in the woman's tooth.

"So, you're a writer?" Tyree turned and grinned at Andy. "Fascinating! I don't know many writers. I'd love to read something. And you paint?" she said, turning back to Elizabeth. "How wonderful, having such creative people living next door. No wonder Mary left her house to you two. I must see some of your work, honeybunch. I'm part owner of a small gallery. Just a dinky little place down in Corona del Mar. But, maybe, you've got something we can show. Well, I'd better get back to my company. See you tomorrow." She gave them a wave, and stepped off the deck, and darted down the sidewalk, her bare feet making little plopping sounds, her long white dress flowing in the breeze.

Elizabeth was left feeling slightly out of breath. "Andy!" she whispered as soon as Tyree was out of earshot. "Did you hear that? She owns a *gallery!*"

"Nice coincidence, huh?" Andy said.

"Oh God! I hope she likes my stuff. It would be a start, at least. And, if they actually sold something . . . we sure could use the money."

"She's oddly attractive, isn't she?" Andy asked, looking after her. "In a bohemian sort of way. But, she sure is inquisitive. Asks a lot of questions."

"Well, that's a lot better than our neighbors in the apartment. Nobody spoke to anyone. It might be nice for a change, to have friendly neighbors."

Andy nodded. "It sure would."

"But what kind of person wears a diamond in her front tooth?"

"Are you sure? I didn't see anything."

"I'm positive. I wonder what Boo looks like."

Andy chuckled. "Maybe he has a bone through his nose."

At that, they both sputtered into laughter.

Inside, the fire felt wonderful and Elizabeth

curled up in the chair next to it, trying to shake the chill from the sea air before she went up to bed. Andy went about locking up the house and turning off all but the living room light. By the time he was through and had gone upstairs, Elizabeth could hardly move herself off the chair. Every muscle in her body ached. She was just about to follow Andy when she remembered Aunt Mary's antique clock that stood at the foot of the steps. Opening the glass door, she carefully wound both the works and the chime. She gave a rough guess as to what time it was. Then, she pushed the pendulum into motion and closed the door. The click, click, click, of the pendulum as it swung back and forth made the house feel as if it had suddenly sprung to life with the motion of the clock.

She turned and gave their new living room another glance. Everything was so much roomier than the apartment. It would take a long time to get used to the change. The drapes were still open. She should close them, but fatigue hung on her like a suit of lead armor, so she decided to leave them alone. She blinked, barely able to keep her eyes open. Then, for just one second, she thought she saw someone outside the sliding glass door looking in. But when she blinked again, the image was gone. No one out there, except maybe a sea bird. She switched off the lights and slowly, her muscles screaming with indignity, climbed the stairs to bed.

A huge harvest moon rose over Saddleback Mountain. Its bright light flooded the foothills and flowed down to the dark ocean, staining everything in its path an iridescent orange. Even though it was close to midnight, determined fishermen still stood on the Balboa Pier, their invisible lines dragging the water, their pails empty of catch.

HE stood at the foot of the pier listening to jazz coming from the Studio Cafe. A breath of breeze ruffled in off the ocean, chilled by October. He didn't feel the cold. All he felt was the flame that had begun to burn inside him again, the ripening heat of the agony. It was too soon! he thought. Far too soon! He never should have peered into the new couple's living room. Not even for that one moment. The sight of the woman, so soft and warm looking, along with the memory of her ambrosial scent, had stirred up the agony to an uncontrollable point. In the beginning, he'd fought it off for months at a time. Recently, however, he'd only been able to keep it at bay for several weeks, sometimes, if he were lucky, a little longer. And it used to come on slowly, giving him time to make careful, undetectable plans. But now it was back, a blazing plague, and only a few days after the last time. He was going into one of his bad periods and the new woman, so close by, had accelerated it. He detested the fact that he wasn't strong enough to control it, or find other ways to subdue the torment.

He walked the length of the pier and back—searching—searching—his body racked with painful spasms. Then, he moved onto the narrow tree-lined street that led to the bay. The area was light and dark, incandescent brightness and midnight shadows. It was a blending of gaudy red, electric blue, and garish purple—the color of his nightmares.

A crowd of mostly teenagers surged around him—a frenzied school of darting fish. He passed the Balboa Pavilion, which stood like an imposing dowager at the water's edge, its roof confettied with bulbs of tiny white light. As he passed, he caught the scent of rotting wood, broiled lobster, varnish, and saltwater taffy. Beside the Pavilion sat the *Catalina Flyer,* the huge catamaran that made the daily twenty-mile trip to Catalina Island. It snoozed in its berth, a bitter salty odor trailing from it like wisps of bad breath. He moved on. Next to the ship was the Balboa Fun Zone with its incessant beeping and flashing of video games, the whirl and dash of the Ferris wheel, and a rocketing of calliope music emanating from the merry-go-round. A powerful humming invaded his head as he walked.

The place was a T-shirt and tennis shoe village. A strong scent of cotton and bleach from stone-washed jeans rose from the crowd around him, along with the smell of chocolate-dipped frozen bananas, pizza, Balboa ice cream bars, and the acrid bite of metallic quarters from the arcade, all blended with the treacly smell of ripe flesh. As more of the odors assailed him, prickles of light began to swim in front of his eyes.

The humming in his head turned to a dull pounding—soft at first, comfortably muted. Then it grew louder and louder—a great bass drum throbbing out its beat—the rhythm set by the movement of the crowd. For a moment, he put his hands over his ears, as if he could stem the pain that came from the pulsing beat. Then he hurried on, left the palpating throng behind, barely enduring the pain that traveled with him. He moved quickly along a sidewalk the color of old tombstones.

A few blocks away from the crowded Fun Zone, in the quiet and half-darkness, he caught a different mixture of scents. A bouquet of London Dock tobacco, Sandalwood, gold fillings, and a hint of lemon throat drops grew heavy in the air. Looking about, he spotted the reason. A jacketed man with a pipe in his mouth had turned the corner and was ambling down the sidewalk a few yards away. He was in his middle years—short and slender, with cropped hair that smelled of sun and salt. The man walked past him, giving him only a momentary glance with pale green eyes, then turned from the sidewalk onto one of the ramps that led to a small sloop, bobbing dockside on the incoming tide.

Somewhere out on the bay, a panic of night birds rose from the water and took flight. The moon was higher now, and no longer orange, leaving a rippling trail of polished light across the deck of the bobbing sloop.

He watched as the man made his way aboard the trim little ship. *Moldy Duck,* the nameplate on the stern said, *Newport Beach.* The ship reeked of polyurethane, hemp, teak and fiberglass. He waited. A light came on in the cabin. He waited longer— smelled limes and vodka and plastic glasses. While he waited, the blood in his veins turned molten, flowed like searing lava through his body. He shook with the fever of it.

Music drifted out of the small vessel. Haunting. Violin-sweet. Piano notes cascading like mellow laughter. The tones reverberated throughout his body—like a shiver of silver bells that continued to peal. Was it Schumann or Brahms? The crystal-sharp recording on compact disc was so clear and glorious it could not be distinguished from the real thing. He'd not listened to music so sublime for many years.

He bowed his head and closed his eyes. He wanted to stand there forever and drown in the layers of symphony. Tears gathered behind his eyelids. For a lingering moment, he considered passing this man. Then, the heat and the hunger rose in him. Throughout his limbs, he felt his burgeoning need. The air was fragrant with one of the countless scents he knew no one else could smell—an aroma of the soothing fluid which would quell his inner fire.

He shook off the hypnotic effects of the music and stepped aboard the *Moldy Duck*. Under his feet, he felt her rise gently with the tide. With feather steps, he made his way to the cabin. The man aboard had failed to close the hatch. Light flooded from the opening along with the lingering strains of music. As he came down the ladder, the man looked up from the magazine he was reading, a tall ice-filled drink in his hand, and stared, a look of abject confusion on his face. Time was elastic—stretching, stretching—while they scrutinized each other.

"Who the hell are *you?*" the man, at last, roared, jumping up from his seat on the ship's bunk. A lantern on the bulkhead swayed with the movements of the sea beneath them. Shadows stretched and shimmied along the cabin deck.

"I am the Dark Angel," he answered, and caught the first delicious scents of anger and fear as they began to seep from the man's pores.

Chapter Two

Ted Bearbower answered the phone with a growl. He felt extraordinarily grumpy. He squinted at the new watch he'd picked up at the drugstore, after his last one had stopped. Five-ten a.m.! Holy Christ! he thought, if this call didn't turn out to be damn important he'd jerk the fucking phone right out of the wall!

"Teddy Bear?" It was Locke's voice.

Ted blanched at the nickname. "It's *Ted!*" he roared. "And, goddamn it, Locke, couldn't whatever the hell it is wait until a little later?"

"It looks like we've got another one," Locke said. "Jesus, *Ted,* police work doesn't wait around until after you've had your breakfast! You get your balls caught in your zipper or something?"

"Shit!" Ted said, then yawned hard. The effort made his jaws ache. He fought off the urge to hang up, disconnect the phone jack and crawl back into bed, although he knew he wouldn't be able to sleep. There was a time when he'd needed a solid eight hours a night, but during the last few years, he'd gotten by on no more than four or five. However, he'd spent the last few days and most of the nights, going over murder cases. He felt about ninety years old. Even with ten hours sleep, he still wouldn't have been ready to cope with a new murder. "Sorry," he said. "I'm just tired."

"This one's really ripe," Locke said. "Coroner says at least three days. A male this time. His ex-wife called it in about an hour ago. Out on the peninsula, a block or so from the Fun Zone. You wanna get a look before they take the body away?"

"Does it match?"

"Throat slashed. Loss of blood. Chunks of flesh missing."

"From where?"

"Don't ask."

"Damn! Where do I find you?"

"On Edgewater. North of the Pavilion. He's on board a boat called the *Moldy Duck*. You can't miss it. Yards and yards of yellow tape."

Even before he boarded the boat, Ted could smell the body. Despite temperatures in the mid-sixties for the past three days, putrefaction had already set in. It was obvious that bacteria in the body had begun to multiply at a rapid rate as soon as death had occurred. It was the unforgettable stench of a human body decomposing.

As he stepped on board the boat, he noticed a faint shoe print branded on the edge of a blue canvas sail-cover lying on the deck. He leaned down to inspect it. It was only a partial print, outlined by a dark substance. Paint? Ink? Tar? It shouldn't take forensics long to identify it. He stood up and made his way across the polished teak deck, steeling himself against the scene he knew he would find in the cabin. He could look at death quite easily now, compared to the way it had affected him the first few years he'd been in police work, but he still dreaded it. He'd never vomited, the way some of his colleagues had, but he'd come close to passing out on one or two occasions. Afterward, he'd gone back to the Department or home and scrubbed his hands and face with soap and water, as if he could somehow scrub away the images of what he'd seen. Then, he'd gone out and treated himself to one of his favorite desserts, or a seven-course meal—a rather bizarre reaction, he realized, but one that had kept him sane all these years.

Inside the cabin, the smell grew worse. The medical examiner, a narrow, pale man with wispy strands of graying hair, was still checking over the body. Locke stood staring out an open porthole and turned to give him only a quick nod when he entered. But in that second, Ted saw the strained, haunted look in the young man's eyes. Locke hadn't dealt with many deaths yet, but he would handle it okay. He had the right blend of toughness and optimism that was necessary.

Ted stood at the bottom of the companionway and began an inspection of the room. He always checked the ceiling first. Or, in this case, the overhead. Nothing out of the ordinary there. The overhead light was on—a hanging lamp that swayed with the movements of the boat. As he looked around, he noticed how quiet the cabin was, except for the lapping of the tide. Two men from forensics were using portable lasers to survey every surface of the cabin for fingerprints. As a rule, death either accelerated or hushed man's idle chatter. In this case, the crew worked silently.

He checked the portholes, the head, the lockers, and a bundle of canned goods tied in a small hammock over one of the v-berths. He noted the overall neatness of the cabin. For a reason he couldn't yet grasp, that fact stirred up something in the deep recesses of his mind. Nothing in the cabin was out of place, except for an overturned plastic glass on the deck surrounded by traces of what had been a puddle of clear liquid—probably a mixed drink. A small pool of dark blood, congealed and unmoving, lay on the wooden deck next to the victim.

"When do you figure it happened?" he asked the medical examiner.

"Three days. Possibly four. There's so much bacterial gas the contents of his stomach have been forced up through his mouth and nose."

Locke made a gagging sound.

"I understand you found some flesh missing?" Ted said.

"Yeah." The medical examiner looked up at him, the corner of his mouth rigid. "One of his balls was . . . well, as far as I can tell, it was bitten off."

Locke moaned and pushed his head further out the porthole.

"Did you find it?" Ted asked.

"Nope," the examiner said. "And there are other pieces of flesh missing."

"Cause of death?"

"Can't say for certain until we get to the lab. But from the look of him, from the small amount of lividity, I'd say he bled to death."

Locke turned away from the porthole. "Okay. But where?"

"Where, what?" Ted asked.

"Where was he when he bled to death? Not here. Not enough blood."

Ted stood for a minute listening to the lap of bay water against the ship's hull. Deep inside his brain, little wheels and cogs began to turn. It was a peculiar feeling, but one he'd grown accustomed to over the years. He took a closer look at the pool of blood. Taking into account evaporation, there was maybe a cup and a half. Two at the most. In every case he'd checked, the victim had bled to death, but there had been very little blood at the scene. Something more was here, too, only he couldn't see it. Something right in front of him. The hook he was looking for.

"Okay then," he said. "Since it's obvious the victims weren't moved, the killer's draining them and taking their blood for God knows what reason."

Locke moaned. "Why would someone do that?"

"A lot of reasons, not the least of which could be satanic rituals. Blood sacrifices."

"Don't you usually find markings on the body in that case? Symbols? That kind of thing?" Locke said.

"Sometimes." Ted stooped down next to the medical examiner. "Anything else we should know?"

"Some deep scratches on his arms. Almost puncture wounds. That's about it," the medical examiner said. "No other marks on the body except a few bruises on the wrists. But who knows, the pathologist may find traces of his attacker's skin under his fingernails, or a dozen other possibilities. Maybe we'll get lucky."

Two uniformed policemen clamored down the companionway. The cabin felt uncomfortably small with so many people in it. Ted had a moment of acute claustrophobia.

"You finished?" the medical examiner asked.

"Yeah," Ted nodded his head. But there was still something about the scene that didn't feel right, something he couldn't quite ferret out.

The medical examiner helped the two patrolmen place the body in a rubberized body bag for delivery to the coroner's lab. Ted felt more comfortable after the uniforms had taken the body away.

"We've got two sets of fingerprints," said one of the forensics men—a tall thin man who had to stoop in the cramped space. "A few complete. A lot of fragments. They're all over the place. My guess is they belong to the owners."

Ted nodded.

"But we've got a shoe print topside that doesn't match this guy's," the tall man said. "Probably male. It's too large for most women. May or may not be something. Looks like tar."

"I noticed that. You mean tar like you find on the beach?" Ted asked.

"Possibly. We found more prints on the sidewalk along the dock and tried to trace them to the origin, but they were completely eradicated by the time we reached the Fun Zone. Too many people tramping over them." The tall man tried to stretch, and bumped his head on the overhead.

A few minutes later the two forensics men left, promising Ted their preliminary report by late afternoon or evening.

It was just the two of them now, listening to the creaking of the boat. Locke had finally stopped looking out the porthole and was busy reexamining the cabin.

"Did you talk to the ex-wife?" Ted asked.

"Yes. She was hysterical. We had one of the uniforms take her to Hoag Hospital for some sedation." As he talked, Locke tugged open the small galley oven and looked inside.

"You said she reported finding him at what? About four this morning? How come so damn early? Isn't that a little strange?"

Locke closed the oven, and went to examine the net sling of canned food. "Seems they were on the verge of getting back together. They'd planned a cruise down to Baja. He'd told her he wanted to leave this morning before sunup. She hadn't heard from him in a few days. But that wasn't unusual, since he didn't have a phone on board. Boy! This guy must love Vienna sausages." He poked the netting with his finger and set it swinging.

"So, she walked right into this mess." Ted slowly moved his bulk around the small space, his eyes checking for the slightest thing that might be out of place. He found nothing. "Any chance *she* might have done it?"

"I don't think she could have managed. Too small. And no sign of a struggle."

That was it! Nothing out of place. No sign of a struggle. Not in this case, and not in any of the other cases. The attacker bled his victim to death and took a bite of flesh, *all without a struggle.* Ted frowned. "Do you remember anything, in any of the other cases we've looked at, about needle tracks or drugs?"

"No. Why?"

"Did they do toxicology reports?"

"Not detailed ones. The cause of death in all of the cases was pretty obvious. Loss of blood. What makes you ask?"

Ted pressed his fingers against his eyes. It was only six in the morning and he was already getting a fucking class-A headache. This was one day he wished he could start all over, much slower this time. "Because," he said, "no one in their right mind is going to just stand still and let someone open a vein unless they're drugged or already unconscious."

"She thinks it was a burglary," Locke said. "The wife."

"Why? Is something missing?"

"Yeah. According to her, an expensive compact disc player, and a lot of discs."

"Doesn't seem to me like enough reason to kill someone," Ted said.

"Maybe it's a junkie looking for something to turn into cash."

"No," Ted said. "We've got a definite pattern here."

Locke ran the tip of his tongue over his teeth in front, where they overlapped, then said, "You're thinking it's a serial, aren't you?"

"We may know more, after we get the forensic report." Ted looked at the tins of Vienna sausages in the net, which continued to sway with the movements of the boat. "Come on, let's get out of here," he said. "I'll buy you a nice big breakfast!"

Locke closed his eyes, moaned and began to climb out of the cabin. "For Christ's sake, Teddy Bear. It beats me how the hell you can go and eat after seeing something like this!"

It had been a long day for Tyree Rattigan. She hadn't gotten much sleep because of thinking about the young couple next door. No one had anticipated Mary leaving the house to them. Everyone expected her things would go to one of the group. Sarah and her sister had mentioned Mary's niece, but she hadn't given it a second thought. Sitting curled up on the den sofa, her needlework in hand, she had the television turned up just loud enough for her to hear. She hated being alone in the huge house at night when her husband, Boo, wasn't home. The great expanse of white walls echoed with loneliness. She looked at her watch. Eleven p.m. Boo was much later than she expected. The evening news came on. Anchorman Jerry Dunphy, looking distinguished with his silver hair, rattled on about the escalating violence in the Middle East, a cargo plane crash in South America, and a fire that had consumed a mattress factory in Huntington Beach.

She'd just finished a row of cross-stitch and laid the work down, stretching to relieve a kink in her back, when she heard the news item.

"Early this morning police discovered the body of a man who was murdered on board a boat in the Newport Beach Harbor area of Orange County," Dunphy said.

Tyree leaned forward and turned up the sound, then sat back and nervously twisted her long red hair between her fingers.

"According to authorities, the victim was Arthur Greene, owner of R and X Electronics in Irvine."

Tyree's hands went damp. Her heart thumped faster than usual.

"Greene was found aboard his sailboat in Newport Beach. His throat had been cut. Medical experts say the cause of death stemmed from a loss of blood."

She jumped from the sofa and began to pace the room like a skittish cat.

"Newport Beach Police told reporters that the body had been aboard the boat for several days before it was found by Greene's former wife, Helen Lurray Greene."

Taking a deep breath to steady herself, she went to the window and stared out on the darkness. Oh God! she thought, not another one! Not so soon!

"Police have no leads in the case as yet."

For a moment, she covered her ears with her hands, trying to block out the words. The sound of the newscaster was barely muted, so she hurried to the television and snapped it off. After that, she returned to the window and leaned her head against the cold glass pane. The coolness was a slight comfort. Still, her hands grew damper and began to tremble with the knowledge that she knew what was happening and why. She could stop it, but it would cost her everything. And it would affect the others. The realization that people were dying sickened her, and she hated herself for her cowardice. She stood at the window for a long time, watching the waves pound against the beach.

Finally, she returned to the sofa and picked up her needlework. Finding the place where she left off, she painfully pushed aside the whole matter and forced herself to become totally involved in the Jacobean bird she was stitching. After a few minutes she stopped, her work poised in her hands. No! They couldn't ignore it! The group *had* to do something. It would put the entire project in danger, but they could manage, if everyone agreed. In the meantime, they had the young couple next door to worry about. She shook her head and went back to her work. How in the hell had they ever gotten into this mess in the first place? she wondered. But in the beginning, they had each agreed it was worth the risk. Besides, they had gone too far, let too much happen, to turn back now. Even still, she found herself afraid of what she knew they were doing to the couple next door. She was directly involved. If something terrible happened . . . well, she couldn't worry about that now. It was too late for that.

HE stood for a long time in the alley behind the house. Even though the night was clear, the air glistened with dampness. The street lamps at the end of the alley frosted white with moisture from off the ocean. All he could think about the past few days was the young couple who had moved into Old Mary's house. The thought gave him both pleasure and pain. The scent of the woman's Ivory soap, a faint aroma of oil paint and turpentine, a touch of White Shoulders cologne, wafted from the house.

The moon hung low in the sky, almost extinguishing itself in the dark edge of the ocean. The couple had obviously gone to bed. The lights were out all over the house. He waited a while longer, wondering what the woman's name was, what her flesh would taste like, how her body would feel against his hands. The young man held far less interest for him—too lean with watery blood. He smelled bland, like the scent of a dry summer wind. Unless the agony became acute, he would never choose him. But the woman . . . the woman was succor. Just the thought of her could bring on the agony.

A stray cat wandered across a cinder-block wall a few feet away, turned large yellow eyes on him, hissing from the depths of its throat, before hurrying on.

The moment the light from the moon dimmed, he moved across the alley, his footsteps muted by the leather sandals he wore, and opened the wooden gate. At the back door, his skilled hands silently worked the long metal picks. The young couple had failed to put the chain in place. How careless. Someone should tell them to be more careful. The door opened with a soft snap, swinging wide, the plumb of the house slightly off. Inside, he made his way through the porch and into the kitchen. From there, he caught the woman's scent again, stronger now. It was no problem for him to find his way into the living room and up the stairs in the darkness. In the upper hallway, the odor of oil paint was almost overwhelming. He moved on past the smaller bedrooms to where he knew the woman slept.

The windows in the large bedroom were open. Outside, the pounding surf generated a phosphorescent glow. What feeble light seeped into the room was the color of old stone. The young couple slept soundly in the antique bed. From somewhere downstairs, a clock chimed three times. The man stirred slightly, settled into another position and quieted.

He moved to the bedside and gazed down at the woman. He'd seen her lovely face somewhere before, but he still couldn't recall where. His nostrils burned with the salty sweet fragrance of her body. In the light, her face looked as pale and soft as candle wax. Her lips were slightly parted, a child's mouth really, her jaw slack, strands of her fine hair spread out on the pillow like a dusty halo. Her innocent vulnerability made him ache. She wore a nightgown of transparent yellow. He could see her heart beating like delicate bird wings beneath the silk fabric. She turned in her sleep, flinging one ivory-skinned arm over her head. He felt as if his own heart had slipped from his chest and was thumping around inside his belly.

Her breasts rose and fell with her rhythmic breathing, her nipples hard in the cool night air. A delicate moan escaped his throat and he was alarmed to see her eyelids flutter. But it was only a flick of lashes and her eyes did not open. He reached down and gently brushed her nipples with his fingertips. The ache intensified and he withdrew his hands, knowing that he invited the agony upon himself. Too soon. Too close to home. He would have to wait. He wanted her, but not with the man lying beside her. He would wait and take the woman when she was alone. Then, the pleasure would be so rare, it would be worth the waiting.

He turned away from the bed and looked at the dresser. Some of her personal things were scattered there. A silver-backed hairbrush, a jar of lemon-scented hand lotion, lip gloss that smelled of her mouth, and a bottle of White Shoulders perfume. He picked up each item, caressing them gently with his fingers, running them across his cheek, before setting them down. Lifting the tube of gloss for a second time, he held it to his nose before slipping it into his pocket. It carried the scent of her lips, sweeter than anything he could imagine. Next time, he might take the hair brush, entangled with silky strands of her lovely hair.

He moved out of the room into the darkness of the hall. It took only seconds to make his way down the stairs through the kitchen and out the back door, which he closed behind him, making only a muted tapping as he set the lock.

It was past eleven in the evening. Ted Bearbower and Steve Locke had just returned to Ted's condo after eating a huge spaghetti dinner at B J's on the peninsula—or, rather, Ted had ended up eating both dinners. Locke still had no stomach for food, thanks to his early morning encounter with a decomposing body. Although he was unable to eat, Locke had managed to down a half-dozen bottles of Corona.

Even after the huge meal, Ted felt hungry. He took a Sara Lee spice cake out of the freezer and put it in the microwave to thaw. Locke sat at the kitchen table, his eyes blinking with fatigue. His sun-bleached hair was disheveled, and his face so pale and drawn the freckles across his nose and cheeks stood out like tiny pieces of brown confetti. He scribbled a few words on a yellow pad and then yawned.

"So what have we ruled out?" Ted asked, setting the microwave timer.

"Revenge, I think. We haven't found any ties between the victims." Locke yawned again.

"Want another beer?"

"Hell, no! One more beer and I'll spend the night sleeping on your kitchen table. As it is I don't think I should drive home." Locke shook his head and scrubbed at his eyes with his fingers.

"You can crash on the sofa."

"Thanks." Locke straightened in his chair and gave his shoulders a stretch. "Damn! I forgot! I had a date with Sandy tonight. But I was so involved with the case I forgot all about it. She's going to be pissed as hell." He shrugged and looked like a contrite six-year-old. "Well, anyway, there doesn't seem to be any tie-in with any particular day, season, or moon phase in these cases."

"How many matches do we have now?"

"It's escalating with all the reports coming in. Including L.A., Northern California, and a preliminary from the FBI, it looks like another fifteen possibles. I've got someone inputting everything we've got into our computer. We'll have a better picture in a day or two." Locke drummed his fingers against the yellow pad on the table.

"Jesus! This guy's been busy!" Ted said. "How far back do they go?"

"Five years. Nothing before that."

"You've checked?"

"I asked for seven. But nothing shows up except for the past five years. Nothing close enough to really consider."

"The guy's probably in his mid-thirties."

"What makes you say that?" Locke looked puzzled.

"Because the average serial killer is between twenty-eight and forty."

Locke drummed his fingers louder, squinted his eyes thoughtfully, then said, "Tell me something. How come no one put all these killings together before this?"

The microwave timer beeped. Ted opened the oven door and pulled out the cake. "I'd bet that up until recently this guy's moved around a lot. Now, he's either gotten lazy or careless, and left a number of victims in the same area. Or maybe he's feeling invulnerable. If he's killed that many people and gotten away with it, he probably thinks he's a first cousin to God by now. With an isolated murder here, another somewhere else, then put some time between them, no one thinks to make a thorough check."

"But still—"

"Take a look," Ted said. "Not all, but a fair number of these people are prostitutes, runaways, street people. The kind that live in society's shadows. No one makes a fuss over their deaths. Lately though, he seems to have switched."

Locke made another note on his yellow pad then set the pencil down. "But, it's so bizarre. Bleeding the victims to death. Taking all the blood. Not to mention his usual M.O. of biting out chunks of flesh. Shit! Why wouldn't something that unusual be noticed right away?"

Ted took two plates out of the cupboard, cut the cake in half, and put a half on each plate. He set one of them down in front of Locke along with a fork. Locke automatically picked up the fork and began to eat.

"It's not all that bizarre. Take my word for it. We get an average of fifty-two homicides a day in the U.S.. And there's been a hell of a lot more grotesque and weird cases on the books than this one." Ted put the other plate down across from Locke, pulled out the chair and sat down. "I remember some guy back east who was collecting his victim's skulls, using them for knobs on his bed-posts. He also collected several dozen vaginas, and sewed them inside women's panties so he could wear them. In his house they found a belt made of female nipples and several chairs covered with human skin."

Locke's hand stopped partway to his mouth, the fork and a piece of spice cake poised in midair. "You gotta be kidding!"

"I wish I were." Ted devoured his piece of cake in a matter of seconds.

Locke lowered his hand, set the fork down and pushed the plate away. "Damn!"

"And there are worse things around than that. So you see why no one made a fuss about a few people having their throats cut, or a bite taken out of them." Ted pointed at Locke's plate. "You gonna eat that cake?"

"No."

"But," Ted said, pulling Locke's plate over in front of him, "the fact of the matter is, *this* is *our* case, since this psycho seems to have settled here. At least, for now. And, it's weird enough for me. I want to put a stop to this guy, ASAP. To do that, we need to know why he's doing what he's doing, which, if we're real lucky, could lead us to him." He took a bite of Locke's cake, considered leaving the rest, then changed his mind and finished it off.

"You got any theories?" Locke rubbed his eyes again.

The poor kid's dead on his feet, Ted thought, but he's still going. Spunky little shit. "A few," he said. "The satanic one I mentioned this morning. That's a bet. Or sex. Maybe blood gives him a hard-on. Then again, maybe he's just got an iron deficiency."

Locke stretched his arms over his head and yawned again. "Yeah, well, maybe he's drinking the stuff, thinks he's a vampire."

Ted nodded. The thought rang a bell somewhere

in the back of his brain. "You know . . ." he started. "You might be right."

"Ah, come on Ted, you don't really believe in such things, do you?" The young man gave him an odd look.

"Real vampires? No. But people who *think* they're vampires, that's something else. I remember some case where a guy back in the fifties in New York, I think it was, went out prowling the streets, sucking people's blood. And, some big mucky-muck in England years ago used to lure people to his plush estate, bludgeon them to death, and drink their blood. If I remember right, that guy used to finish off the whole thing by eating the rest of his victim."

"Ah, cripes!" Locke groaned, then put his head down on the kitchen table, his cheek against the yellow pad. He let out a sigh of exhaustion. "I gotta call Sandy," he mumbled. "Don't let me forget to call Sandy."

"There's something more here," Ted said. "I can't put my finger on it—not yet anyway. I need to make some phone calls tomorrow." He thumbed through the forensics report. They had one possible lead. The shoe print on the deck. It didn't belong to the victim or the victim's ex-wife. Hopefully, it wouldn't take long to find out what kind of shoe, and where the tar came from. That would tell them something about the killer's size, and about where he'd been walking just prior to the killing. Of course, it was possible that the owner of the shoe might not have anything at all to do with the kill-ings. When he looked over at Locke, he saw that the

young man was sound asleep. He quietly picked up
the forks and plates, and set them in the sink. Looking at his watch, he saw that the stupid thing had
stopped again!

"Come on," he said, trying to rouse Locke.
"You'll be more comfortable on the sofa." But
Locke only wiggled his fingers and let out a soft
moan. His breathing settled into a deep rhythm.
Ted went into the living room and brought back
one of the afghans that his wife, Sylvia, had crocheted. He couldn't remember an evening when she
hadn't had her 'busy' work in her hands. For a
moment, he pressed the Afghan against his face,
hoping it would still carry her scent, but it only
smelled like dry wool. He snugged the afghan
around Locke's shoulders. The nights were getting
chilly. Then, he turned off the kitchen light.

"Yeah, kid," he whispered. "You've got the right
idea. Sleep tight." With that, he made his way out
of the dark kitchen, down the hall, and into his
bedroom.

Even though his body was tired, his mind was still
clicking like a runaway computer. He knew he
wouldn't sleep for a long while yet. His mind was a
clutter of facts that needed sorting out. He put on his
robe, and sat down in the overstuffed rocker by the
bedroom window, and looked out on the night. Now,
all he had to do was put everything he knew about
both the current and past cases into neat, logical little
piles. You could figure out even the hairiest puzzle,
he told himself, if you just went about it right.

* * *

During the first week, after they moved into the beach house, Andy lumbered out of bed before sunup every morning, put on his velour warm-ups, padded downstairs, made coffee, and disappeared into his new office. He announced to Elizabeth that the sea air was acting like a tonic. He slept so soundly, and awoke so rested, that he overflowed with creative ideas in the morning. He'd finally broken through his writing block.

"I've banished my old enemy!" he said, early one morning, flourishing the yardstick that Elizabeth had been using to measure for wallpaper. He whipped the stick around like a sword. "I'll never be plagued with it again!" He thrust the stick into one of the sofa cushions, carrying on a make-believe duel for a few minutes, before sheathing the sword down the front of his warm-ups and marching triumphantly to his office. Elizabeth thought he looked perfectly idiotic. A little pang of jealousy stung her.

She wished she could catch his mood. She kept putting off starting her own work. Every time she passed the bedroom where she'd stored her art supplies, a sense of panic swept over her. Maybe when the house was more settled, she told herself, she would lose her fear. She knew the problem. Her work had been rejected so many times, she couldn't bear putting her heart and soul into another painting, only to have some snooty gallery owner tell her it "wasn't quite right." Instead, she got busy measuring for new wallpaper, cleaning and painting the wicker furniture, and dusting miles of wooden shutters.

She had the TV cable hooked up even though they couldn't afford it, otherwise all they got was snow. She located the supermarket—which was too far away, and much more expensive than her old one—found a little newsstand that carried a variety of magazines and newspapers, and blew a hole in their tight budget by buying five pounds of macadamia-nut coffee from a specialty shop in Fashion Island.

Every evening, just after sundown, Tyree Rattigan came rushing over from next door with a steaming casserole dish in her hand.

"You really shouldn't go to all this trouble every day," Elizabeth kept insisting.

"Hey, it's just until you get settled," Tyree said. The tiny blue-white diamond in her front tooth sparkled as she talked. "Besides, I adore trying out new recipes, and I don't get the chance to experiment often. Now be sure you eat every bite. Moving is stressful. You need all the nutrition you can get."

Elizabeth didn't care much for Tyree's cooking, although she was touched by the woman's thoughtfulness. However, it made her feel somewhat obligated, and she wondered how she might return the favor. She tried to coax Tyree into visiting awhile, to have coffee and, of course, to take a look at her paintings. But Tyree always begged off, claiming she wouldn't think of intruding until they were settled. Andy thought the food was delicious and wolfed it down, taking second helpings, which was unusual for him. His normal appetite wouldn't have fed a mouse. Elizabeth thought the casseroles had an odd, cupreous taste, and she only nibbled at them. And the few times she did eat a full meal, her stomach had become upset. And, then there were the nightmares. She'd never been plagued with bad dreams before. She figured it was either Tyree's rich cooking, or the change of climate, or maybe even the new house. She felt as if she dreamed most of the night, and woke up exhausted in the morning. Just the opposite of Andy.

Determined to get started with her painting, despite her fatigue, Elizabeth finally forced herself to fashion the small bedroom into a workable studio. She pulled the coverings off the skylight, and stacked her blank canvas against one wall, and her completed paintings against the other. Then she set up a card table to hold her paints and other supplies, and arranged her three easels so the light was right.

She pulled out what she thought were her four best works and hung them on the studio wall in anticipation of the time when Tyree would agree to look at them. They didn't look nearly as good as she had hoped. The old familiar dissatisfaction returned as she studied them. She had wonderful technique—her scholarship at Otis-Parsons had taken care of that—but she sensed an emptiness, a lack of emotion in them. They were too tightly done. Too much like an architect's renderings. "Damn," she muttered aloud. She'd have to do better if she were going to be accepted as an artist. She rummaged through her paints and brushes for what she needed, then set up a blank canvas.

As soon as she had everything in place, she perched herself on her 'painting stool' and spent some time trying to decide what to paint next. Sea-scapes would be good, with the surf at her front door—or the old houses along the peninsula—even the wild-looking teenagers who zoomed along the narrow sidewalk that ran in front of the house along the edge of the sand. The fact was, she had to find something with more guts to it than the cutesy cot-tages she'd been painting the past two years. She sat there for a long time, waiting for the muse to strike. But, nothing happened. She looked around at the awful wallpaper. How could anyone work with all those things peering at them? Disappointed, she fi-nally slid off the stool and went downstairs, a pain-ful knot growing in the pit of her stomach. This must be the way Andy felt when he had writer's block, she realized.

She decided to call Judy Bird, her closest friend. Judy was always a good catalyst for her art work. Elizabeth had promised to call her as soon as they were settled. Poor Judy had been devastated when she'd announced that she and Andy were moving out of the San Fernando Valley. She and Judy had been as close as sisters since kindergarten.

"I'll never see you again!" Judy had wailed.

"Don't be silly. We're moving to Orange County, not Jupiter. It's only about sixty miles away."

"All that traffic!"

"Not on the weekends," she had insisted. "Now that you and Alex are divorced, you can come and stay over. We'll get the guest room set up for you. And, you love the beach."

Elizabeth smiled as she picked up the phone. Yes, that's all she really needed. A good gab-fest with

Judy. Invite her down for the weekend. Maybe splurge and have lunch out somewhere elegant. Take a long walk on the beach. Collect shells. Maybe together they could get some of the awful wallpaper in the house changed, since Andy was so busy with his writing. It could be that the atmosphere in the old place had stifled her creativity. It was enough to unnerve anyone. She quickly dialed Judy's number. Surely her old friend would help her dispel the nightmares.

On Thursday evening, Elizabeth and Andy were stripping off the hideous Egyptian wallpaper in the living room when Elizabeth turned around suddenly and saw an elderly woman standing outside in the fog. She had her nose pressed against the glass of the sliding door, and was grinning in at them. Elizabeth let out a loud gasp, which made Andy jump and drop the bottle of stripper he was holding.

"Damn!" he said, catching the bottle before any of the liquid spilled on the Persian carpet. "What is it, Lizzy?"

Elizabeth regained her composure and gave a halfhearted laugh, pointing to the glass door. "I think we have company."

"Oh, dear-heart!" the woman said when Elizabeth slid open the door. "How rude of me. Sarah and I were just out for an evening stroll. I saw you working away, and I was curious to see what you were doing. Now isn't that just like an old busybody?"

"Oh, . . . that's okay," Elizabeth said. "I guess if

we don't want anyone to see what we were doing we should pull the drapes." Despite her words, she did feel a trifle invaded. "Won't you come in?"

"Goodness, no. You're busy. But we wanted to say hello since we live just next door. I don't suppose you remember us, do you? You were so young. I'm Mable Zipper and this is . . ." The woman looked around. "Sarah? Dear, come over here, and say hello to our new neighbors. My sister Sarah's a bit shy until she gets to know you. Then you can't get rid of her. You know, we used to watch you playing on the beach years and years ago, when you came to visit your Aunt Mary. We live just to the north of you, but I don't suppose you remember us."

"No, I'm afraid not," Elizabeth said.

The two women looked almost exactly alike. Elizabeth wondered if they were twins, but didn't ask. Both of them had to be in their seventies, plump, with short and precisely waved silver hair, pointy noses, watery-blue eyes, and thin pink mouths. The difference was in the way they dressed. Mable wore a bright flowing caftan in orange and red silk while Sarah had on a black polyester pants suit with a gold lapel watch safety-pinned at the neck. Another difference was evident when they talked. Or, rather, when Mable talked, since Sarah didn't. She merely stood in the doorway next to Mable, and smiled, bobbed her head, and fingered the gold-rimmed glasses that hung around her neck on a long chain.

"Why don't the two of you come in?" Elizabeth said, suddenly swept up in a wave of compassion for her two elderly neighbors. They looked so lost and lonely standing in the doorway. "I'll put on some coffee. We need a break. We've been stripping this paper for hours."

At the suggestion, Sarah Zipper looked panicked. The color in her face drained. She gripped Mable by the arm, her fingers pressing so hard that Elizabeth thought it must hurt, but Mable didn't reflect that it did.

"That's terribly nice of you, dear. But we wouldn't think of just popping in. Another time." Mable smiled sweetly. Sarah appeared relieved.

"Maybe when we get the new wallpaper up," Elizabeth suggested.

"Yes," Mable said, tipping her head to inspect the work they had done in the room. "My, I really did love that wallpaper Mary had. It was so . . . stylish! But, like all good things, I suppose it's seen its day."

"Yes, I'm afraid it has," Elizabeth said.

Sarah looked into the living room, shook her head, and gave a little cluck, as if she disapproved of what they were doing.

"Well, the fog's moving in, so we'd better get on home," Mable said. "It's nice to see you again. You certainly have grown up."

Almost instantly, the two of them were gone, swallowed by the darkness and the swirling mist. Elizabeth stood in the doorway staring out at nothing. "For heaven's sake," she complained, "everyone keeps coming by and introducing themselves, but so far no one has come inside to have coffee or anything."

"Maybe we've got dragon breath or something,"

Andy teased. "Besides, you don't want to get those two old farts in the habit of coming in anyway."

"Andy, that isn't nice. They seem pleasant enough." Elizabeth took the bottle of stripper from him, and began wetting down another swath of wallpaper.

"Sure. They're okay. But old people get lonely and start to cling. That's all I meant."

"Well, at least they're a friendly lot—the people we've met so far."

Andy climbed the ladder, and began tugging the wallpaper away from the wall. It gave off a moldy smell, and Elizabeth put her hand over her nose. "Whew! That's awful!" she said. "This stuff must have been up here for ages." She put the bottle of stripper down on the newspaper-covered coffee-table and stretched. Her arms were aching, and her back was tired. "Do you suppose Tyree is really going to have that get-together for us next Monday, the way she said? She hasn't mentioned it again. And my paintings. She hasn't mentioned them either."

"Ask her, why don't you?"

"It seems kind of pushy. I mean, after all, just because she owns a gallery doesn't mean she's obligated to look at my work. Besides, she's been so nice about bringing over dinner every night. Even if I don't care much for her cooking." She grimaced.

"Well, then, *don't* ask her," Andy grumbled. "Is Judy coming down tomorrow?"

"No, the day after. On Saturday. Friday night the traffic would be impossible. The two of us are going to get busy and put up the new wallpaper. But on

Monday, I really have to get started with my painting. I think I'll try something a little more sophisticated for the Newport Beach area." Elizabeth wiped the stripper off her hands on an old rag. "By the way, when do I get to read your stuff?"

"What?" Andy looked startled.

"Read. You know, written words. Books. *Your* book. You've been so excited about it. When do I get to see some of it?"

"Ah . . . pretty soon. I'd like to get enough done so you can see if the plot holds together. A few weeks more, maybe."

Elizabeth gave him a puzzled glance. "You usually hand me the pages the minute they come out of the printer."

Andy frowned. "This time I'd rather wait a while. That last bout of writer's block scared the shit out of me. It's going so well now, I don't want to jinx it."

"Fine," she said, a sinking sensation in the middle of her stomach. "I never really thought of myself as a jinx before."

"Oh, come on, Lizzy, I didn't mean it like that." He frowned at her. His dark eyes looked slightly angry.

She shrugged. "No, I don't suppose you did. I guess I'm just tired." After all, she thought, it should be enough that he was working again. But she still felt hurt. She yawned, and purposely changed the subject. "I'm really beat. Let's call it quits for tonight."

Andy nodded. "Sure. I'll be up in a while. I've got more polishing to do on my last pages."

A pang of disappointment hit her. Ever since he'd started writing again, he'd stayed up until all hours of the night. And before that, his writer's block had all but erased their sex life. She missed making love with him, falling asleep cuddled next to him. Right now, it was almost as if he were on a manic high. She hoped he would level out soon. Or, at the least, that she would catch the same fervor about her own work.

Getting ready for bed, she scrubbed her face and inspected herself in the small, round mirror in the bathroom. The beach air must be good for her. Her cheeks were ruddy, and her skin clear—which was a switch for her since she usually had such pale skin. The fine lines around her mouth had softened and almost disappeared, making her look younger. And her gray eyes had a brightness to them she liked. In the bedroom, she stood in front of the dresser for a moment, giving her hair a quick brush before climbing into bed. Her lips felt dry, and she tried to find her tube of lip gloss, but it seemed to have grown legs and skittered off someplace.

She fell off to sleep easily, but as usual, found herself bouncing in and out of disturbing dreams. She was stripping wallpaper off the floors, which in her dream didn't seem the least bit unusual. Then, Tyree came by and handed her a huge bowl of beet soup with a great dollop of sour cream in the middle. She thanked Tyree, but told her that Andy couldn't possibly eat all that sour cream because he was watching his cholesterol. Then, the soup turned into a glob of oil paint, and Elizabeth found herself lifting the brush and painting the oddest picture she'd ever seen.

The house felt chilly to Andy. Or maybe it was because he wasn't feeling good. A touch of flu perhaps. His head ached and his stomach felt queasy.

Sitting alone in his office after Elizabeth went to bed, Andy shivered. He would have to get a small space heater, he realized, since his office appeared to be an add-on, and the central heating ducts hadn't been extended to cover the area. But, chilly or not, he liked the room. It was large enough for his computer and desk, as well as their old sofa and over-stuffed chair. Being at the back of the house, just off the kitchen, he found it quiet. Quiet was a commodity that had been in short supply in their old apartment. The walls there had been like tissue paper, and the arguments of neighbors seeped through like strong brewed coffee through a paper filter. Perhaps the peaceful nature of the beach, and the quiet atmosphere were the reasons his writing had suddenly taken on a whole new dimension.

Something certainly had sparked his creativity the past week. Actually, it was damn strange the way it began. One morning he woke up feeling as if he might be coming down with the flu. He'd put his head down on the desk to rest. Some time later, he'd found a stack of pages on his desk, all printed out. A whole new plot. The type of thing he'd never done before. At first, he thought it was a joke that Lizzy had played on him. But on inspecting the material,

he found it was his own writing—no doubt about
the style. The fever must have blotted it from his
mind. But, fever or not, he was certain it was some
of the best work he'd done in a long time. Fortunately, that was the only time he'd worked, and not
remembered it.

After the first fifty pages or so, he'd called Marc
Cline, his agent, in New York, and discussed the
work with him. Marc had been excited about the
new plot. Andy felt a touch of regret at having upset
Lizzy by not sharing his new book. But, he wanted
to be positive the whole thing jelled before he told
her. God knows, he'd made a number of false starts
before. Even so, the fact that he was writing again
was enough to make him ecstatic.

Outside his office window, the wind started blowing in off the ocean, moaning around the eaves like
someone in pain. The leather of his chair seemed to
suck up the cold and transfer it to his body. It made
his ass and balls ache. He really had to get a heater.
He checked over the last few pages he'd roughed out
that day. Although it seemed impossible, he'd
managed almost thirty! He'd never worked that fast
before. The muse was definitely with him. With a
shake of his head, he turned off the word processor,
stacked a few stray books, and went into the
kitchen. A shot of brandy might help warm his
chilled bones and aching head.

He heated the brandy in a small glass, savoring
the sharp bite as he sniffed at it. Then he chug-a-
lugged it, something Elizabeth would have been ap-
palled to see him do. It burned a comfortably hot
trail from his mouth to his stomach. He started to

heat another shot when suddenly he heard a rasping noise close-by. He was certain it was the sound of the wooden gate out back being opened. He waited a moment, then a tiny metallic clicking cut through the silence, as if someone were trying to open the back door. The sound died, and was replaced by a scraping noise, like that of a long fingernail rasping against the wood siding of the house. For a moment, he stood rigid wondering if he should investigate. A raccoon? A tomcat on the prowl? The chill that had touched him earlier deepened, despite the brandy.

Finally, he set the glass down on the sink, and turned off the kitchen light. Standing in the darkness, listening, he felt the way he had as a child alone in his bedroom, imagining a low keening from inside his closet, or an unearthly slithering under his bed.

Quietly, and with far more bravado than he felt, he made his way to the service porch, pulled back the yellow cotton curtains on the back door window, and looked out. He half expected to find a ghastly apparition of old Aunt Mary waving skeletal arms at him, but the yard lay pale-blue and empty. Nothing stirred, except the wind, a lonely wail skittering around the eaves. When he checked, he found that neither he nor Lizzy had remembered to put on the chain lock. He picked it up, and pushed it into place. Careless, he thought. With all the strangers who wandered the beach, they'd better be more careful. Tomorrow, he would go out and buy a dead-bolt and install it, just to be on the safe side. He looked around the yard once more, but all that moved was a flutter of leaves and dry grass buffeted about by the wind. The metal wind chimes that hung from the edge of the roof clanged restlessly. The chimes, he rationalized, must have been what he'd heard.

He made his way into the dark kitchen, and continued on into the living room. He stood there for a second, listening for anything out of place. The surf, in its eternal restlessness, rumbled in against the sand. The wailing of the wind became a snarling growl. He heard nothing else except the tick ticking of Aunt Mary's old clock. Then, he quickly mounted the stairs, two at a time, wanting more than anything not to be alone—to feel the warmth of Elizabeth's body next to him, and her breath against his cheek.

Elizabeth woke up all twisted around Andy, who had managed to slip into bed without waking her. The sheets were tightly woven between the two of them. From downstairs, she heard the grandfather clock strike three. Outside, the surf sounded furious. She untangled herself, got up, and walked to the window. A stiff breeze had swept away any trace of fog, and it was sparkling clear. The moon, though almost down, was full, and she could see for quite a distance. Sure enough, the waves were at least six feet high, and thundering in along the beach. The house was only a short distance from the area surfers called The Wedge, where waves were trapped between the beach and the jetty—dangerous, unless you were an experienced swimmer, and extremely strong.

She was just about to go back to bed when she noticed someone surfing—a dark form riding in on one of the towering waves. Now that, she decided, was foolhardy—surfing near the Wedge at night, and apparently alone. Turbulent as the water was, he managed to ride the wave all the way in without being wiped out. She watched him, fascinated by his daring. On the beach, he shook off a spray of shimmering sea-water, picked up his board, and walked across the sand toward the boardwalk in front of the house.

The last of the moonlight flooded the beach like silver vapor, and she caught a good look at him as he passed below her window. He resembled a young Robert Redford—chiseled features, muscular, sandy-haired. Silently, he lifted his surfboard and carrying it under one arm, made his way between their house and the Rattigans'. Just before he disappeared between the houses, he stopped and looked up at her. She sucked in her breath, wanting to move, but felt her body freeze in place. His teeth glowed in the moonlight as he smiled up at her and gave a slight wave with his free hand. Then he moved on between the houses. She let out her breath and raced back to bed.

He was only a neighbor. A surfer. But riding the waves at an ungodly hour. Suddenly, the bedroom seemed filled with shadows. She pulled the covers up around her ears, and closed her eyes. New places had unfamiliar sounds, different shadows. It would take her quite a while to get used to the ones here. Curling closer to Andy, feeling safe against the warmth of his back, she tried to remember if they had put the chain locks on the doors downstairs. She burrowed closer to Andy. His body smelled sweet and musky. A sudden warmth surged through her and she began to run her hands over his arms. She would kiss him, wake him. But before she could act on her impulse, she felt herself being sucked into a deep, dark sleep. This time, the nightmares stayed away.

Elizabeth found herself awake before sunrise, wondering if the Robert Redford surfer had been part of a dream, or if he'd been real. She slipped into a pair of jeans and a sweatshirt, and went downstairs to make coffee. It was Friday, and she had promised herself that today she would go through and clean all the upstairs cupboards and closets.

Andy came plodding into the kitchen, rubbing his head.

"You okay?" she asked, pouring him some coffee.

He took a long swig of coffee, and sighed. "Just been working long hours."

"Give it a rest, why don't you? Take a walk on the beach."

"Maybe later. I hate to interrupt the flow when it's going so damn good." He leaned down, and gave her a kiss.

Temptation prodded her to kiss him again. They could go back to bed. Make love. It would be lovely, with the sound of the surf outside. Then, looking over at him, she realized how totally preoccupied he'd become with his writing. She hated the catch 22 routine they'd fallen into. Andy had writer's block, so they didn't make love. She had a painting block, so they didn't make love. The ridiculous part was now that Andy was on a writing high, they still didn't make love. What it all boiled down to, she realized, was that after five years of marriage their lovemaking had changed from a lusty romp once a day to a halfhearted quickie once a month, or less. The thought depressed her. They were much too young for such a routine.

"What would you like for breakfast?" she asked, pushing thoughts of sex out of her mind. A marriage resembled the ocean's swells. That's what her mother used to tell her. At times you were at the top of the crests, sometimes at the bottom. It all balanced out, if you were lucky.

"Coffee will do. I'm not really hungry."

"You should eat something."

"Later, maybe. I want an early start this morning. How's your painting coming along?"

"Haven't begun. But, by Monday, I'll be set up and ready to go," she said, pleased that he had asked.

"Great." He picked up his cup and refilled it. "I'll take this along to my office. See you later." He turned, and padded through the kitchen toward his office.

Elizabeth called after him. "Oh, hey! I forgot to tell you. I saw Robert Redford last night."

"What?" Andy called from the porch.

"I saw Robert Redford on the beach last night—surfing."

Andy poked his head around the kitchen doorway. He gave her a mischievous grin. "Sorry, dear, I don't have time to chat. I've got Kathleen Turner waiting for me in my office."

The rest of the day Elizabeth worked around the house. She put new sheets on their old bed in the guest room, and set out fresh towels in the bath for Judy's visit the coming weekend. After that, she clipped a half dozen of the roses growing in a wild tangle in the backyard and arranged them in a vase on the coffee table.

In the afternoon, she finally tackled the upstairs cupboards, searching for some of Mary's personal things. The only items she'd found were a small blue-and-white cameo pin in the top drawer of the dresser, and five gold hairpins in the bottom cupboard in the bathroom, along with a cut-crystal perfume atomizer. She wondered what had happened to all the lovely silk caftans, and the gold earrings. And, what had Mary done with all those bracelets? If she remembered right, Mary used to wear at least a dozen of them.

The hall cupboards turned out to be almost bare, except for something she saw glinting in a back corner. The cupboard was deep, and she had to crawl halfway inside to reach it. As soon as her fingers closed on the item, she realized it was another of Aunt Mary's plastic bags filled with brick-colored powder. There were two of them, in fact. She pulled them out, and stared at them. What the heck *was* this stuff, anyway? She opened one of the bags. Just like the one she'd found in the large, salt-crusted box in the bedroom. It had no odor. She picked up a pinch of the powder and examined it. It felt extremely fine and smooth. She couldn't think of a damn thing it might be. Rust-colored cocaine? She laughed. Pretty exotic. Andy was probably right. It was some kind of roach powder. She shouldn't be handling it.

On the top shelf, she found a leather-bound photo album. When she opened the dusty book, she found it crammed with photographs. Most of them were of people she didn't recognize, and, from the look of the clothing and the quality of the photos, most of them were extremely old—perhaps taken somewhere around the turn of the century. But, sure enough, looking no more than twenty, but unmistakable, was Aunt Mary. Elizabeth squinted at the dim photos. Mary had been a small, plumpish woman, with wide gray eyes, a prominent nose, and a thin, determined-looking mouth. Her hair, gold and curly, was swept up on top of her head in the style of the era. Near the end of the album, she found several loose photographs taken at a much later time, from the look of the clothes. On the back of one was the date of March 15, 1973. In the photo was a much older Aunt Mary and a youngish, tow-headed man. Mary's son, no doubt. So handsome. Elizabeth wished he'd not always been away at school when she'd visited. After all, he was her cousin. Her only one, and she'd never seen him. What a tragedy, she thought, dying so young. Mary must have been inconsolable.

She sighed and closed the album, setting it aside to take downstairs to show Andy. Maybe she'd use some of the older photos as a basis for a new series of paintings. There was something quite fetching about them. For a moment, she found herself wanting to pick up a sketch pad or a brush. That was a good sign. But she would wait until Monday, since Judy was coming for the weekend. Give her creative juices a chance to really boil.

That night, just after dark, Tyree came by carrying another casserole. She handed Elizabeth the dish. "Just heat it when you're ready to eat." Tyree blinked her marble-blue eyes at Elizabeth.

"You really shouldn't go to all this trouble every night," Elizabeth urged. She felt a stab of guilt because she'd been putting a lot of the casserole into the garbage. After a few bites, she just couldn't manage the odd spices Tyree used. She usually made herself a peanut butter sandwich instead. Andy continued to not only clean his plate, but go back for seconds. But Elizabeth's stomach had been a trifle upset the past few days, and she blamed it on Tyree's cooking.

"It's no trouble at all. I know how young people eat when they're as busy as you've been." Tyree tilted her head to one side. "You *have* been eating what I sent over, haven't you?"

"Yes. Well, actually, some of it. I mean, Andy just gobbles down everything. But . . . I'm afraid my stomach is a bit sensitive right now. Probably from the move and all. So, I haven't really done it justice. That's why I hate to see you go to all this trouble."

The blue in Tyree's eyes went dark. "Upset stomach?" Her face sobered. "You do look a bit peaked. As if you might be coming down with something. It's probably wise not to eat too much when you feel that way. But, do try to munch a little of what I bring over, at least. You need the nourishment. Okay?"

Good grief! Elizabeth thought. The boss lady! "Sure," she said trying to keep the irritation out of her voice.

"Good girl." Tyree's eyes softened, and she smiled gently. "Well, are you settled yet?"

"Close. Except for some paint and wallpaper. New drapes. That kind of thing. But we're on an awfully tight budget, so some of it won't get done for a long time."

"Then I've got to take a look at those paintings of yours, honeybunch. If they're any good, maybe we can sell a few."

A sudden panic hit Elizabeth. She wanted to show them to Tyree, but what if she didn't like them. She wasn't up to another rejection right now. But then, if she did like them, and she could sell even one, it would be a great help for their budget. "Would you like to see them now?" she finally said.

Tyree pursed her lips, considering the idea. "I'd prefer to wait and have Amber with me. She's my partner in the business, and a damn remarkable painter herself. She and her husband live just a few doors down from here. How is Monday, sometime before we have the little get-together we're having for you two?"

"That would be fine." Elizabeth felt slightly relieved. A short reprieve. She imagined for a minute she could hear Tyree's voice saying, "They're lovely, honeybunch, but not quite right for us, I'm afraid." She grimaced at the thought.

Tyree gave Elizabeth a little pat on the shoulder. "Don't you-all forget Monday night, now. I've asked everyone on the entire block. Eight o'clock?"

"That sounds wonderful. Can I bring anything?"

"Just yourselves."

"I'm really looking forward to meeting every-one."

"Well, believe me, honeybunch," Tyree gave her a grin, and as she did, the diamond in her tooth winked, "they're just as eager to meet you."

Chapter Three

On Friday, Ted felt as if he'd fallen into someone's nightmare. While Locke was out doing legwork, Ted spent the entire day at the department going over the forensic details of a half-dozen more cases that resembled their two. As always, he put everything into neat, logical little piles so he could start assembling the puzzle. After fitting together the pieces, he didn't like what he saw. The evidence bore out the fact that all the slayings had been done by the same person. Each victim had an artery severed with a sharp instrument, or with the killer's teeth. All of the victims had their blood drained. In most cases, the killer also took one or more bites of flesh. He found no evidence they might be connected with devil worship, other than the fact that blood sacrifices were commonly used in such cults.

The cannibalistic nature of the cases threw him, however. They weren't that rare, but they still kept him from putting the whole thing into some neat little slot. What bothered him the most was that none of the victims appeared to have put up a struggle. *Why not, damn it?* Why had so many different types of people gone to their deaths like sheep? It made no sense. But there it was, in every case in front of him. He'd ordered a thorough toxicology test on the boat victim, and had asked the doctors at Hoag Memorial to run a panel of highly sophisticated toxicity tests on the Duff girl's blood. Maybe they would turn up something of value.

At the moment, one of his main worries was a possible leak in the department which would alert the public to the fact that this might be a serial killer. If that happened, they would have to hold a fucking press conference. Something he hated with a passion. Newspapers went for the throat. They jumped on every juicy tidbit and sensationalized it. But one leak, and the chief would order them to talk with the press. And what the hell could they tell them at this stage? Ted sighed and tapped his fingers against the stack of folders on his desk. No easy answers. Hardly any answers at all.

Late in the afternoon, Locke came roaring into the department, slapped some papers down on Ted's desk, pulled up a chair, and gave him a shit-eating grin.

Ted glanced over at him. "You look like you've got a bee up your ass."

"Yep," Locke said.

"Okay, talk to me."

"Birkenstocks."

"What?"

"That's the kind of shoe our killer wore."

"Ah."

"And the tar. The shoe print on the boat deck. It

didn't come from the beach like we thought. It's the kind of tar used to re-asphalt roads."

"Good. What roads? And where?"

Locke's expression changed, and he frowned. "Ah, damn! You know what? I was so busy with this tar thing, I forgot to call Sandy."

"The lady better get used to it."

Locke shrugged, and shook his head. "Not Sandy. She wants a perma-pressed, nine-to-five civil servant."

"In that case, you're in the dumper. Come on. Keep talking."

Locke nodded, and brushed his hair off his forehead, as if brushing his thoughts about Sandy away. "I checked, and there were at least two dozen places in the county where they've been resurfacing or sealing roads this past week. Two in Brea, four in Anaheim, three in Huntington Beach, five in Orange, one in Modjeska Canyon, two in San Clemente . . . the list goes on and on. But then I spotted the clincher. Balboa Boulevard near Peninsula Point!"

Ted jolted forward in his chair. "Are you shitting me?"

"The reason we weren't aware of it that morning is because they'd been working on the entire length of the street during the past few weeks, and had just finished up the morning of the killing. By night, it was still somewhat soft, but they'd removed the last of the barricades."

"What does forensics say?"

"Their analysis shows that the prints on the boat had to be from the work on the peninsula. The other asphalt jobs had slightly different compositions. Fractional, but different."

Ted took a deep breath. "Well, that doesn't mean we'll find our killer there. But whoever it was had been walking the peninsula that night. We'd better follow up."

"We could do a door-to-door. Even a boat-to-boat in the bay." Locke picked up some of the papers from the desk and looked through them. "We should check everyone's shoes around here. Find ones with tar on them."

"Hell, a lot of people probably walked in that tar," Ted said. "And a lot of people wear Birkenstock sandals. Especially at the beach. Even if we do find the guy, he may not be involved in this. But if he is, and he should happen to live down there, a door-to-door might scare him off."

"You got a better idea?"

"No. Let's do it. It's a manageable area."

Locke nodded. His rainwater eyes deepened. "The two of us and a couple of uniforms?"

"Yeah, that's fine. It's too bad we don't have a sketch. But since the Duff girl is still in the hospital, I doubt we'll get a better description. I stopped by there at lunch to see how she's doing. Seems she's developed a fever and infection. I understand you can get some nasty things from being bitten by a human."

"Ah, damn it! I'm sorry to hear that," Locke said. "Well, if we're going out on the street, we'd better get started. I'll arrange for the uniforms."

"And keep this quiet. No talk around the department. Let's try and keep this contained if we can.

We don't want public panic. When we talk to the people on the peninsula, we tell them it's just routine."

"Right."

"And we'll start tomorrow morning. I'm hungry and beat tonight."

"You're always fucking hungry," Locke grumbled. "If we don't go tonight, I won't have any excuse not to get this thing with Sandy straightened out."

"Lottsa luck!" Ted grinned. "You should find someone like my Sylvia. I don't think she understood my obsession with work, but she always tolerated it."

"I should get so lucky." Locke paused. "You still miss her a lot, don't you?"

"It never goes away."

"Listen, Sandy is already pissed as hell at me, so how much worse can it get if I don't mend the breach until tomorrow? Let's have dinner tonight and go over the case."

Ted looked over at the young detective. The last thing he wanted was pity. But he didn't see any of that in Locke's eyes. Actually what he saw was eagerness—a reflection of what he'd seen in his own mirror for so many years—an urgency to find whoever was perpetrating such grisly deaths on fellow human beings.

"If you're sure," Ted said.

"If I see Sandy, all I'll be able to think about is the case. She wouldn't appreciate that."

"Okay, then." Ted got up from his chair, and put on his jacket. "Come on. I'm gonna take you to a place where they make the most fantastic boudin you've ever tasted this side of Baton Rouge."

Locke laughed. "Actually, I've never tasted any bou . . . ah . . . whatever. I'm more of a McDonald's kind of guy."

Ted threw him a look of mock horror. "Remember what someone once said, 'To eat is a necessity, but to eat intelligently is an art.' I think it's time we got serious about your gastronomic education."

On Friday evening, Elizabeth fixed lamb chops and salad for herself while Andy prefered to eat some of Tyree's casserole. Neither she nor Andy felt well, so they just picked at the food. Andy had a touch of flu and a nagging headache, which he didn't mention to Elizabeth. Elizabeth's queasy stomach had gotten worse. She would ask Tyree to stop sending over any more dinners. They were obviously too rich for her. She kept taking a few bites, and then would feel ill. It was time for them to eat more simply—fresh vegetables and lean meat or chicken.

After dinner, Andy announced he needed some research books and wanted to make a trip to the library. Elizabeth didn't feel up to the drive, since their old Toyota was in worse shape than ever and had taken to joggling and jolting. Before long, she knew they would have to scrape up the money to have it fixed. As it was, they kept the battered little car hidden away in the garage with the door down so their neighbors wouldn't notice. To Elizabeth's chagrin, she had discovered that the only cars on the block were BMWs, Mercedes and a Lexus. But, at the moment, their budget didn't allow for them to buy a used car, or get the Toyota fixed. Their bank account was dwindling fast, since neither she nor Andy had had a sale in a long time. The thought depressed her. It had been awful in the apartment, but at least they weren't living around so many people who were obviously quite well off.

After Andy left for the library, Elizabeth washed up the supper dishes, then decided that it might make her feel better to take a walk on the beach. The cold sea air revived her. It stung her cheeks and made her skin tingle. As she walked, she enjoyed the blaze of lights from the houses along the shore, and the rush of surf as it rumbled in against the sand. Toward the end of Peninsula Point, she could make out the faint figures of several fishermen casting their lines into the water. In the other direction, she saw the outline of the Balboa Pier, and a number of bonfires on the beach.

She didn't want to go too far, so when she reached the first fisherman, she started back in the direction of the house when suddenly a soft, wooly fog began rolling in. From somewhere close by, she heard the strains of a symphony. Someone had a radio or hi-fi turned up quite loud. The music was lovely, some kind of piano concerto. She glanced across the stretch of sand toward the Zipper sisters' house—a one-story, California craftsman cottage, painted white with yellow trim. Through the mist, she saw the elderly faces of the two sisters as they peered through a large picture window, like two frogs peeping from a pond. She waved at them, but the fog was thickening, and apparently they didn't see her since they didn't wave back. She wondered if the music might be coming from their place. Perhaps they turned it up extra loud because they were a bit hard of hearing.

The fog thickened rapidly, coming in off the ocean in great moist webs. Shoot! The heavy mist would put an end to her walk. Well, she'd give it another try in the morning, if it turned out clear. She headed toward the house, only now she couldn't tell exactly where it was. The piano music had stopped, and the crashing of the surf was muted by the fog. In fact, it seemed to echo about, coming first from one direction, then another. Damn! She should have moved faster. She hadn't realized how quickly the white vapor could move in. After a few tentative steps in one direction, she decided that was wrong, then turned about, unable to decide which way to go. The fog brought with it an uncomfortable suffocating sensation. She took a few more steps, and suddenly found her feet in the icy surf, the foamy water splashing against her tennis shoes.

"Damn!" she said, jumping away from the water, but not before it had soaked through her shoes and the edges of her jeans. Well, at least now she knew the direction of the house. She scrambled along the sand, hoping she was moving in a straight line away from the surf, when suddenly, directly in front of her, a huge dark form loomed. In a quick frenzy, she sprang back, her whole body prickling with fright. Jesus! she said to herself. What in the hell is that?

* * *

From his bedroom window, HE had seen the artist woman leave the house and stroll along the beach. As he watched her, the familiar fire kindled in his blood. The agony rippled through him, teasing, threatening. God! How he wanted that woman. No matter what the risk.

He imagined how glorious her skin would feel against his mouth, the soft, suppleness as his teeth entered her flesh, the sharp, sweet scent of her fear. The agony should not be tormenting him this soon. For a moment, he felt nothing but contempt for himself. It had only been a few days since the man on the boat. Yet, what could he do? The agony controlled him. He lowered his head, almost drowning in a wave of helplessness. Then, he straightened up and quickly made his way outside, jogging toward the beach and the woman.

As the fog rolled in, he made his move. Silently he crept along the sand, wrapping himself in a cloak of mist. The vapor was so thick he could see only a few feet in any direction, but it would be easy to find her by the scent of her Ivory soap and faint odor of oil paint. He suddenly saw a vision of how she had looked asleep in her bed, her sheer silk nightgown pressing against her erect nipples. The agony inside him flared, licking at the very center of his being. He cursed his affliction and, at the same time, gloried in it.

He quickly picked up her scent, and flames shot through his blood like fiery bullets, searing his veins. He moved toward her, so close now he could hear her breath against the gauzy air. He stood in the gathering mist, inhaling slowly, filtering the aromas, trying to locate exactly where she was. Then silently, shrouded by the mist, he began circling his prey.

The dark form in front of Elizabeth wavered and flowed, as if it were liquid. Then it dimmed, until it became only a gray shadow veiled by fog. Perhaps it had been her imagination. She trembled, then took several deep breaths, trying to steady herself as she gazed through the mist. She shivered a little, despite her quilted jacket. She felt eyes staring at her, a presence so strong it made her skin prickle.

"Hello?" she called feebly. "Is someone there?" She squinted through the fog, but saw nothing. She was thankful she hadn't wandered too far from the house. But the damn fog kept growing thicker, until she couldn't tell which direction was which. Taking a blind guess, she began to trudge through the cold, damp sand again.

When she'd gone a hundred yards or so, cursing the fact that the beach was so wide, she heard something, and paused, listening. Over the pounding of her heart came a rushing sound, like papers tossing in the wind. She moved again, sprinting this time, hoping any second to see the glow of house-lights through the mist. Her breath came in short gasps, and she railed at herself for being so out of shape. She increased her speed. Her tennis shoes made soft, sucking sounds. The damp sand tugged at her feet, making her legs ache. Then, to her horror, she heard a second set of footsteps, muffled, but clear, running close behind her. Her impulse was to keep running, but she had an ache in her side, and an oxygen debt that made her light-headed. Where the hell was the house, anyway?

She slowed for an instant to catch her breath, hearing the footsteps closing on her. Then she increased her speed again, but too late, for just as she moved, someone grabbed her arm. She let out a scream, struggling to free herself. Thin, sharp fingers dug into her arm. A second hand tugged at her, almost shaking her out of her shoes. She let out another scream, and twisted around to face her pursuer.

"What the hell are you doing out here, Elizabeth?" It was Tyree. She appeared like a banchee out of the mist, her whorl of red hair twisting about her shoulders. "Are you out of your mind?" Her voice was a low growl.

Elizabeth's knees went weak from relief. "My God, Tyree! You almost gave me a coronary!"

"Well, it serves you right, honeybunch." Tyree's voice smoothed. She loosened her grip but didn't turn loose of Elizabeth's arm. Instead, she linked arms with her, and quickly escorted her off the beach. "Haven't you been reading the papers, or listening to news reports? We've got some nut running around this area killing people."

"No, I didn't realize . . . I've been so busy getting the house settled. I only intended to take a short walk on the beach." Elizabeth looked up to see the welcome sight of house-lights glowing like a myriad of halos through the vapor. Her thundering heartbeat still echoed in her ears.

"Please," Tyree said, giving her a glowering sideways glance, "stay off the beach at night!"

"I will," Elizabeth assured her. "I couldn't find my way back, that's all. How did you know I was out here?"

"I saw you leave, and when I checked back a few minutes later, the fog had come in."

"So you came dashing after me . . . alone. That wasn't too smart either, was it? Where's Boo?"

They stopped on the deck outside the sliding glass door to Elizabeth's house. "He has a meeting tonight. Andy?"

"Library. But he won't be long."

"Good." Tyree gave her a mirthless smile. The misty light from the house reflected like a flicker of firelight off the diamond in her front tooth. "Sorry if I gave you a scare, honeybunch, but I guess I panicked, seeing you out here all alone. Now scoot inside and lock your door." With that, Tyree, her flame-red hair glowing in the drizzled light, gave a little wave, then turned and ran toward her huge art-deco house next door, the mist curling around her as she went.

Once inside her own house, Elizabeth made certain the doors were locked. She found her teeth chattering, although she wasn't certain if it were from the dampness, or from the incident on the beach. On reflection, she realized it had been pretty careless of her, wandering around alone like that after dark. She changed out of the wet jeans, and put on her nightgown and robe. Then she built a fire in the fireplace, wrapped the afghan around herself, and snuggled down on the sofa. In only minutes she fell asleep, and was hardly aware when Andy came home and helped her to bed.

That night she dreamt she was riding on a surfboard with Robert Redford. A giant wave lifted them up and carried them toward the shore. Robert Redford wiggled the board, and it tipped over. She fell, swirling around in a whirlpool of foaming seawater, sucked down into the endless, dark green of the night sea.

She jerked awake, wrapped in a cocoon of sheets, hardly able to catch her breath. She was incredibly thirsty, and her mouth felt dry, as if someone had packed it with cotton. In the bathroom, she drank two full glasses of water, and still felt parched. When she went back to bed, she drifted off to sleep easily and, thankfully, without dreams, or if she had any, she couldn't remember them in the morning.

On Saturday morning, Elizabeth's childhood friend, Judy Bird, was due to arrive sometime after ten. For the first time since they'd moved, Elizabeth overslept, and so did Andy. She woke up sluggish and thirsty again, and on top of that, she had a nasty headache. It wasn't the best of days to have a house guest. But, then, Judy was more like a sister than a guest.

She swallowed two aspirin with her coffee, toasted two English muffins, and set out the marmalade. Her head pounded furiously. Andy didn't appear too chipper either, so they ate their English muffins in silence, sipping their coffee. After his second cup, Andy announced that what he needed was some fresh air and exercise. He decided to go outside and weed the rose bed, and spend some time planning what to do about the rest of the small rear yard.

"Any suggestions?" he asked as he made his way out through the laundry room. "Flowers or shrubs? Maybe some grass?"

"Not at the moment," she said, the headache pulsing at her forehead. "I've got all I can handle getting ready for Judy's stay."

After he left, she realized she was thirsty again, and took a glass from the cupboard, filled it with water, and drank it down without taking a breath. The cool liquid made her feel a little better.

Judy arrived just as Elizabeth had finished washing up the few breakfast dishes. She stood on the back porch, her overnight case in one hand, a large garment bag draped over the other, staring up at the house.

"My God, Liz!" Judy gasped. "I was expecting more of a tilt-to-one-side beach shack, for some reason. This is incredible! Totally Cape Cod! What a great style!" Judy was her usual, exuberant self. She wore an exquisite I.B. Diffusion sweater in cream cashmere with a cowl neck and a matching pair of skintight leather pants. Her hair was lighter than Elizabeth remembered from the last time she'd seen her, cropped short and slightly spiked. Her large, lavender eyes blinked rapidly as she scanned the house.

Elizabeth thought she would have been heartbreakingly beautiful, except for the underlying tightness to her skin, the tremor of tension in her muscles. Well, a weekend at the beach was just the ticket. By Monday, she'd be so relaxed, the thought of her ex-husband wouldn't enter her head. Maybe, with a little luck, she might even meet some nice, rich, young bachelor sunning on the beach.

"Oh, Liz, I parked in the alley next to the garage, is that okay? Is this the front door or the back? I guess the front is toward the beach."

"Your car's fine. And, you're right, we really don't have a front door. Company has to come in the back, through the alley, since all we've got in front is sand."

"Well, come on, show me through the place," Judy insisted. "And then you can feed me. I'm starving. I skipped breakfast so I could get down here."

Elizabeth took Judy's overnight case, and led her through the kitchen and into the living room.

"Wow! Holy Mary!" Judy howled as they entered the living room. "Will you look at this! All these high ceilings and fantastic wicker stuff. I love it! I absolutely love it!"

When Elizabeth pulled back the drapes so they could see the ocean, Judy let out a long sigh. "I'd never get a bit of work done if I lived here. I'd just sit and watch the waves roll in. This is my idea of pure heaven!"

"Well, heaven or not, you and I are going to get the living room wallpaper done," Elizabeth announced. "You promised to help. I'm sorry, but the guest room still has some awful Egyptian stuff."

"Don't apologize," Judy said. "That decor is all the rage now. You see it in all the best magazines."

"Come on, I'll I give you the grand tour," Elizabeth said.

Upstairs, Elizabeth showed her the studio where her blank canvases still stood on their easels. "I haven't started yet. But, I've promised myself to give it a try no later than Monday." She ran her fingers across the top of one canvas. "I think . . ." she began, remembering quite vividly the way the row of beach houses had looked in the fog last night, with their lights all defused and eerie. "I think I'll do a series of paintings of the local houses." She realized that was exactly what she was going to do. Paint them in different light, different moods, weather. But she needed bigger canvases, much bigger. And she would add the boldness of a pallet knife along with a brush. She would also try some portraits, based on the photos in Aunt Mary's album. A myriad of ideas began to flash through her head, and she felt a rush of excitement.

Without thinking, she picked up a pad and pencil, and began sketching a scene that had formed full blown in her mind. The idea flowed from her head and onto the page like a stream of warm water— effortlessly. Yes, that was what she wanted! The excitement grew. In her mind, she saw the colors, muted, yet rich. In order to mix them, she'd have to find an art store since she didn't have a large enough palette.

"Liz? Did I lose you?" Judy called from somewhere down the hall. "What happened to my tour of the house?"

She'd forgotten all about Judy in the rush of creating. She put down the pad. It could wait until

Monday, since she'd waited this long. Although Judy would have understood if she'd disappeared into her studio. That was the nice thing about their life-long relationship.

She helped Judy settle her things in the guest room, then continued the tour. In the master bedroom, Judy rushed over to the low chest with its Egyptian paintings.

"Hey, look! It's a float tank! What do you know! I've never seen one painted like this one. Kind of a neat idea."

Elizabeth came over and stood beside her. "A what?"

"A flotation tank. You know, one of those things people use for meditation and that kind of stuff. It's something that developed back in the sixties, I think. During the hippie era."

"Why would Aunt Mary have one of those?"

Judy shrugged. "She might have been into Eastern religions. Or, maybe she had high blood pressure and the tank helped her to relax and lower it. I read a lot about these things in one of my psychology classes. Or, was it a science class? Anyway, it's kind of neat."

Elizabeth lifted the lid and looked into the chest. Like Andy had said, it looked rather like a closet turned on its side, with the door on top. It was long enough for a tall man to lie in, with room to spare. Maybe Judy was right. "Look, it's coated with salt crystals," she said.

"Yeah, that's right. You fill it with water which is warmed by a small heater. Probably that thing on one end of it there. And then you put a ton of

Epsom salts into the water. That makes a person buoyant as hell. You bob around like a cork, from what I've read."

Elizabeth frowned. "But how does it work?"

"A person gets in, just like a bathtub. Then you lower the lid and just lie there and float. It's something called sensory deprivation. No light. No sound. No feel of gravity. And with the water the right temperature, no sense of feeling."

Tugging the lid down, Elizabeth sat on the chest and looked up at Judy. "Why would anyone want to do that?"

"I hear a lot of people swear by it. I've always wanted to use one." She grinned. "Hey, maybe we can get this thing working, and I can try it out."

"Are you serious?"

"Dead. Look," Judy sat down next to Elizabeth. "Inside this thing, with no sensory stimuli at all, your brain gets hungry. It wants stimulation. Craves it. And when it doesn't get it, it makes its own. Entertains itself, sort of. But, a lot of people say it puts you into a theta brain wave state. All kinds of creative things come out of that. Some people use motivational tapes, after a long period of isolation. I understand they're pretty effective used that way." Judy put her finger on what Andy had pointed out was a tape player attached to the box. "Maybe, it could help me with my screen writing. I haven't had the heart to do any of it since . . . since Alex and I broke up." When Judy looked back at Elizabeth, a dull veil had suddenly covered the usual gleam in her eyes. "You know . . . all those ideas that never got written." She sighed, then shrugged and looked away. Standing up, she walked to the window, pushed open the shutters and looked out. "I can't believe this view. You know what? I'm dying to go beachcombing. What do you say?"

"Sure," Elizabeth said. "As long as we do it in the daylight, and no fog." A faint chill whispered over her as she recalled the incident of the night before. "Besides, I want you to meet a few of our neighbors. We've got some real doozies! To the north of us are the Zipper sisters. Two rather nice old ladies."

"Zipper? Are you kidding me? I love it!"

"And on the south side are a couple named Rattigan. Boo and Tyree. Can you believe that? I haven't met Boo yet. But Tyree seems nice enough, although a little overbearing and take-charge. She's insisted on feeding Andy and me all week long. And she has this tiny blue-white diamond imbedded in her front tooth. Try not to stare at it, will you?"

"Oh, honestly, Liz. Give me more credit," Judy said, giving a little bark of a laugh.

"Did you bring your warm-ups or joggers or something?" Elizabeth asked.

"Sure did. Brand new. A little something by Givenchy. And, a bathing suit by Gottex. Plus, of course, some Nike Air Cushions."

"Good grief, don't you own anything that isn't a name?"

"Not if I can help it."

"Well, come on. Let's change. Then I've got to clean out Tyree's dish and take it back to her. After that, we can beachcomb."

In the kitchen, Elizabeth started to scoop the leftover contents of Tyree's latest casserole into the garbage.

"Hey!" Judy said. "Don't toss that. It looks delicious. And I'm hungry. Mind if I eat what's left?"

Elizabeth shrugged. "No. I'll put it in the microwave for you. But, I find it a bit rich for my stomach."

"You know me. I can eat anything. And, don't bother to heat it. I like stuff cold from the fridge." Judy took a fork out of the drawer and started eating. "I was right. This stuff is good. Lots of curry."

Judy ate every bite, then helped herself to some toast while Elizabeth washed out the dish.

On the way to the Rattigans', she told Judy about seeing Robert Redford surfing. "He was gorgeous," Elizabeth said. "Of course, it wasn't *really* Robert Redford, and it was pretty dark when I saw him. Actually, it gave me a real start, to have him stop under my window and grin up at me. Burrrr!"

"Maybe I'll take up surfing while I'm here," Judy said, brightening. "I certainly wouldn't mind meeting up with someone who looked like Robert Redford. In fact, I wouldn't mind meeting up with a guy who looked even half-way human." The brightness left her face. "God, it gets lonely, Liz. Lonelier than you can imagine."

"I know," Elizabeth said. For an instant, her anger at Judy's ex-husband surfaced. Judy had always been such a special person, filled with eagerness and a sense of adventure. Or, at least, she had been until the divorce. Now, in tiny, but perceptible ways, it seemed Judy was changing, growing older much too young. And cynical. Damn you, Alex Bird! she said silently.

They rang the Rattigans' doorbell four times before Tyree finally answered. She opened the door a tiny crack with the chain guard still in place. Her hair hung down in crimson streams across her face, and her eyes were squinched together against the light. Boy, Elizabeth thought, looking at her watch, when Tyree says she sleeps late, she really means late!

"Who is it?" Tyree asked, her voice thick.

"It's Elizabeth from next door. I brought your casserole dish back."

"Oh, thanks, honeybunch. Just set it on the porch. I'll pick it up later. I'm not dressed right now. Stayed up late working on a new quilt for the art museum."

"Sure. Listen, why don't you come over later? I have a friend here I'd like you to meet."

"That would be great. Sorry I growled at you last night, honeybunch." She yawned and shut the door.

"Now that's what I call *red* hair!" Judy exclaimed. "But I didn't see the diamond in her tooth." She sounded disappointed. "And, what was that all about? Her growling at you last night."

"Oh, nothing really. I took a walk on the beach after dark, by myself. She didn't think that was such a good idea. She's kind of a mother hen. But, I guess we've got some nut running around and I should be more careful." Elizabeth laughed. "At least, we don't have to worry about a car jacking. No one in their right mind would steal our battered old

Toyota." Elizabeth tugged on Judy's arm. "Come on. Let's explore the beach. I really haven't had time since we moved."

The breeze changed to a warm Santana bringing the wind in off the desert instead of the ocean. They took off their shoes and walked on the wet sand, dodging waves that rolled in. Elizabeth looked around, remembering her fright of the night before. How friendly the beach seemed in the daytime with a number of people about—surfers, young girls sunbathing, children playing.

As she walked, she had bright little flashes of her own childhood when she had come to visit Aunt Mary. She remembered how she'd loved running on the beach, paddling in the surf, making huge castles in the warm sand. She would have stayed forever, if her mother had let her.

"God bless you, Aunt Mary," she said, lifting her arms toward the cloudless sky. For a moment, she felt like a child again, running carefree on the beach.

"What's that all about?" Judy asked.

"I didn't much like the house, at first. But now, I think it's wonderful! I'm so glad to be out of that awful apartment. Even if we can't afford to repair the house yet, it's a lot better than that place."

"I could live in a shack, if it sat on the beach. Given the chance, I might move in with you." She gave a laugh. "It's nice to have rich friends."

"We're so rich, I'm worried about what we're going to do for food money next month. Not to mention house taxes the first of the year. If only I could sell a few of my paintings. If Tyree decides not to show them, maybe some of the local decorators will take them. I sold several that way in the Valley. Maybe, I should give up on the galleries, and just become a hack." Elizabeth dug her toes into the cool sand as she walked, marveling at how wonderful it felt.

"Hey, don't knock being a hack. After all, that's what I am. I fix *other* people's screenplays, instead of writing my own. Since Alex wiped himself out on cocaine, along with our bank account, I have to make a buck any way I can."

When Elizabeth looked over at Judy she saw a gleam of tears in her violet eyes. As she watched, Judy ruffled her pale hair with the tips of her fingers. The gesture, Elizabeth knew, was the harbinger of the depression that swept over her from time to time since the divorce. She'd known Judy since kindergarten. They'd gone through grammar school, junior high, high school, and then graduated from UCLA together. They'd grown up like sisters living next door to each other, borrowing clothes, makeup, schoolwork. Judy's father had died of cancer when Judy was seven, so she'd adopted Elizabeth's dad.

After UCLA, while Elizabeth went off to Otis-Parsons to study art, Judy stayed on at UCLA to attend graduate school as a budding screenwriter, determined to set the industry on fire. She completed a script that attracted a lot of attention, but, for whatever reason, never sold. Both she and Judy fell in love with the same man—Alex Bird—an aspiring actor with crow-black hair that ruffled around his face in casual waves, wide shoulders, narrow hips, and the tightest buns on campus. Alex had been first prize, and Judy won. Elizabeth took second prize—Andrew Rosemond, a striving writer she'd met while still at UCLA. In the long run, Andy had turned out to be the real prize.

Alex made seven movies, all small feature roles, then got hooked on cocaine, and no matter what Judy did, she couldn't rescue the marriage, or Alex. Judy lived alone now, worked for a studio as a script doctor, and seemed to be collapsing in on herself.

As if plugged into Elizabeth's thoughts, Judy said, "What do you think? Should I go back to my maiden name now that the divorce is final?"

"Klankhammer?" Elizabeth laughed. "You gotta be kidding!" Judy laughed along with her, and she was glad to see some of the old sparkle return.

The beach was a patchwork of beige—the wet sand fading into dry mounds of tangled kelp swarming with thousands of sand-hoppers, and studded by a gloss of tiny seashells. Judy stopped to pick up some of the seashells as they walked, stuffing them into the pockets of her warm-ups, until she looked like a roly-poly doll, despite her long, leggy figure. When they reached the end of Peninsula Point, they turned and strolled back toward the house. Elizabeth splashed her feet in the icy water, her bones aching with the cold.

They stopped at a large mound of kelp where Judy found a treasure of shells, and watched a large crab scavenge for lunch. Elizabeth tugged on a kelp strand, shaking it to see if she could dislodge more shells for Judy. Suddenly she saw something sticking out of the seaweed. She tried to drop the piece of kelp, but it clung to her hand, cold and clammy.

"Dear God!"

"What?" Judy said.

Elizabeth pointed, and backed away, almost tripping over her own feet in the soft sand. She blinked hard, praying that the image wasn't real—a bloated bare foot, the skin milk-pale, the toenails painted bright red.

"Holy Mary!" Judy jumped, jarring some of the seashells out of her pockets. "Mother of God!"

"We should call someone," Elizabeth whispered, but found herself unable to move. She stared at the foot with morbid fascination. Then slowly, not really conscious of what she was doing, she delicately began to peel away more of the seaweed, as if unwrapping the remains of an ancient mummy.

HE had spent a tormented night sequestered in his bedroom, windows closed, drapes drawn, in flickering candlelight, playing Chopin, Brahms and Tchaikovsky on his newly acquired compact disc player. Through sheer strength of will he managed, through the night, to subdue the agony. However, it remained precariously close to the surface, ready to ignite at the slightest encouragement. The flames had been replaced by cold chills, and a damp sweatiness slicked his body.

The music helped. "To soothe the savage beast," he told himself, walking the length of the room, and back again, unable to rest, although it was now mid-morning. The carpet was a deep reptilian green that whispered under his stockinged feet. The air in the room hung musty and cold, heavy with the oily resinous smell of candlewax.

It happened for the best, he realized—the aborting of his mission on the beach last night. The agony, having flirted with him again, overrode all sense of danger. His hunger for the woman had outweighed any rational thought. He wanted her, but he knew someone watched him. He'd been within a few feet of her when the red-headed Xanthippe had snatched her away from him.

Nevertheless, he would endure; he would hold back the agony until he'd conjured a safe way to have the woman. But if he couldn't manage to stem the terrible pain, he would go to another part of the county to ease it. He would find a vagrant—one of humanity's many dregs—a body no one would care about, or mourn over. It was a way to ease the agony, but would bring him no particular pleasure. For a moment, he damned his affliction, but allowed himself only a small measure of self-pity. What he was, what he had become, was of his own doing. He could blame no one else. He detested what he was, but could not fight the desires, the agony, the incredible pleasures it brought. But it was also a level of human suffering that even Dante had not imagined.

He went to the window and tugged it open, then closed the drapes to shut out the light. Only a thin stream of air filtered in through the drapes but it was fresher than the air in the room. Outside he heard a muffled commotion—sirens, the stir of people, voices. He went back to the window, pulled the drapes a fraction, and peered out. Sunlight raked at his eyes, sending a lightning streak of pain through his head. He blinked rapidly against the light, searching the beach. Just to the south he spotted a lifeguard's jeep, and a dozen or so people gathered around a mound of kelp. Only it wasn't just kelp, he realized. In the middle of the mound was a body. He jerked back from the window.

"Damn!" he growled. It was the girl! The heavy surf should have carried the body to the south. She had washed ashore only a few yards away from where he had put her into the sea. He hadn't wanted to draw attention to this area again so soon. But there was nothing he could do about it now. He'd fucked up because of his greed in wanting both the young women. The first one had managed to live, and might be able to identify him. Although, she'd only seen him for a few moments. And, now, this body was almost at his doorstep. Shit!

He should get the hell far away from here as fast as he could. But he loved this place—the atmosphere, the sharp smell of the sea, the fog, the sight of a trim sailing ship. It was the only life he'd ever known. Of course, he'd been sent away many times. But he always came back. Besides. The others needed him. He was both an embarrasement and a necessity. Still, there might be those who would turn on him, decide they could do without him. Yes, perhaps he should make plans. He could move quickly, leaving no trace. The others would never find him. But, if he moved, he would have the artist woman before he went. No one had sent such pangs of longing and pleasure through him before. He would enjoy her slowly, drawing out the experience, savoring it. Perhaps, he would be sexually intimate with her—something he only did on rare occasions. As a rule, he found little pleasure in sexual contact with his prey since they were so quickly subdued. Still, he longed for passion, and even more he hungered for a closeness with someone. He yearned to feel once more the tender, loving touch of a woman. He'd known it for such a short period of time. He'd been segregated by necessity—set apart from others by the dark blessing that plagued him. A hellish plague of his own making.

He crossed the room to the dresser where he'd put the disc player, and slipped in a recording of Puccini's *Turandot*. He picked up the small tube of lip gloss he'd taken from the artist woman, inhaled its sweet scent, and put it down. Then, he crawled into bed, pulling a dusty quilt over himself, suddenly feeling a great weight of weariness. Yes, he would make arrangements to move. Most all of his personal things would have to stay behind. He would take care of everything, so he could leave the moment he'd finished with the woman.

"Nessun dorma! Nessun dorma!" the tenor on the recording sang. *"Tu pure, o Principessa, nella tua fredda stanza—"* The words wound through his head. "None shall sleep! None shall sleep! Oh Princess in your icy seclusion you too are watching the stars which tremble with love and hope! But my secret is locked within me, no one shall know my name!"

With the glorious music still swelling in his ears, he finally slept.

* * *

Andy heard the grandfather clock chime and tried, without success, to keep track of the chiming. He had no idea how long he'd been working. A sudden thirst came over him, his mouth as dry as old newspapers. He made his way out of his office into the kitchen, put a half-dozen ice cubes into a glass and filled it with water. He drank greedily, then refilled the glass, sipping more slowly this time. He still felt as if he had a touch of flu, and it was beginning to get him down. But, he didn't want to mention it to Lizzy. She had her hands full enough with the move and Judy's visit.

He wondered where the two of them had disappeared. The kitchen was empty. So was the living room. He called upstairs, but only an echo of his own voice tumbled back. He had worked rather lazily in the rear yard for an hour, hoping the fresh air would revive him. Then, after Judy's arrival, he'd greeted her, excused himself, and settled in front of his word processor. Already he'd done close to ten pages of new material—all of it quite good. Or, at least, he thought it was good. Never in his life had he worked so rapidly or so effortlessly. The words literally jumped into his mind, and then seemed to tumble out of his fingers onto the keys. It was a writer's dream. And, the pages only needed a minimal amount of rewriting, which astounded him. Always before he'd worked and reworked, never satisfied, until he reluctantly put it to rest, still hungering to improve his words. But, of course, his critique might be wrong. The true test would come when his agent and editor read the material. Well, at least he would know soon enough. Another day or two and he would Federal Express the first two-hundred pages to them, that is, if he were able to continue the frenetic pace he'd set.

"Lizzy," he called again, but got no response. "Judy?" He sat down on the wicker sofa in the living room, noticing that sometime during the week Lizzy had stitched up new slipcovers in a sea-shell pattern. They looked remarkably good, he thought. He wondered how much the fabric had cost. Their bank account was in miserable shape and they would have to be careful if they were going to hang on to the house.

The jangling of the phone jarred him out of his thoughts. It took him a moment to remember where it was in the new house. It hadn't rung much in the short time since, they had moved in. He finally located a yellow cordless extension in the kitchen.

"Hello," he said.

"Andy? Jake Tyson." Tyson was the lawyer who'd been named the executor for Mary's will.

"Oh, sure, Jake. How are you? Everything okay? You didn't happen to find any cash old Mary had stuck away, did you? We sure could use it." Andy laughed.

"As a matter of fact, I may have something. Not cash. At least, not yet. But, I did get a call from a firm back East. They're sniffing around asking about that one drug patent Mary left Elizabeth."

The cordless phone crackled and Andy wondered if he'd heard right. "Did you say patent? But I thought it was a useless drug. Something about FDA testing, wasn't it?"

"It probably is. Still, if these guys are sniffing

around, it might mean something. They wanna know if you have any records on it. All they have is the patent info."

"Just Mary's journal. Not much in that."

"Well, even if they want it, I doubt they'd pay much."

Andy gave a short laugh. "Look, Jake. Even five dollars would help right now. Things are pretty tight. We may have to sell the house. But it needs so many repairs and with the market off, we'd loose a hell of a lot on it. Besides, I like it here. I'm working again. Hopefully, I'll have a sale before long to save us. That is, if we can manage to feed ourselves until then."

"So, if they make an offer, you're interested?"

"I am. But the decision is Lizzy's, not mine."

Jake was silent on the other end of the phone for a moment. "Listen, we could try for a royalty. If the drug breaks out, it might mean some bucks."

"Like I said, Lizzy is the one who'll have to decide." He paused, thinking, then asked, "What's this drug for, anyway? Something important I hope."

"I don't know much more than you do. Mary used to call it her 'brain booster.' "

"Come again?"

"Well, I'm not a neuroscientist, but from what she explained, it's a substance they hoped would enhance various functions of the brain."

"Could something like that actually work?"

"This company that's sniffing around obviously hopes it will. With time and testing. I don't know though. Mary was all hot on it for a long time, then suddenly, dropped it. Said, it was a disaster. But, we won't tell this company that. Anyway, if they make an offer, what should I do."

Andy thought for a moment. "I'll to talk to Lizzy, and get back to you."

"ASAP, buddy. In the meantime, I'll tell them you haven't run across any notes on it."

"Yeah. Sure. Thanks." After he hung up, Andy stood feeling his pulse race, and his heart pounding hard against his chest. "Well, I'll be damned," he said.

Standing on the beach next to the body of the young girl, Ted felt himself blanch. The girl was only about fifteen. She had been in the water for sometime. Tangled in a web of seaweed, her arms and legs twisted in unnatural positions, she looked like a doll someone had discarded. She was nude, except for her shoes, her hair a matted tangle of webbed fibre. The skin on her face had turned gray-white, and was crazed like an old piece of china. In places the crazing was covered by a thin film of slime caused by the growth of organisms such as algae and molds. One of her eyes was open, and it stared straight at him. The other eye was missing, leaving only a dark, cavernous hole. She looked as if she were smiling, a wide, tooth-flashing grin, and he realized suddenly that most of her lips were missing.

At his side, Ted heard Locke gasp. He put an arm out to steady the young man. It was impossible to be prepared for a sight like this. Floaters—bodies that had spent some time in the water—weren't a pretty sight. The water, because of the cold and lack of oxygen, helped to keep the tissue from decomposing too rapidly. But portions of the young girl's body were bloated by the formation of gas which had caused it to float. It was difficult to tell right off what had been done to her before exposure to the water, and what had been caused by the time spent in the ocean.

The front of the girl's throat had been ripped open on the right side, and her body was riddled with teeth marks—at least a dozen—where chunks of flesh had been bitten away. Pathology would tell them if the bites were of human origin or caused by fish.

"It's the younger Duff girl," Ted said. "Even as bad as she is, I recognize her from the photograph her parents gave us."

"Good Christ!" Locke whispered. "I've never seen anything like this."

Because they were still canvassing the area, questioning residents in the next block over, they had arrived on the scene only minutes after the call came in. The two young women who had made the grisly discovery stood beside Ted, clinging together, shivering, even though the weather was comfortably warm. Ted noticed that one of them looked so bloodless and pale, he feared she might faint.

"Are you okay?" he asked, steadying her with his hand for a moment.

"Ah, yes. I guess so." The woman blinked. Her eyes looked sunken, as if withdrawing from the scene.

He reached into his pocket for his pen and notebook. "May I have your name," he asked gently.

"Eliza—beth, ahh . . . Rosemond. And . . . and . . . this is my houseguest, Judith . . . ah, Judy . . . Bird." The woman's hands trembled.

"Do you live close by?"

"Yes," Elizabeth said. "Just over there. The large Cape Cod."

"And you were out walking when you found the body?"

"Yes." Elizabeth took in a deep breath, but continued to tremble.

"And you went home to call the police?"

"Ah . . . no . . . I . . . that is, we . . . we saw the man in the, ummm, the lifeguard in the jeep there, and ran to tell him."

"He called in on his radio," the other woman said, holding on to Elizabeth's hand so tightly it made deep indentations in her skin.

"That's fine," Ted said. "I don't think we need to ask you anything more just yet. Why don't you go on home. Take some time to get over the shock of this. We'll stop by later to talk with you."

"Good." Elizabeth bobbed her head and swallowed hard. "That would be good."

The two women, still clutching each other, walked across the sand toward the beach house.

"There isn't much more we can do here," Locke said, his eyes avoiding the body of the young girl. "Why don't we let forensics and the medical examiner finish up while we go on with our door-to-door. We'll pick up their report later."

Ted nodded. He looked down at the dead girl. So young, he thought. She'd hardly lived. "I think we'd better go by the Duff residence first," he said. "They'll have to go in and make a positive ID."

"Yes. Well, at least the older sister is still alive."

"That's a blessing, but no consolation."

Locke moved away, but Ted stood for a moment looking at the girl. He felt a flash of anger. They could at least cover her naked body. Not even a dead person should have to suffer the indignity of being stared at. Death was too personal to be displayed that way. He started to pick up a turquoise beach towel he saw lying on the sand a few feet away, to drape over her. But then he realized that would contaminate the investigation, and he needed it to be done right. Absolutely right. He ground his teeth together. They had to get the son-of-a-bitch who'd done this, before his sick mind sent him out to do it again.

"I think I'm going to throw up," Elizabeth whispered to Judy as they left the police detectives and walked across the sand toward the house. Then, she turned away and began to vomit, hot chunks of her breakfast burning the back of her throat.

"It's okay," Judy said, holding an arm around Elizabeth's waist. When the heaving stopped, she offered her a shell-studded Kleenex from the pocket of her warm-ups. "I feel the same way. Come on, let's get back to the house."

As they walked, Elizabeth gripped Judy's arm to steady herself. Her legs felt as wobbly as old rubber bands. It wasn't often that death washed up right at your front door. She wiped her mouth, and took in a long deep breath.

Judy's face looked crumpled. "Jesus, she was so young!"

Andy met them at the sliding glass door. "What's going on?" he asked. "What were all the sirens?"

"A body on the beach." Elizabeth's voice shook. "A girl."

"Oh God!" Andy said. "Wasn't there anything they could do?"

Elizabeth shook her head. "No. The . . . her body washed up on the beach. Judy and I found it in a tangle of kelp while we were out walking."

"Lizzy!" Andy took hold of her hand. "You should have come and gotten me."

"I don't think I'll go swimming while I'm here after all," Judy said, her voice low and shaky. "Do you think she drowned? You don't suppose a shark got her, do you? Are there sharks around here?"

"No," Elizabeth said. "I think a shark would have done a lot more damage. She must have been swimming alone, and got caught by an undertow. Maybe knocked around on the breakwater."

"I may never go swimming again." Judy rattled the shells in the pockets of her warm-ups.

"Does anyone know who she is?" Andy asked. He steered them into the house, and closed the sliding door.

"I don't know. I mean . . . we just . . . it all happened so fast. That's all I know," Elizabeth said, gripping his hand tightly.

Judy slumped down in the wicker chair next to the fireplace, and stared out at the beach. Elizabeth curled up on the sofa, and Andy sat next to her, still holding her hand.

"You okay?" he asked.

She nodded.

"You look pale. And your hand's ice cold."

"I'll be fine. It's just such a shock, something as awful as that. She looked so. . . ."

Judy gave a little moan. "I've never seen anyone who was dead before, except my dad. And I was so young I don't remember." She kept blinking her eyes rapidly and sighing.

"I never saw a person dead before either," Elizabeth said. "At least I don't . . . oh, yes, my grandfather. I saw my grandfather. But, he didn't look anything like that girl."

"He didn't drown in the ocean," Judy said.

"He was over eighty and died in his sleep."

After that, they sat for a long while, attempting to make small talk, avoiding the subject of death, glancing furtively at the beach now and then. Elizabeth wasn't aware of time passing. She felt as if her body had gone numb. She kept hoping she'd wake up, and all of this would be just another one of her nightmares. Some terrible delusion induced by the move or fatigue. Every time, she closed her eyes, she saw the face of the dead girl, with its ragged mouth grinning up at her.

After a while, the grandfather clock at the bottom of the stairs began to chime. Elizabeth counted five. It couldn't be that late, could it? But, she realized, it was dark outside. Someone had turned on the two lamps in the living room. She didn't know who. The three of them sat passively staring at their own re-

flection in the dark glass of the sliding door. The
surf outside was invisible, but she heard it rumbling
against the sand. Their reflection showed how wan
they all looked. Elizabeth got up and pulled the
drapes. That was better. Maybe she should start a
fire in the hearth. That would cheer the room. She
fumbled with kindling, added some newspaper, lit a
match, and relished the sudden warmth of the fire as
it took hold.

"It's almost dinner time, and none of us ate
lunch. Should I fix something, or what?" she asked.
"I don't think I could eat a bite after all this, but.
. . ."

"No," Andy said soberly. "I'm not hungry."

"Me either," Judy agreed.

"We've been sitting here for hours." Elizabeth
forced herself to get up. Her legs cramped painfully
from having been curled under her for so long. "We
should *do* something."

Suddenly, she realized something weird. What
she really wanted to do was go upstairs to her studio
and work. Ideas—what seemed like brilliant ideas
for paintings—had begun to stream through her
head. Scene after scene presented themselves. Glorious rich colors. It was no doubt due to the morning's trauma, but, nothing like this had happened to
her before. And, to make the whole thing more
peculiar, the headache she'd woken up with that
morning had returned with a vengeance. It nagged
painfully behind her eyes, but that didn't impede the
flow or quality of the ideas that were assaulting her.

What she needed were some aspirin, she thought,

and excused herself for a moment while she went to
the kitchen where she kept a bottle of Bayer. Taking
two aspirin out of the bottle, she washed them down
with a glass of cold water. Then she returned to the
living room and ambled about for a few minutes,
stirring the blaze in the hearth, turning on the television, plumping pillows, desperately wrestling with
her desire to go upstairs and, at least, sketch out a
few of the ideas that were bombarding her. What if
she put it off, she wondered, and by Monday morning, they were all gone—the whole flow of ideas
sucked up the chimney like curls of smoke? But she
couldn't just leave Judy, who still looked pale and
stricken. No, she wouldn't go off and paint as if she
were some temperamental artist, not even if the
stream of ideas were brilliant, which they probably
weren't. They were obviously the result of trauma,
and would no doubt turn vapid the moment she
tried to put them on canvas.

She shook her head to stem the colorful flashes
that kept appearing in her mind. Rummaging
through the etagere, she found a jigsaw puzzle of
Aunt Mary's that had never been opened, and put
it on the coffee table. Judy responded by moving to
the floor and sitting cross-legged, then she opened
the puzzle and spread it out on the table. Elizabeth
sat across from her. Andy began pacing the room,
and she sensed his restlessness.

"Andy, why don't you try and work," she said to
him. "Do something to take your mind off all this."

"Would that be okay?"

"Good idea," Judy said. "Keep busy, Andy."

"Well, if you're certain. Oh, by the way Lizzy, with all that was going on, I forgot to tell you your lawyer called. Jake Tyson."

Elizabeth looked up at him. "Anything important?"

Andy paused for a moment, then shook his head no. "Just some details. We can talk about it later. We're all too upset right now." He gave Judy a peck on the check, then hugged Elizabeth. "Don't stay up too late you too. You've had a hell of a day."

As soon as Andy left, the two of them began picking up pieces of the puzzle and fitting them together, the details of that terrible morning unspoken, but hanging about them like a pall of dark smoke.

The grandfather clock chimed six. Just seconds after it finished, someone rapped loudly on the sliding glass door. When Elizabeth opened the drapes, there stood Tyree. Her long red hair was piled in curls on top of her head, and held in place with rhinestone combs. She wore a Kelly green jumpsuit—her figure spectacular, with a tiny waist, and full, round breasts.

"Thanks, honeybunch," she said when Elizabeth slid open the door. "Did you hear what happened on the beach this morning? Can you imagine, I slept right through all the commotion?" Tyree stepped into the room, and in the firelight the tiny diamond in her front tooth flashed brilliantly. "I didn't know until those policemen came pounding on my door to ask questions."

"Oh God, Tyree," Elizabeth said. "Judy and I found the body."

"You didn't! How awful for you!"

"Yes," Elizabeth said, blinking hard to dislodge the horrible memory of that morning. "We called the lifeguard, and then had to stay there and wait for the police."

"It's appalling, isn't it, when a young girl like that isn't safe in her own neighborhood?" Tyree sounded angry.

"Yes, it sure is," Elizabeth said. "Do they have any idea of what caused her to drown?"

"Drown? Didn't the police tell you? It was one of those two sisters who were attacked on the beach. The older one is still alive and in the hospital."

Elizabeth stared at Tyree, her face going bloodless. "It wasn't an accident? I mean, we just assumed that—"

"Honeybunch, I told you . . . some nut is loose out there. Why do you think I was so concerned about you being on the beach alone last night? All this has the neighborhood in a panic. I think we should get together and talk about protecting ourselves." Tyree wrinkled up her forehead. "Not right now, but soon. At the moment, I have to dash. Boo and I are on our way to the ballet at the Performing Arts Center. We're sponsors, you know. But, I wanted to come over and meet your friend."

"Oh, yes. I'm sorry. This is Judith . . . Judy Bird, my friend from the San Fernando Valley. We've known each other forever."

"How nice to meet you, Judy," Tyree said. "You'll have to come over on Monday night. We're giving Elizabeth and Andy a welcome-to-the-neighborhood party."

"Thank you," Judy got up, and stood beside Elizabeth. "But, I'm afraid I'm only here for the weekend."

"Oh, do try and stay over, won't you? We'd love for you to come." Tyree smiled, and the diamond sparkled again.

"I might do that." Judy nodded.

"Gotta run, honeybunch," Tyree said. "Boo will have a fit if I'm late." She headed toward the door. "And *please* stay off the beach . . . both of you . . . until we . . . until they stop this looney. Don't go anywhere alone."

"You'll get no argument from me," Elizabeth called after her, then carefully, locked the door.

By ten-thirty, Elizabeth felt limp all over, and her hands still shook whenever she tried to hold something. Andy was sequestered in his office, so she didn't disturb him. "I'm ready for bed," she said, yawning.

"Yeah, me too," Judy agreed. "Exhausted. What a hellish day." She stood up and stretched.

"I hope you don't have nightmares," Elizabeth said to Judy, as they climbed the stairs. "After all that's happened."

"I'm too damn tired to have nightmares," Judy said, stifling a yawn.

It was Elizabeth who ended up having the nightmare. In her dream, the bedroom was filled with cats. Wide-eyed cats who prowled around, growling low in their throats, and Elizabeth had to get up and open the window to let them all out. Just as she was about to close the window, Tyree appeared, outside her window, her red hair waving around her head like a halo of crimson snakes. The diamond in her tooth glittered, as if some horrible light were shining out. For some reason she didn't understand, the sight of her made Elizabeth's heart pound, like a heavy mallet beating against the inside of her chest.

"May I come in, honeybunch?" Tyree asked.

"No," Elizabeth told her, her heart still pounding painfully. "Not right now." Elizabeth willed her heart to ease its uncomfortable hammering. What a bizarre dream I'm having, she thought. But then dreams usually were.

"That wasn't very polite," scolded a shadowy man, from where he sat on Aunt Mary's brightly painted float tank. He was wearing a white robe and a little skull cap, but she couldn't see his face. She thought his silhouette looked like that of the man she'd seen in the alley the day they moved in. I should run and get my brushes, Elizabeth thought, so I can paint all this. But, by the time, she had scampered into her studio, she had forgotten what she had come for and why. And, then the dream was only colors. Bright cubes of red and yellow and royal purple. Elizabeth felt herself being absorbed by the colors and she tried to shout herself awake. But all that happened was that the cubes turned into glowing orbs that sucked her up, until she didn't exist anymore.

Chapter Four

It was after nine. Andy had apparently gotten up early, made coffee, and retired to his office. Judy hadn't come down yet, so Elizabeth banged around the kitchen, found a cup, and poured some coffee. Her head ached fiercely, the way it had the day before, and her fingers felt unusually stiff and sore. She was either reacting to yesterday's scene on the beach, or else coming down with a miserable case of flu. Just what she needed! She poured two aspirin out of the bottle from the kitchen cabinet and swallowed them with her coffee. The aspirin burned the back of her throat.

By the time she finished her coffee, her head was throbbing even worse. She tried to ignore it, and began mixing batter for pancakes. Just as she finished, the Zipper sisters rapped on the back door. A wooly fog had rolled in during the early morning, and when Elizabeth pulled open the door the sisters appeared like unearthly spirits materializing out of grizzled wisps of vapor. It gave her quite a start. Both Mable and Sarah wore identical large-brimmed red hats, long grey dresses, gloves and sunglasses.

"Hello there." Elizabeth smiled grimly. "On your way to church, ladies?" *Oh please!* she said to herself, *please don't let them ask to come in.* She felt too miserable to cope with even the simplest conversation. Her head gave a throb.

"To where?" Mable asked.

"To church. It's Sunday. You're all dressed up. I just assumed you were going to church."

"Oh, dear heart, no," Mable said. "Although I'm sure we should be." She lowered her voice to a whisper. "Especially, after all that dreadful business on the beach yesterday. Can you believe such a shocking thing?"

"Shocking thing," Sarah echoed.

"Some pretty awful things happen nowadays," Elizabeth agreed.

"Well, it's not acceptable," Mable sounded angry.

"No, not acceptable at all," Sarah said.

Mable pinched her pink lips together for a moment, then said, "We really must *do* something. It's getting out of hand." Her soft, elderly face took on the stern look of a zealous vigilante. Then, as if realizing how she sounded, she chuckled, and gave Elizabeth a gentle smile. "Actually, we were just out for a stroll, and thought we'd stop by and see how you were getting on."

"Our morning stroll," Sarah said. "And, then, we may take in a movie."

"Yes, yes. An afternoon movie," Sarah nodded. "We adore movies."

Mable turned her pointy nose toward Elizabeth and smiled. "We sometimes treat ourselves to a matinee."

"I see," Elizabeth said.

Mable lifted her head, and looked over Elizabeth's shoulder, peering into the kitchen. "You don't happen to have some coffee on, do you? We'd simply *love* a cup of coffee."

Her head gave a painful throb. "Ah, well. . . ." she began, then sighed. Here they were just trying to be neighborly, and she was acting like a prima donna. Besides, they were probably lonely. The aspirin would take hold soon, and she'd feel better.

"Well, as a matter of fact, I do have some coffee on." She gave a weak smile. "Why don't you come in. I've got a friend visiting. I'd like you to meet her. She should be up soon."

Sarah frowned, poked her head inside the door, and craned her head as if inspecting every corner of the kitchen. Mable took her arm and gave it a tug.

"It's okay, Sarah," she said. "Just the same as it used to be when Mary lived here." Mable stepped into the kitchen, and beckoned to her sister. "Poor dear, she's so shy."

Sarah took off her sunglasses and actually sniffed at the air. Elizabeth had to swallow a laugh. Poor old lady, she seemed a bundle of nerves. The woman took a second sniff, nodded her head yes, gave a grim smile—allowing Elizabeth a glimpse of several gold teeth—and came trotting into the kitchen after Mable.

"There, you see," Mable said, taking off her sunglasses. "She won't be shy long."

"What kind of wallpaper are you going to put up in the living room?" Sarah asked.

"Something with seashells is what I'd planned." Elizabeth rubbed her aching forehead, not wanting to be rude, but she wished the two of them would go away and come back sometime when she felt better.

Sarah knotted up her face. "Yes, well, that is certainly going to be *different!*"

Judy came bounding into the kitchen, still in her robe and slippers, her hair rumpled into little gold spirals all over her head. "Liz! They are *wonderful!*" she trilled. "Absolutely won-der-ful!"

"What's wonderful?" Elizabeth asked. Then, noticing the expectant expression on the elderly women's faces, she said, "Oh, yes, Judy, I'd like you to meet the Zipper sisters. Sarah and Mable. This is my friend Judy Bird."

"Hello," Judy said, giving the two women a flash of her bright smile. "Liz, you must have been up *all night!*"

Elizabeth gave Judy a quizzical look as she filled four cups with coffee. "What are you talking about?"

"Your paintings."

"But, you've seen all of them before," Elizabeth said. "Come on, let's sit at the breakfast bar and have our coffee." A little more caffeine, she reasoned, might help her head. Her hands had gone clammy, and her heart thudded heavily against her chest. The tenderness in her fingers seemed to be increasing. She was beginning to feel as if she'd jumped off a fast-moving freight train!

Neither of the sisters removed her hat or gloves,

but sat like two very proper Victorian ladies. Sarah wanted real cream in her coffee, none of that imitation stuff, and she took three spoonfuls of sugar, while Mable had hers black. Elizabeth felt a bit like a guest at the Mad Hatter's tea party. She had to stifle a strong urge to say, "Move down, move down!"

"Now this is what I call delicious," Mable said, taking a sip of coffee.

"It's a luxury, I'm afraid," Elizabeth explained. "Macadamia nut coffee."

"This is great," Judy said. "I should get some for myself."

"It's nice to have young people in the neighborhood who are adventuresome, isn't it, Sister?" Mable said. "Except for the Rattigans, and a few others, they're all getting to be old fuddy-duddies like us."

"Fuddy-duddies," Sarah echoed.

"Where are you from, dear heart?" Mable asked Elizabeth.

"The San Fernando Valley. Andy was born in Bend, Oregon, but he's lived in California since he was five."

"Do you have brothers and sisters?" Sarah asked.

"Andy has a sister, Betsy, who lives in San Francisco, but I'm an only child."

"Yeah, me too," Judy chimed in, running fingers through her crop of gold hair. "Liz here is the closest thing I've got to a sister."

"That's a shame," Sarah clucked and shook her head. "I don't know what I'd do without my sister."

"So you're an artist," Mable said to Elizabeth. "I understand Tyree's excited about seeing your work. And, I hear tell your husband's a writer."

"Yes, he is."

"Would we have read him?" Sarah asked.

"Well, he wrote *Dolphin Dreams* and *The Orange Juice Man.* Both were in paperback. He hasn't had a new one out in some time though."

Mable shook her head, no. "I'm afraid I'm mostly into Hemingway this year, and Sarah adores those hot and heavy romances by Suzanne Forster." She drained her coffee, and rattled the cup back onto the saucer. Giving a glance out the window, she squinched her eyes together. "Dear me, it's getting late. We'll miss the early matinee if we don't hurry."

"If we miss it, we'll go tonight," Sarah said. She seemed already to have lost some of her shyness and acted as if she would like to stay.

"We can make it, if we hurry," Mable urged.

They both put on their sunglasses at exactly the same time. As they did, Elizabeth heard Judy start to chuckle under her breath. She gave her a don't-you-dare-laugh-at-these-poor-old-ladies-glare, and Judy's laugh turned into a cough. Clutching each other's arms, the two sisters made their way out the back door.

"Now don't forget. We'll see you tomorrow night at the Rattigans'," Mable said, as she gave a gloved wave. "I do love our little get-togethers at the Rattigans'."

"Love them," Sarah chirped over her shoulder.

The two scooted off toward their house so fast

Elizabeth was surprised they didn't stumble. They were certainly spry for their age.

"Can you believe them?" Judy whispered, watching them go. "Aren't they the oddest things."

"In an upscale place like Newport Beach, they call it eccentric," Elizabeth said, rinsing out the sisters coffee cups. "Are you hungry? I'm making pancakes." Maybe, she reasoned, if she ate something, she'd feel better.

"I'm starving."

"What was all that stuff about my paintings, anyway?"

"I was talking about the *new* ones." Judy helped herself to a second cup of coffee, and perched on the edge of a bar stool.

"New ones? I haven't done a new piece in ages."

"But . . . well, of course you have. I just looked at them." Judy frowned, and set her coffee cup down. "Come on, Liz, what's the big secret? Wasn't I supposed to look?"

"No secret." Elizabeth gave the pancake batter a stir. "You've just forgotten. That's how long ago I did them."

"Liz," Judy said seriously. "The paintings I looked at are *still wet.*"

Elizabeth stopped stirring, and looked over at Judy. Her head throbbed furiously. She wasn't in any mood to play games. "Wet? That's impossible. I mean, oils take a long time to dry—some of them months—but all of the ones upstairs are at least six months old."

"Then someone else in this house has taken up painting. And whoever it is, is terrific!"

Elizabeth put down the spoon and wiped her fingers on a dish towel. "Look, I'm sorry, but I feel lousy this morning. My head's splitting. I'm really not in the mood for practical jokes."

"Honey, why didn't you say something?" Judy tilted her head to one side. "Did you take something?"

Elizabeth nodded.

"But Liz, this is no prank. I'm serious. Three wet paintings are sitting upstairs that weren't there when you showed me your studio yesterday."

Elizabeth stood at the end of the breakfast bar staring at Judy, kneading her temples with her fingertips, trying to massage away the headache. "Three . . . paintings? But who . . . ?"

"Liz, they're *good!* Like nothing I've ever seen you do before!" Judy peered over the edge of the cup with serious eyes.

"You're not joking, are you? Has someone been fooling around with my stuff?" Elizabeth strode out of the kitchen, ignoring the throbbing pain in her head, and bounded up the stairs.

The upstairs hallway smelled strongly of fresh oil paint and turpentine. She rushed into the studio and stood in the middle of the room staring at the sight in front of her. There, propped on easels, were three of the largest canvases she owned. As she looked at them, a small bubble of hysteria crept up her throat. Then, suddenly, she couldn't catch her breath. She gulped for air. Her head pounded furiously as she stared at the paintings. Behind her, she heard Judy's footsteps.

"You must have been up all night working on

these!" Judy strode from canvas to canvas. "They're wonderful!"

Elizabeth took in a long, difficult breath. She gazed at one painting then another. One was a house, drifting in mist, a golden light spilling from its windows—exactly the way she had imagined it when she'd decided to change her style of painting. The second canvas was of a woman with flame-red hair blowing in the wind. Tyree! The way she'd looked in her dreams last night. The third was of a shadowy man seated on Aunt Mary's float tank— the man she'd seen lurking in the alley her first day in Mary's house. Her dream again! The colors were vivid and strange, like globs of crayons melted together, making new colors she could have sworn didn't appear on the spectrum.

"Liz, you were just putting me on, weren't you?" Judy said. "I'm sorry I spoiled your surprise, but these are the best I've seen you do."

For a moment, Elizabeth thought her legs were going to wobble out from under her. She steadied herself against an easel. *The paintings had to be hers. But that was impossible!* She recognized her brush-work, something as identifiable as a signature. But these paintings had more fire, more life, more excitement than anything she'd ever done before. Was she losing her mind? She didn't remember a thing about painting them. Could she have done them in her sleep? Some sort of dream-walking? She closed her eyes and shook her head. The pain popped against her forehead. She wiggled her fingers. A dull ache gnawed at the joints. They'd been hurting since she'd climbed out of bed. Could it be from holding a brush for a long period of time? What the hell was going on?

"Lizzy," Andy came dashing into the room. "I'm starving. How about some break—" He came to a sudden halt in the middle of the room, his eyes growing huge as he saw the paintings. Slowly, he pivoted on his heels, gaping at the paintings. "When did you . . . I mean, I didn't know you'd started . . . ah . . . Jesus! These are *incredible!*"

"But Andy," Elizabeth said, feeling her entire body go slick with sweat, her head hammered with deep pain. "I don't remember doing them!" Her legs gave away then, crumpling like twigs. She felt herself falling.

"Lizzy! Baby!" Andy's voice sounded as if it were miles away. He reached for her, and she tried to reach back, but her arms just hung at her sides, heavy as dead tree limbs.

She folded to the floor in what felt like slow motion. As she looked up, she saw Andy's thin, serious face, the fan of dark hair across his forehead, the boyish mouth, for only a moment. Then she was sucked into a thick, smothering blackness. Oh my God! She thought. What the hell is happening to me?

Andy sat stiff-backed on the living room sofa, staring out through the sliding glass door. His eyes refused to focus on the long row of white-foamed waves breaking on the sand. Something was terribly wrong, only he didn't know what it was. He felt as if a big fat worm were gnawing away at his insides.

A violent shudder seized him. Perspiration seeped from the niches and hollows of his body, and flowed in thin trickles down his skin. He flicked his tongue over his lips and took in a deep breath.

Upstairs, Elizabeth was sleeping. After she fainted, he had insisted they take her to the hospital to have a doctor check her over. But, she protested, despite the bright spark of panic in her eyes, saying it was only a touch of flu, and that she'd be okay if she could just sleep it off.

He'd been under the weather all week himself, until this morning, when he began to feel better—a little shaky still—but better. So, why was he so damn frightened all of a sudden? He tried to sort out the reason for his fear. Part of it was caused by the torrent of words that continued to tumble from his head—pages and pages—almost thirty a day! Fresh new exciting work that hardly needed any rewrite. At this rate, he'd have the book completed in a few weeks! And, if he were any judge, the material was damn good.

But, the real fear had hit when Lizzy told him she *didn't remember doing her three new paintings.* Although he was aware of all his writing now, that was the way it had started with him. The day he felt the worst, he'd obviously written all day, but couldn't remember doing it. Yet, the printed pages were there, letter perfect, as proof, the style unmistakably his. He'd tossed it off as a result of feeling ill. But now Lizzy. Her three new paintings were remarkably good. And apparently she'd done them all in one night, an impossible task. But there they were!

Maybe, he told himself, the flu bug was one of

those weird hybrids. One that pumped a person full
of adrenalin, putting both him and Lizzy into a
work frenzy. He laughed grimly. A creative virus! It
didn't made sense. But, whatever the hell it was, it
was still active.

He'd been in his office since five that morning. By
ten, he'd completed close to twenty pages. Unlike,
the first time, he could remember every word he
wrote. The words just popped into his head—ideas,
scenes, characters, plot—flooding his brain and
flowing down to his fingers and into the word
processor. He'd been delighted at first. It was all so
easy. But now, as the phenomenon not only continued, but grew, fear began to gnaw at him. He had
such an alien feeling, as if he'd been invaded. But by
what, he didn't know. He kept expecting the alien
feeling to go away, but, if anything, it increased.

Judy came bounding down the stairs, two at a
time, shaking him out of his thoughts. He shifted
away from the window and looked at her. He could
still feel the sweat oozing out of his pores.

"Andy! You look terrible!" She came over and
sat down beside him on the sofa. "Come on. Relax.
Liz is okay. Just a bug. Everyone in the Valley's got
it." She gave him a bright smile. "She has a pretty
high fever, so I made her drink a glass of water and
take some more aspirin."

Andy nodded. He desperately wanted to confide
his fears in Judy, but if he did, she'd probably think
he'd lost his marbles. After all, what could he tell
her? That he and Lizzy had caught a virus which
had turned on some kind of creative flow?

"Hey, you okay?" Judy put her hand on his shoulder.

He nodded again. "Yeah. Fine."

"Can I make you anything to eat?"

"No. I'm not hungry." Andy dabbed at some of the sweat that had collected in the hollow of his neck.

"Well, I am. There's pancake batter all mixed. Do you mind if I make some for myself?" Judy yawned and rubbed at her eyes. "I slept like a log, thanks to the sound of the surf pounding away outside."

"Help yourself. Listen, after you eat, would you do me a favor? Would you read a chapter or two of my new book? I'd like to see what you think of it."

"Sure. I'd love to."

"But please," Andy said. "Don't tell Lizzy I let you read it. She hasn't seen it. I don't want to hurt her feelings. Our relationship's been strained lately. What with both of us lolling around in the doldrums with our careers. And, to be honest, I get pretty selfish sometimes. I forget she's got as much ambition as I have. We've been sniping at each other a lot. And the move sure hasn't helped."

"Andy . . . I'm sorry. Maybe I should read it later, after Liz does. I wouldn't want to cause a problem."

"Look, I really need an opinion," Andy said. "Right away. Before I send it to my agent. And since Lizzy's not feeling well, I don't want to bother her." He knew Judy was a excellent story analyst and he valued her opinion. He had to know if his new work was as good as he thought.

"Okay then," she agreed.

"Great. The manuscript is in my office on the desk," Andy said. "Judy? What did you think of Lizzy's new paintings?"

Judy grinned at him and in an awed whisper said, "Amazing! I always thought her stuff was nice, but it lacked something. Too pedestrian. I think she knew it too. But these new ones . . . God, how do I describe them? Provocative? Exhilarating?"

Andy nodded. "Yes." He paused momentarily, feeling a sudden pang of guilt. After all, there was no reason to expose Judy to their flu. "Look, on second thought, maybe you shouldn't stay here. Maybe you should go on home."

Judy gave him a startled look. "Why?"

"Whatever Lizzy's got, I've had, too. So, you're probably exposing yourself to the flu. I wouldn't want you to get sick on our account."

"It's too late. I've already been exposed. Besides, I don't mind hanging around. I'd like to help."

"I was hoping you'd say that."

Judy got up, and started toward the kitchen, and then turned back. "It will be okay, Andy. You and Liz. Things will smooth out. You'll see."

Andy gave her a weak smile. "Yeah. It *has* too. I love her. A lot."

"I know," she said. "Okay, then, first, pancakes and coffee, then I'll read your manuscript." She jogged out of the room, her sandals making little clicking noises against the back of her heels.

Andy felt relieved. Whatever peculiar things were going on with them, it would be comforting to have her around. After she read his work, and if she thought it was as good as he did, then maybe he'd tell her about what had been happening. She might have some explanation other than the ones he'd come up with. But, something was definitely wrong. Something out of sync. And, the more he thought about it, the more it scared him.

Elizabeth slept fitfully all morning. She woke feverish from time to time, and Andy sponged her down with a wet washcloth and some alcohol. He sat on the edge of the bed and looked down at her. Her cheeks were flushed bright pink, but the rest of her skin looked pale and damp. He scolded himself for not insisting they find a family physician right after they moved. The only thing he could do was take her to the emergency room at Hoag Memorial Hospital. It was the closest place he knew of. He'd let her sleep a while longer, but when she woke, he'd bundle her up and see if they could give her some antibiotics.

She stirred in her sleep, making little moaning sounds, and he shook the washcloth to cool it, then folded it carefully across her forehead. It was a good thing Judy had offered to stay over. He wasn't terribly good with sick people, although he tried to be. He remembered when his sister, Betsy, had had the measles. She'd been feverish and incoherent for several days. He was certain she was going to die. He'd wanted to comfort her but, instead, he'd stayed in his room, a pillow over his head, until his mother finally came to get him. Two weeks later, he came down with the measles and hardly felt ill at all.

He heard the doorbell ring downstairs. Damn, who could that be? Maybe Judy would get it. She was still ensconced in his office reading. She had finished the first two chapters of his new book and instead of stopping, she'd waved him away, making it clear she intended to read every page he'd written so far. If the writing was lousy, he reasoned, she would have stopped. No. It was good. He knew it was good. He only wanted that knowledge validated.

He gave the washcloth another shake and rearranged it on Elizabeth's forehead. The doorbell chimed again. He sighed. Judy obviously hadn't heard it. He tucked the covers around Elizabeth, then kissed her gently on the cheek. She didn't stir.

Downstairs, he went to the sliding glass door, then realized the only door with a bell was the one off the kitchen. As he made his way through the dining room, the bell made another impatient sound.

"Okay!" he grumbled. "I'm coming!" Pulling the curtains on the kitchen door aside, he saw Tyree standing on the back porch. In her hand she held a large polished-wood box. Her red hair was pulled back in a thick French braid. Little curls had broken free and were fluttering around her face like licks of flame.

"Hi, honeybunch," Tyree called through the glass.

Andy pulled open the door. Tyree was wearing a white jersey jumpsuit snugged together with a gold belt. On her forehead she had a white sunshade and a pair of mirrored sunglasses were propped on her nose. Andy jumped slightly when he looked at her. Instead of seeing her eyes, he saw a distorted reflection of himself.

"The Zippers told me that Elizabeth didn't seem too chipper this morning. Thought I'd stop by and see if she was okay."

"Well, as a matter of fact," Andy said, "she's feeling awful. Running a fever. I guess it's the flu. I've had a touch myself this week."

"Oh, dear," Tyree moved past him. As she did, she gave his face a gentle touch with the tips of her cool, dry fingers. She had a way of dancing into the room before you invited her in, her lithe body doing all sorts of floaty things that made her look as if her feet never touched the floor. "Tell me, has she been eating okay lately? How about the food I brought over? Did she eat most of it?"

Andy hesitated. He didn't want to hurt Tyree's feelings, but he thought he should be honest. "Some. But I think it was too rich for her. Upset her stomach. But maybe it was just this flu she was coming down with." He smiled. "But I made a pig out of myself. Thanks, for being so thoughtful."

Tyree frowned, a deep crease appearing across her forehead. "Poor baby. You should have called me the minute she got sick," she said. "Of course, you had no way of knowing I have a cupboard full of herbal medicine. Elizabeth's Aunt Mary gave me most of it. I'm sure you know she was in pharmaceuticals. She had a dozen researchers on her staff at one time. All of them collecting native remedies from the rain forests. Sumatra. New Guinea. All over the place. She doctored the lot of us." With that, Tyree glided over to the breakfast bar and plunked down the wooden box. Then she quickly skimmed to the stove, picked up the teakettle, and proceeded to fill it with water.

"Well, I don't know if. . . ." Andy started. "I mean, I'm planning to take Lizzy over to Hoag and have a doctor look at her. Maybe give her some antibiotics."

Tyree set the teakettle on the stove, and turned on the burner. "That's a good idea. But let's give the folk medicine a chance first. Can't hurt. Not as much as some of those modern medications. After all, a lot of native tribes have used these for centuries. Even though Mary's company made some pretty sophisticated stuff, she always prefered the natural cures. Besides, it's probably just the old misery. I hear it's going around. Let me steep up some herbal tea. That may take care of it. And the Zippers will be over in a while with some of their soup. It's so potent we call it the Lazarus concoction." Tyree chuckled. "Raise a person right up out of the grave."

"Tyree, I don't know. Rain forest herbs? Sounds kind of—"

"Oh now Andy, don't panic. There's nothing in any of it that can hurt a person. It's all natural." She pulled a cup and saucer out of the cupboard, then turned to look at him. "How are *you* feeling? You look a bit peaked yourself."

"I should have said something to Lizzy. Maybe if she'd stayed away from me, she wouldn't have caught it. I'm better today, though."

"Uh, huh. Still you'd better have a cup of my tea.

Makes all the difference. Try it. You'll see." Tyree
pulled out a second, cup and set it on the breakfast
bar.

"I'm not much of a tea drinker."

"Nonsense. Do you good."

"Still, I'd rather not." Andy shook his head.

Tyree put her hands on her hips and gave him a
scolding look. "Honestly, you'd think I was trying
to poison you or something! Now stop being such a
baby." She opened the wooden box, pulled out a
small tin, lifted the lid, and scooped out two tea-
spoons of dark leaves into each cup. The teakettle
began to whistle. She poured the steaming water
into the cups, covering the leaves, which swirled
around for a few moments before settling to the
bottom.

Andy watched, halfway amused by her tenacious
mothering. He didn't know how old she was, but he
guessed her to be in her late thirties, too young to be
such a mother hen.

"Now," Tyree said, handing him a cup. "I don't
want to hear another word out of you. Just drink it
down like a good boy, you hear? I'll take this one up
to Elizabeth."

"Yes, ma'am," Andy smiled submissively. "I
guess it can't hurt."

"And no dumping it down the sink while I'm
gone," Tyree warned over her shoulder as she
wafted out of the kitchen on her way upstairs.

Andy stared down at the liquid in the cup. It had
a muddy look to it he didn't like. What on earth do
you suppose it is? he wondered. A pinch of fever-
wort? A sprinkling of tannis root? He gave a little

laugh. Bubble, bubble, toil and trouble. Witch's brew! He took a small sip of the dark liquid. It tasted like sweet raspberries. "Son of a gun!" he said, and quickly drank down the rest. "Not bad. Now, let's hope I don't grow hair all over my body and howl at the moon."

The doorbell rang again, and this time Andy found the Zipper sisters standing on the back porch, both of them dressed in blue housedresses covered by bright patchwork aprons. They tramped past him into the kitchen. They both smelled like basil, garlic, dill weed, saffron—a walking herb garden. One of them-Andy wasn't sure which one, because they looked so much alike—carried a covered pot.

"Ohhh please, out of the way, dear heart," the one with the pot said. Must be Mable, Andy supposed. If he remembered right, she was the one who called everyone *dear heart*.

"Yes, we don't want to spill our lovely soup," Sarah chimed in, trailing after her sister. "It's nice and hot. You'll love it."

"It's nice of you to—"

"Oh, for pity sakes. That's what neighbors are for," Mable said, plunking the pot down on the range top and turning on the burner. "I could just tell that Elizabeth wasn't herself this morning. She looked so peaked. Poor darling. That nasty old bug is going around like crazy."

"Is Tyree here?" Sarah asked.

Andy nodded. "Yes. She took some tea up to Lizzy."

"We'll just run up and see how they're doing." Mable adjusted the flame under the pot, and then the two of them scampered off through the dining room and up the stairs. Andy could hear their heavy shoes as they clomped up the landing.

"Christ! It's a circus," he said aloud. He certainly hoped this wasn't going to happen every time he or Elizabeth sneezed. A little concern was nice, but this was getting out of hand!

By the time Tyree and the Zipper sisters came downstairs, Andy was feeling better than he had in a long while. The tea had been soothing. He sat at the breakfast bar in the kitchen, his mind on his writing, wondering how long before Judy would be finished reading. She certainly must be absorbed in his plot, not to have been disturbed by all the coming and goings. He could hardly wait to get back to his computer and do some more work. The ideas were beginning to pile up in his head.

"Well," Tyree said, setting Elizabeth's empty cup on the sink. "Did you drink it all?"

"I did. And it works great. In fact, you ought to patent that stuff."

Tyree grinned. "Told you so. Now, all you need is a bowl of the Zipper sisters' soup, and you'll be good as new."

Andy looked at his watch. It was after noon, and he hadn't eaten anything yet. "As a matter of fact," he said, "I am getting hungry. The soup smells wonderful."

"I'll take a bowl up to Elizabeth," Sarah offered, opening the kitchen cabinet and taking out a pottery bowl.

"And I'll fix some for Andy," Mable said. "Oh, we should set a place for your friend, too. What's her name?"

"You mean Judy? She's in my office reading one of my manuscripts. I'll get her."

Tyree took hold of his arm. "Andy, before you go, I want to ask you something," she said, with eager, glistening moves of her eyes. "I happened to peek into Elizabeth's studio on my way back downstairs. She's got three paintings in there I'd die for. Especially that one of *me!* What a lovely surprise. I'd like to buy that one myself. The brushwork is wonderful. And those colors! Do you suppose she'd let me take the other two down to show at my gallery? I know they're still wet, but I've got a couple of clients I think would kill for them."

"I'm sure she'd be happy to let you show them. But, I suppose you'd better ask her."

"I'll ask for you," Sarah chirped, as she filled the pottery bowl with a ladle of thick yellowy soup, and started out of the room.

"Tell her I can get a good price," Tyree called after Sarah. "I hope she'll do a lot more of them for me."

"She's got a bunch of others," Andy said, warming to the conversation. They could certainly use the extra money right now.

"Yes, I looked around at all the others, but they are . . . ummm . . . how can I put it?" Tyree gave him an apologetic smile, the diamond in her tooth shimmering blue-white. "They're very nice, but they just don't have the same . . . ah . . . special quality as those three on the easels. If she can keep up that new style, she's got it made. Seriously."

Andy smiled. "She'll be excited to hear that."

"I'd be thrilled to handle her work," Tyree said. "Good business. She'll be a money-maker. I'll bet on that."

Andy felt a lick of anxiety. Elizabeth couldn't remember having done the paintings. Still, if Tyree wanted to buy one, and maybe sell the others, it sure would ease their finances.

Mable placed two bowls of soup and two spoons on the breakfast bar, then rummaged through the cupboard and found the paper napkins. Andy watched, fascinated, as she deftly folded, turned, twisted, and manipulated the napkins until they both resembled flying birds.

Mable saw him watching, and chuckled. "Just something I learned as a child. I was a bit . . . well, backward they said. But, my father thought I should learn some type of art, so he taught me origami," she said. "Now it's a habit I can't break. Give me a piece of paper, and I automatically turn it into an animal or a bird, or an odd-shaped box. Silly, isn't it?"

Andy shook his head. "No. Not at all. You make it look so easy. Listen, I'd better get Judy before the soup cools off."

Andy turned and headed toward his office. Just as he got to the doorway Judy came bounding through, almost colliding with him.

"Oh, Andy! I'm sorry! Listen, I finished reading and it's wonderful!" Judy cried. "It's going to be a best seller. I just know it!" She stopped suddenly and looked around the kitchen. "Oh, hello. I didn't know anyone else was here. What smells so good?"

"Tyree and the Zipper sisters came over to doctor Lizzy. I highly recommend their herb tea. It made me feel a hell of a lot better."

Judy sniffed at the pot of soup. "Ah, ha! Chicken soup, I bet."

"Potato cheese," Mable said proudly. "Chicken soup is highly overrated. I've poured a bowl for each of you, so sit yourselves down and enjoy."

Judy pulled out a bar stool, and picked up her spoon like an obedient child. "This is nice of you."

"No trouble at all," Mable said. "There's plenty more on the stove."

"Just good neighbors." Tyree carefully packed up her box of herbal tea.

Sarah trotted into the room. The soup bowl in her hand was still full. "I couldn't get any of it down her." She looked at Tyree and gave a little shrug of her shoulders. "But the tea seems to have helped her miseries. The fever's broken, and she drifted back to sleep."

"She's . . . a little rundown, I think." Tyree pursed her lips together, and shook her head. "Probably the move and all."

Mable took hold of Sarah's arm. "We'll leave you in peace now. Enjoy the soup, you two."

"Yes," Tyree agreed. "You have to be in good shape for our neighborhood get-together tomorrow night. After all," she patted Andy on the shoulder, "the whole evening's just for you."

As the Zipper sisters started out the door, Sarah

turned to Tyree. "Oh, yes, Elizabeth said that of course you can show the new paintings. She was so pleased."

Tyree, following on Sarah's heels, nodded, and said, "Fine. I'll get them first thing tomorrow. That way, Elizabeth will be feeling better, and we can chat about them."

"Ta–ta for now," Mable said over her shoulder. Sarah gave a little wave.

Tyree hesitated in the doorway. "Andy? Please try and get Elizabeth to eat a little of that soup. Not too much. But a few spoonfuls every four hours or so."

"Yes. Sure. I'll try."

Tyree stood on the threshold, the frown still creasing her forehead. She looked as if she were going to say something more, then shook her head again, and went out, closing the door quietly behind her.

Andy and Judy sat at the breakfast bar, spoons in hand, staring at one another.

Judy let out a giggle. "Talk about your friendly neighbors!"

"Aren't they." Andy sipped at the soup. It had a wonderfully sharp cheese taste mixed with dill. "Hey, this is good!"

"It is," Judy agreed. Let's hear it for nosey, but friendly neighbors." She picked up one of the napkin birds Mable had folded. "Look at these! Aren't they adorable?"

"Mable," Andy said. "I think it was Mable who made them."

"Clever. Just like you and your writing. Honestly, Andy. I can't believe how good your new work is. It's inspired me to get busy and try my hand at my own screenplay again. Got a lot of new ideas going in my head. And Elizabeth! Can you imagine, those new paintings? They say the sea air does wonderful things. I think I'm a convert. Mind if I stay here forever?" Judy laughed.

A small shiver passed over Andy. He thought again about his earlier concerns. He'd been so frightened. But of what? What was so scary about the fact that Elizabeth was finally hitting her stride? After all, she'd worked long and hard for that. The same was true of himself. It was about time he broke through his block. And, about time he wrote a great book. He'd certainly paid his dues.

"It *must* be the change of climate," he said, not realizing he had spoken aloud.

"What?" Judy looked at him quizzically.

"Oh, I was just thinking. . . ." he paused. "Maybe it *is* the move. Or the salt air. Both Lizzy and I . . . we really have found our stride."

"I'd say so," Judy looked over at him, her eyes wide and earnest.

Andy nodded. He felt a momentary thrill. What more could he ask for? But, then, a sensation of unease crept over him. A new fever of fear. He twisted slightly, and felt a fresh bundle of aches and pains. For a second, he swayed, leaned against the bar, felt perspiration dampen his skin again. That alien feeling—like an invader sitting inside him—an unbalanced, unsympathetic Philistine come to terrorize him.

He looked over at the window above the sink.

Sunlight poured in through the glass panes, bubbling and bouncing around the room, bleaching the air with its bright light. He wanted to put his mouth against the light and feed on it, the way he was feeding on Mable and Sarah's hot soup. He wanted to suck the warmth out of it because he suddenly felt so chilled. His skeleton lay under his flesh like knobby sticks of ice. He gave a great shudder.

Ted Bearbower hadn't eaten a bite of food all day. He wrote it off as a case of acute frustration over the two unsolved murder cases. By four, Sunday afternoon, his hunger overwhelmed the frustration and he persuaded Steve Locke to join him for an early supper at Bangkok 3, a Thai restaurant on the Balboa Peninsula.

"So, how goes it with your lady friend?" Ted asked, after they were seated.

"What lady friend?" Steve said with a pensive look and a shrug.

"Oh, oh. That bad, huh?"

Locke gave another shrug, his rainwater eyes blinking slowly. He took out a cigarette and lit it, blowing the smoke out in small doughnut shapes. "I guess police work and romance are like the proverbial oil and water."

Ted nodded. "We've got a high rate of divorce on the force. Can't deny that. But, there's someone else out there. You'll find the right one."

Locke gave a begrudging smile, revealing his slightly crooked front teeth. To Ted, he didn't look a day over eighteen, but he'd graduated from college with a degree in police science, and had been on the force for four years. He'd gone from uniform to detective in record time. His sandy hair and freckled complexion were exactly like Ted's late wife's. If he and Sylvia had had a son, Ted liked to think he might have looked a lot like Locke. Having the young man as a partner was almost like having a son take up his trade. And, like himself, Locke put police work before everything else. It's too bad there weren't more young people out there willing to sacrifice part of their own life, in order to make it safer for others. Then, suddenly, Ted gave a brittle laugh. What an old fool you are, he told himself. An absurd idealist. Shit!

Locke's pale eyes scrutinized him carefully. "What's so funny?"

"Nothing. I think I'm getting giddy from not eating all day."

"Yeah, well, that's got to be a record for you."

Ted laughed again, this time with more humor. "Probably."

The waitress, a tiny, exquisite woman with dark-crystal eyes and pale mocha skin, came to take their order.

"Try the beef satay with peanut butter sauce," Ted suggested. "It's not as spicy as some of the other stuff."

After they ordered and the waitress brought them each a glass of plum wine, Locke took out his notepad and checked it over. "So, where are we with this whole mess anyway? Do we have anything that counts, or not?"

"Yes. And no. And maybe," Ted said, not being at all facetious. "It all depends. We're positive the two homicides were done by the same person. Looks like a good number of the older cases, in other jurisdictions, were too. At the moment, however, I'm only concerned with what's happened in our own territory."

"It looks to me like we're dead in the water. Our canvas of the peninsula didn't turn up much."

Ted sipped his wine for a moment, thinking. "I'm not so certain that it didn't." He took another sip, savoring the sharp, flower-like taste of the wine. "Nothing concrete, of course, but I did notice something."

"You did?" Locke leaned forward, an eager expression on his face. "What? They all told us pretty much the same thing."

"It's not what they said, but rather, the way in which they said it. Body language. Facial expressions. An odd use of language. Could be my imagination though. Wishful thinking."

Locke leaned back, disappointed. "Body language? Hell, what good is that?"

"Subtleties are sometimes important. Especially, when they begin to pile up."

"Okay, Teddy Bear. Stop feeding it to me bite by bite. If you've got something, give me the whole enchilada."

"I will, if you'll swear to God you won't ever call me Teddy Bear again!"

Locke chuckled. "Ahh, where's your sense of humor. We call you that because we love you. And because you *look* like a Teddy Bear."

"Great! Fat jokes before dinner. Just what I need."

"I promise I won't call you that again . . . tonight."

Ted fought back a smile. It was true. The nickname was a term of endearment. But Jesus! Teddy Bear! Couldn't they have come up with something more forceful? Like Duke, or Rambo, or even Frankenstein?

"So, tell me about the body language."

Ted pulled out his own notepad and flipped through it. "Well, on this one particular block we had a flicker of an odd reaction most everywhere we went. You didn't notice?"

"If I had, I would have made a note of it. Where was this?"

"A small strip on the ocean side of Balboa Boulevard near the end of the peninsula. Maybe twelve houses, plus several small apartments over garages. The oceanfront places look right out onto where the floater was found."

"Yeah, okay. We covered part of it yesterday, and the rest this morning."

"Right. That's the area."

"So, what was unusual about it?"

"First of all, the places where we stopped last night, no one asked us in. Hardly talked at all. Shook their heads, is about all. You'd think they would be anxious to talk about this. Help out if they could."

"They were probably all hung over. Saturday night parties. Or maybe a reaction to that grisly find on the beach, so close to home."

Well, whatever it was, they weren't too agreeable.

Then, when we told them the reason for our visit, we got . . . I don't know what it was we got, exactly. But at one place, the only place where the husband and wife ushered us inside—remember? They offered us coffee? I told them what we wanted. I don't know. Maybe it was a look they exchanged. A tightness around their mouths. Another place, you know, where those two elderly sisters live? All they could do was fidget. Nervous people make me nervous. Suspicious, too."

Locke picked up his wine glass, and inspected the purple liquid. "I think you read a whole lot more into it than I did. It just sounds like some rather uptight people. After all, two old ladies who live alone. I'd probably fidget too. This whole business has everyone on edge."

"Yes, well in this case, we talked with people from nine of the homes, and all but one of the apartments. You remember, I didn't have us bother the two young women who found the body. Figured they'd had enough for now. But, at all of the other places where people were home, I got the same feeling from every person I spoke with. They were more than just on edge."

Locke stubbed out his cigarette in the ashtray, and took a swallow of his wine. He made a face. "Ahhh, geeze! This stuff tastes like fucking flowers! You *like* this stuff?"

Ted grinned. "Love it. Would you rather have a beer?"

"Yeah. Please."

"It's oriental beer, but pretty good." He signaled the waitress.

"Thanks."

Ted drained his wine glass and pulled Locke's over in front of him. "Anyway, I haven't put it together yet. But there's *something* there. I sense it. We're going back again tomorrow. See if we can't shake enough sandboxes to make something rise to the surface."

"Are you Detective Beerboor?" the young waitress asked as she approached their table.

"Bearbower," Ted said.

"Yes. Yes. You have a phone call, please."

"Thanks. Where can I take it?"

"At the front desk."

Locke frowned at him. "You leave this number? What's wrong with your pager?"

"I've got some tests I asked for, from some special places. Told them to call me anywhere, anytime, if they got them done."

"Maybe we got a break."

"Maybe." Ted got up and strode to the front desk, being careful not to let his bulk swipe any of the place settings off the neatly arranged tables.

"Bearbower," he growled into the phone. It was Doctor Kimmijuju from the Department of Health Services. Ted took out his notepad, made notes of the conversation, thanked the man, hung up, and headed back to the table. He knew he had a huge smile on his face.

"Okay," Locke said, sipping a glass of beer the waitress had brought. "What's that shit-eating grin for?"

"Well, at least we've found one thing the victims had in common."

Locke put down his beer. "I'll bite."

"Endorphines."

"What?"

"Endorphines. A lot of endorphines in their bodies."

"You mean they were on drugs?"

"No. More like they were souped up on a natural high."

"Like a runner's high?"

"Yep."

"Well, how the hell does that fit in? You think they were all out jogging before they were killed?"

"No. Too much of the stuff in their blood. But, it explains the one thing that's been bothering me the most." Ted picked up Locke's leftover wine and gulped it down, letting out a long sigh as he put the glass back on the table.

"Which is?"

"Which is," Ted said, "why there were no signs of a struggle in the Newport killings, as well as the others."

"They were shit-faced on endorphines?"

"Feeling no pain."

"But, how the hell could they be *that* high? What were they doing to cause it? Long-distance running? Like you said, even that wouldn't juice them up that much? And how come we didn't know about this earlier."

"We did. It was right there in the medical reports. But all it said was a large amount of endorphines. It didn't appear important. At least not until I started thinking about how they all died without any sign of a struggle. I wanted to recheck the latest victims.

The Duff girl, the one that's still alive, was by far the lowest, but some of it still showed up. Which is strange, because it should be gone by now. That stuff doesn't usually stick around too long after you stop the activity that caused it."

"Are you sure they weren't injected with something?"

"No needle tracks. Only a few deep scratch marks, probably fingernails. And some bruises."

"Okay, then maybe that's why this guy takes a bite out of their flesh. To conceal the needle tracks. Or maybe they ingested the stuff orally."

Ted thought about that. "Yes. That's possible."

"Or maybe it's caused by fear."

"Fear raises the adrenaline level, not the endorphine level."

"Christ! I'm more confused now than I was before." Locke downed his beer and sat staring into space, his boyish face looking troubled. "This guy . . . our killer . . . goes to all the trouble of picking out someone who's pumped up with so many endorphines he or she can't put up a fight. Then, our killer cuts or bites their throat and takes away most of their blood, as well as some chunks of flesh." Locke stared into his empty glass. "Nah, I can't buy that. How would the killer know if the victim was sky high on endorphines? Bite 'em first and see if they yell?"

"I'm not sure how the stuff got there. Or, how it fits into the pattern. Not yet, anyway."

"So, what's the motive here? Shit, Ted, none of it makes any fucking sense, does it?" Locke pulled out another cigarette and lit it. "It just doesn't come together."

"I think it will . . . eventually."

"Ah, come on, Ted! That's like putting an apple and a pork chop together and saying it might make a pig, if you look at it long enough." Locke concentrated on blowing little white rings of smoke.

"But it's *something,*" Ted said. "And something is at least a little more than we had before."

"So what do we do now?"

"Now, we do the most important thing of all," Ted said, unfolding his napkin and spreading it out on his lap. "We eat dinner."

Tyree Rattigan paced the carpeted floor of her upstairs bedroom. A feeling of helplessness nagged at her. She couldn't breathe. Her muscles were all wire and tight springs, but her lungs were lax, like heavy bellows. Her pulse throbbed restlessly at her temple. With a quick movement, she opened the window, and let a soft flutter of tangy sea air into the room. That was a little better. The night was clear, no sign of fog, and the stars were coming out. With her fingers, she combed the long red tangles of her hair.

"Damn!" she said to the night. "What the hell are we going to do?" She shook her head. It was the helpless feeling that bothered her the most. She stuffed her hands into the pockets of her sweatsuit, her fingers tight and bunched, then resumed her pacing. Every damn thing that could go wrong, had!

The police had left the area for the time being, but

they would be back. Of that she was certain. And, she could help them. She felt certain she knew who was responsible for what was happening. But, if she told them what she knew, it would involve them all. They would lose everything. They needed more time. Time to finish what they'd started with Elizabeth and Andy. But, time was the one thing they didn't have. If they let the killings continue, they would be as guilty as the killer.

"Damn!" she said again. Her voice felt like a tight little ball in the back of her throat. What was she supposed to do? She stopped her pacing, pulled her hands out of her pockets and stood in front of her dresser. She looked for her comb, but unable to find it, picked up a tube of lipstick, then peered at her image in the mirror. The palest of faces looked back at her. The stress was taking its toll. A slick of color on her mouth helped some. She sighed, turned away from the mirror and went back to the window. Leaning against the sill she watched the surf. The waves made green and white fires in the darkness. In the pale light, she saw something surface, a dolphin perhaps. Whatever it was, breached in a rush of creamy foam, spraying emerald diamonds of sea water in the air, and then disappeared.

"What I really need," she said, watching the spot where the creature had left a fan-shaped impression in the green-sequined water, "is a stiff drink!" She shook away the mesmeric image, closed the window, and made her way across the room.

Downstairs, she rummaged in the refrigerator and found the pitcher of Bloody Marys she'd made that afternoon. She filled a tall glass with the thick red liquid, added an extra jolt of Tabasco, two ice cubes, and a small stalk of celery. Then she took the drink into the living room and sat down in the overstuffed rocking chair, making certain her cassette player and headphones were on the end table beside her. She didn't bother to turn on the lights. It was nice, just sitting there in the dark looking out on the beach. The waves broke on the sand in bright little splashes of phosphorus. God, how she loved this house—this place. Now it was all going to bloody hell! And all because of *him*. Her heart gave a painful little twist. But then again, without him, they wouldn't have the house. Or the money. Nothing. Without him, Boo wouldn't have been able to accomplish so much in such a short time. Damn! There had to be a way out of all this.

She took a few sips of her drink, and felt herself relax slightly. There had to be an answer, a workable solution. The group had plunged the young couple next door into this thing without their knowledge or permission. What would happen when they found out? How would they react? Would the process work? Could they count on their hunger for money? Well, she wouldn't think about all that now. First things first. They had to find a way to stop the killings. Then, they could deal with the rest of it.

Tyree stirred her Bloody Mary with the celery stalk, then took several long swallows. The drink caught fire in the center of her belly and spread its warmth through her veins. Better. She reached over to the end table and picked up a set of headphones and put them on. She turned on the cassette player, leaned her head back and listened to the sounds. Focus, she told herself. Focus, and all of the answers will come.

She sat there for a long time, listening, tuning, waiting. She couldn't afford to make a mistake. Even a small mistake would be too costly.

At four-thirty on Sunday afternoon, Elizabeth stirred in bed, heard the sound of the surf, smelled the briny breeze through the open bedroom windows, and wondered for a moment where the heck she was.

Her sleep had been so long and sound that she felt totally disoriented. She expected to find herself in the dark, cramped little apartment she'd shared with Andy for the past four years. Instead, she looked around the large bedroom, at the black marble fireplace, the huge baroque cherrywood bed and matching dresser, and the odd box thing of Aunt Mary's. Then her memory shifted into gear with an almost audible click. She was in Aunt Mary's house, of course. No, that wasn't exactly right. The house belonged to *her* now.

In response to her thoughts, she heard the grandfather clock downstairs chime once, for the half hour. She stretched out in the bed and wiggled about, savoring the feel of cool sheets through her nightgown. A vague thought crossed her mind, like a wispy shadow not quite formed. Something had happened to her. She shook her head and sucked in a deep breath of the moist salty air that flooded the room. The flu! That was it. She'd had a fever. And

nightmares. Her entire body had ached like an in-
flamed tooth. But she felt a lot better. Her head
twinged a bit when she looked at the fading afternoon sunlight, but that was all.

Then she remembered that something else had
happened just before she'd become ill. She sat up
and swung her legs over the side of the bed. *The
paintings!* Yes! She'd done some new paintings. Or,
at least, she thought she had, even if she couldn't
remember doing them. Or, was that all part of her
fevered sleep? Well, she'd find out quickly enough.
She reached for her terry-cloth robe at the foot of
the bed and put it on. The floor felt cool under her
bare feet, but she didn't take the time to find her
slippers.

She went to the window for a moment to gaze out
at the sight of the ocean pounding in along the
beach. Such a glorious sight! How fortunate they
were to have Mary's house. She hadn't liked it
much, the day they moved in. But it had quickly
grown on her. Now, if they could just hang onto it.
If they could make enough money to keep paying
the taxes and make the repairs. She sighed, pulled
the shutters closed, and made her way across the
room and down the hall. Pushing open the door to
her studio, she held her breath, half expecting to
find the paintings a delusion of the flu. But, there
they stood! All three of them, the oil paint still
glistening. She quickly inspected each of them with
a critical eye. Were they as good as she'd thought?
As good as Andy and Judy had said?

The first painting, the one of Tyree, had a glow to
it that was almost mystical. Yes, it was good! Like

nothing she'd ever done before. The second, the one of the large old house on the beach, shrouded in fog—why she could almost hear the gulls crying. The last one had a whimsical touch to it. The shadowy man from her dream. He had a mischievous gleam in his eyes, and his skin tones were remarkable real. How, in God's name, had she managed to paint three such fine pictures, virtually in her sleep? And, so damn fast? Was it simply that she was finally hitting her stride? The same way Andy seemed to be doing with his work? Yes, of course. It was her turn now. Her turn to really become an artist, not just a painter. It was the flu that had caused her not to remember doing them.

She rummaged through her boxes of paints. Did she have enough colors? She pulled out a clean paper pallet, laid out the paints she had left, set up a clean canvas, and selected several brushes and a pallet knife. For a few moments, she stood thinking about what she wanted to paint. But she couldn't think of anything that excited her. She stood poised, rolling a charcoal stick between her fingers. *That's when it happened.*

It was like an audible click inside her head, and then she began to sketch. In her mind's eye, she saw the finished painting. Misty, muted violet. Pale gold. Grayed turquoise. Pale moonlight dappling the restless surf. The vaguest outline of a surfer, his wet form reflecting the metallic light, riding the curl of a giant wave. Her fingers moved swiftly, catching the right lines, the sense of movement. The vision expanded, flooding her mind until it almost blinded her. She continued to sketch, outlining every detail. Now and then she stood back to view the work, then continued in almost a frenzy. The drawing took shape exactly the way she saw it in her mind, flowing from her brain like a swift river cascading into her hands, through her fingers and onto the canvas.

The sketch completed, she stood staring at it. Downstairs, the grandfather clock began to chime, but she didn't keep track of the number. Time didn't matter. All that mattered was completing the painting. She began to mix the oils, only faintly aware of what she was doing. She lay in the background, working dark to light, watching like a bystander as the colors came to life on the canvas. The clock chimed again, only once this time, for the half hour. She heard it as a spiral sound that wound up the stairs—a soft peal that curled around her, and continued on its way without disturbing her hiatus.

Andy stretched in his office chair, trying to work out a small cramp that had gripped the calf of his leg. He looked at his watch. It was after six. Judy had gone upstairs some time ago to take a nap, saying the sea air made her lazy. He'd been working all afternoon. The new pages of the book that he'd completed so far that day were spitting out of his computer printer on the fast draft mode. He had the feeling the work he'd completed this morning was even better than what he'd done yesterday, or the day before. Still, that little worm of fear gnawed at him. He couldn't shake the sensation that something was not quite right—that being able to write in such a prolific manner wasn't normal—that the remarkable change in his style was somehow not the gift it appeared to be.

He looked at his watch again, realizing that he hadn't been up to see Lizzy in some time. But, the last time he'd looked in on her, she'd been cool and sleeping quietly. He thought it best not to disturb her. He looked out his office window. Earlier in the day, the sky had been the same soft blue as over-washed jeans. Now it was deep blue, but sparkling clear. He wondered if Lizzy would be up to taking a short walk on the beach. The fresh air would be good for her. Maybe even work up an appetite.

The printer stopped, and he reached over and tore off the pages of his manuscript. He ruffled through them, satisfied that they were as good as he could make them. But he'd take another look later. If they were as good as he thought, the book could make him and Lizzy a great deal of money. He tried to imagine a life-style where they wouldn't have to fret about money, but found it impossible. They had pinched and skimped for so long, it felt natural.

Suddenly, he remembered Lizzy's paintings. The new ones. If what Tyree said was true, maybe they would sell. With all the potential money, they could keep the house, have it redecorated, and get a heater for his fucking-cold office. He grinned and got up, making his way through the kitchen into the living room. He stood in front of the sliding glass door. The beach was deserted, except for a few joggers. Yes, even a short walk would be good for them both.

He took the stairs two at a time, stretching out

the tendons in his legs that seemed to have shrunk from so much sitting. At the top, the familiar odor of oil paint and linseed oil hit him. It made the house feel more like home. He felt a sudden pleasure at the thought of Lizzy's painting again.

"Lizzy?" he called as he strode down the hall toward their bedroom. "Come on, Sleeping Beauty. How about a short walk, and then something to eat?" When he opened the bedroom door, he found the room empty, the bed unmade. "Lizzy?" he called, but she didn't answer. Out in the hall, he noticed the door to her studio was closed. "Of course!" he said. "She's at it again. Must be feeling better."

He opened the studio door and took a step inside, then stopped and stared. Elizabeth stood in front an easel, a paintbrush in one hand and a large palette knife in the other. She turned and looked at him, her eyes blinking as if she didn't recognize him. Her hair was tousled the way it usually was when she'd been sleeping, but her cheeks were slicked an odd color of rose, and her skin looked drawn. Her hands, face and nightgown were splattered with a rainbow of oil paints. She resembled a wild gypsy festooned with jewels of glistening color.

"For God's sake, Lizzy! What the hell . . . ?" He moved toward her.

"I had to find out," she said, her eyes finally focusing on him with recognition. "Andy . . . I had to find out if I could really paint the way I've always wanted to. And I could! I had it . . . everything working perfectly. But then . . . I . . . I couldn't . . . it just . . . stopped. It . . . didn't work anymore."

She let out a sob. "I can't do it. Look." She waved toward the canvas set on the easel.

Andy was struck by the oddity of what he saw. A detailed sketch of a surfer riding a huge wave, some of it covered by rich, but muted colors, parts of it finished to perfection, and other areas dabbled at like a child's finger painting. An incongruous mess, with a rather insane air about it, yet it had started out brilliantly. It stood on the easel in the middle of the room like an aborted fetus.

"Lizzy, it's okay. You're just not over the flu yet." He tried to calm her.

"No, it's not that. It flooded over me, the images, the ideas, the colors. And I was doing it. *I was doing it.*" She let out a little cry. "Then it all drained away. Like someone pulled the plug. And I couldn't do it anymore." She started to cry, rubbing at her eyes with fingers smeared with oil paint.

"Honey, please. It's okay. Tomorrow. You can do it tomorrow. You'll feel better then."

Tears streamed down her cheeks through the maze of colors. She whimpered slightly, and looked down at herself. "I was messy, wasn't I?" With that, she gave a deep sigh, as if letting go of the painting process. Slowly, she slipped out of her nightgown. "I'd better shower." Her tears slowed, and she swiped at them again with the back of her hand. "Come on," she said. "Take a shower with me. You can help scrub off the paint."

Andy looked at her standing there nude, and his desire for her suddenly flamed. Jesus, she looked wonderful! She'd lost some weight, he thought. Her legs looked longer, slimmer, but her breasts appeared fuller than he remembered. It had been such a long time since either of them had initiated making love. She reached out and tugged off his shirt, then helped him to remove his shoes and jeans. Just the touch of her hands increased his desire. He felt himself grow hard.

In the bathroom, they locked the door in case Judy should happen by. Elizabeth turned on the old-style shower above the bathtub, adjusted the water temperature, and then pulled the shower curtain around the ring to keep the water from splashing on the floor.

"Honey, are you sure you're up to this," Andy asked, having a moment of doubt because she'd seemed so ill earlier in the day.

"Yes." She climbed into the tub. "I'm positive. I need something to take my mind off that fiasco in my studio." She gave him a smile, obviously rid of her frustration of a few minutes ago.

The water was almost too hot, but Andy hardly noticed. He took the bar of soap, and began to suds Elizabeth from head to toe. Her skin felt as soft and silky as the petals of a rose. When he'd covered every inch of her with soap he took the washcloth and scrubbed her, watching the various colors of oil paint as it ran down the drain. By the time he was done, he was so hard and wanted her so much he could hardly stand it. He reached for her, snugging her close, but she pulled away.

"No," she said, taking the soap from him. "It's your turn now." With that, she began to suds him, teasing him with her fingertips as she did. He responded with a moan. When he could stand it no

longer, he tugged the soap from her hands and
tossed it out of the tub. He kissed her mouth, finding it tasted like salty tears. His hands found her
breasts, felt the nipples harden, pressed his mouth
to one of them and sucked, tasting the bite of Ivory
soap in his mouth, which heightened his desire even
more. Then he lifted her up so she was straddling his
waist, and slowly slid her down, impaling her on his
penis. She let out a soft cry as he entered her. The
steaming water poured over them unnoticed. He
moved rhythmically, feeling his orgasm rushing
upon him much too fast. But already Elizabeth was
undulating wildly, an animal growl coming from
the back of her throat that grew into a savage cry.
He gave into it, felt himself burst inside her, loving
her more than he had ever loved her before, feeling
more pleasure than he ever thought possible.

Elizabeth sat in the kitchen on the bar stool, sipping
a cup of coffee, and watching Andy stir up a Span-
ish omelette for supper. Omelettes were one of the
few things Andy could manage. He seldom tried his
hand in the kitchen. She knew the reason he was
doing it now was because they had just made love.
He always managed to find some totally unrelated
way to let her know how much he enjoyed it.

Thank God his writer's block had lifted. This was
much more like the Andy she knew and loved. She
thought about her own skills, the ones she'd gained,
and then lost so dramatically. *They'll come back,*
she told herself. Just like Andy had reassured her.
They *would* come back. They *had* to. She couldn't

bear to go on as just one of the dime-a-dozen paint-
ers. She'd worked too long and hard to let that
happen. She pushed the thoughts of her work out of
her mind. It didn't do any good to dwell on it.

"Should I get Judy?" she asked.

"In a few minutes. Let me get everything ready
first."

"So, how's the writing going?" she asked, not
really wanting to discuss his work, but knowing
how much it meant to him.

To her surprise, Andy's face paled. He stood over
the bowl of eggs, blinking, staring into space, his
mouth set into a tight line. She was sorry she'd
spoken. Maybe he'd lost it, too. The same way she
had. The idea both cheered and depressed her. She
felt jealous of his sudden creative urges, but she
much preferred the man who was happy with them.
A mixed blessing.

"My writing," he began, then paused, stabbing at
the eggs with the wire whisk. "My writing is . . . ah.
. . ." He put down the whisk and looked at her. The
brown of his eyes had turned almost black. "It's
going along so well and so fast that I'm convinced
something is wrong."

She gave him a puzzled look. "That's an odd
thing to say."

He laid the whisk down on the breakfast bar.
"It's true. Can't you see? Something is happening.
Something that's not right."

"What on earth are you talking about?"

"I'm talking about the way you painted those
three pictures. I'm talking about the fact that they
are by far the best work you've ever done. And, I'm

talking about the fact that I've written almost a third of my new book in the short time we've been living here. And it's good. All of it. Goddamn good!"

Elizabeth straightened up, her eyes wide with surprise. "You've done that much already? Why didn't you tell me?"

Andy frowned, picked up the wisk and began beating the eggs. "Because, at first, I was afraid it was just some crazy aberration caused by the flu. I felt rotten all week."

"You didn't say anything."

"I know. I should have. Maybe you could have avoided getting it if I had. But I was so damn driven to keep working. It didn't matter that I felt bad. The words just kept flowing and flowing until it became frightening."

"What's scary about having your work come easily? God knows you've been blocked long enough. Me, too. I think that's why those three pictures came flooding out when I was sick. And it started again this morning. But I must have drained my creative bank account for now. But it will come back. You said so yourself."

"Andy stared at her, his eyes filled with a curious mixture of alarm and wonder. "But that's just it. Don't you understand? People don't suddenly become so prolific. And they don't develop an extraordinary talent overnight."

Elizabeth reached out and touched his hand. "Well, of course they do, when they haven't yet reached their full potential. We're just hitting our stride, is all. You're a little ahead of me but I'll catch up."

"Lizzy, it's . . . not right!" Andy said, the pitch of his voice rising.

Elizabeth pulled back her hand, feeling as if Andy had stung her. "Well, I don't know about you, but I don't think it's so unusual for me to have found my style. I've been looking long enough. I've worked hard and had enough training for ten people." She knew she sounded angry, but she couldn't help it. What the hell was wrong with him? Did he resent the fact that she might succeed with her painting to the same degree as he could with his writing? "I've found something special. By tomorrow, I'll be back on track and painting up a storm."

"No, I don't think you should do that," Andy said seriously. "I think you should stop for now. Until we know what's happening."

"What! Now that I'm finally on the right track, you don't want me to break through?" She felt the color in her face rise, her skin burning. The son of a bitch, she thought. *He is jealous!*

"Of course I do, but I think we should investigate what's been happening, and find out why."

Elizabeth grabbed her cup, and went over to the coffeepot. First he gets moody when he's blocked. Now he gets moody when it's going along so well. Talk about your insecurities. What the hell does it take to please him anyway? She poured a cupful of fresh coffee, carelessly slopping some of it on the ceramic sink top. She tried to wipe it with her fingertips, but only managed to burn herself. "Shit!" she hissed. "Double shit!"

She sat down at the breakfast bar again and tried to compose herself. "Okay, so you think something's wrong. So explain to me what's happening."

Andy looked away and sighed. "I can't." He looked down at the bowl of beaten yellow eggs, his face so tight and white Elizabeth felt a touch of alarm.

She shook her head. He looked so vulnerable, like a gangly Puck—Shakespeare's hobgoblin—as he perched awkwardly on the edge of the bar stool. His fan of brown hair had gotten so long and unruly, it almost hid his eyebrows. He was dressed in a faded L.L. Bean plaid shirt and pale-blue jeans.

"Come on, Andy. What's that old cliche you like so much? Don't look a gift horse in the mouth? After all, it was you that said the sea air was therapeutic, remember? Well, you were right." She put down her coffee cup, and touched his forehead with the palm of her hand. "Maybe you're having a relapse of the flu. That can make you edgy."

"Yeah. I suppose." His voice was flat, his face strained and colorless.

Elizabeth looked at him for several minutes, wondering what the hell had gone wrong. They'd made love and it had been so sensual, after such a long abstinence. And now, both of them were making great strides with their work. Granted, he was moving faster, but, nonetheless, the future looked a lot brighter than it had a few weeks ago. Why the heck was he trying to spoil it for them? Was he afraid of success?

"Lizzy, you have to admit that you did your paintings while you were feeling pretty sick. And when, you tried again this morning, the fact that you couldn't keep it going almost crazed you. I think it would be wise not to try for a while. Wait and see if things get back to normal."

Elizabeth stared at him, hard. He refused to flinch under her gaze. He was deadly serious. "You don't want me to do any more painting, but I suppose it's okay for you to go ahead with your book."

Andy thought for a moment before speaking. "I think I have to. And then send it to Marc in New York, to see if it's as good as I think, or not. If it's good then . . . well, then we need to take a hard look at why the sudden change. If we don't find anything, then I'd say it's okay to go ahead with your work."

Elizabeth shoved her coffee cup away, almost upsetting it, feeling a great surge of anger welling up in her. "I'll be goddamned if I'll let you take over the spotlight and try to sabotage my work. You're just being mean and jealous."

"Who's being mean?" Judy asked, as she walked into the kitchen.

"Andy, the bastard!" Elizabeth jumped up from the stool so fast, it clamored against the side of the breakfast bar. "And he can damn well sleep down here in his office from now on." She stormed out of the room and up the stairs.

The last thing she heard as she left the kitchen was Judy who said, "Whoops! Bad timing on my part, huh?"

Upstairs, in the bedroom, she took off her clothes

and, since her only nightgown was covered with oil paint, she slipped into bed nude. A sudden heaviness had descended upon her, and she felt totally drained. With the fatigue came tears. She'd somehow lost her newfound talent, and now she had probably lost Andy, too. She turned on her side, and beat her fist against the pillow, sobbing softly. She didn't want to sleep alone. She wanted Andy there next to her. But, he'd been so damned paranoid, she just couldn't forgive him. At least not yet.

The streets on the Balboa Peninsula had turned quiet. A few teenage couples wandered about, a middle-aged woman walked a short-legged fuzzy dog, and an elderly couple who were so withered they looked as if they were being consumed by their clothing, strolled arm in arm down the sidewalk. HE was glad the agony wasn't with him, since the prospects at that moment looked depressingly slim. The stars were out, and a bright moon hung like a huge silver bowl over Saddleback Mountain.

After a night of roving through the back streets of San Diego, he had finally gorged himself on a new victim—a tired, elderly bag lady who smelled like rotten oranges. He'd found her asleep behind a Ralph's Market. Then, he had driven back to Newport Beach and quarantined himself in the bedroom of his apartment. Sleep evaded him, so he'd listened to music all day on the compact disc player he'd taken from the man on the boat. To the strains of Vivaldi, Salieri, Mozart and Tchaikovsky, he'd made his plans for moving.

Tomorrow night, he had reservations to fly to France. He spoke the language fluently. He would use the passport he had in another name—a passport kept current for just such a time as this. He would walk out of the apartment with just his brief-case. He had deposits in a Swiss bank. His mother had seen to that. They would wire him funds when he arrived in France. It would take care of him until he could think what do. He would have to let go of the money his mother had settled on him here. Nothing he could do about that if he were to remain free. He would need at least one more feeding before leaving, to insure the agony would not torture him during the trip. It was a long flight to Europe.

Now, at one a.m. on Monday morning, he felt a restlessness, his mind yeasty with thoughts of his new life, his ears still ringing with the strains of Vivaldi's *The Four Seasons.* He strolled the streets, not in search of death, but to celebrate life, to drink in one last look at the beauty of the harbor. When he reached the gaudily-lit Fun Zone at the edge of the bay, he found the merry-go-round just closing, the arcades billeted with their iron gates drawn shut and padlocked. A sweet, fleshy smell of an earlier crowd still lingered in the air, faint, but perceptible. None of the food shops were open, except for one that sold frozen bananas and Balboa ice cream bars.

The young girl behind the counter was cleaning up, but he persuaded her to sell him a chocolate-dipped frozen banana crested with peanuts. She took his money, and returned an impish, though tired smile, licking her full, pink mouth with the tip

of her tongue. She was interested in him. It was
obvious. He smiled back, and noticed how intensely
blue her eyes were, the color of clear cobalt glass.
She smelled of Jasmine bubble bath, Juicy Fruit
gum, and starched cotton. If she hadn't been so
young, he might have asked her to a late movie, or
perhaps to join him bodysurfing in the ocean. The
waves were high—perfect for riding. And he knew
without a doubt that under her flamingo-pink uniform, her body was lean and tan, with tiny firm
breasts tipped with nipples the color of baby roses.
His sexual desires had been sublimated for so long
now, he almost let them free. But, she couldn't have
been more than sixteen, and it wouldn't be wise to
make himself too noticeable now that his plans to
leave the area were settled. And besides, there was
the young artist woman. It was impossible to keep
her out of his thoughts.

The heat could rise in him fairly soon—the old
woman he'd fed on had not been all that satisfy-
ing—and he was afraid the agony would quickly
refill his body. He had decided that the artist
woman would be his last here. The one that would
sustain him until he reached safe ground. And with
her he would satisfy both the agony and his newly
awakened sexual longing. Tonight, he would once
again get close to her while she slept. But, he would
not take her until just before he left the area. At the
moment, he only wanted to see her for a few moments, to fill himself with her scent. Maybe touch
her pale skin. The thought of that sent a surge of
pleasure through him. He took a large bite of the

frozen banana, savoring the rich chocolate covering and the feel of its icy coldness in his mouth.

All the lights were out in the young couple's beach house, when he opened the rear gate and let himself into the backyard. The back door was locked, and the safety chain was in place. He decided not to fool with it, since it would make too much noise. Scanning the house, he noticed the small window that led into the upstairs bathroom was partway open. He finished the remains of the frozen banana, and tossed away the stick. Then, soundlessly and with little effort, he shinnied up the heavy drainpipe, eased his way hand over hand along the edge of the roof, pushed the window full wide with his feet, and swung himself inside. He knew he was only there to satisfy his curiosity. It was not yet time to satisfy his final needs. But it would not be long, for even now he felt the first tiny flicker of flame in his blood.

He made his way down the hall toward the large bedroom where the couple slept. At the doorway, he stopped. He could not smell the thin, papery scent of the young man, but he recognized the sweet odor of oil paint lingering in the air along with the clean smell of Ivory soap of the woman. He made his way toward the top of the stairs, and then caught the man's scent emanating from somewhere on the first floor. The man was not in his bed, but perhaps working, writing, even at this late hour. How wonderfully convenient. He stifled a laugh, and turned in the hallway to notice something else. Something slightly different. A new scent. Could it be another presence in the house?

Yes, that had to be it. An intriguing scent like the musky smell of burning incense mingled with flower fragrances. He felt the flame in him increase. Not yet. Not yet, he told himself. Too soon. Must wait. He stood in the middle of the hall inhaling both the scent of the artist woman, and that of the new person. His need burgeoned, his craving grew. Two of them, he thought. He could have two of them. Now. Tonight. And find another to sustain himself for the trip. Suddenly, he realized his greed. How had he become like this? How had it all gotten so out of hand? He waited for the usual sense of guilt and remorse to fill him—to stop him—to send him away from here before he took another life. Maybe two. But it would not come. His appetite, so ravenous, precluded any other sensations. He could not stop. He would never be able to stop. His hunger grew malignant.

He stood in the hallway, filtering out the different scents. He wanted both. But which one first? The artist woman, certainly. He'd hungered for her day and night since she had moved here. He walked to her bedroom door and opened it, then crept across the room on the quiet feet of a night animal and looked down at the woman. She lay on her back, arms flung up above her head against the pillow, the coverlet pushed to one side, the sheets rumpled and twisted below her ankles. The soft curves of her face familiar again. Certainly he'd seen her face before. But where? His eyes ran down the length of her body. She wore no night clothes! He held his breath for a moment, then let it out in an almost inaudible hiss.

Outside, the moon was high, casting a stream of silver light through the window. The room glowed metallic. As he watched, the woman moved slightly, her pale skin trembling like a ripple of white velvet. Her lashes, strands of yellow silk, lay softly against her cheeks—her hair a spray of pale gold across the pillow. As he watched, she turned delicately in her bed, slid her long-fingered hands across the sheet, and let out a whisper of breath. Her movements brought his attention to her full breasts. The tips tilted upward, the nipples gilded pinkish-silver by moonlight from the window.

On the bedside chair he spotted a pair of velour warm-ups. He picked up the top, and buried his face in its softness. The scent of her body permeated the fabric—a warm, earthy tone mingled with the clean scent of Ivory soap, and a touch of oil paint. He reached for the bottoms, took in their fragrance with a long, deep breath, and felt his erection begin to grow. He took a small vial out of his pocket and set it on the night table, then removed his shirt, slipped it off, and let it slide to the floor with a soft whisper. Then he took off his trousers and the bathing suit he'd worn underneath in the event he'd decided to go night surfing.

Looking at the woman, he decided they made a good match, for her skin was pale, almost as pale as his, and it was quite obvious her body had not been exposed to much sun—its milky tone reflecting the moonlight—a paragon to his.

He found a lacy bra on the back of the chair, and ran the silky material lightly over his face, inhaling the rich moist odor of her body that clung to the garment. With his other hand, he gently teased himself, brushing his fingers lightly over his erection.

Carefully, he approached the bed, not wanting to wake her too soon. It wouldn't do to have her bolt upright in bed and let out a sound that would bring the others. But he wanted to have more time to drink in the sight and feel of her before it was necessary to subdue her. Keeping his fingertips a fraction of an inch above her flesh, he skimmed them across her body—across her lovely breasts, down over her firm abdomen, over her soft mound of golden pubic hair, around each side of her slender thighs. It felt to him as if her skin gave off tiny sparks that made his hands tingle. The heat of her radiated through the night chill.

He eased himself down on the edge of the bed, and felt her stir, turning, drawing one leg up. He wanted to slip his fingers between her legs and feel the heat and dampness of her. But instead, he moved his hands to her breasts and cupped them gently, the warmth from her body spreading through his fingers. Her eyelids fluttered. With that, the desire in him burgeoned until his entire body ached.

"So lovely," he whispered. "So beautiful. It will be only a dream for you. A waking dream." With that, he leaned down and pressed his mouth against hers, catching the corner of her lip with the sharp edge of his eyetooth. He bit down, breaking the skin. She let out a tiny whine of pain, her eyes opening wide. He pulled back and smiled at her. Even in the ashen light of the room he could see the soft gray of her eyes as she blinked up at him, not yet aware of what was real and what was not. Reaching for the vial he'd put on the bedside table, he uncapped it and poured a small amount of the liquid it contained, onto his finger. With a gentle movement, he rubbed the liquid into the tiny cut on her lip. It only took a second before her entire body quivered, her back arched, and she let out a soft moan.

Then, he leaned down and took one pink nipple into his mouth and sucked gently, the skin satin-smooth against his lips. He still had hours before sunrise. He would not be finished with her until then.

Elizabeth had fallen asleep listening to the relentless tumbling of the surf. The argument she'd had with Andy kept haunting her. He'd taken her at her word and chosen to sleep on the sofa in his office, the first time in their married life they had not slept together.

After her disappointment with the painting, she had needed him, wanted him. And, he'd responded. Their lovemaking in the shower had been exciting. She thought their relationship was finally back on course. And then Andy's words had stung her so. He didn't want her to succeed. Or, if he did, it appeared he didn't want her to be too successful. Perhaps it had been Tyree's raving about her paintings that made him feel insecure. What had happened to them, anyway? Why was it going wrong? They had been so much in love, and now it all seemed to be falling apart. She didn't want to end up like Judy, divorced, living alone, depressed. No!

She pushed the thought out of her mind. It wasn't the same. With Judy it had been cocaine that had ruined the marriage. She and Andy had a lot more going for them. At least, she hoped they did.

"Andy, you lovable bastard," she had muttered to herself just a few minutes before finally falling asleep.

At first, it was a deep, uncomfortable sleep, like being swept underwater. But then, Andy came to her rescue, tugging her up from the depth, lifting her head, and leaning down to kiss her. Sweet dreams. She responded warmly. But his dream kiss sent a tiny, sharp pain across her lips. She tired to open her eyes. Tried to push away the dream.

Now, her eyes were open. Wide open. She was certain of that. But sleep still dogged her, the abyss still sucked at her, her vision blurred, unfocused. Through the haze, she finally saw it wasn't Andy at all, but a young Robert Redford, the one she'd seen surfing that night, his body dappled by moonlight, leaning over her, and she felt a sudden but momentary pinch of alarm. But then, she understood the absurdity of it all and let out a giggle. Of course! It was her surfer boy, the one she had tried to paint that afternoon. She had managed to incorporate him into her dream. His fingertips rubbed gently over the spot on her lip that hurt. The pain stopped. She arched her back and moaned. A remarkable sensation wound its way throughout her body. Floating. She was floating on golden sunshine. How lovely!

"I saw you on the beach, didn't I?" she asked, and heard her voice echo oddly around the room.

The voice had the hard edge of reality to it, and yet.
. . . Was she dreaming or waking? Or in that twilight
time between both? Had she taken a nightcap? A
brandy, perhaps. She didn't remember doing so,
and yet, too much brandy had a way of invading her
sleep with odd delusions such as this.

She closed her eyes and sighed. Soft, cool hands
touched her bare breasts. A warm mouth caressed
one of her nipples, and sent a charge of excitement
through her body. Christ! She hadn't had a sexual
dream in such a long time. The hands stroked the
length of her thighs. Suddenly, she felt both fragile
and wild, like a newborn deer. Her lovemaking with
Andy earlier must have awakened the sleeping sen-
suality she'd stifled for so long.

"Nice," she murmured, "Lovely!" And once
again she was startled by the reality of her voice.
This *wasn't* a dream. But, it *had* to be! She struggled
to open her eyes again, to break through to the
waking world. Or, perhaps she could shout herself
awake. But her eyelids, her throat, her limbs, all felt
so languid. Her muscles had turned into useless
floating tendrils. Finally, with tremendous effort,
she managed to open her eyes partway again. Or,
was it only in her dream that her eyes opened? She
couldn't be certain.

Poised above her, the surfer boy smiled. He still
looked like Robert Redford. She was having an
erotic dream about Robert Redford. But no, not
him, not really. Someone who resembled him.
Someone with dark golden hair and skin, and eyes
the color of deep ice. He leaned down again and
kissed her neck, ran the tip of his tongue along the

edge of her ear, and then grazed her mouth with his. She expected to feel more alarm, but instead, her body responded with a terrible longing. As if sensing this, he pressed his mouth against hers. She let him explore the inside of her mouth with the warmth of his tongue, then returned the exploration to discover the wet satin curves of his.

She gave up the fight to keep her eyes open, surrendering to the dream's persistence. From whatever corner of her mind she had conjured him, she welcomed, even craved, his touch. He was beside her now, turning her toward him, fitting his body against hers. He felt both hot and cold. Fire and ice. And she wondered how that could be. Dreams didn't contain hot or cold. But the sensation rocked her, sent great pangs of desire through her belly, and surged into flame between her legs.

She felt no harm in being swept along by an erotic dream. Her body was fulfilling its natural function. She would go with it. Enjoy it. This dream man's skin felt good next to her, and smelled so good—like musk and honey. With that, she reached out and touched him, ran her hands over his silken body. His muscles were hard and well-defined, his flesh smooth and hairless—quite unlike Andy who had such a dark furry chest.

"Who are you?" she whispered to the dream lover.

His voice was deep, but breathy, in her ear. "I am the Dark Angel," he said.

"No, really. You're someone I've dreamed up, but who?"

"Shhhh," he said, his fingers tracing circles across her shoulders. She moaned, her body writhing against his. His hands became more demanding as he pressed her against the pillow so that she was lying on her back. She lay there looking up at him, his smile silver in the moonlight. Such a strange dream. She'd had so many dreams lately. Her head felt so peculiar. A strange whirring echoed between her ears.

He began to stroke her body, his hands burning now, and she felt the heat transferred to her own flesh. She let out a little cry as he slipped his hands between her legs and separated them, resisting him for only a moment. His fingers slipped inside her, hot, exploring, probing, invading. She tried to pull away, but he held her firmly with his free hand. He pressed his fingers into the depth of her, and she found herself twisting, arching her back, delirious with the ripples of pleasure that began to spark through her body.

"Oh, God!" she whispered, and heard his husky laugh in the darkness as he gently removed his fingers and effortlessly, soundlessly, moved his body over onto hers. She could feel the steel hardness of his muscles, the spark of fire on his skin. The whirring in her ears increased, the room revolving slowly, as if she had taken too many Valium. Part of her wished to awaken from the dream, but part of her did not. One moment she was convinced it was all a dream, the next she felt certain it was reality. She turned that over in her mind, trying to make sense of it. Had Andy come to bed after all, wanting to make love again? Wanting to make up for their argument? If so, why did he look so strange?

When he pressed his hardness between her legs she felt a dull pain which made her cry out softly. To silence her, he covered her mouth and slowly, but relentlessly, continued to enter her. The pain turned to burning, his flesh so hot between her legs it felt like flame. She tired to move, to twist away, to cry out for him to stop, but his mouth stayed on hers, and his hands held her firmly in place while he pressed into her.

She felt a sudden helpless terror. The size of him! The heat! The strength of his hands! He lifted his mouth from hers, and she looked into his eyes. Brilliant eyes now, with sparks of red, fierce, filled with haunted shadows. And then, with one final thrust he was completely inside her, and this time she let out a breathy gasp, feeling as if his hugeness had bruised her.

Her terror mounted as he began to move, his flesh searing her insides. She gasped again as he withdrew from her and then penetrated her once more. He continued to move, his motions taking on a rhythm which suddenly began to awaken a sense of pleasure in her, and to her surprise, the terror subsided. At first, the pleasure was only a ripple, then ripple upon ripple running like soft flames throughout her body, echoing, ringing, growing like the brilliance of a light, until she was molten inside. She moved with him, her body demanding, urgent, swinging like a bell, clinging to him, wanting him, needing him deeper, deeper, deeper still.

Like a liquid drop of fire, she felt the swell of her orgasm take hold and grow, budding, building, almost reaching culmination, when suddenly he stopped his movements, held her still with hands of steel while she writhed and moaned, her lips begging him for the release he had almost given her.

"Not yet, sweet thing," he said. "Not quite yet." He lifted one of her arms and kissed the inside of her wrist, his mouth as hot as glowing coals. Then, the heat turned to something close to pain, but not quite, as he quickly punctured her skin with the sharp points of his teeth. When she looked, she was horrified to find he had torn away a tiny piece of flesh from the vein in her wrist. Even in the metallic moonlight, she could see a thick trail of blood flowing down the pale softness of her skin. But before she had time to understand what had happened, he pressed his mouth to the wound and drank from it, the sensation so perverse, so lurid, she felt her climax building once more. He moved inside her again, slowly, allowing her to enjoy the whirlpool sensations that swirled throughout her body.

But before she found release, he stopped once more and took his mouth from her wrist. The flow had ebbed and he laid her arm down against the pillow where it slowly made a small red stain. Then lifting his own arm, he made the same small wound on his own wrist that he had made on hers, and pressed it against her mouth.

"Drink," he whispered softly. As the first few drops of his blood entered her mouth, she opened her eyes in surprise. The liquid tasted bittersweet. Like a frightened animal, she flailed, tried to pull away, but he deftly kept her mouth in place as he began again to move inside her. "Drink," he repeated, stroking into her so that she was filled with overlapping flames of pleasure. With a tiny, inarticulate cry, she opened her mouth and began to suck at the wound. The thick, bittersweet fluid flowed down her throat, biting hot. She swallowed and felt the heat seep into her belly, but was more conscious of the exquisite sensations between her legs, than those caused by the blooding.

She felt him quiver for an instant, and then his semen exploded inside her, burning like acid, filling her from below the way his blood was filling her from above. He moved his wrist from her mouth and placed his lips against hers, sealing the scream that had risen in her throat as the tide of pleasure consumed her.

Chapter Five

Ted Bearbower arrived at the department at seven-thirty Monday morning, a bag of chocolate-chip croissants in one hand, a thermos of French vanilla coffee in the other. He had a good feeling about the day. Hopefully something would break in the case.

He spread out a paper towel on his desk for the croissants, and then went to the coffee room for his mug. He loved coffee, but the stuff they made at the department could have lubricated a diesel, so he brewed his own at home, and brought it in every morning.

After bringing his mug back to the desk, he sat down, poured a steaming cupful, and read through his stack of messages that had been left on the desk. The first one was from Locke. He would be in a little late. Had to get a haircut. Five of the messages were from out-of-state agencies reporting back on Locke's inquiries. He thumbed through them. He'd let Locke deal with those.

The next message was from one of the people he'd interviewed out on the peninsula—a Mrs. Tyree

Rattigan. All it said was, "Call me." An unusual name, Tyree, one you didn't forget. If he remembered correctly, she was the exotic-looking woman with long red hair and a diamond set in her front tooth. He looked at the message. She had called at seven a.m. He set the message by the telephone, then took a croissant out of the bag. It was fresh and flaky, with little jewels of chocolate throughout. He finished the croissant, then picked up the message from the woman on the peninsula and dialed. It rang for quite a while before someone picked it up.

"Hello," a female voice answered.

"This is Detective Bearbower, returning a call from Tyree Rattigan." Ted drained the rest of the coffee from his cup, and set it on the desk.

"Yes . . . of course . . . I'm Mrs. Rattigan."

"You called me?"

"Yes, about the . . . the body you recently found on the beach."

Ted screwed the lid off the thermos with one hand, and poured more coffee into his cup. "Did you think of something that might help us, Mrs. Rattigan?"

"Yes." The woman didn't continue.

Great, Ted thought, I'm going to have to pull it out of her. That's the way it was so many times. People called wanting to help, but then they balked, had second thoughts about getting involved. "When we first talked," he went on. "you said you didn't know anything that might help us. Has that changed?"

"Yes." Again, silence.

"You suspect someone?" Ted asked, then took a sip of his coffee. He forgot how hot it was, and burned his tongue. He covered the phone with his hand. "Shit!" he hissed, sucking cool air into his mouth.

"I don't suspect, I *know* who it is."

Ted put down his cup to let the coffee cool. "Then suppose you tell me."

"I'll give you his name and address," she said. "He lives here on the peninsula. But I have to warn you, he's clever and cunning."

Ted frowned. "Mrs. Rattigan, what makes you suspect this guy's the one?"

"I've known him for a long time. He's had . . . problems. Serious problems."

"I wish we could just take your word for it. However, we need concrete evidence."

"Yes, of course. Maybe his doctor can help. He'd have all his records."

"Can you tell me what kind of problems you're talking about?" Ted picked up his coffee cup.

"He has a . . . disease. It makes him do terrible things."

Ted took a sip of coffee. It tasted bitter. "Is it mental?"

"You really should talk with his doctor." Tyree paused for a moment. "The police have been pretty vague about the various killings, haven't they? No detailed facts have been made public?" She didn't wait for him to answer. "I can tell you what those facts are," Tyree said. "First of all, there's a lot of blood missing. And second, the killer has taken a bite, or a number of bites of flesh out of the victim."

Ted blanched. How the blazes had she found *that* out? He had purposely kept that particular item away from the media. Anything that smacked of cannibalism dredged up the basest of human curiosity.

"Also," Tyree continued, "in the small amount of blood that's left, you've found large amounts of a strong drug—a form of beta endorphin. And the killer takes a memento with him. Something personal from the victim."

Sucking in his breath, Ted cursed to himself. All he needed was a leak in the department. He'd have someone's head when he found out who had been blabbing. The only place where Tyree had missed was concerning the mementos. Wait! That wasn't quite true. The man on the boat—his wife had reported a CD player missing.

"I knew his mother. We all did. A group of us here on the peninsula. We know she tried to get help for him. But apparently the disease is out of control again."

"Maybe if I could speak to his mother? Or some other family member."

"She died recently."

"If you've been aware this man is dangerous, why haven't you been to the police before now?" Ted asked.

"We thought he was better. That they'd found something to help him," Tyree said. "Listen, you'll find all the evidence you need in this man's apartment."

"What kind of evidence?"

"The mementos I mentioned. Personal items from each of the victims."

"Okay. Maybe I can bring this guy in for questioning."

"If you do, be careful. This disease makes him extremely strong."

"Is he on something like PCP?"

"No."

"Well, I appreciate your calling. I'll need his name."

"Whatever you do, don't let him *touch* you. Don't let him draw blood or anything."

"Is his disease contagious?" Ted felt a moment of alarm.

"His name is Barry Brownstone," Tyree said, ignoring his question. She gave him the address and the name of his doctor then abruptly hung up.

Ted sat there for a moment, a prickly feeling bothering the back of his neck. He wanted to ignore what she'd told him. Wanted to write it off as just another weirdo looking for fifteen minutes of fame. But he couldn't. He knew this was the guy. He didn't know *how* he knew, but he did.

Andy, waking from an odd dream about wildly painted clowns, found himself on the sofa in his office. It was the first time in their married life that he and Lizzy hadn't slept together. But he'd been so tired and angry about their argument that he'd said to hell with it. He'd bedded down on the sofa with a crocheted afghan pulled over him.

He sat up and stretched his legs, one of his joints cracking as he did. The window behind the sofa was open and through it he heard the sound of surf breaking on the beach and the cry of gulls scavenging for breakfast. Elizabeth had been right. Their energy and talent had no doubt been waiting for just the right time and place to maximize. And what better place than here, he thought. After all, men had been proclaiming the virtues of living by the ocean for centuries. He owed Lizzy an appology.

He got up and made his way into the kitchen. No sign of Lizzy yet. The house had a breath of shadowed, early morning coolness about it. A measured hush. No creaks, no groans, no settling noises. Only the sound of the sea outside, and the tick of the grandfather clock in the living room. The sudden ringing of the doorbell chime shook him out of his reverie. Through the kitchen door window he saw Tyree standing on the back porch step. Her long red hair was tucked under a wide-brimmed purple hat, and she wore bright purple sunglasses, a white jumpsuit, and a pair of purple gardening gloves. He unlocked the door and opened it, chuckling to himself over how outrageous she looked. She flashed him a smile that made the diamond in her front tooth glow blue-white.

"Hi, honeybunch," she said as she wafted past him into the kitchen. "How are you feeling today? Better? And Elizabeth? Better, too? Any coffee on? The Zippers have been raving about Elizabeth's macadamia coffee." She pulled off her sunglasses, and set them on the breakfast bar.

"No, sorry. I just got up."

"Oh dear, I do apologize. I know it's early. I can come back later. Just wanted to see if you two were up to par today. I'm full steam ahead with that little party for you tonight. That is, if you're both up to it."

"Ah, well, I don't know how Lizzy is. She's still asleep."

"You do think she'll let me take those two paintings down to the gallery today, don't you? I have some clients lined up who want to see them. I'm going to set a high price right from the start."

"I'm sure she'll be eager for you to take them."

"Great. Now, why don't we go up and wake the sleepyhead?" Tyree grinned. "Get her started painting. I can use all the work she can produce."

"Look, Tyree. Lizzy had a bit of a setback yesterday with her painting. But I think it's because of the flu. She was feeling pretty bad."

"Well then, let's go up and see." Tyree waved a purple garden glove, then turned and strode out of the kitchen.

Andy jogged along behind her, surprised he was having difficulty keeping up with her long strides. Then, suddenly, from somewhere upstairs, he heard a piercing scream. The sound wound through the old house, echoing, and growing louder as both he and Tyree raced up the stairs.

HE lay stretched out on his bed, his head propped on large feather pillows that were encased in velvet covers. The drapes in his room had been drawn against the early morning sun. Only a few thin rays of dusty light managed to filter in through the ragged tears in the shabby material. He felt brittle. As if his bones were made of thin crystal. As if he would shatter, melodically, if he were to fall from the bed. For a moment, he almost wished he could replace the brittle sensation with the agony. As terrible as it was, he'd become accustomed to that torment. This feeling was different, one that he had not felt for so long, it was both unrecognizable and disturbing.

To help quell his unease, he had brought a bottle of iced champagne to his bed, poured it into a tall crystal glass, and now lay there sipping slowly, relishing the delicate taste of fermented sunshine. He had put on a compact disc recording of Mozart's "Eine Kleine Nachtmusik." Streams of music filled the room like a vibrant, but soothing, liquid. He'd lit some incense that made the bedroom smell of moss and lilacs—the damp smell of the earth mixed with the honeyed scent of a flowered field. It reminded him of life and death—of birth and demise.

Last night had been a terrible mistake. The memory of the woman's lovely body next to his haunted him. She had been so warm, so filled with life, and he had drawn such pleasure out of her. He had not expected it to be that way. The celibate habits of the past years had brought him a certain comfort, a detachment, that kept him from thinking about what he'd become, and what he did. Now, he longed for what he had missed, what he had been cheated of. He wanted to love, and be loved in return.

He tried to put the thoughts out of his mind. After all, he was leaving in the morning. Starting a new life. He poured the last of the champagne, and quickly drank it. By dark he would be rested, and able to move without detection. He would take one small case. Nothing more. Simple, clean, quick.

He put the glass down, cursing the fact that the liquid had done nothing to soothe him. Restless, he got up and went to his closet shelves, scanning the array of items he had taken from those who had given him their life force. He fingered a length of pearls, pink-tinted and perfectly matched. He remembered the woman who had worn them, an older woman with upswept silver hair and eyes the color and shape of a cat's. He picked up a spoon, carved at the end with twining roses, and held it up. A narrow shaft of sunlight, which had escaped from the torn curtain, reflected off the silver. Its owner had been a young girl saving it for her hope chest. He shook his head. If it were not for the fact that their lives had been traded for his own, the guilt of all he'd done would have overwhelmed him.

For just a second, he caught a glimpse of his reflection in the bowl of the spoon, twisted grotesquely by the concave shape. He shuddered and dropped it. Then he laughed. There was a monster in his closet. And the monster was him! It was wise, he knew, to recognize what you were. Otherwise, the world held far too much danger.

It was after one, and Ted Bearbower was tempted to go out and find a good place to lunch. A nice plate of pasta with pesto perhaps. Garlic bread dripping with butter and cheese. His stomach rumbled just thinking about it. But he didn't want to get too far away from the station, in case the search warrant he'd asked for came through. It was a million-to-one shot that he'd get it. He had nothing in the way of evidence against Barry Brownstone. Nothing except the insistence of Tyree Rattigan plus her knowledge of some of the facts in the case—and his own gut feeling. He was suspicious that a number of other people on the peninsula knew about this man too. From what Tyree said, and also the odd way some of them reacted when he'd interviewed them, he knew something was going on down there. But what the hell was it? Were they involved in some sort of cult? Satanic crap, stuff like that? The idea made him shiver.

He looked at the piece of paper where he'd written the information Tyree Rattigan had given him. It read: BARRY BROWNSTONE, 14 OCEAN-FRONT, GARAGE APARTMENT. Dr. FOX-HOVEN, 125 SUPERIOR BLVD., SUITE C. He'd run Brownstone's name through the computer, but that name had no priors. If he could manage to get a few of his fingerprints, they might pull up another identity.

Where the heck was Locke? he wondered. It shouldn't take a whole day to get a haircut. He needed to get *his* feel on this new development. Was the Rattigan woman just one of those nuts who crawled out of the woodwork during a crime spree?

"Hey, Teddy Bear!" Locke came rumbling into the room. He was wearing a crisp new shirt, a deep maroon tie, and a brand new silk suit. His sandy hair had been styled so he looked like a goddamned actor. Ted could smell Locke's aftershave. Something new. Lemony.

"You must have made up with Sandy."

Locke grinned. "Wrong. Sandy won't even talk to me."

"Oh, so you did all this for *me*. Well I appreciate it."

"Ha!" Locke snorted. "Actually, I did it for another lady. Have you seen that new beauty in dispatch? Jennifer Amber Harvey? She's tiny, but has legs as long as a giraffe's neck. Long hair, down to her ass. Real nice. We're going to have dinner tonight if this damn case doesn't get in the way."

Ted grinned. "We could be working pretty late. I've got something new. Let me tell you what happened while you were out getting brewed, screwed, and tattooed."

The phone on Locke's desk rang just as Ted completed detailing the events of that morning. "Steve Locke," his partner barked into the phone. "What? Yeah, he's here. What? Oh, great, he'll be tickled pink to hear that. Shit! Why didn't you ring *his* number? Oh. Okay. Thanks." Locke hung up, gave Ted a hangdog look, and shrugged. "Sorry, they denied the warrant on this Brownstone fellow. The guy didn't want to talk to you. Said you usually blew up when you didn't get what you wanted."

"Damn.." Ted banged his hand down on the desk, causing several yellow pencils to jump. "We need to get a look inside that apartment. Just bringing him in for questioning won't cut it." Ted stared at a series of small scratches on his desk. "What we can do, is put a stakeout on his apartment. Watch his every move."

"You really do think there's some validity to this information, don't you?"

Ted nodded. "I'm not sure why, but I do." Fatigue had settled in on him far too early in the day. Maybe it was time to take an early retirement. Let someone else hash it out.

"Okay, so what do we do first?"

"First," Ted said. "I see the doctor who's been treating this guy. While I'm doing that, you make arrangements for the stakeout."

Locke looked toward the window. "Got a storm brewing out there, I think. Lots of clouds. Looks pretty serious. Bad night for a stakeout."

"In a case like this," Ted said. "Any night is a bad night."

The doctor's complex resembled a glass bubble. The office, looking out on a courtyard filled with glossy green plants, had rows of convex windows across the front. Ted got the sensation he was entering an aquarium. Inside, the nurse behind the reception window gave him a curious look.

"I'm sorry," she said, "but doctor doesn't see patients on Monday."

Ted glanced at his watch. Damn! It had stopped again. He shook his wrist and checked it again. The second hand started moving. "I'm not a patient," he said as he reached into his jacket and pulled out his badge. "I'm Detective Bearbower. I need to speak with the doctor concerning a case."

The nurse frowned, the bridge of her nose wrinkling like a piece of soft pink silk. "Oh. Well, let me check and see if he's still in his office. He has a tennis game on Monday afternoons." She got up, gave his badge a cursory look then turned away and headed down the hall out of sight. Ted heard her white nurse's uniform whispering against her legs as she walked.

He put his badge away, and checked his watch once more. The second hand had stopped again. Maybe he should wear an old-fashioned pocket watch. That might work better. He joggled his wrist but couldn't get the watch going. A moment later the nurse reappeared, her face beaming, the pink skin around her mouth wrinkling the same way her nose had.

"He's still here. Go on back to the office at the end of the hall." She stepped away from the window and opened the reception room door for him. "I just caught him."

"Thank you," he said. "I appreciate that."

The doctor's office was decorated with an array of old comic books—collectors items—individually framed in black metal. An obviously expensive collection. Foxhoven, a tall, silver-haired man that Ted estimated to be somewhere in his fifties, had a strong face with chiseled grooves down each side of his mouth. Outside of that, time had been good to him.

Foxhoven motioned for him to sit down on one

of the jade-colored office chairs. "What can I do for you, Detective, ah. . . ."

"Bearbower. Newport Police Department. I'm investigating several homicide cases, and one attempted killing."

"Yes. I thought so. Someone called me and let me know you were coming."

"What? Who?" It had to be the Rattigan woman, Ted thought. But why?

"Not important. I understand you're interested in a former patient of mine. Barry Brownstone." The doctor pursed his lips, looked away from Ted, then back again. "As you know, I can't reveal anything specific about any of my patients without their written permission, or a court order."

"The person who gave me his name believes this man has a disease which caused his killing spree." Ted stopped and caught the doctor's eye. He saw more there than just mild interest. Foxhoven's eyes held his intently. "My question is, is that possible?"

After a long pause, through which Ted waited patiently, the doctor finally spoke. "What I can tell you is that this man was, at one time, my patient. But I was of little help to him. After a few years, he sought treatment elsewhere." Foxhoven set the pencil down on the desk, lining it up carefully with the edge of the desk blotter.

"Would the nature of this disease make him homicidal?"

Foxhoven shrugged and gave a grim smile. "Not even doctors know where the mind and body separate, if, in fact, they do."

"But it could be the work of a nut and have nothing to do with a physical disease."

The doctor's face tightened. "Disease is disease, detective. More and more science is discovering that even when it's labeled 'mental' disease, it's still a physical malady. Blood chemistry, hormones, genes, all kinds of physical things come into play." Foxhoven gave a reluctant shrug. "Actually, I believe that killing is a natural act for man. Restraint is what's unnatural. We've made rules. Do not kill. Otherwise we could not live together as a civilized society. But that doesn't mean it comes naturally."

"So, Brownstone is not influenced by the rules of society? Isn't that the description of a sociopath?"

"Yes, but there can be other reasons for that type of behavior. I'm afraid that's all I can tell you."

Ted got up from the chair. "Later, if there's anything more you think of that might help, I'd appreciate your giving us a call." He reached into his pocket and took out a card. "I'll leave this with you."

Foxhoven took the card from him and scrutinized it, still silent. Ted reached out and shook his hand then turned toward the door.

"Detective. . . ." the doctor said softly.

Ted turned back. "Yes?"

"Have you ever heard of something called genomes?"

"Gee nomes? No, I don't think so."

"Very interesting subject."

"Do they have something to do with our Brownstone fellow?"

The doctor shook his head. "Understand, Detective, that I'm not talking about anyone in particular. I'm just discussing a subject. Something scientists have been exploring for some time."

Ted nodded and sat back down. "I'm listening," he said.

Foxhoven leaned back and looked at the wall behind Ted. "I'm no expert in this field, but I know a little about it. You see, gene mappers—that is, people who spend their time mapping and sequencing genes—are attempting to map and sequence all the genes that make up a human being. One of the things they've discovered along the way is that the human genome is probably far larger than first believed. One of the things they think is responsible for this larger size is an accumulation of dormant or redundant genes. In other words, genes which are not being used. One would have to have the entire human organism jump through some pretty fancy physiological hoops before these genes would do their thing."

"Okay," Ted said, wondering where the doctor was going with this information. "I'm with you so far."

"Some people believe that in the past, perhaps as far back as the beginning of man, these genes were necessary—genes that set into motion traits enabling mankind to survive. But later, when man's survival wasn't as severely challenged, these genes fell asleep." The doctor turned his eyes back toward Ted. "But needed or not, they remain a part of man's DNA. Now, if something were to wake them up—make them jump through those hoops—we might see something quite unusual."

"Just exactly what would do that? And what would happen?"

"Chemicals might do it. Drugs. That kind of thing. And what could happen is . . . now this is conjecture, remember, none of this has been proven, as yet . . . but one or more of these dormant genes awakened could bring out various behaviors in a person that primitive man might have had. We don't actually know what early man was like. Our view of him is based on very little evidence. He might have had some pretty nasty habits. Habits that allowed him to survive."

Ted sat there, trying to sort out exactly what it was the doctor had told him. "In other words," he said, "early man could have had say . . . for the heck of it, let's say cannibalistic traits. Maybe a taste for blood. Things like that?"

Foxhoven didn't show any expression. "Possibly. He might have been far more like other animals than he is today. If his usual game turned out scarce, he might have eaten his own kind. Survival was all that counted. He might also have had a heightened sense of smell, something other animals still retain. He might have had better night vision . . ."

Ted leaned forward, intently. "Then it's possible for something to wake up these dormant genes, set them into action?"

"Yes, it's possibile. Genes are remarkable things. Everyday, people are engineering genes in the laboratory. But these are *planned* changes. In a few years we'll have disease-resistant fruits and vegetables, lower fat foods that taste good, plants that will absorb more carbon dioxide to help avoid the greenhouse effect. We'll be able to make mankind resistant to disease. We might even be able to undo nature's mistakes. Mistakes that cause tragic things like Huntington's chorea, multiple sclerosis and retardation."

"Okay, let's say that something does wake up these genes. What else besides drugs could do that?"

"Well, a person could be born with these genes already awake. A billion to one shot, but it could happen. In earlier times we might call this person a throwback. Then there's gene therapy. But as I said, drugs are a good bet."

"So any one of those could cause a person to become . . . a cannibal? But wouldn't this kind of craving, or hunger, occur only if the individual were, say, starving?" he asked.

"Not necessarily. We don't know exactly how these awakened genes would affect modern man. Circumstances are far different today. Man may now be using genes that were dormant in his prehistoric ancestors. Put the modern genes together with the primitive ones, and we have no idea what might happen. We could get some pretty aberrant behavior."

"Okay then, tell me, if drugs were the cause, how or where would someone get such drugs?"

The doctor shrugged. "I'm afraid I'm no help there."

All the synapses in Ted's brain begin to whirr and click. Son-of-a-bitch, he said to himself. This guy is telling me exactly what happened to this Brownstone guy. Good God almighty!

"That," Foxhoven said, "is all I can tell you. I don't know if this will help you or not, but it may give you some idea of what you may be up against."

Ted nodded, felt numb. He got to his feet, shook the doctor's hand again and made his way to the door. "Thank you," he said. "You've been quite helpful." Ted walked down the hall and out the reception door, giving the nurse a wave of his hand as he went.

Outside in the fresh air, he took in several deep breaths. So where did he go from here? How the heck did he get enough evidence for a warrant? Just knowing the cause, didn't cut this guy any slack. Anyone who went around drinking their victim's blood, and making a picnic lunch of flesh, had to be taken out. One way or another.

He suddenly thought about his own appetite. How he craved certain foods. No matter what he did, he couldn't curb his hunger. Whenever he dieted, the torment was so terrible he always gave up. He wondered if Brownstone felt much the same. If so, he had to feel a speck of compassion for the guy if what the doctor had told him, was true. But only a speck. The part he couldn't understand was how this guy could bring suffering on others, just to feed his aberrated appetite. He gave a brittle laugh as he climbed into his car and sat there for a few minutes. What the hell did he do now? he wondered. He looked at his watch. The second hand was running backward. Great! He'd had watches do that before when he was wearing them. But just then, watching the tiny silver hand running counter to its natural orbit, he got the uncomfortable feeling he was about to crawl into some kind of quirky space-time continuum that would change him forever.

It took Locke and Ted four hours of phone calling to find what they wanted. They contacted every laboratory from San Diego to Eureka, that might possibly give them even a thread of information to help get a warrant for Barry Brownstone's arrest. Even then, Ted wasn't certain he'd found the right place, or that it would be of any value. But he had to follow up.

"Wouldn't you know," Locke said. "We call the whole damn state, and the only place where we get even a spark of info, is just down the road in Orange County. Should we both go and meet with this guy?"

"Yep," Ted said, putting on his jacket. "He's waiting for us."

"Hope he's not just shining us on."

"No reason for him to do that." Ted picked up the scratch pad with the name and address of where they were going. "Irvine Industrial Center. Just a short hop. The guy's name is Walter Schafler. Said he thinks he knows something about a drug that was being developed some years ago, a drug that went wrong. That's all he'd say on the phone."

"I'd bet a lot of drugs have gone wrong. This may not have anything to do with our case."

"I gave him the details. He seemed to think they fit."

Locke nodded. "Let's go then."

* * *

BioChem turned out to be a four-story building butted up next to the 405 freeway in Irvine. Sleek dark glass walls made the building look like it was wearing an array of sunglasses. Inside, the building was hushed. Cool, gray marble floors squeaked delicately as they walked up to the reception desk and gave their names. Almost immediately, a woman wearing a red suit, red shoes, and a silver broach shaped like a violin pinned on her lapel, came out to greet them.

"I'm Sherry Schafler," she said, extending her hand to shake first Ted's then Locke's. "Walter's daughter. I'm the PIO here. He asked me to bring you to his office as soon as you arrived." The woman's long sleek black hair swung gracefully as she turned and began walking down the hallway at a good clip. She had to be in her mid-forties, but Ted couldn't help noticing her graceful figure. Full, but not overly so. The two of them followed her, their shoes once again squeaking against the marble floor.

"Come in, come in," the man behind the desk said. "I've had Sherry put together as much stuff as I could find. As I understand it, you wanted some information about a certain drug, right?"

Ted pulled out his notepad and pen. "Yes, but as I told you on the phone, we have no idea what it's called, or who made it."

"But from your description, it had an adverse effect on genetic structure, correct?" The old man leaned back in his padded leather chair and gave an abject sigh. With his worn face and tuft of soft gray hair, Ted thought if he'd been wearing a long black robe, he would have made a dignified judge. "Genetics," Schafler went on without waiting for a reply. "Fascinating subject. Lots of work being done in that field. One prominent pharmaceutical company in Costa Mesa is researching a program to develop drugs designed to selectively inhibit genes that cause disease. They use a system they call oligonucleotide antisense technology. Pretty fancy, huh? But we haven't gotten into that area much. Maybe one of these days. Probably the wave of the future. Right now we're working on drugs that enhance the immune system. AIDS of course, but also drugs that may help with a lot of other diseases as well."

"You said you'd heard of something like I mentioned." Ted tapped his pen against his pad. No matter how anxious he felt, he realized he couldn't hurry this guy.

"A rumor went around the pharmaceutical world some years back. None of the Johnny-come-lately's would know about it. But us old codgers, well it was a real interesting piece of scuttlebutt back then."

"Scuttlebutt?" Locke said.

"Poop," Schafler said. "Word had it that one of the labs in the area was onto something really big. A drug that could, if it worked and got past the FDA, make billions. Naturally, we were all interested. It was supposed to turn on dormant portions of the brain, all those parts we don't use. You know, don't you, that we only use a tiny portion of our brains? Well this drug, the scuttle says they nicknamed it *Sunshine,* had a lot of side effects. Some of them highly beneficial. Some of them pretty appalling."

Ted frowned and wrote down the word *Sunshine* on his pad. "Tell me the good part first."

The old man shifted in his chair. "It killed pain. Completely. Like nothing else we've ever seen, or so the rumor went, and gave you a high to beat all highs. Those elements alone, if they could be isolated from the rest of the compound, would be worth a fortune."

"Tell me something," Ted said, thinking about what Schafler had said. "This pain killer. Could it be something that could raise the endorphine level?"

Shafler pursed his lips, thinking. "I don't see why not. Yes, from the description we got, it could easily have been something like that." He nodded his head, staring into space contemplatively. "From what we heard, it also woke up the brain, so to speak. Enhanced thought processes, all types of cognitive thinking, as well as the more esoteric kind. Back then, we didn't know exactly why. But today, from some other work of this nature, I'd say it was caused by either changing the DNA, or waking up portions of it that had been snoozing."

"So in that respect, it was successful," Locke said.

"It was a total disaster, from the word go."

"Why's that?" Ted asked.

Schafler leaned forward, almost whispering. "It killed all the test subjects."

"People died using it?" Locke said.

"No, of course not. It never got to that stage. I meant mice, to begin with. It got as far as simians. Evidently, it worked so well at first, no one could believe it. But even though the subject's learning and creative ability went sky high, they always went into convulsions and died after the first few doses."

"So they abandoned it?" Locke asked.

"That was the word. But only after a lot more experimenting and testing. Then they finally gave up. But . . ." Shafler leaned forward again, as if sharing a secret. "The owners were bent on eliminating its toxicity. My company worked with their R & D department for a time. We had some things going then that might have made it possible to do just that. But nothing worked."

Ted felt a surge of hope. "So, you *knew* the people who developed this?"

"Oh yes. Too bad, the world could use something like that. Do you know where they found this almost miracle drug?"

Ted and Locke both shook their heads, no, at the same time.

"From a bright, sunny-yellow flower one of their people found at the top of the canopy in a South American rain forest. From the distillate they synthesized it."

Ted poised his pen. "You can tell us their names, then. The owners?"

Schafler frowned. "I couldn't remember them offhand, but I had Sherry dig through our archives." He reached for a manila folder on the corner of his desk. "It's all here. The short dealings we had with them. Yes, it's too bad. We all would have made a ton of money, if it had been successful." He pushed the folder over in front of Ted, who eagerly opened it.

"Warren Pharmaceuticals," he read. "Is this place still operating?"

"No," Schafler said. "Not for years. Shut down when . . . well we heard that the owner's son died. But the scuttle was that when he couldn't get the FDA to approve testing, he tested it on himself. And that he *wasn't* dead. That the drug did some pretty awful things to him. But if he lived, Mary Warren, the company's owner, kept it mighty quiet. Must have messed him up badly."

Ted quickly thumbed through the folder. Then the name jumped out at him. *Barry Warren! Barry!* That could be their man. Changed his last name. "Locke, look at this!" He pushed the folder over in front of him. "It's not proof, but it sure looks as if we're on to something."

"That's it, I'm afraid. Can't tell you much more. The whole thing has been pretty much forgotten. You fellows mind telling me why you're asking about this?"

"Just a case we're working on. Can we get a copy of this file?"

"Sure," Schafler grinned. "No problem. I'll have Sherry take care of it."

He pressed a button on his phone and Sherry's voice echoed out of a speaker.

"Yes, dad?"

"Need some copies of this archive stuff."

"Sure."

Schafler picked up the folder, closed it and

handed it to Ted. "She'll meet you in the lobby. Won't take a minute."

Ted and Locke stood up. "Thanks," Ted said, offering his hand. Shafler shook it with a firm grip.

"Glad to be of help."

Outside, Locke looked at him with an odd expression on his face. "Jesus, Ted, you don't really think that some goddamn yellow flower from the top of some rain forest can be the cause of this maniac running around making meals out of people, do you?"

"God only knows," Ted said. "And maybe not even him."

When Andy and Tyree opened the bedroom door, the room was a shambles. The bedside lamp lay on its side, the small alarm-clock had been smashed, and bits of glass littered the floor beside the bed. Elizabeth lay sprawled nude across the bed, her gray eyes wide open, the sheets tangled like snakes around her ankles.

"Lizzy!" Andy yelled, kneeling on the floor next to the bed. He touched her face, then took her wrist, and felt for a pulse. "What's wrong with her?"

For a moment, Judy stood entranced by the horror of the scene. She found it difficult to take in the whole thing. When she finally looked down at the motionless form of her friend, she saw pools of deep red staining the sheets and one of the pillowcases. Stunned, it took her a moment to realize what it was.

"She's bleeding!" Judy cried. "She's bleeding to death!"

Tyree quickly took Elizabeth's free hand and examined it. For an instant, Judy thought she saw a touch of panic in Tyree's eyes. But, then Tyree shook her head, her eyes narrowed, and said, "No. It's from a cut on her wrist. It's already stopped bleeding. She must have broken the clock with her arm and a shard of glass cut her." She looked up at the two of them. "Christ! She's burning up. I can't get a pulse!"

Judy stood frozen, hearing her own breath echo back in her ears. She felt as if she couldn't catch her breath. She remembered Liz telling her about some problems in their marriage. Then last night she'd walked into their argument. Had Liz become despondent and taken an overdose of something?

Tyree deftly untangled the sheet from around Elizabeth's legs and pulled it up to cover her. Then, she touched her fingers to Liz's neck, against the carotid artery. She shook her head, and moved her fingers slightly, then frowned.

"Is she breathing? I can't see her breathing," Judy cried.

For a moment, Tyree closed her eyes, her face pulled into a mask of taut lines. Her shoulders slumped. Then, she straightened up and regained her composure. "Honeybunch, call the paramedics! Hurry!"

"She isn't dead, is she?"

"No. But her pulse is terribly faint and thready."

Judy reached for the phone on the nightstand.

Her fingers trembled uncontrollably as she tried to dial 911. She dialed three times before she finally hit the right numbers. "Please," she whispered. "Please, don't let her die!"

"Emergency," came the voice on the phone. "Do you need assistance?"

Judy sucked in her breath, but her throat felt so tight she could barely get any air in her lungs. "Yes. Someone's sick. Hardly breathing. I don't know what's wrong."

"Give me your name, please."

"We don't know what to do."

"I need your name and address."

"Judith Bird. Ah, I think it's 15 Oceanfront. On the Balboa Peninsula. Send someone, please. Hurry!"

"Stay calm. I'm dispatching paramedics immediately. Was there an accident?"

"No, we just found her. She's terribly sick."

"Did you say she isn't breathing?"

"It doesn't look like it. Her eyes are open. But she isn't moving. And there's . . . ah . . . blood all over."

"How's her color? Are her lips blue or dark?"

"Yes." Damn it! Judy's mind screamed. Stop asking questions and get someone here!

"Do you know how to do CPR?"

"No. Yes. I think so. But we need a *doctor!*"

"Paramedics are on their way. Stay calm. If she doesn't seem to be breathing, start CPR."

The voice started to say something else, but Judy slammed down the phone. "They're on their way. They said to start CPR."

Andy was already leaning over Liz, breathing

into her mouth. His face was ashen, but he seemed to know what he was doing. He wouldn't let her die.

"They're coming," Judy said again, feeling herself begin to shake all over.

Tyree came over and put her arms around her. "It's okay, honeybunch. I think she's got the flu. Pneumonia possibly." Tyree's voice held a throaty tone. "Listen, if you like, I'll call my doctor. Have him meet the ambulance at Hoag Hospital. He's a good friend, and besides that, he's the best in the county."

"Between breaths Andy said, "Yes. Please. We don't know anyone here."

Tyree headed for the door. "I'll phone from downstairs. You two spell each other with the CPR." With that, she disappeared down the hall.

"Come on Lizzy!" Andy shouted. "Come on, damn it! Baby, please breathe! Lizzy, I love you!"

Judy watched as Andy continued to breathe rhythmically into Liz's mouth. But she wasn't responding. Her lips turned bluer, the rest of her face already marble-white. Her eyes stared unfocused, not moving, not blinking. Judy moved to the opposite side of the bed from Andy, sat down, and reached a trembling hand out to touch the side of Liz's face.

"Don't be dead! Please, don't be dead!" she said. "Liz! You just can't die. We're Siamese twins, remember? Joined at the brain." Liz's skin felt dry and burning hot. If she were dead, Judy suddenly realized, she'd be cold. She'd be cold as ice. Tyree was right, it was probably pneumonia. That damned flu! They could give her some antibiotics and fluids, and she'd be just fine. If only the paramedics would hurry up and get here.

Tyree appeared in the doorway. "I reached Doctor Foxhoven's office. He wasn't in, but they know where to find him. Hopefully, he'll be waiting for us by the time we get to the hospital."

In the distance, Judy heard the faint wail of the siren as it wound its way down the narrow peninsula road. It seemed like forever before she finally heard it turn off Balboa Boulevard, and into the alley behind the house.

Andy paced the dark hospital carpet, a styrofoam cup half-filled with lukewarm coffee in his hand. Why were they taking so damn long? Where was the doctor, anyway? Lizzy had been in the emergency room for almost two hours, and no one had come out and said a word to them. He looked at Judy huddled in a miserable lump on a green plastic sofa. She looked so thin. He'd never seen her so thin before. Her face crumpled, as if she were going to cry at any moment. She kept glancing about the room like a frightened deer.

He wished Tyree had stayed with them, but she'd dashed off shortly after Lizzy had been taken into the emergency room, promising to be back as soon as she took care of some important errands. She had to cancel the neighborhood party that evening, and then show Elizabeth's paintings to a client. If Andy didn't mind, she'd run by their house and pick them up. Andy gave her their spare house key, sorry to see her go, but relieved that at least someone was able to function in a normal manner.

They had met Doctor Foxhoven for only a moment when they first brought Lizzy in. A tall white-haired man, in his mid-fifties, spare, tan, and muscular, with piercing green eyes set off by heavy dark eyebrows, he'd come bounding into the hospital wearing a dazzling white shirt and shorts that matched his white hair. It appeared he'd come straight from the tennis court. Nevertheless, Andy had been impressed by his firm, take-charge manner. But, he wished someone would come and tell them what the hell was happening.

"Andy?" Judy said, her voice barely a whisper. "She isn't going to die, is she?"

Andy put the plastic cup down on the table next to the sofa, and sat down beside her. "Don't even say that, Judy. She just has that awful flu we both caught. People don't die of the flu anymore. They have all kinds of medication for things like that."

Judy shook her head. "But they *do*. People do die of the flu!"

Andy put his arm around her. "Not Elizabeth. She's not going to die." But inside him, he felt the little worm of fear that had been plaguing him the past few days. He couldn't imagine life without Lizzy. They'd planned their life together. All their hopes and dreams. The children they would have. If only they hadn't had that silly argument last night. Lizzy wasn't up to par, and she'd been so upset. It probably brought on a relapse. If she died, he would never be able to tell her how sorry he was. If she lived, he would make sure they talked things out. He'd never let something like this happen again.

"What are they *doing* in there?" Judy asked. "Why is it taking so long?"

In answer to Judy's question, Doctor Foxhoven suddenly appeared in the waiting room, the expression on his face grim. "Are you the young lady's next of kin?"

Judy went rigid. "Oh, my God!"

"No, no. I'm sorry," Foxhoven said, raising his hand. "I didn't mean to alarm you. We've gotten her somewhat stabilized for now. But I'd like to get hold of whatever medical records she might have. Allergies, things like that."

"I'm her husband. We went to a medical center in Van Nuys," Andy said, his voice trembling. "Chapman Medical, I think it's called."

"Fine. If you'd sign a release, we can have her records faxed. That would help us a great deal."

Judy leaned forward. "What's wrong with her? Is it the flu?"

Foxhoven pursed his lips for a moment, his eyes hazy, as if thinking. "We really aren't sure yet. Besides, losing a lot of blood, her temperature was one-hundred and five when you brought her in. And, her white count is astronomical. It's definitely an infection. We're trying a wide-spectrum antibiotic, giving her several units of blood, and keeping her in isolation, until we know exactly what we're dealing with here."

"But, she is going to be okay?" Andy asked.

"I'm hoping for the best. We're keeping her in CCU. No visitors, at least for today. Tomorrow perhaps, for a few minutes."

Andy felt his pulse race. At least she was alive.

They'd gotten her here in time. She'd be okay. She had to be.

Foxhoven looked at Judy, then at Andy. He seemed to study them for a moment. "You know what? I'd like to take a quick look at the two of you. You say you've had the flu recently?"

"Yes," Andy said. "I did."

Judy shook her head. "No, I haven't had it."

"I'd still like to do some blood work—just a few things. It won't take long."

"Doctor," Judy said, "are you thinking it could be . . . well, something like meningitis?"

Foxhoven stood up and gave them a confident smile. "We won't put a name on it just yet. Okay? Now, why don't you go on into the emergency room? They'll draw some blood and do a little work-up. I'll be back in a few minutes."

Andy helped Judy to her feet. She seemed reluctant, holding back, her eyes blinking rapidly as if she weren't exactly certain what was happening. She gave him a puckery little smile, as a nurse pulled a white curtain around them and told them both to sit on the edge of the examining table.

"The man from the lab will be here in a short while to draw your blood," the nurse said. "Try and make yourselves comfortable." With that, she disappeared outside the curtain.

The two of them sat in silence looking around the sparse little cubical. The room was icy cold and dingy. It smelled sharply of antiseptic. The examining table was uncomfortable, and the overhead fluorescent light gave everything a greenish cast. Andy saw Judy shiver. The chill in the room seemed to seep up from the hard tile floor. God, how he hated hospitals. But then, didn't everybody? Judy shivered again.

"Do you want my jacket?" he asked.

She shook her head, no.

"I'm sorry, Judy. Sorry you had to come down here with all this going on."

"Andy, Liz is my closest friend. We're closer than most sisters. When she gets . . . when she gets well, she's going to need some help around the house. I can get some time off work. I want to stay. I wouldn't be able to work anyway, worrying."

Andy folded his arms around her, and tried to quell her shivering. "A little better?"

She gave him a flicker of a smile. "Yes. Thanks." She lowered her head for a moment, then looked up at him; her gold-ringed eyes had slight shadows beneath them. "Why couldn't I have met a nice guy like you, Andy? I had to pick a shit like Alex. Elizabeth has no idea how lucky she is."

"I'm not such a bargain," Andy said, thinking about how self-absorbed he'd been, worrying about his writing block instead of supporting Lizzy's painting.

"Well, all I can say is one of these days I hope I meet someone exactly like you. And, believe me, I'll pounce on him."

"Andy laughed softly. Yes, he thought. He and Lizzy were lucky. Sometimes, they forgot just how lucky. But he'd see to it they never did again.

The round black-and-white clock on the wall behind the examining table ticked metallically—the only sound Andy heard, except for the occasional whispering of a nurse's soft shoes against the floor. "I think they've forgotten us," he said, after what seemed like a half hour. They continued to sit there, clinging to one another, listening to the monotonous ticking of the clock. Finally, Dr. Foxhoven pulled the curtain partially open and stepped in.

"I'm sorry to keep you waiting so long. But we've had our hands full with Elizabeth."

"What's happened?" Andy gasped, feeling the pulse in his throat jump.

"It's the fever," the doctor said. "A fever that high often leads to convulsions."

Judy took on a ghostly pallor. "Oh, my God!" Sitting there with her hands clasped tightly together, rocking nervously back and forth on the edge of the examining table, she resembled a fragile praying mantis. Andy wondered if he looked much better himself.

"I know that sounds scary." Foxhoven patted Judy's hand gently. "But it isn't always as bad as it sounds. I think we've got it pretty well under control. Her fever's down some now, and the transfusion is helping. So let's get *your* blood work done," he said pleasantly, his elegant bedside manner suddenly in evidence. "Then I'll take a quick look at the both of you. Tyree said to tell you she's back and waiting to drive you home. There's no use in your sticking around all night. Now, please, roll up your sleeves."

Andy took off his jacket, and unbuttoned his shirt sleeve. "But I thought they were sending someone from the lab."

Foxhoven dabbed icy alcohol on Andy's arm,

wrapped a tight elastic band above his elbow, and then took a syringe out of a plastic package. "It's time for a shift change. I don't want to keep you here any longer than I have to."

"Are you Tyree's doctor?" Andy asked.

"Yes. We've known each other a long time. Move in the same social circles, so to speak, here in Newport Beach. Fine lady. Talented, too. Ever seen any of her quilts?"

Andy shook his head, no.

"Well, ask her to show you sometime. Very avant-garde, not traditional. Her creations are commissioned. She gets an astronomical price for them. I know, my wife bought one."

With an odd sense of fascination, Andy watched the sharp tip of the needle the doctor held slip painlessly into the blue vein in his arm. For some reason, he always expected blood to be a bright, crimson red. And it always surprised him to see the small glass vial fill with thick, dark liquid the color of bruised strawberries. In spite of the chill, he felt himself begin to perspire. Moisture seeped like a glistening tide from his pores. After that, the doctor took Andy's blood pressure, listened to his chest, then flashed a tiny point of light into one of his eyes which sent a knife of pain cutting through his head.

"Sorry," Foxhoven apologized. "A little sensitive I see." It was the same with the other eye. The light crawled in like a razor-sharp probe, piercing his brain with a pinpoint of pain. When he finished with Andy, he went through the routine again, this time with Judy.

"That's it for now. Go home, both of you, and

get some rest," Foxhoven finally said. "Let us take care of Elizabeth. We'll call you immediately if there's any change."

Tyree stood in the waiting room, still wearing her white jumpsuit and purple sunglasses. "There you are," she said. "I bet you're exhausted." She moved between the two of them, and put her arms around them. "She's in the best hands possible here. Believe me."

Tyree led them out through the glass doors toward the parking lot. As Andy passed by the door, he caught a quick reflection of himself in the glass. He stopped. Good Christ! Was that *him?* A gaunt skeleton of a man—his eyes peering back at him like brown jelly-eggs sunken into caverns of white bone. The flu, his working too many hours, the shock of Elizabeth's illness, had all taken their toll. He stood gaping at the reflection for a moment. Then, Tyree tugged him away, and steered the two of them toward the parking lot.

He took a deep breath, glad to be rid of the antiseptic smell of the hospital, relishing the bite of brine in the air as the breeze blew up from the ocean. It was late afternoon, and the sky had turned the color of day-old bruises. Curtains of purple-gray clouds were scudding up from the south.

Tyree looked at the sky. "According to the news reports, we're getting a nasty storm up from Baja. The edge of a hurricane named Terrance. Probably have wind and rain before midnight. And some pretty high tides. If it gets too bad, we may have to sandbag our houses."

"Oh, great!" Andy moaned. His eyes pained

anew from a burst of daylight that struck him just before the sun slipped, like a shiny gold coin, into a pocket of dark clouds. "A storm. High tides. Just exactly what we need!"

Chapter Six

HE awoke suddenly from the heat of his dream-filled sleep, plunging into the chill of his rapidly darkening bedroom. It was as if the thundering sound of waves breaking on the beach had recalled him from some twisted, violent, otherworld to the sane reality of a stormy evening. It took him a moment to adjust. For a time, the echoing violence of his dream seemed more real than the rhythmic pounding of combers against the sand.

He reached out in the darkness and turned on the bedside lamp, flooding the room with a river of yellow light. He lay there trying to remember what it was he had to do. Something urgent. He pushed back the covers and swung his feet over the side of the bed. Then suddenly, a flood of memory erased the spill of dream phantasma that paralyzed his brain. He had to catch a plane. His briefcase was packed. All he had to do was casually leave the apartment, as if going to some kind of job, and never return. But before that, he had things to do. He had a passport, and enough money to get by until he could get to the Swiss account his mother had set up. But his heat-filled dreams told him that the agony would envelope him before long. He would have to subdue it before boarding the plane. He had purposely taken as little from the artist woman as he could. He had tried not to harm her. The feelings she evoked in him had outweighed his need. So even though the encounter had satisfied his lust, it had done little to quell the agony.

He picked up his watch from the bedside table and looked at it. Only a few hours, but he could not leave until he did something about the agony. And perhaps he might find a way to see the artist woman one more time. His night with her had awakened emotions in him he thought no longer existed. Had he harmed her? Vaguely, he recalled hearing the sound of sirens close by. Had he hurt her more than he realized? Had they taken her to the hospital? He tried to remember how she'd been when he left her, but his mind refused to function properly. The agony gathered around him, closing in, sucking from him all reason. He tightened his fists and beat them against the mattress. He did not want to be the way he was. Wanted to go back before it all happened and lead a normal life. Wanted a chance to make the choices again. The right ones. But he could not undo his mistakes. He had to live with what he had done.

His fists went limp and he got up from his bed and went to open the drapes. The sun had just gone down, its final arrogant light slashing across the turbulent sea like a smear of blood. Overhead, great clumps of dark gray clouds had gathered to hang like heavy wet rags. He opened the window and sniffed the air. The tang of seaweed, which had been churned up from the ocean floor, stung his nose. From the south he smelled heat and ozone. The storm would be violent. The scent of dolphin and whale was absent from the sea. All the cetaceans had moved their pods away from the approaching maelstrom. Perfect weather for him. Tropical storms hit Southern California so seldom, it would put people off balance. He would be free to roam and find someone to ease his agony.

He leaned out the window once more, testing the air, straining its scents through his nose and lungs. Everything in its place. Wait! Something else out there. New people on the block? Teenagers strolling where his eyes could not see? He squinted into the darkness but saw no one moving. Yet his acute sense of smell told him someone was there. Someone not familiar. Close by. He inhaled again, but could not define the odor. The heavy scent of brine that flung itself from the churning sea, permeated everything. Then, from the corner of his eye, he caught a slight movement. A car parked several houses down the alley. An unfamiliar car. The engine smelled hot. It had not been there long. Someone seated inside, moving about. Two people. Were they watching him? He pulled back from the window. No, just two people talking. Nothing to be concerned about.

Enough time wasted. He would take care of the agony as quickly as possible. To hold off the agony until his plane landed, he would need two people. Difficult, but necessary. After that, he would come back for his case which held his passport, plane tickets, and money, and then walk away. He dressed in black pants and shirt so he could melt into shadows. He would not be gone long. The air smelled of danger. Time now to begin a new life. Perhaps he might even find a new doctor in a new country, someone who could help him, who could take away this nightmare in which he lived.

He left the apartment lights on and put a stack of compact discs in the recorder. It was his habit lately to play music whenever he was home. He would do nothing different from usual. Nothing to arouse anyone's suspicions. Just in case he was being watched.

To the strains of Mendelssohn's Violin Concerto, as deftly as a night-cat, he made his way out of the apartment and folded himself into deep shadows. The wind freshened around him, howling like a lost soul, as the coming storm fortified itself.

Ted rattled the electric switch on the seat of the late model Oldsmobile. The damn thing wouldn't move back any further, making him claustrophobic. One disadvantage to being a large person was having to shove himself into spaces designed for midgets. He let go of the switch, gave a roar and banged his hand against the padded dashboard.

"Hey!" Locke said. "Calm down. You're as uptight as a piece of dried catgut tonight. We've got this guy covered. With you and me holding down the alley, and Fitz and Melborne staked out over on

Balboa Boulevard, we'll be right on him if he tries to leave. It was your idea to stake this guy's apartment. What's got you so jumpy?"

Ted leaned back in the car seat and tried to find a comfortable position. The girth of his stomach pressed against the steering wheel and made him feel as if he were locked behind one of those bars on a roller coaster. He let out a deep sigh and tried to relax. He slipped off his tight shoes, which helped a bit. But it was a stupid thing to do. Especially, if he found it necessary to get out of the car and make a chase down a dark alley.

"This whole damn case," Ted growled at his partner. "makes me jumpy as hell." One moment, he was convinced they were on the right track. The next, he found himself wondering what the hell they were doing sitting in a cramped car, the wind blowing up a gale, rain as thick as syrup, watching for some surfer who might be a psychotic killer. One minute, the case made sense, the next it didn't. Shit!

"Hey, check it out! The large window. I saw someone moving," Locke said, motioning toward the apartment.

Ted looked at the window. Through the onslaught of rain, he caught a fleeting glimpse of a dark shadow. "Someone's in there."

"Okay buddy, make your move," Locke said to the shadow.

They watched in silence for a few minutes, but saw no further movement.

"You're wearing that new aftershave," Ted said, trying to keep from being so jumpy.

"New West," Locke said. "Like it?"

"Yeah," Ted said. "Smells like lemons. The new girl, huh?"

Locke grinned. Even in the dim light, Ted could see the freckles across the young man's cheeks, almost luminous in the dark. The beginning of young love, he thought, so filled with illusion, so hopeful. Perhaps this time it would be the right girl. Locke deserved someone special. Someone as special as his Sylvia had been.

"Wait a minute," Ted said. "I hear music. Do you hear it?"

"Yep. Is it coming from the guy's apartment?"

"Can't quite tell, what with the heavy wind and rain." Ted rolled down his window. "Yeah, it's music. Classical shit. Mozart, isn't it?"

"Mendelssohn."

"Ah, ha," Ted shot him a teasing look.

"Used to play violin. Hours and hours of violin. I joined the police department just to get away from the fucking violin. Honest to God."

"Well, everything else aside, you gotta admit this fuck may be crazy, but he's got good taste in music." Ted rolled the window up against the wind. The storm rolling up from Baja was really kicking up its heels. Just what they needed during a possible all-night stakeout. And to top it off, fifteen-foot breakers were already cresting in along the beach. It promised to be a wild night.

"Hey! Did you see something just then?" Locke leaned forward. "I thought I saw something on the stairs to that guy's apartment."

Ted stared into the darkness, checking the dim

corners of the house, the stairs, the balcony. "No, nothing," he said. "But get on the radio and check with Fitz and Melborne, just to be safe."

"Probably just something blowing in the wind." Locke picked up the radio and made contact with the other car. "Thought I saw some movement over here. You guys spot anything?"

"Just a horny cat," the other detective answered.

"I don't think that's our perp," Locke grumbled and replaced the phone.

"Damn this storm! Can't see a fucking thing!" Ted drummed his fingers against the steering wheel. The longer he sat there, the more fidgety he felt. What he really wanted to do was drive over to the Pavilion and have a nice Irish Coffee, listen to some music and watch the lights reflecting off the bay.

"I wish you'd been there with me this morning," he said.

"Been where?" Locke asked.

"At the Rattigan house. I don't know what it was, but I'd bet anything they know a hell of a lot more than they told me."

"You don't think this is some kind of wild-goose chase they've sent us on, do you?"

Ted shook his head. "No. That's just it. I think they've actually fingered the guy. How and why, I don't know. But we have to find a way to get into that apartment. Legally."

Locke shrugged. "Well, let me know when you figure out how the hell we can manage that. Without a warrant. . . ."

There was a sharp little silence. Ted closed his eyes. They couldn't just crawl in a window. They had to have a viable reason. Wait! Windows. He opened his eyes and looked out through the darkness. "Windows. How many windows are in that apartment?"

"What?"

"Are all the drapes closed except that one? Or are some of the others open?"

He searched the darkness with his eyes.

"I think the one on the left has a gap."

"Check with Fitz and Melborne. See what they can see from their side."

"What the hell are you up to?" Locke asked.

"Do you have a list of those items he may have taken off some of his victims?"

Locke patted his pocket. "Right here. I must admit, that part of it got my attention. The Duff girl's parents said a gold locket is missing from one of the girls. Has her initials on it. And a ring from the other girl is missing, an opal, her birthstone. Then there's the compact disc player, and one of those New Age crystals on a silver chain. It's a long list. Once I got to calling people this afternoon, I found something was missing from most all the victims. So it appears that the Rattigan woman scored on that point."

"That would be all the evidence we needed. If we found even one or two of those items in this guy's apartment." Ted's eyes took on a glow of excitement.

"Yeah," Locke nodded. "But we can't do that without a warrant. It's called breaking and entering. That way, you and I go to jail, and the nut-case goes free. Besides, the evidence we found illegally couldn't be used in court anyway."

"Yes, but if we *saw* some of them before we went in, or had good reason to believe they were there. Then we could go in."

"You mean we play peeping Tom?"

"Something like that."

"And if he caught us staring through the windows?"

"Worry about that if or when it happens."

Locke looked back out at the dark alley. "I don't know. Sounds risky."

The wind roared up, buffeting the car. The black night grew heavier with rain every minute.

"And what if it isn't the right guy?" Locke went on. "The landlord says he's lived here for some time. He's quiet, soft spoken. Lives on a pension of some kind. Could be a vet. If we pick up some fingerprints from the outside of the place. The staircase maybe. We might get some AKA's."

"What do you say we alert Fitz and Melborne. Call for another car. As soon as it gets here," Ted felt his pulse quicken. "we turn into peeping Toms."

"We see anything at all that looks like it might be a part of the case, we go in, right?"

"One item," Ted said. "That's all we need. One item on that list in your pocket."

"I just wish I was convinced this is our man. It's going to be pretty embarrassing if we have to confront some poor guy who doesn't know what the hell is going on."

"This is our guy," Ted said, peering through the

rain at the glow of light coming from behind the drape in Brownstone's apartment. "Don't ask me how the fuck I know. After all these years, I feel it in my gut. I just wonder how the hell this Tyree Rattigan and her little group knew about him. Where do they fit into this? After we break this case, they're going to have one hell of a lot of explaining to do." He turned to Locke. "Because something around here smells to high heaven!"

"Oh, yeah? Well then, for God's sake Teddy Bear, put your shoes back on!"

A strong gust of wind blowing in off the ocean rattled all the windows in the old house and made the timbers groan. The storm coming up from Baja moved in fast and savagely.

Judy poked at the fire with the iron, then sat down on the sofa. She pressed the palm of her hands against her eyes and sighed. Liz just had to be okay! She would *will* her to be okay. Andy had recovered from the flu, and Liz would too. She couldn't imagine Andy living without her. Outside of Liz's early crush on Alex, neither one of them had ever really been in love with anyone else. And even if they had been fighting a bit lately, it was just one of those periods that all marriages go through. It would be okay. It had to be.

From the kitchen, she heard Andy snap shut a cupboard door. She was glad to be away from that dreary hospital. Tyree was right, there wasn't anything they could do for Liz by staying there. Restless, she got up from the sofa and strode to the sliding glass door. She opened the door a crack, listening to the thunderous crashing of water against the sand. The tide had turned and the water was pounding dangerously close to the houses on the ocean side of the peninsula. It would be awful for Liz to come home from the hospital and find the house swept away to somewhere down in Mexico. She tugged the sliding door closed and turned to find Andy bearing a tray filled with cups and a coffeepot.

"I thought this might help," he said, looking like a lost child.

"She'll be okay, Andy."

He set the tray down on the coffee table. "Yes. Of course. I know that, but still. . . ." He shook his head. "Here," he said, pouring her a cup full of coffee.

Judy took it from him and curled up on the sofa. "I'm tired."

"Maybe we should call the hospital."

"I don't imagine they have anything new to tell us yet."

"I guess you're right."

Judy looked at him. His face seemed so thin and tired. Liz always called him her wonderful, talented, gangly gnome—how she adored him. There was a time, she remembered, that she'd felt that same love for Alex. But it had been short-lived. The son-of-a-bitch had turned nasty the first year they were married. But it was the cocaine that did it. Right now he was probably in a rehab hospital somewhere, trying to kick the stuff for the tenth time. He had been gorgeous when they first married. His skin so pale and his hair so black. Unlike Andy whose hair was soft brown.

"You need a haircut," she said.

Andy gave a soft laugh. "You sound like Lizzy."

"I need someone to fuss over, the way Liz does you."

"You'll find someone. Someone nice. Wait and see. Look," Andy said. "Why don't you go upstairs and rest for a while. I'll lock up and spend some time in my office." He looked at his watch. "It's only seven. I'll call the hospital in a few hours. Maybe we can rustle up something to eat after that." A gust of wind rattled the glass of the sliding door and shuddered through the room. "This is quite a storm."

Judy got up and started toward the stairs. "I'll go on up and change into some fresh clothes, maybe take a short nap."

"Good," Andy said. "I'll be working in my office if you need me."

Upstairs, Judy changed into a pair of new Levis she'd bought especially for the weekend. All these lovely clothes going to waste. Well, she'd put them on anyway. What the hell. Rummaging around in her suitcase she found the new I. B. Difusion sweater she'd bought just yesterday morning, and slipped into it. Black, with a clown face in colors of red, yellow and blue, it shouted in primary colors. She went into the bathroom and checked herself in the mirror. Not too bad, considering what she'd been through that day. She finger-combed her hair, put on some lipstick and then nodded her approval.

Her body looked trim, her breasts full. And with that sweater, she could certainly turn some heads.

Another blast of wind hit the house, its timbers crying out in anguish. The wind wailed along the eaves like a distressed child, the staccato rap of rain beating fiercely against the wooden shingles of the roof. She couldn't remember many storms like this one hitting Southern California. Once in a while they slipped up from Baja. Hit and run as a rule. But this one sounded as if it were settling in. She took one more look at herself in the mirror, then headed downstairs. She felt tired, but not at all sleepy. She couldn't possibly sleep, what with worrying about Liz and having all that racket going on outside. No way. She would go downstairs and turn on the TV. Andy would probably work for a long while yet. She hadn't brought her laptop computer, so she couldn't do any of her own work. But she had to do something to keep her mind off Liz. Then it dawned on her what she was going to do.

She thought about the idea for a moment. Liz was bound to have a raincoat around the place somewhere. And an umbrella. She didn't have to go far. Only a few blocks. She remembered a lovely place, what was its name? Sitting right out on the bay. Had a nice cozy bar. The Pavilion, that was it. She'd bet a lot of people would be there, riding out the storm, having cappuccino, watching the ships in the harbor rearing at the storm. What the hell! It was better than just sitting there. And Andy could call her if he heard anything from the hospital. She could be back in minutes. Yes, that was the ticket.

Do her good. She might even meet an interesting guy. Someone rich and single who hadn't wanted to stay home alone during the storm.

Andy wasn't too keen on the idea of her going out in all that rain and wind. But he helped her find a raincoat and umbrella, then looked up the number of the place where she would be so he could call if there were any news about Liz. Then he phoned the Pavilion to make certain it was open, but all he got was a busy signal.

"If they aren't open," Judy promised. "I'll come right back. I won't go off the peninsula."

"Drive carefully," Andy said, going to the back door with her. "It's dangerous out there. The water's already pretty deep. Don't let your brakes get wet."

The wind almost lifted her off her feet before she could get the door to her car open. Inside, she started the engine, slipped it into gear, and carefully pulled out of the parking space into the alley. Andy was right, she would have to be careful. The wind came in blasts and rocked the car like a cradle. Rain sluiced down the windshield so thick the wipers did little good. She giggled to herself. Her fatigue had lifted. An adventure! For the first time in a long time, she was actually having a new adventure. She'd been tied to the memory and pain of Alex and hadn't allowed herself to really live. Well, that was enough of that. With Liz coming close to dying today, she realized how ephemeral life was. Might as well get on with it, and enjoy it.

She reached the intersection where she had to turn to go to the Pavilion, only to find it completely flooded. Slowly she eased the car through the water, remembering Andy's admonishment about not getting the brakes wet. She heard a crackling sound and suddenly, the motor stopped. She turned the key, and the starter hummed, but the engine wouldn't turn over.

"Well, hot damn!" she said. "Missed the brakes, but shorted out the engine!" Now what? She couldn't just leave the car in the middle of the road. She had to get it over to the curb. The Pavilion was only a few yards away. She could walk from there.

She stepped out into the deep water and felt it sluice into her shoes, and soak up her Levis. Well, you found your adventure all right, she scolded herself. Putting her shoulder to the inside of the car's door jam she gave it a push. The car sat there like a piece of concrete. You'd think with all this water the dang thing would float! She gave it another try with no more success.

"Need a hand?" someone said.

She turned to find a tall, muscular man dressed in black standing next to her. "Yes!" she said. "I sure do."

He smiled, his straight teeth glowing in the darkness. "Got the sparks wet," he said.

She laughed. "Guess so." She stepped aside and he took her place, pushing with apparent ease. The car moved slowly to the side of the curb. He stopped it and set the brake.

"Thank you, so much," Judy said. "I wasn't sure what to do, what with this storm and all. It would probably be hours before the Auto Club could get here."

"Glad to help."

"Well, now that we're both soaked, it might be a good idea to have a nice hot toddy for the body. Can I buy you a drink," she said, motioning to the Pavilion just ahead of them.

"Yeah, I could use a drink," he said, smiling again. "But I know a better place."

He took her arm and steered her away from the Pavilion. "Okay," she agreed. "But the drinks are on me."

"That's the best offer I've had today," he said.

As they made their way down a side street, she turned and studied his profile. Even in the dim light she could see his straight features, reddish-blond hair, and icy-blue eyes. Well, she told herself, if this isn't my lucky night!

HE stood on the street corner, leaning into the wind and rain. He loved the night when it filled with such extravagance. The bestial side of nature never failed to intoxicate him. For most people, the ferocity of the storm was a deterrent. The streets were empty. His agony in retreat, he felt no rush to find his second victim. He pulled the memento from his recent victim out of his jacket. Such a lovely sweater, the front adorned with a bright clown in red, yellow and blue. He held it to his nose, the sweet scent of the woman who had worn it still fresh. Then his throat tightened. He didn't have time for remorse and tried to push it away, but the terrible sensation washed over him anyway. He had to get help. Had to stop living like this. If they caught him, they would never understand his torment. But until then, he had no choice.

A slash of lightning, followed by a rumble of thunder reminded him that even though he felt no urgency, he had little time left. He would have to swallow back the remorse and find his second victim quickly, get back to the apartment for his few things, and meet his plane. He tucked the sweater back inside his jacket. The marquee light from the Lido Theater gleamed wetly across the gray pavement. Next to the theater, the video store appeared deserted except for a dark-haired young man who stood behind the counter with his arms folded, gazing out into the night. The young man, though tempting, would be a dangerous choice. His absence would be noticed far too quickly.

He turned up the collar of his aviator-style leather jacket to forestall the stream of rainwater running down his back. The inclement weather proved both a help and a hindrance. He could move about without being noticed, but his choices were few, unless he were willing to go farther afield. His chancing upon the lovely young woman with the stalled car was sheer luck. It would not be so easy the next time. He looked around the deserted street. He needed to find someone soon. Someone who would not be missed for at least a few hours. Across the street stood a small store that catered to tourists, its window filled with suntan oils, beach towels and sand buckets. Although it was usually open twenty-four hours, the storm had caused the owners to close early, their customers hiding out in motels and rented beach cottages.

He perused the area, checking and rejecting possibilities. Then he turned back to the theater. It was playing an Italian/English film titled *Thief of Hearts*. He wondered how large an audience would be attracted on a stormy Monday night. Not many, he guessed. But it was worth a try. He walked to the box office, and bought a ticket.

"The film's already started," chirped the young blond girl behind the glass window. Her words whistled through a set of silver-wire braces. "But, you can stay over, because it plays again at nine."

"Fine," he said, and smiled. She flushed, then gave him a flirtatious grin, her face as round and shiny as an autumn apple. Be thankful, he told her silently, that you're working tonight. Be thankful that I'm in a hurry and can't wait outside the theater until the last show is over. She smelled of chocolate candy, and the silk of her blouse. Inside, he bought a tub of popcorn, and made his way into the darkened theater.

He sat in the rear of the theater where he could look over the audience. Only fifteen people had braved the storm. He inhaled. A rush of scents invaded his nose. It would take a few moments to sort them out. He looked about in the dim light for people who sat alone. He spotted five, two women and three men. Inhaling, he began to sort, catalog and identify the fragrances.

Quietly, he stood up and moved farther down the aisle, seating himself behind a lone woman who smelled of roses and sherry. She wasn't young, but not old either. From the rich sweet smell of her flesh, he guessed she was about thirty-five. He liked the warmth that emanated from her. She was vital, healthy. Finding her had been much easier than he expected. Now, he could sit back and relish the movie, then at the end of the film he would follow her outside.

The movie was narrated by a young man recounting his youth—a youth which had been filled with all the wretchedness and all the euphoria that was a part of life. Sitting there with the flickering lights playing upon the screen, he felt a mellowness he seldom experienced. For a few moments, he was that boy on the screen, living a normal life, experiencing friendship, love, hate, fear, death—all of the things he would never again encounter. At this thought, he shook his head, cleared his mind. It did no good to fret about his plight. He breathed deeply, putting his attention on the woman in front of him.

A spicy aroma invaded his nose. One that he had not noticed before. He sniffed at the air. It was not coming from the woman in front of him. It was strong. Familiar. Close. He glanced around. Two rows ahead of him to his right, he saw two women seated together. He breathed in again. Yes, the scent was coming from the two of them. Their heads were close together, and he could see that they were talking softly. He pulled back in his seat. Damn! Damn them!

One of the women turned around, her elderly face in deep shadows, but the white of her hair glistened in the flickering backlight from the screen. Then slowly, the other woman turned to stare at him. He lowered his head, closed his eyes, swallowing hard as the bitter taste of gall rose in the back of his throat. *The Zipper sisters!* Of all the places he could have chosen on the entire peninsula, he'd managed to run into those two. With a little cry, he jumped from his seat, and blindly made his way up the aisle.

In the lobby, the young girl who had waited on him looked up startled. "You didn't like the movie?"

"I forgot to put money in the parking meter," he said, rushing past her through the doorway, and out onto the wet sidewalk.

"It's after six," the girl called after him. "You don't need to."

He stood on the sidewalk for a moment, regaining his balance. The wind screamed around the buildings on the corner, carrying great streamers of silver rain. He'd been so close—the woman in the theater would have been so easy. In the past, Tyree and her group had tried to find help for his condition. But he supposed his value to them had about run out, and they were no fools, they knew what he'd been doing. He doubted they would let him continue. The whistle was about to be blown. He could tell from the look on the elderly sister's faces that something was in the works. He had no choice now, he'd get home as fast as possible, grab the few belongings he could take, and get the hell out of there. If they guessed he was going to make a run for it, they would be looking for him at John Wayne, or LAX. But he'd made arrangements to fly to San Diego from Ontario, and catch his nonstop flight to Paris from there. He really needed his second victim, but perhaps he could find someone at the airport just before his flight.

He stepped out from under the shelter of the theater marquee into the wind and driving rain. It felt good against his face. The reflection of lights off the watery street was a dark rainbow of colors. Then, for just an instant, a flash of lightning turned the night to daylight. He blinked, then began to move, slowly at first, then faster. He turned at the corner and made his way toward the end of the peninsula. He moved like a black shadow down the sidewalk, hearing the thunder of his own heartbeat synchronize with the thundering of the surf just a block away. The tide surged, black waves rolling in along the main street through the peninsula. The water swirled around his legs, growing deeper with each step. It seemed to him that all the fury of nature was calling out to him—hurry—hurry— hurry!

Andy's office didn't feel as cold as usual—in fact it was almost comfortable. For the most part, he ignored the moaning of the storm. Despite his concerns about Lizzy, his work continued to give him a sense of exhilaration he'd never experienced before. Even if he did say so himself, the novel was shaping up in spectacular fashion. It felt quite natural now, the keen way his words flowed, and he wondered why he'd ever felt a sense of anxiety. Lizzy had been right. They had both broken through, and were on their way to success. Then a picture of Lizzy, alone and ill, in a dreary hospital room almost overwhelmed him. If only he could be with her. Since the hospital hadn't called, he had to assume she was doing okay. With rest and medication, she would be just fine. She had to be. He pushed the thought out of his mind and continued to concentrate on his work.

He'd completed almost seven pages of new material, when he began to feel drowsy. He yawned, then took in several deep breaths to try and refresh himself. He leaned back in his chair and slid down so his head rested on the back. Maybe he would take a little catnap, and then do a few more pages. By then, Judy might be back and they could fix a late snack. If he hadn't heard anything from the hospital, he would call. Maybe Lizzy would be feeling good enough to talk to him.

He had no idea how long he had dozed, when he awoke suddenly with a start, hearing a great cracking sound. Every nerve in his body jumped and tingled.

"Jesus Christ! What was that?" he yelled, bolting upright in the chair. The room suddenly plunged into darkness. The glow on his computer screen faded. For a few seconds, he saw only blackness. The wind and rain howled around the corners of the house, and the surf rumbled like a brigade of drums across the sand.

His night vision finally took over, and he could make out a faint outline of his office furniture. "Well, damn!" he said, realizing that what had startled him was a bolt of lightning that had struck close by. Thank God, he'd put a surge protector on his computer.

In the kitchen, he rummaged around in the dark, hunting for a flashlight or candles. But there didn't seem to be any. He checked in the dinning room buffet, but came up empty. Where would Lizzy have put them? The upstairs cupboards were mostly empty, he knew, and he hadn't seen any in their closet. Another bolt of lightning struck, not so close this time, but still too close for comfort. He thought about Lizzy again. She was terrified by lightning. He wanted to sit beside her and hold her hand, the way he always did during a thunderstorm. Stupid hospital rules! Tomorrow morning he'd be there, no matter what. And, he'd stay with her until they bodily threw him out.

He checked the entry closet, but saw no sign of either a flashlight or candles. He took out his heavy jacket, and put it on. Judy had the only umbrella they owned, but it was only a short distance to the Rattigans', and he was sure they would have a flashlight to loan him. Outside, the wind and rain was much stronger than he'd expected. The tide had brought the surf rolling in over the sand, flooding the sidewalk along the front of the house, and running between the houses. If it hadn't been for their deck, the house would have flooded. He stepped off the deck and found himself knee-deep in foaming seawater.

"Shit!" he yelled, feeling the cold seep into his shoes, and soak into his trousers. He battled the wind and the press of rain, moving slowly toward

Tyree's house. Her lights were out also, as they were in all the houses along that strip of the peninsula. He wondered how widespread the power failure was. From Tyree's front window, he caught sight of a soft glow. It appeared she had candles lit. That was a good sign. Knowing Tyree, she wouldn't mind sharing a few of them. God only knew how long the power would be off.

He stood on the Rattigans' front porch, which faced north rather than west toward the ocean, sheltering him somewhat from the onslaught of the storm. Someone had snugged several sandbags against the front door, to keep out the water. He rapped loudly, but the storm quickly drowned out the sound. He pressed the bell, then felt foolish when he realized it wouldn't ring without electricity. He gave another pound on the door, louder this time, and waited. A giant comber, at least fifteen-feet high, curled in from the sea. He watched with both fascination, and not a small amount of fear, as it approached the beach, arching only fifty yards or so from the house. Spume from its white edge blew in tattered ribbons against the dark sky. Then it tilted down, curled inward, and crashed against the sand, its momentum carried a flood of dark seawater which shot a foaming rivulet of velvet-black water between the houses. The water caught him by surprise and almost buckled him over. He grabbed for the latch on Tyree's door, and held on. The water ebbed quickly, sucking back, tugging against his feet. In the distance he saw another wave foaming.

"Enough of this!" he shouted, wrenching the

door latch. The door flew open and he jumped the sandbags, stumbling inside and shoving the door closed behind him. He stood for a moment in the hall, horrified at the prospect of dripping water on the Rattigans' hardwood floors. But someone had placed a small candle on a maple tea wagon in the hall, and when he looked down, he was relieved to see that someone had also put down a bundle of thick terrycloth towels.

"Tyree," he called. "It's Andy, from next door." He slipped off his wet shoes and rolled up his pants legs, squeezing the material as dry as possible. "Tyree?" He stepped off the mat of towels, and padded barefoot toward a pair of louvered doors. He hoped the doors led to the living room.

"Hello?" he called. "Tyree?" From behind the louvers, he heard the hum of numerous voices, along with the clink of ice in glasses and plates rattling. It had to be the living room. Did Tyree actually have a house full of company on such a stormy night? He hadn't noticed any cars parked in the alley.

He pushed open the doors slightly, not wanting to make an intrusive entrance. In fact, he was just about ready to retreat and forget about the candles or a flashlight, but his curiosity got the better of him. Through the small opening, he squinted at the crowd of people milling about the huge living room, drinks and plates of food in hand, talking in hushed voices. The room glowed with an orangy light from a blazing fire in the fireplace, and from several dozen large candles set about the room. Suddenly, it dawned on him, Tyree had gone ahead with the neighborhood party after all! She had not phoned anyone and called it off, the way she'd told him she had.

Easing the louvered doors wider, he looked around. The scent of smoking candle wax curled through the opening, mingled with a strong, spicy scent—some kind of perfume or incense. Then, in the strange fluidity of candlelight, he surveyed the room again. What he saw caused the saliva in his mouth to thicken, and made the pulse at his temple throb. The room swam in rippled golden-orange light, giving him the impression that he'd stumbled upon a den of elegant thieves wallowing among their treasures.

A half-dozen white iron cages filled with birds met his eyes. Silvery finches, emerald-winged parrots, ebony ravens, a jeweled peacock, and cockatoos—fluttered and squawked. Tables overflowed with bowls of flowers—roses, gardenias, chrysanthemums and orchids. Most of the crowd stood talking quietly, their eyes dark and serious. But it was the walls of Tyree's living room that suddenly caught his attention. The walls were studded with a brilliant array of paintings. From what he'd learned from Lizzy, he realized that if they were the real thing, they had to be extremely valuable. He noted paintings from every school of art—Flemish, Der Blaue Reiter, Lombard, Neapolitan, Pre-Raphaelite, Tuscan, Venetian—the array overwhelmed him. Elizabeth would have been stunned. The Rattigans' obviously had far more wealth than he'd imagined.

He stood there in the doorway, his head swirling

with the puzzle of the whole thing. Tyree must have decided it was too late to call off the party, but why had she lied about it? And then, through it all, like a strong black line through a colored painting, ran a familiar voice. Someone moved, a gleam of emerald silk, a flash of fire-drenched red hair. Thin strong fingers gripped his arm.

"Well, well, honeybunch! How nice of you to join us." Tyree slanted a brilliant blue eye at him, and steered him into the room. "Oh, Boo, do get him a drink. He looks like a drowned puppy. Come along, Andy, and sit by the fire. Any news about Elizabeth?"

"No," Andy said, watching as Boo, a tall, slender man with porcelain-white skin and inky eyes set off by hair as sleek and dark as feathers on a blackbird, gave Tyree a salute, wheeled around, and made his way to the bar on the other side of the huge room. So, that was Boo Rattigan, Andy thought. He wondered why they had not met before now.

"I didn't think you'd be up to going out tonight," Tyree said. "After all that happened today. You really shouldn't have gone out in all this weather. But I'm glad you did. We can help take your mind off Elizabeth. As you can see, just about the whole neighborhood is here. Except for Mable and Sarah, who'll be along a little later." She made a sweeping motion with her arm. "Since I'd already arranged everything for the party, I figured we might as well go ahead with it. Do you like it?"

"Pretty fancy," Andy admitted.

"Yes, well we do indulge ourselves now and then. It's really all for you and Elizabeth. What a shame she can't be here. But we'll do it again, when she's feeling well."

Andy allowed himself to be led along by Tyree, passing people who appeared for a moment, glowed colorfully in the light of so many candles, then swam into deep shadows. Tyree seated him on a plump brocade pillow on the hearth, where the warmth from the flames felt good against his damp skin.

"I can't stay. The hospital might call. I only came to borrow some candles. I didn't mean to interrupt anything."

"That's perfectly all right." She smiled down at him, a tiny blue-white spark from the diamond in her tooth escaping before she turned away to address the crowd. "I'm sure your friend, what's her name? Judy? will come and get you if they call."

"No, she went out. Storm and all. She was restless, and awfully worried about Lizzy."

"Now that you're here. You must stay. We can call the hospital and give them this number." She raised her voice and said, "Listen, everyone. One of our guests of honor has joined us after all. I want you all to meet Andy Rosemond. No word on his wife, Elizabeth, I'm afraid." Then she turned back to Andy, and looked down at him, her eyes narrowing much like a cat's, her face stained gold from the firelight.

There was a little silence. Andy stared up at her. The emerald folds of her silk dress revealed a medallion of gold, sprinkled with glowing jewels—yellow ones, that splayed out light like the rays of the sun.

She lifted her hand and fingered the medallion, her nails gilded coppery red.

"You know," she finally said. "It's probably a good thing you came over. We've been discussing something. I think we have to tell you about it. We can't put it off any longer."

Suddenly, a sword-gleam of lightning cut through the orange haze in the room, followed by an explosion of thunder. At the same moment, the doors to the room burst open, and Mable and Sarah Zipper stumbled in wild-eyed, their clothes soaked, silver hair plastered to their heads, both of them dripping rainwater across the floor.

"Tyree!" Mable said. "We just saw him! He's out there. I think he's going to do it again. There must be some way we can stop him!"

Ted Bearbower and Steve Locke had been sitting in the stakeout car awaiting two backup patrol cars when the bolt of lightning struck a transformer only a block away. The transformer exploded in a shower of fluorescent white sparks, shooting up into the night sky like a fireworks display, then trailing off to a stream of smoke. The rain began to pelt down in such a squall it kept the strike from igniting the wooden pole to which it was fastened.

Ted radioed in the incident, dismayed at how many more homes had lost power. Several blocks of the peninsula had already been plunged into darkness by the storm, and now at least two-thirds of it was without power. At least before the strike, the light from the surrounding homes had helped illuminate the area around Barry Brownstone's apartment. Now, the entire alley was as dark as the inside of a bat cave.

When, after fifteen minutes and the back-up cars still hadn't arrived, Ted said, "I think we should go ahead and move on this. We've already got Fitz and Melborne. Besides, in this heavy rain, our suspect could slip out of there at any time, and we'd never see him." He put on his shoes.

Locke was silent for a moment. "I don't know," he finally said. "It doesn't feel right to me."

"A piece of cake. We take our flashlights, go up there, take a look through the windows, and hope we're lucky enough to find something suspicious."

"And if we don't, and he confronts us?"

"We tell him we were checking out the neighborhood after the lightning strike. Making sure everything was okay."

Locke nodded. "Yeah. But I doubt he'll buy that."

"Come on. I can't stand being cooped up in this damn car. Between the rain and darkness, we can't see a fucking thing anyway. We're useless here."

"Right," Locke said, but his voice told Ted he wasn't completely convinced.

"We want this guy, don't we? If he's the guy, we want him bad."

"That's for damn sure."

"Then let's move, before we lose him."

"Okay," Locke agreed. "But be careful. We've got water all around us. It's still coming down hard, and the tide's way in."

Ted picked up the car radio. "Fitz? We're gonna move. Get in close and give us some backup."

"Where are our black-and-whites?" Fitz asked.

"The storm's keeping them busy. We have to move anyway. We're totally blind over here. For all we know, the guy's skipped already. See if you can get us a chopper. You guys ready to go?"

"Yeah. I'll take the alley, and Melborne can take the front."

Ted put down the radio, fumbled for his flashlight, slipped it into his pocket, and opened the door on his side of the car. The wind caught the door, buffeting it about so roughly he could barely keep control. "These gusts are goddamned rough," he said as he stepped out into the alley, and found himself knee-deep in swirling water. "Damn it to hell! The tide's in further than I realized." He felt the chill of black seawater run through his bones.

"Surf's up!" Locke gave a humorless laugh as he stepped out into the water on his side of the car. "Watch out for sharks!"

"If this keeps up, the entire peninsula will be underwater by morning. That's probably why the patrol cars haven't arrived."

Lightning flared, and Locke peered up at the night sky, his wet face slicked platinum-white. The dark alley around them flared with opalescent light, then wavered, and faded to black once more. Thunder exploded in their ears, rumbling glass windows, garden gates, and garage doors.

"Holy shit!" Locke said after the ruckus died down. "This is *some* weather!"

Ted slushed through the dark water, swearing under his breath about his ruined shoes and trousers. "I should be home right now," he said in a stage whisper. "A fire in the fireplace, a brew in one hand, and a plate of pasta in the other."

"And I should be at a fancy restaurant with my new date," Locke grumbled.

"Come on," Ted motioned to him. "Let's get this over with so we can go drip-dry." Silently, they made their way toward the stairs that led up to the apartment.

"Listen!" Locke whispered suddenly.

"What?"

"Nothing."

"Huh?"

"Listen to *nothing.*" Locke punched the word nothing.

Ted stopped and looked at him, wondering what the hell he meant. Then it dawned on him. Nothing! Up until the power failure, they had been listening to classical music. Beethoven, Mozart, Tchaikovsky, Mendelssohn—music turned up so loud it could be heard over the storm. Now all he could hear was the howl of wind, and the incessant staccato rapping of the rain.

"Silence. It's fucking eerie after all that music." At the foot of the stairs, Ted pulled out his two-way radio. "Fitz?"

"Right behind you."

"Melborne?"

"On the street side of the house."

"Good. What about the chopper?"

"Officially, they can't. But they're gonna try anyway. May not stay up long, with all this wind and lightning."

"Okay, we're going up." Ted put the radio in his pocket, and took out his flashlight.

They made their way up the stairs to the narrow balcony that fronted the apartment. Ted kept his flashlight gripped in his left hand, leaving his right hand free to draw his gun. The front door to the apartment had a small diamond-shaped window. Ted squinted through it, but could see only a few dark shapes. He drew his revolver, then turned on his flashlight, held it to the window, and swept the interior with the beam.

"See anything?" Locke whispered.

The beam of light stopped on an object. "A briefcase," Ted said and clicked off the light.

"Anyone moving in there?"

"Not that I could see," Ted said.

"Okay, I'll try the windows in front. You cover the one on the side. We can't reach any of the others."

Ted moved around to the side window which was high, and covered with a heavy drape. Nothing there. The wooden floor of the balcony was slippery in the driving rain, so he holstered his gun, and took hold of the balcony railing as he made his way back to Locke. The wind gave an abject moan as it curled around the eaves of the garage-top apartment. It roughly flapped the collar of his jacket against his face. He shivered, feeling the wetness soak through to his skin. I'm getting way too old for this, he told himself. It's time to quit and let the young guys like Locke take over.

When he reached Locke, the wind suddenly died, leaving the air oddly silent, except for the rain. Now he missed the music they had been listening to even more. "You see anything?" he said to Locke who was flashing his light through a small opening in the drapes.

"No. I think this guy's given us the slip, unless he's holed up in the bathroom. No sign of anyone at all. Take a look."

Ted turned on his flashlight, and inspected the small studio apartment. "What a mess!" he commented. "Look at the dust in there. And the burned-out candles." An unmade double bed, an overstuffed chair, clothes strewn about, a bookshelf filled with moldy looking books, a small refrigerator, a stove with a string of onions hanging like white pearls from a metal hook on the wall beside it, bottles of wine, and a wall shelf with a few framed pictures—that was about it.

Without any warning, the lights in the apartment flashed on. The theme from Tchaikovsky's Piano Concerto rang in their ears. Both of them flicked off their flashlights, and jumped back against the wall. Ted felt a jolt of adrenaline, and his heart jerked nervously in his chest.

"Shit!" he hissed, looking at the lights coming on in the houses around them. "Great timing!"

"Good old Tchaikovsky. Now what?" Locke whispered. "No more windows we can reach."

Ted leaned his head back against the wall, and closed his eyes. "I guess we call it a night. I didn't see anything that would justify our breaking in without a warrant. I'd settle for some evidence of drugs, anything to get us in there."

"Let's get out of here!" Locke moved toward the stairs, shoving his flashlight in his pocket. "I didn't like this idea from the start."

Ted stood against the wall, his eyes still closed, listening to the music. So close, but no ball game. He couldn't even bring the guy in for questioning on what little they had. If only he'd spotted one or two of the missing items. The ring. A gold locket. Or had seen blood stains on some of the clothing. Anything at all. He sighed, opened his eyes, and started for the stairs. Then something rattled at his mind, something . . . but he couldn't quite make out what it was. He started down the stairs behind Locke, stopped, then started again. The wind picked up once more, blowing the heavy rain into long silver ribbons. Wait a minute! The music! That was it. That's what was rattling at his brain. The music. It had been playing for over an hour while the power was on. Was it a radio? No. He'd heard no voice, no commercials. A record player? Perhaps. But then maybe, just maybe, *it was a compact disc player!* He didn't remember seeing it, but then he'd been looking for other things.

"Locke!" he gave a short bark.

"Yeah?" Locke had reached the bottom of the stairs.

"Did you see where the music was coming from?"

"Sure. A CD player on the bookshelf."

Ted stood staring down at the young man. Rain dripped off Locke's youthful face, his sprinkling of freckles glowing bronze in the hazy light. Locke stared back at him.

"Jesus Christ!" Locke almost yelled. *"A CD player!"*

"This could be our probable cause. Let's check it out."

Locke took the steps two at a time, both of them reaching the top at the same time. The lights in the houses flickered around them, dimmed, came on again, then went out. The music stopped.

"Make up your fucking mind," Ted growled at the lights. "Can you see it?" he asked Locke who had directed his flashlight through the narrowly parted drapes in the front window.

"Yes."

"Is it a single disc, or changer?" Locke said, flashing his own light through the gap in the drapes.

"Changer!"

"Goddamn!"

"You got the description of the stolen disc player on that list in your pocket?"

Locke fumbled through his inside jacket pocket, his fingers trembling. Ted wondered if it was from the wet, or the tension. "A Sony DiscJocky CD player and changer," he read from the paper. "Holds six discs. We've also got a partial list of some of the missing discs."

Locke snapped off his flashlight. "Now we can go in. Right?"

"It's flimsy. Lots of people own disc players. Just pray it's the right brand." His voice cracked with excitement.

"You think the guy's in there?"

"I think we lost him for now. I think he slipped out with the storm. If we're lucky, the chopper will spot him." Ted took out his hand radio. "Fitz? Melborne? We've got probable cause . . . I hope. Keep your eyes on the street and the alley in case our guy is still here, and makes a break for it."

"Got ya," Fitz said. "Hey! Here come the black-and-whites. And the chopper's circling. The wind's eased a little."

"Great." Ted put the radio away and took out his gun. "At least, we're well covered."

Locke drew his gun, and stood to one side of he front door while Ted stood on the other. Ted rapped loudly on the door. "Police! Open the door." Silence. The wind stirred and whistled around the eaves. "Police! Open up!"

Locke reached over and tried the doorknob. "Locked."

"Kick it in!" Ted ordered.

Locke gave him a surprised glance.

"You're a hell of a lot younger than I am," Ted growled.

"Sure," Locke grinned, his crooked white teeth glistening like tiny ice cubes in the dim light. "That's half the fun." He gave the door a violent kick, breaking the lock, splintering the wooden door frame, and sending the door flying open.

Inside, the apartment smelled of stale candle wax and cold, damp dust. The two of them fanned out, and made a careful, but unsuccessful, search for the suspect. Then Ted went to the disc player and checked it out. Bingo! A Sony 6 DiscJocky! Exactly the way it was spelled out on his list. Next to the disc player was a stack of gold discs, all of them classical music. Schubert, Liszt, Handel, Chopin—and all of them on the list.

Locke opened the closet door, and let out a long, low whistle.

"What?" Ted asked.

"Take a look at this, will you! All this stuff! I'd bet you even money we'll find a lot of these items on our list. There's an opal ring here that fits the description. And a gold heart! Jesus! We've hit pay dirt!"

Ted took a look, flashing his light up and down the shelves. "Talk about your sickos!"

"I'll check the briefcase." Locke took the case to the bed, and snapped open the briefcase. "Christ! It's stuffed with money! And here's his plane tickets," he said, opening up a travel folder. "Out of Ontario, to San Diego, then to Paris. For tomorrow morning, early. A few more hours and we'd have missed him." He gave a grim smile.

"Yeah, but where is the guy now?" Ted said.

"Ahh, Ted . . . listen," Locke's voice was a whisper.

"We've got a passport here," Ted said looking through the rest of the stuff in the case. "Barry Brownstone, age 32. This sucker looks a lot like that movie actor, what's his name?"

"Ted!" Locke called, his voice husky. "Get a load of what I found."

"Robert Redford!" Ted said. "That's who he looks like. Should be easy to spot."

"Teddy Bear!"

"What?"

Locke held something up, but Ted had trouble getting it in his flashlight beam. "Come here, and take a look at these!" Locke sounded breathless.

Up close, Ted flashed his light on the object in Locke's hand. "A pair of shoes?"

"Birkenstocks! With tar on the bottoms!"

"I'll be damned! Fall in a pot of jelly and find some peanut butter to go with it!"

"I'd bet my paycheck they'll match the prints on the boat."

"Locke, my boy, I love you!" Ted inspected the shoes carefully. On the top of one he found a number of brown stains. "And if my guess is right, these are blood stains. Probably one of our victims. It won't take long to see if we've got a match."

"You think our forced entry will hold up in court?"

"You bet. We only came here to question him. We saw the luggage and the disc-player and the bloody shoes when we looked through the window. With the evidence we've found, it's open and shut. We only have to justify the entry."

"Yeah, but. . . ."

"If you want to make certain this holds up, then we saw the shoes through the window, too."

"Right."

"A technicality."

"Right."

"No." Ted frowned. "On second thought, *I saw the shoes, not you.* I'm not going to drag you into this. You've got a long career ahead of you."

Ted knew it was wrong. But he was willing to do anything, even perjure himself, to get this maniac out of action. Whenever he'd tried to sleep the past few nights, he'd dreamt about the anguished look on the face of the hospitalized Duff girl, and the bloated and mutilated body of her slain sister. He'd never made a false statement in court. But he'd never personally run across anyone like this Brownstone guy—someone who left a trail of dead bodies so long he wondered if they would ever come to the end of it. He'd make sure this case was nailed shut, then he'd get out of the business—buy a small place down near Julian, nestled in the pines—maybe open a gourmet restaurant. And he'd sleep real good nights, knowing this demented son-of-a-bitch wouldn't be out there draining someone's blood or chewing on a chunk of their flesh like an after-dinner mint.

"Better call forensics," Ted said. "And I want a round-the-clock watch on this place until we pick this guy up. I'm sure we've scared him off by now, but on the off chance that he comes back, I don't want to miss him."

"I'll put out an APB. Let me have the passport photo for a description. He can't have gone too far. Someone was moving around in here earlier. And he's gotta be on foot. There's no way we would have missed a car. The chopper will spot him." Locke took the passport, and turned his flashlight on it. "You're right, he'll be easy to identify. Hot damn! It's open and shut! This is gonna be easier than I expected. And you can thank the Rattigan woman for the tip."

"Yeah," Ted said, musing about that for a moment. "But I'm going to want some straight answers from her about this whole thing. How she knew about this guy. And what the hell she had to do with all this. Something's way off center here."

"We can let forensics take care of the rest of this," Locke said, and turned toward the door. "You and I can get out there and find this guy." Suddenly a deep-throated growl echoed through the darkened room. "Ted? Hear that? I think the guy's got a dog!"

"Nah, we checked." The growl came again, from the darkest corner of the room.

"Then what the hell is growling at us?"

"I don't know," Ted said, feeling a rash of goose-bumps raise on his skin. He cautiously flashed his light toward the sound. The beam outlined the white porcelain door of the small refrigerator, then the small stainless-steel sink. In the far corner it picked up something large and dark, something moving slightly.

"Shit! What is *that?*" Ted cried. He put his hand on his gun and raised the flashlight beam. Its round circle of cold light found the outline of a man, not an animal. He looked almost like a street person, his black overcoat sagged, his dark cap pulled down almost to his brows, his hair jutting out from the sides of the cap. And the eyes! Jesus Christ! The eyes were like the dark fixed pupils of some corpses he'd seen. The flashlight glinted off the eyes, turning them ruby-red, the way a wolf's shine in the head-lights of a car.

"What the hell!" Locke cried. "How did he get in here?" Locke drew his gun.

"Police," Ted said. "Do you live here?"

The man moved forward slightly. Ted drew his gun, slowly, so as not to alarm him. Locke steadied his. The man looked at Locke, and then back to Ted. "I said, do you live here?" Ted repeated. "Are you Barry Brownstone?"

"It's him, all right," Locke said. "The guy in the passport photo."

"Okay," Ted said, keeping his gun leveled on the man. "Let's make this easy. You're under arrest. Anything you say may be used against you in a court of law. You have the right to an attorney. . . ." He rattled off the man's rights. The guy stood there staring at him. A real psycho. The man didn't flinch, didn't protest. He wanted to get him cuffed as quickly as possible, but he wasn't taking any chances. He put down his flashlight, and pulled out his pocket radio.

"Fitz? Melborne? We've got our suspect. Get up here and give us a hand."

"Coming right up," Fitz answered.

Ted heard the detective's footsteps on the wooden staircase. Two uniformed officers, guns drawn, jogged up the stairs behind Fitz. Ted let out a small sigh of relief. The five of them should be able to handle this.

"Melborne's on his way," Fitz said.

Locke moved toward the suspect. "Turn around, skuzzball," he ordered.

"Pat him down good," Ted warned, keeping the guy in his gun sights. "We don't want any surprises."

"Hands against the wall," Locke shouted. "Legs spread!" But the man only stared at Locke.

"Wanna play hardball? Okay." Locke reached for the man, grabbed his arm, and started to twist him around toward the wall. Suddenly, with one hand, the man swung at Locke, palm open, bashing the young man across the face. Locke flew backward, eyes wide with shock, his legs scrambling to find a hold on the floor. The man moved toward him. Locke, still off balance, fired his gun. The bullet grazed the man's shoulder, but didn't stop him as he moved toward Locke again.

The two uniformed policemen jumped to either side of the man. "Hold it!" one of them yelled, his gun aimed at the suspect. But the man continued to move on Locke who had lost his flashlight but had found his footing. He held his gun firmly in both hands. The man was almost on top of Locke, and showed no signs of stopping.

"Goddamn!" Locke said, and aimed his gun to fire again. The man didn't slow, but instead, he lunged at Locke before he could squeeze off another shot. One of the uniforms, a panicked spark in his eyes, fired a wild shot hitting the man in the leg. But the guy didn't flinch. Instead, he grabbed Locke by the arms, ripped the gun from his hands and instead of turning it on him, tossed it aside.

Fitz took aim, ready to fire, but Ted yelled at him. "No! You might hit Locke!" Ted rushed the man. With a snarl, he grabbed him around the neck with one arm, and pressed hard with a choke hold. The man gave a tremendous shake, and threw him off as easily as a panther shaking a bird off its back. Ted slammed roughly against the wall. The suspect went back to Locke, and ripped away the sleeves of his coat and shirt with one tremendous movement. He grabbed Locke's bare arms with both hands, and dug his fingernails deeply into the skin. Blood oozed out of the wounds. Locke let out a piercing screech.

"Get this guy off me! For God's sake! He's killing me!" Locke flailed, trying to break free, but the man's grip didn't slip, his nails continued to penetrate Locke's arms. Even in the dark room, Ted could see a trail of glistening blood wind its way down between Locke's fingers.

"This son-of-a-bitch has to be on PCP!" Ted yelled. "All that shit about latent genes!"

All four of them piled on the man and jerked him backward. Ted tried to keep his hold on the man, but found it impossible. The moment he got a hold, the guy shook him off. He shook them all off, one after the other. Each time they tackled him, he broke loose almost instantly. Ted felt a nasty bite of adrenaline hit, and his heart thumped painfully. Jesus! This guy was really crazed!

"You okay, Locke!" Ted yelled, straining to get a grip on the man's right arm so they could cuff him.

"Yeah," Locke said. "But now I'll have to get a fucking rabies shot! Just get him the hell off me!"

Fitz roared, trying to get the man's left arm twisted around for Ted to cuff.

With a vicious back swing of his arms, the man struck both Ted and Fitz. The blow caught Ted in the gut. The pain hit him like a knife and he retched. He fumbled for, and found, his gun and flashlight, but for an instant he couldn't breathe. He sucked in, panicked by the sensation that all the oxygen had been slammed out of his body. He retched again, then managed to pull in a long, rasping breath. Fitz, a large lean man about five years younger than Ted, doubled over and slumped to the floor.

The two uniformed officers moved in holding their guns, ready to fire, but with Locke in the way, they hesitated. As they did, the man turned and took them both out with wicked kicks, the soles of his heavy shoes cracking sharply against the side of their heads. One of the officer's guns fired wild before he dropped.

"Locke! Shoot him! Get some lead in this guy, for God's sake!"

The man turned back toward Ted. Once again, his face had that hollow look, and his eyes stared like two dark-blue crystals, icy and unblinking. Ted felt himself go feverish, a slick, hot sweat breaking out all over his body. He'd seen this type of thing before, someone so psycho or pumped up on drugs he could probably take a dozen bullets and keep on ticking. You had to hit them just right. Take their brains out through the back of their head. That's about the only thing that would stop them. The Rattigan woman had warned him this guy would be strong.

"Locke, can you reach your gun?" Ted took a quick look in Locke's direction. The young man had slumped into the crazed man's arms, his eyes open, but his body limp. "Locke? What's wrong." Locke's mouth moved slightly, but no sound came out.

"Locke!" Ted yelled. "Ah, Christ!" The crazed man took a step toward him. Ted couldn't fire, not with Locke in the way.

Melborne, a short, stout detective suddenly bolted through the open door of the apartment, gun in hand. "What the hell's going on in here? Jesus!"

The man swung around and glared at Melborne. Then, with an agile twist, he folded Locke's limp body over one arm, and headed for the front door. Locke just hung there, limply. Ted heard a slight moan, and saw Locke's hands fanning the air feebly.

Melborne raised his gun, started to fire, but hesitated, obviously afraid he'd hit Locke. The small, round detective blocked the doorway, a look of total surprise on his face as the man reached him, lifted him off the ground and, with his free hand, carried him out onto the balcony. With little effort, he chucked him over the railing. Melborne hit the water-flooded pavement below with a dull thump like a bundle of dirty laundry, then let out a piercing screech.

By the time Ted reached the balcony rail, Melborne was sitting on the pavement, seawater up to his stomach, nursing one of his legs and groaning loudly. Brownstone and Locke had disappeared.

"You okay?" Ted called.

"Leg's . . . broken," Melborne moaned.

"Sit tight."

The lights suddenly came back on again, lighting the rainy night with a jarring incandescence. Behind Ted, the CD player jolted on, pealing out the last strains of Tchaikovsky's Piano Concerto, while overhead the police helicopter's rotor throbbed rhythmically, circling the area. Its searchlight penetrated the heavy rain relentlessly. There was no sign

of the suspect or Locke. The night had swallowed
them up. What the hell had been wrong with Locke?
Shock? No. The fucker shot him up with something.
The same stuff he'd used on his victims.

Ted bolted down the stairs three at a time, and
fought the floodwater to his car. His legs felt like
over-stretched rubber bands, and he could barely
move his arms. He grabbed for the mike and contacted the chopper.

"Ocean One, we've lost the guy," Ted said. His
fatigue made his voice shake. "He's got a hostage.
Detective Locke. He can't get far. You should be
able to spot them."

"We'll check," came the reply.

"If you can get a clean head shot, waste this guy.
Just don't hit our man!"

Ted picked up the radio again, and called dispatch. "We've got a nine, nine, nine here," he
yelled. "Several officers down. Get us an ambulance, code three! Our suspect is loose, and has
taken one of our men with him. Get everything out
on the street you can muster, storm or no storm."

"Yes, sir!"

Ted hung up, got out of the car, and stood beside
it. He searched the dark shadows of the alley
around him. The wind whipped in a frenzy around
him, rattling windows all along the alley. The rain,
blowing in Ted's face, had turned much colder. He
shivered. Fitz appeared at the top of the stairs, rubbing his head. He sat down on the top step and
looked at Ted.

"Holy Christ! What in green hell happened?"
Fitz moaned.

"He's got Locke."

"How in the fuck—"

"He used something on him . . . I don't know what. Whatever it was, it put him out of it. Totally." Ted looked around the alley again. He ground his teeth together, something he did under extreme stress. It made his jaws ache. "How are the two uniforms?"

"Coming around. A couple of broken ribs maybe."

The car radio crackled on. Ted leaned in and snatched it up. "Yeah?"

"Ocean One here. Sorry, we don't see anything moving out there at all. Nothing except the flood tide. Wind's getting too strong. Gotta go in."

"Hey! We're up to our asses in water down here! You have to help find this guy! We can hardly move!"

"Sorry, Teddy Bear. Too dangerous. We'll be splattered all over the peninsula if we don't put her down in a hurry. We went out against orders as it was. Gonna get our asses chewed."

"Get us some more black and whites," Ted yelled.

"Afraid not. Got another homicide a few blocks from the Pavilion. Young woman. Looks like your perp has been working overtime. We've got every available man out on the street. Going to try for a SWAT team, but it'll take some time."

"Ah, shit!" Ted yelled, slamming the mike down. "Fitz, get down here. We've lost the chopper. No more uniforms for now. Let's roll."

"What about the others?" Fitz said, making his way down the stairs."

"I've called it in. They'll be okay. Come on."

Ted started the engine while Fitz folded his lanky legs into the car. They moved slowly, edging through the surging water. Ted scrutinized every dark corner for the slightest movement. They'd find the motherfucker! He couldn't last long dragging Locke with him. And when they did, Ted would have the great pleasure of blowing the creep into so many chunks he'd look like a five-thousand-piece puzzle.

"Hang on, Locke," he growled, checking the brakes to make certain the deep water hadn't damaged them. "We're coming to get you, fellow. We're coming to get you."

A wave of guilt swept over him. Locke had been reluctant about moving on the apartment. The guy had a gut feeling. If there was anything Ted had learned to trust, it was that gut feeling. He should have listened. Damn it! *He should have listened!*

Chapter Seven

The room had an odd smell. Elizabeth opened a door on the darkness that had overwhelmed her for so long. A white light stabbed at her eyes. She let out a little moan, and closed her eyes. Where the hell was she? What had happened to her? She opened her eyes again, slowly this time.

White walls, a strange bed, and that odd smell. Then it hit her. She was in a hospital. But why? An accident? No, wait, she'd been sick with the flu. That was it. And something else had happened. Something she couldn't remember. She couldn't even remember how she'd gotten here. The only thing she recalled was the fight she and Andy had. She'd stormed off to bed, angry. And then the dreams. Strange, disjointed dreams.

She tried to lift her arm, but it felt like damp clay. She wanted to find the bell so she could ring for the nurse and find out what was wrong with her. Was Andy here? She lifted her head slightly, but the effort sent a sharp pain through her head.

"Andy?" Her voice was barely a whisper, but it

echoed around the small room. Glass walls? The room had glass walls. How strange. She moved her arm again, this time lifting it so she could see her hand. A long silver needle was imbedded under the skin on the back of her hand. Attached to the needle was a thin, plastic tube. She tried to see where the tube went, but couldn't move her head enough to manage it.

"Andy?" she called again. The effort exhausted her. She let her hand fall back on the bed, and closed her eyes. She wanted to reach out and touch Andy, to have him hold her hand and stroke her aching head, the way he always did when she was sick. Damn. Why wasn't he here? She let out a soft sigh. She didn't have the strength to be angry.

The darkness sucked at her again, pulling her into it, out of the light. She let go, and allowed herself to drift in an endless black void.

HE moved through the wind and rain, his heavy load, along with the wound in his leg, slowing him. At last, he reached the entrance to the Balboa Pier. No one else had braved the weather. Gone were the usual fishermen, the restless teenagers, and the hungry patrons of Ruby's Cafe at the far end of the pier. The only sign of life was the iridescent glow from Ruby's pink neon sign that wavered through the watery night.

His captive, slung over his shoulder, squirmed mildly, and gave a quiet moan. "Only a short distance more, my friend. I'm sorry to drag this out so long. But I had no choice." He made his way up the ramp and out along the wooden planks of the old pier. His leg burned where the bullet had pierced the tissue. But he felt no real pain. Beneath him, giant waves pummeled against the pilings. The pier undulated under his feet like the whipping tail of some prehistoric animal. Timbers groaned. Sea foam sprayed across his path.

When he reached the end of the pier, he put the man down, and propped him against one of the fishermen's benches. He looked around. The air was filled with the strong smell of ozone mingled with an aroma of stale hamburgers, grease-soaked French fries and milk-sweet malts. A sign on the door of the cafe read: CLOSED DUE TO STORM. A flash of lightning off to his left startled him. It was an awesome night. It was too bad he didn't have more time to enjoy the energy that churned around him.

He knelt beside the young man and lifted his face with his hand. So handsome. So bursting with life. The man's eyes flickered open, unrecognizing, unfocused. Beautiful brown eyes with sandy lashes. The youth smelled of spicy aftershave and traces of Irish Spring soap, peppermint Life Savers, and the rich silk of his suit. He rummaged through the jacket pockets and found a leather folder. On opening it, he found a police badge and ID. The name jumped out at him. STEVEN EDWARD LOCKE. Damn it to hell! He hated knowing the name of his prey. It made the whole thing too personal. He stuffed the ID into the young man's left hand, then lifted the other hand, and found a school ring marked "Orange Coast College," slipped it off the man's finger, and put it into his own pocket. At least, he had his lucky talisman.

In the distance, he heard the faint wail of a siren through the noise of the storm. He had only minutes now. They were close, and even the storm could not hide him—not from a violent retaliatory group of men. After all, he'd taken one of their own. He stood up and flung off his ragged overcoat. In his shirt pocket he found his blade. The pier rumbled, twisted, swayed, but he held his stance and bent back down to the young man. The young policemen looked at him, blinking, trying to fathom what was happening. He pulled open the man's jacket, took off his tie and then peeled the damp shirt away from his neck.

"Who. . . ." But that was all the young man could say.

"I am the Dark Angel," he whispered. Then, his gleaming blade poised, he began his work. The man's skin turned warm under his fingers as a rich gush of blood flooded from the small wound. The clean-sliced opening on the neck of the robust young man felt even warmer as he placed his thirsty mouth against it and drank.

Rain blew so hard against the window of the police car that the windshield wipers couldn't clear it away. Ted squinted through the watery blur. Where was the bastard, anyway? It didn't seem possible he could have made it this far. The son-of-a-bitch had probably taken refuge in one of the houses along the beach. Well, by God, they'd road-block the whole damn peninsula and do a house-to-house search. No matter how bad the storm got. He'd bring in the whole fucking Marine Corps, if he had to!

Fitz suddenly leaned forward, "What's that?" He pointed in the direction of the pier.

"Someone's moving out there!" Ted swerved the car, and headed toward the pier. "Only a fool or our maniac would be out there in this storm. Damn! I wish we had the chopper."

Fitz picked up the radio. "This is 43-210. I think we've spotted the suspect at the end of Balboa Pier. Where the hell's our backup?"

The radio crackled. "We've got three cars searching the immediate area. But it's slow going with the flood."

"Well, get them over here! Let 'em swim if they have to."

"Is the hostage with him?"

"We can't tell yet."

Ted hesitated for a moment, doubting the good sense of taking a car out onto the end of the pier in such foul weather. Several piers that lined the Southern California coast had snapped away in storms less violent than this one. He knew that if he went over the side, or if part of the pier broke loose, that would be it. It would be difficult, if not impossible to survive in that sea. Then he thought about Locke. His foot hit the gas pedal. The tires lost traction, and the engine raced as he drove out onto the wooden planks. The pier swayed beneath them. Ted's stomach lurched as the car slid sideways toward the slender railing. Even in darkness and rain he could see the monstrous breakers rumbling in against the pilings. The dark waves surged in almost as high as the pier itself. He turned the car into the slide and managed to gain some control.

As they approached the end of the pier and the white building that housed Ruby's Cafe, Ted saw a dark figure standing on the edge of the railing. It was their suspect all right, doing a tightrope act on the rain-slicked edge of wood. "How the hell can he do that!" he cried. "In all this wind?"

"Not for long, he won't," Fitz said. "Jesus! He's gonna go over!"

"I hope the bastard breaks his fucking neck! Do you see Locke?"

"No. Wait! Yeah, he's over there . . . by that bench."

Ted floored the gas pedal once more, and swung the car around to the side of Ruby's Cafe. He prayed the brakes hadn't gotten wet as he slammed them on. The car skidded several feet on the slick wood and stopped. "Use the Taser on the guy. That should stop him." He climbed out of the car, grabbed his Taser in one hand and a shotgun in the other.

"Locke?" Ted called. Only the howl of the wind and sea answered him. He ran around the width of Ruby's cafe, his shoes sliding precariously in the wet. He stopped about ten feet from where the suspect stood poised on the narrow pier railing, his arms arched in the air, somehow keeping his balance against the furious wind and rocking of the pier pilings. Then, just to his left, Ted saw Locke propped up against one of the wooden benches. His eyes were open, but he wasn't moving.

"Locke! Damn it Fitz, cover me will you? I'm gonna get Locke out of there and into the car."

"Go for it," Fitz said.

Ted sprinted toward Locke, all the time keeping his eye on the man poised atop the railing. He put down his guns when he reached Locke, lifted him away from the bench, and cradled him in his arms. "Locke? Buddy? You okay? Come on. We're gonna get you out of here ASAP."

"Hey!" Fitz yelled. "What the—"

Ted looked up just in time to see the man on the rail lower his arms toward the violent churning water below the pier. Then he pushed off with the soles of his shoes, and plunged head first into the ocean. The noise of the storm was so loud he couldn't tell when the man hit the water.

"Son-of-a-bitch! He jumped!" Fitz raced to the side of the pier and stared into the water. "Christ! A humungous wave hit him. Slammed him into the pilings. That's all she wrote for that guy! We'll probably find the body somewhere off Point Magu in a few days."

"Okay, get on the horn and get some medics out here quick," Ted ordered. "Or see if there's any way the chopper can pick us up. Locke doesn't look good." He put his fingers on Locke's carotid artery. That's when he saw the wound. A small, clean slash. Only a small amount of blood oozed out. "Ah, Jesus. He's cut! The fucking bastard cut him! Let's get him into the car. I think it's faster if we take him to Hoag ourselves." Ted lifted his partner. Locke's body was dead weight. "Hey, buddy, you got a late date tonight. Remember? A pretty lady." But Locke didn't respond. His eyes, wide open, their sandy lashes beaded with water, looked at nothing. Ted felt a cold sickness creeping over him. In the distance he heard the wail of their backup cars approaching.

"Let's move it," he told Fitz. "Flood or no flood, we're gonna get him to the hospital."

In the car, Fitz drove while Ted sat in the back seat cradling Locke's body. "He's ice-cold. All this damn water. Come on fellow, talk to me! You're okay. We've got you."

Ted looked down at Locke. Christ! He didn't look right. He didn't look right at all! His hands were paper-white, and in one of them he was grasping his police badge and ID like an infant holding a rattle. What in the hell had that guy done to him?

Andy sat by the fire in Tyree's living room, feeling a giddy wave of intoxication roll over him. He wasn't certain if it were from the Bloody Mary Tyree had given him, or the comforting warmth of the fire. He shouldn't just sit there, he should be on the phone to the hospital. But the effort of finding the telephone in Tyree's house seemed too much for him to manage.

Tyree and the Zipper sisters were huddled together in the corner of the room, discussing something. Andy couldn't help notice how agitated they all seemed. But then, maybe what he was drinking made it appear that way. When he moved his head, the entire room tilted. He lifted the glass of Bloody Mary to his mouth and took a swallow. Just *one* of these, he told himself. Then he had to go home and call the hospital. Jesus, the stuff was hot! It felt as if it glowed on the way to his stomach. He raised his glass again and emptied it.

He looked over at the bar, where Boo was mixing drinks. Beauregard Rattigan—now there was an odd, but rather likeable man. He'd chatted with him for a few minutes after the Zipper sisters had made their dramatic appearance. Gallant, humorous, and handsome, in a peculiar way. His nose was cut a bit too narrow, and his mouth was round and soft— almost feminine. But he'd slapped Andy on the back in a warm greeting, and expressed genuine interest in his book.

Tyree and the Zippers continued their conference. Andy glanced around the room at the rest of the people. Two young women stood by the front window gesturing rather wildly as they chatted. One of them was almost six-feet tall, with golden-blond hair. She wore a puffy yellow dress of raw silk that made her look like a giant snapdragon. The other woman was short and plump, in a long flowing purple dress, with ropes and ropes of pearls twined around her neck. He wondered what all of them were discussing that made them so animated.

Finally, Tyree turned away from the two older women and raised her arms, trying to get the attention of everyone in the room. "It's time," she said. Andy noticed a tight little twitching of the skin under her eyes. "We must start our meeting," she said. "We have some terribly important things to discuss. Andy, won't you come over and sit on one of the sofas?" Tyree took his hands in a motherly fashion, and led him over to the grouping of sofas and chairs which were full. But as they approached, two people got up and made room for him.

"Could I use the phone first?" Andy asked.

"This won't take long. Besides, I left a message for you with Dr. Foxhoven. If there's any change, he'll call you here."

Andy sat down on the sofa, a little stunned by Tyree's audacity. Lizzy was his responsibility, not hers. Yet, she constantly seemed to be taking charge. Well, as soon as their little meeting was over, he'd get out the car and, storm or no storm, he would get to the hospital, and stay there until he knew Lizzy was okay.

Tyree picked up a small glass bell from the coffee table and rang it. The sound cut through the hum of conversation in the room. Within seconds the room was silent, except for a cough or two. A few people cleared their throats.

Tyree stood in the middle of the room, and turned slowly around until she'd made a complete circle. Then in a low throated voice she said, "We must begin." She paused, and looked over at Andy. For no reason that he could think of, her look washed over him like a chilled breeze. He broke out in a rash of giant goose bumps. "It appears," she said, "that we have run out of time."

* * *

In the emergency room, silence held court. The large round clock on the wall did not have an audible tick. No machines whirred. Even the nurse's shoes were silent. Ted wanted noise. He wanted a hurdy-gurdy band, a rock video, a blaring TV, a drum-and-fife-corps—loud, discordant, nerve-jarring noise! Anything at all to break the terrible silence. Silence was death.

Fitz stood leaning against the far wall. He stared into space, unblinking, his mouth slightly ajar, his breathing shallow, his face the color of aged parchment.

"We'd better take him now," the orderly said to Ted, putting his hand on the gurney.

"No!" Ted ordered. "Not yet!"

The orderly backed off, and went to stand next to Fitz who coughed and shifted his position against the wall.

Ted looked down at the leather folder in his hand. Locke's badge and ID. He turned them over and over, wondering what he was supposed to do with them. He finally slipped them into his pocket where he couldn't see them. But their weight pressed against his side, more burdensome than the weight of his revolver.

"Ted—" Fitz began.

"In a minute!"

Ted looked down at his partner on the gurney. The young man's chest was bare. Here and there a gel-like substance glistened where the trauma crew had placed electric paddles in a vain attempt to restart Locke's heart.

"We could keep trying," the doctor had said.

"But he's been without oxygen for a long time. He lost too much blood. There are some things worse than death."

Ted understood. Locke would not have wanted to continue living with half a brain, or less. He'd been too robust, too active, to live like a vegetable for the rest of his life. Ted picked up the shirt that Locke had been wearing. Despite the soaking rain, it still smelled strongly of Locke's new aftershave. He lifted Locke, and tugged on his shirt, buttoning it carefully. Then he took the silk jacket that Locke had bought that morning and pulled it on over the shirt. That was better. Somewhere else, someone else would take them off again. But when Locke arrived in the bowels of the hospital in whatever room they used to cut up people after they died, Ted wanted him to look dignified. He deserved that. With his fingertips, he gently brushed back strands of sand-colored hair from the youth's forehead, settling them neatly into place. Then, for just a moment, he gathered Locke up in his arms and held him close.

"Okay, son," Ted said, letting him go. He arranged the young man's pale hands so they wouldn't slip off the side of the gurney. He let his fingers linger for a second on the sprinkling of amber freckles on the back of Locke's hand, then pulled away. He turned toward the orderly. "You can take him now."

The orderly nodded. He unfolded a sheet and covered the young man, then pushed the cart through the trauma room door and down the hall.

Ted felt in his pocket for the folder. "What

hould I do with this? And the rest of his personal hings?" His throat ached. He tried to swallow, but ound it impossible.

Fitz stood up away from the wall, shoved his hands nto his pockets, and shrugged. "Next of kin?"

Ted thought about it. "He's got a mother. Nancy. She lives in Portland, Connecticut. I should be the one to call."

Fitz nodded. "Unless you want the chief to do t."

Ted shook his head. "No." His belly tightened and felt as if a tangle of hot wires had invaded it. "And there's . . . a girl. He had a date." He looked at his watch. "She'll be waiting for him. I should let her know he . . . isn't coming." Ted stood in the middle of the room, not knowing where to go, or what to do first. The ache in his throat intensified. The silence of the room overwhelmed him. The only thing he could hear was the slight thumping of the gurney wheels from somewhere down the hall. Even that small sound faded.

Fitz walked over to him. "Come on, Teddy Bear," he said softly. "We'd better go. We've got a lot of reports to write." He took Ted's arm and gently steered him toward the door. "You okay?"

"No. I'm not okay." Ted swallowed, and finally managed to get rid of the pain in the back of his throat.

"Yeah, well at least the son-of-a-bitch who did this is at the bottom of the ocean now. A big chunk of fish food."

Ted stopped, and turned to look at him. "We're not absolutely certain of that."

"Well, if he's not," Fitz said. "Then the guy's indestructible, for Christ's sake! I mean, who could live through all that? What do you think? That this guy can tap dance on water?"

Ted shook his head, and began to walk, slowly at first, then faster, feeling some sense of destination nagging him. "I've got questions. I want answers."

"We'll find them," Fitz said, dogging his heels.

"I'll find them."

Outside, three patrol cars stood empty. Their occupants huddled together in the open parking lot, braving the wind and rain. One of the uniformed men was smoking, using his hands to cup the cigarette to keep it dry. When Ted approached, they all turned and looked, the question written on their faces. He walked up to the men, and looked at each one of them. Young men about Locke's age, men whose lives had just begun.

He shook his head, no.

"Shit!" said the man with the cigarette, dropping it on the asphalt, and crushing it with the heel of his shoe. The others were silent. They dispersed slowly, climbing back into their squad cars. But, for an instant, he had read in each of their faces both grief and relief. The grief for the loss of Locke's life. The relief that it was someone else who had died, not them. Not this time.

"Fitz, will you get a ride with one of the black-and-whites?"

"Aren't you going back?"

"Not yet. I've got something to do."

"Look, Ted, whatever—"

"No! It *can't* wait until morning."

Fitz looked at him for a long moment, then nodded his understanding. "See you whenever. Take it easy."

Ted got into his car. It smelled of Locke's new cologne. He sat there until all the other cars had left the lot. Then he let out a yell. It sounded, he thought, like the trumpeting of an injured elephant. Locke would have said it sounded like a wounded Teddy Bear. He yelled again. Blood rushed to his face and stung his cheeks, which made him feel better. He started the engine, then turned on the radio and windshield wipers. The rhythmic beat of the wipers pleased him. He liked the loud music that blared from the radio speakers. He liked the howl of the wind and drumming of the rain. No more silence.

He pulled the car out of the lot, and drove down Superior Avenue toward the peninsula. The flooding had increased. Lightning flashed somewhere up ahead. Thunder rumbled, a long, low, continuous sound that seemed to go on forever. Once on the peninsula he drove slowly, the deep water beneath him seeping into the car along the bottom edge of the doors. Familiar places looked strange in the storm. Buildings he'd seen hundreds of times appeared warped, like the reflection in a fun-house mirror. It felt as if he were moving through some nightmare where everything was lifelike, but distorted.

Two-thirds of the way down the peninsula, something inside the motor shorted out. The car stopped dead in the middle of the street. Without a word, he climbed out of the car, and began wading through icy black water that flowed around his knees. His destination was still a long way, especially in this foul weather, but nothing in heaven or hell was going to stop him from getting there.

HE was tired. The sea's churning undercurrent did its best to drag him down to the ocean floor. Great tubes of seawater sucked at him. But he managed to break free long enough to catch his breath just at the moment when his lungs took fire and threatened to consume him. The pain from the bullet wound in his leg gnawed at him like a vicious little animal with long, sharp teeth. His bones throbbed from the pounding he'd taken against the pier pilings. His feet finally hit firm sand, and at that moment he knew he would survive. The combers roared in and broke over his head, but as long as the sand was there, he could make his way to shore.

Several yards out of the churning ocean, he stopped to rest on a sharp embankment of rock that was higher than the floodtide. The storm swirled around him, its briny smell invading his lungs. He sat with his legs drawn up and his head resting on his knees. It was imperative to make new plans as quickly as possible. He had no way to get to his passport now, or his plane tickets, but he still had the keys to a safety-deposit box with enough money to get him by. He could replace the passport and take on a whole new persona. The blood ran thick and slow through his veins, and an overwhelming fatigue tugged at him. But he couldn't give in to the exhaustion. Not in his weakened state.

With considerable effort, he wrenched himself off the embankment and began to slosh through the floodwater. He headed toward Coast Highway above the tidewater. As he walked, he thought about the artist woman with the gray eyes. He saw her pale hair gleaming in the soft night light—remembered the sweet clean scent of her body. Just the thought of her renewed his energy. The usual wave of regret rolled over him. Had he taken too much from her? Had she died? He'd heard the sirens and knew she had been taken to the hospital. He had to know. Going to the hospital would put him in extreme peril. But he needed to know if she'd survived. Whatever vile acts he had committed in his life, this was one time he prayed to have failed. He crossed Coast Highway, noting that the usual heavy traffic was thinned by the storm, and headed up the hill on Superior Avenue toward Hoag Memorial Hospital. The sharp bite of pain from the bullet turned to a burning sensation. Lightning flared, turning night to day. A car slowed and stopped next to him, and a man rolled down the window.

"Can I give you a lift?" the man asked. "Bad night to be walking."

He turned to smile at the man. "Thanks. But I'm too wet. I'll ruin your car's seats." Then he looked down at his leg, and at the blood stain on his pants. "Besides, I took a tumble and cut myself. Appears I'm bleeding some."

The man reached across the seat, and opened the car door. "Don't worry about it."

He paused for a second, then dutifully got into

the car and closed the door. Never pick up a stranger, he told the man silently. "Thanks," he said aloud.

"Going to the hospital?" The man was quite young, but had thinning hair and crinkly eyes.

"Yes"

"I'll take you to the emergency entrance then."

He nodded. It was a good thing he'd taken succor from the young policeman. Otherwise this good Samaritan would have done his last good deed. He smelled of sweet aromatic tobacco, vodka, shoe polish, and Bay-rum aftershave. The scents made him feel better. He would get through this somehow. As soon as he found out about the woman, he'd get the hell away from here.

"Need some help getting into the emergency room?" the young man asked.

"No. I'll be fine. No sense both of us getting soaked. "Thanks."

The man let him out directly in front of the emergency room door. As soon as the car disappeared into the night and rain, he began to walk. He would blend into the shadows. It was far too late for visitors. The hospital would be quiet, and anyone wandering about would be noticed. They might be watching for him. Tyree would know who was responsible for the woman's condition. He had pushed things too far. And from the look on the faces of the Zipper sisters, none of them would tolerate him any longer. He made his way to the rear of the hospital where it was pitch-dark. The best way in was through the belly of the building. He'd find his way up to the artist woman's room using the fire stairs. He would never forget her scent. It would lead him to her. That is, if she were still alive.

He found an unlocked window at street level and opened it. Slowly, silently, he snaked through the opening, thankful he was still wearing his black clothing. He made his way through dark rooms and dim corridors, then wound his way up back stairs. The aromas around him were both terrible and intriguing. The smell of death and birth. He reached the third floor without finding the scent of the woman. He leaned heavily against the wall, hoping none of the nurses would venture out of their station to check on patients right at that moment.

The burning of the bullet wound turned to a deep ache. It throbbed, uncomfortable, but reminded him he was alive. Yet, the thought gave him no comfort. The promise of continued life held no pleasure. If he had not taken the woman—had not experienced the warmth and closeness, the passion—perhaps it might have. But now it only filled him with anguish. He moved away from the wall, made his way to the stairwell, and began his climb.

The instant he stepped out into the fourth floor corridor, he recognized the special fragrance of the woman. It was mingled with the bite of medicines and antiseptic, nonetheless unmistakable. Ivory soap. Oil paint. Sweet lemon. She was here! She was alive! Cautiously, he moved down the hall toward the aroma. It came from a large room filled with small glass cubicles. The nurse was nowhere to be seen, although he could hear her voice from the far end of the room. He checked the first five cubicles, but smelled only illness. At the next unit, he discov-

ered the scent again. He pushed open the glass door.
In the dim glow of a bedside light, he saw her profile. Her arms were connected to plastic tubes that
ran into bottles and bags hanging on a metal stand
beside the bed. Her wonderful gray eyes were
closed, her face colorless. Suddenly, he knew why
she'd looked so familiar to him. It had been long
ago, and he'd only seen pictures of her, but he remembered her face. My God! he thought, what
have I done?

He inhaled deeply, intoxicated by her scent. Remorse filled him. If only he had been more careful.
Death had become so routine for him that he had
lost his sensitivity. He was the Dark Angel—a monster of his own making. He wished he could undo all
that he had done. He wished he could hold her in his
arms and comfort her. She should have more succor
than just sterile tubes and bottles.

Looking down at her quiet form, he filled with the
desire to take her away from here to where he could
cradle her in his arms, feel the warmth of her body.
He'd brought her to this point, he could at least give
some measure of compassion. Perhaps he was seek-
ing atonement for past deeds. Perhaps he'd fallen in
love with her. No matter what the reason, he had to
do this. He'd find refuge in the basement of one of
the old homes nearby. He knew of several that were
vacant. If he waited much longer to leave the area,
they might catch him. He didn't mind, as long as he
could have some time with her. Quickly, he pulled
the needles from her arms. She stirred, her eyelashes
fluttering.

"Andy?" she said softly.

"No," he answered.

Slowly her eyes opened, blinked, closed, then opened again. In their gray color he saw recognition.

"You. . . ." she whispered.

"Yes." He smoothed her hair from her forehead. "I came to get you." With that, he folded the crisp white sheet around her, and lifted her into his arms. He carried her out through the corridor, into the stairwell, and made his way downward, and out through a service entrance.

The rain pelted them as he made his way toward the parking lot in search of a car he could use. Noise ripped the night open, as thunder rolled around them. In a flash of lightning, her face, brilliantly lit, looked more beautiful than anything he'd ever seen.

CHAPTER SIXTEEN

Chapter Eight

Elizabeth felt herself being carried out into the storm. Rain pelted her face, cooling her feverish skin. Wonderful, sweet rain. All the needles and tubes that had been attached to her arms were gone. The man who carried her felt strong, muscular, not quite like Andy. But who else could it be? She tried opening her eyes, but found it almost impossible.

"Andy?" she said as loudly as her weakened state would allow. "Did you come to take me home?"

"No. Not Andy."

"I know you. . . ." She managed to open her eyes for a moment. "My dream. You're the one in my dream." She felt a sudden tug of fear. Something wasn't right.

"Yes."

"Where's Andy? Are you taking me to him? He'll be worried about me."

The man fell silent. He stopped by a blue car in the parking lot of the hospital and opened the door, lifting her into the passenger seat.

"Shhhh. Be quiet now," he said.

"All just a crazy dream," Elizabeth whispered and closed her eyes. Maybe she was hallucinating. So real. The rain on her face. The darkness. The smell of hospital antiseptic fading. She opened her eyes again, and watched as the man slid into the driver's side of the car. Robert Redford? Yes, the surfer on the beach. Why wasn't Andy in her dream? Oh, it was all too much to understand. The fear nagged at her, but she pushed it away. So tired. She closed her eyes and let herself drift asleep, listening to the thump, thump of the windshield wipers against the car window. The dream would end soon, and Andy would be there holding her hand. He always was.

HE parked the car he'd stolen from the hospital parking lot, in the darkest section of the alley behind a Victorian house on the bay side of the Peninsula. It wouldn't do to have the police spot the car. The house was old and empty—an aged lady whose layers of paint were flaking in great patches, like discarded skin.

The place had warped timbers and broken panes of glass. He'd used it as a sanctuary on occasion, and knew it had been vacant for at least a year. Probably in probate. He'd taken two of his prey there, both of them society's outcasts. People no one would miss. He'd made a ritual out of their deaths and the partaking of their flesh. If he took care not to let any light show through to the street, he could keep the woman in the basement for as long as necessary. He lifted her out of the car still swathed in the hospital sheet. She clung to him, her eyes closed, her face swept clean by the violent rain which pelted them.

The smell hit him the moment he pried open the back door and made his way into the kitchen. It was a dank, fermented odor like an old-fashioned cold pantry where potatoes had putrefied. In the kitchen, he found the door to the basement standing open, swaying with gusts of wind that wreathed through minute cracks in the old house.

No light penetrated to the basement stairs. The darkness below opened like a hungry mouth, threatening to swallow anyone who might venture into it. He'd left candles down there in that yawning black hole after his other stays. Carrying her carefully, he stepped downward into the darkness, sensing each wooden landing before his foot touched it. Other odors drifted up to him as he descended. The oily scent of cold candles. Damp, musty plaster. Cobwebs. Fetid boxes of clothing. The moldy stench of crumbling wicker furniture.

The bottom of the stairs was swathed in total blackness. His feet touched the cement floor, the chill of it soaking through the soles of his shoes. He remembered there was only one small window in the basement, located at ground level and covered by a piece of coarse, black material. The woman felt boneless in his arms as he made his way across the cement floor. His shin bone hit something solid. He let his leg explore it. It turned out to be a wicker sofa. Gently, he set her down on the rotting cushions.

"I'll find a light," he said softly. His fingers

groped across the cement, searching for the candles he'd left behind the last time he'd used the basement. He touched something soft. Fur. A dead rat perhaps? He moved his hand in a different direction. If memory served him, he'd left three thick candles on the floor not too far from the wicker sofa. He'd also left a butane cigarette lighter, because he discovered matches didn't work well. The room held too much damp. The tips of the matches only crumbled when he tried to strike them.

He heard a murmur from the woman. "Only a minute more," he said. He reached farther away from the sofa. Something moved close by. Scurried. A tiny sound. His fingers touched something chilled and slick. A candle! He patted the floor with his free hand, and found the small lighter on his first try. He flicked the flint and the flame jumped high. He tilted it over the candle, which took a moment to light because of the damp wick.

Even with three candles lit, the room was shadow-struck. Pools of orange light wavered into dark corners. He sat on the edge of the decrepit sofa, and looked down at the young woman. "Are you comfortable?" he asked.

She nodded. He picked up her hand, which had gone as limp as folds of crushed velvet. Her fingers were icy. He wished there were some way he could warm her. He unwound the wet sheet from around her body, tossed it aside, and slipped off the crumpled hospital gown. Then he pulled an elderly blanket out of a nearby box, spread it over her, and lay down beside her, pressing his body against hers, hoping he had enough heat left in him, to share with her. He felt her shiver slightly, then let out a murmured sigh.

"Your name is Elizabeth," he said. "I remember it now."

There was a long pause before she answered. "Yes, Elizabeth," she said in a tiny voice.

"I used to look at your picture, years ago, and wish we could meet." He smoothed the wet hair off her forehead. In the candle glow, her skin took on the burnished tone of old gold. But, he saw how transparent it had become. He'd taken far too much from her. He'd also let her drink too much of his own blood. He'd satisfied his longing for supreme intimacy. The ultimate orgasm. Now that the agony was at bay, he cursed the fact that his appetites had no constraints.

If only he'd been more careful. The bitter taste of self-hate welled up in the back of his throat. His actions were geared to the rhythm of a life he'd lived for too many years now. He ran his hands over her body, alarmed at the fluidity of her flesh. He wrapped his arms around her, and held her tightly. The old house gave a lamenting voice to the wind and rain that battered and twisted around ancient timbers. As he touched her, he felt his desire for her stirring. It was not the agony. But he knew she was in a dream state, and that it was her husband she longed for, not him. The thought saddened him. He needed someone with whom he could be close. It didn't have to be physical. Just someone for him to love who would love him in return. But, of course, that was impossible. His mother had loved him. Right up until her last breath. She'd protected him.

Tried to help him. In fact, she blamed herself for his problem. But he knew that wasn't true. This whole nightmare was of his own making. It had been his craving for success, his need for recognition, that had caused it. He laid his head down next to hers.

"Where's Andy?" she said softly.

"I'll stay with you."

She closed her eyes, and gave a little shudder. How could he have known that this woman would stir up such feelings—feelings he had long buried in order to survive. He felt the tears well up in his eyes, and a deep searing pain gripped his throat. Thankfully, he felt some of his body heat transfer to her. She lay silent and motionless in his arms. Had he been wrong to take her from the hospital? Perhaps he'd taken her last chance for life away from her. He shook his head, trying to clear his confusion. His thought processes felt odd. He'd only wanted to comfort her. Or had he wanted to comforted himself? The guilt for all his other deeds stung him. His desire to live had always outweighed the destruction he caused. As he rocked her gently, a terrible fatigue swarmed over him. He was tired of the hunt, of the killing, of the running, the hiding. He wanted asylum. Surely someone, somewhere, could find a way to help him. He heard himself let out a sob. They'd tried. So many of them. All those hospitals. Doctors. His mother paying for all of it. Medications. Always new medications. None of them worked. Nothing helped. And he'd done this terrible thing to himself. He had no one else to blame.

Somewhere nearby, he heard the scurrying

ounds again. Night creatures, coming out to feed.
Creatures smaller, but not unlike himself.

He rocked her, singing softly, feeling the warmth
in her grow. He should take her back to the hospital, let them help her. She wasn't like him. The
medications could make her well. But he didn't
want to let her go. It had been so long since he'd felt
the touch of another's skin, and not hungered for it.
He couldn't bear it, not having her there in his arms.
He let his head rest against her shoulder. Maybe if
he kept her warm, kept her dry, he could keep her
from harm. He would hold her all night, and the
next day if he had to. She would get well. And
perhaps he could take her with him to France. They
could go together. He rested his head against her
shoulder and began to cry. His thoughts were only
wishes—wishes he knew would never come true.

Driving rain pelted the Rattigan house. Lightning
flashed and thunder shook the beams and walls
causing candlesticks, glasses, flower bowls, plates
and coffee cups to chatter wildly.

To Andy, the room looked slightly blurred, colors running into colors, objects melting into objects.
"Damn Bloody Marys," he muttered, looking into
the near-empty glass in his hand. He'd managed
two drinks in a short space of time. He knew better,
since he seldom drank anything stronger than iced
tea. But it felt good to just relax and let go, after all
he'd been through that day. Tyree was talking in a
low voice, but he couldn't quite make out what she

was saying. "Greet our . . . neighbors . . . both. . . ." He only caught a word or two. Concentrating, he narrowed his eyes and watched her lips as she spoke. Since this party had originally been for Lizzy and himself, he felt he should pay attention. "Hope . . . join . . . Sunshine," he heard her say. He looked around the room and saw that everyone was listening with rapt attention.

Tyree paused, turning about in the center of the group. "They are not aware of what part they play. Or of the great gift we are about to offer them."

Gift? Andy wondered. Whose gift? Was it someone's birthday?

"I think, however, they have some idea, now, of what it's like."

Andy shook his head, trying to clear the effects of the Bloody Mary. He had trouble keeping his mind on the words Tyree was saying. Instead, he again checked out the pendant she wore around her neck. Now that was some piece of jewelry! A polished gold medallion studded with what looked to him like yellow diamonds surrounded by topaz, glittered in the firelight. The piece glowed with light, like an aurora. Must have cost a fortune!

Tyree came over and sat down on the coffee table in front of him. She fingered the pendant around her neck. "Andy, we want to talk to you about our special group. We want to invite you to join, something we rarely do. Of course, we know you can't speak for Elizabeth. But perhaps if we tell you about it, you can convey it to her when she's feeling better."

Andy sat up straighter on the sofa, a little alarm

bell going off in his head. "Ahh, a group? Like a club?"

"Yes. A club. A very elite club." Tyree nodded.

Andy felt himself cringe slightly. What had he gotten himself into here? Were they Jehovah's Witness? Mormons? Born-agains? "I don't think—"

Tyree held up her hand. "No, don't make any judgments yet. Wait until you've heard the entire . . . ," She looked around the room, gave a little laugh, then turned back to Andy. "our entire spiel. Then decide. You see, we've been very bad, actually. Done something we shouldn't have. But I want you to know that it was done only because it's the best way for you to discover the truly miraculous privileges enjoyed by the members of our . . . club. Believe me, this group is made up of the highest stratum of our society. You will be one of the haut monde, if you decide to join us."

"The what?"

Tyree laughed again and this time most of the others in the room laughed too. "The gentry. Aristocracy. Creme de la creme. Whatever you want to call it. Meaning those with privilege. Those with money. Those with a special station in life."

Andy leaned forward, his interest perked. Probably a new Amway approach, he warned himself. Whatever it was, he thought it in bad taste to start the dog-and-pony-show now, with Elizabeth critically ill in the hospital. But since he couldn't do anything about Lizzy at the moment, he might as well go ahead and listen to what they had to say. Who knew, perhaps they were onto something that might help them become financially secure. But, he told himself sternly, if it sounds too good, remember, it probably is! He gave Tyree a nod, indicating he was interested and listening.

"We call our group Sunshine. Boo and I are the elected leaders of the group. Before us, Elizabeth's Aunt Mary was host. It was Mary who led us to this point."

"Old Mary belonged to your club?" Andy said. "I don't think Lizzy is aware of any club she belonged to."

"Elizabeth hadn't seen her aunt for many years. Except for the . . . club, Mary wasn't social at all for the past fifteen or so years. Not since. . . ."

"Since her son died," Andy completed Tyree's sentence. "Lizzy said she stopped having family gatherings."

Tyree looked down at the floor for a moment, fingered the pendant around her neck, sighed, then looked up. "Andy, Mary's son *did not die.* He was ill, yes, but he did not die. Mary made up that story to hide the truth."

Andy narrowed his eyes more, trying to decide if he was still a bit drunk. The room had come into sharp focus so he thought not. "Truth?"

Tyree stood up suddenly and walked away from the sofa to stand by the fireplace. She ran nervous fingers through her blaze of red hair. "I think we should start with something else. Something that involves you and Elizabeth. We'll get to Mary's son later."

Andy gave a little I-couldn't-care-less shrug of his shoulders. All of this was becoming a nuisance. What he really wanted to do was go home, change clothes, and get to the hospital where he could wait until they would let him see Lizzy. If this club had something really great to offer, they could tell him about it later.

Tyree put up her hand, as if she knew what he was thinking. "Give us just a few minutes, Andy. I know you are worried about Elizabeth. But what we have to say, will ease your mind. And perhaps give you something you have dreamed about for a long time."

Andy settled back into the sofa, convinced that if he wanted to get out of here, it would be easier if he listened to their pitch first.

"Good. Now, if you'll be patient for a bit, we'll get to the bottom of all this. First, let me ask you if you would like to have all the money you'll ever need?"

Andy looked around at the others who were smiling at him, nodding their heads, yes. "Of course. Who wouldn't?"

"Would you like to have all the books you write be successful? Would you like for Elizabeth's paintings to sell the minute they are painted?"

Andy gave her an are-you-kidding look.

"Naturally you would. Over and above this, would you like to have a generous, steady income?"

"Tyree," Andy said, a bit impatient. "Are these purely rhetorical questions, or do you actually have a reason for asking?"

Tyree gave a sly grin. "A big reason. And for that, I'd like Boo to please take over from here." She motioned in the direction of her husband who came out from behind the bar and made his way across the room and stood beside her. Tyree smiled and sat down on the fireplace hearth, looking up at Boo.

Here it comes, Andy thought. The big song and dance. How he could save them income tax money. Or maybe it was a pyramid scheme. Still, his curiosity prodded him and he continued to listen.

"As I'm sure you're aware, Andy, your wife's aunt, Mary Elizabeth Warren, owned and ran a pharmaceutical company for a number of years." Boo leaned one arm against the fireplace mantle, giving him a casual air. But his deep voice carried a tone of intense seriousness. "Her son, Barry—to say he was a brilliant scientist is an understatement—was given full control over their research and development department, along with a generous allowance to run it. Both he and Mary had one main goal in mind. They wanted to develop something that would help people use their minds to the fullest." Boo paused, pursing his lips as if trying to coordinate his next words. "Mary believed that we only use a tiny portion of our brains—something other scientists concur with—and that with the right method, we could be turned-on, or tuned-in to using the rest of it. Her concerns were benevolent. She wanted not only to raise the level of intelligence in humanity as a whole, but to also be able to address such things as mental retardation. She began by experimenting with everything out there. Meditation. Isolation tanks. Hemisyncing. Light machines. Alpha stimulation. Electro biostimulation. You name it, she tried it. All with some, but still rather limited, results."

Something about this sounded familiar to Andy. But he couldn't remember what. He nodded at Boo, who was looking directly at him. His inky dark eyes penetrating. Andy didn't understand where all this was leading but his curiosity had grown.

"When Barry went to work for Warren Pharmaceutical," Boo continued, "he and Mary put all their hopes and money into discovering some form of chemical stimulation that might be the answer. Barry became obsessed with developing a drug, or a compound, that would bring out the latent ability of the human brain. He knew that some states of mind such as fear, hate, serenity, and love, were controlled by neurochemicals. If this was so, then certainly such things as imagination, intelligence, insight, were undoubtably also controlled by various brain chemicals. He brought in a geneticist in hopes he might discover some important portion of the human genetic makeup that could be utilized to stimulate the brain. One chemical compound after another was tested on animals. However, Barry felt these tests were not valid, as the brain systems were not similar enough. He longed to test them on humans, but couldn't get FDA approval for any of them. Many of the drugs had adverse, as well as downright lethal side effect, on animals."

Boo paused again, pacing a small path in front of the fireplace. Andy had the feeling that he was trying to decide just how much of this to tell him. The others in the room appeared to be paying rapt attention.

"It wasn't until he came across what we now call Sunshine, that Barry became excited."

"Sunshine?" Andy said. "The name of your group, or club, or whatever?" Now that was peculiar, naming a club after a drug.

"Yes. The original drug was a distillate from a bright yellow flower some of the Warren researchers found in a rain forest, at the top of the canopy. Fortunately, the compound could be synthesized. I say fortunate because that area of this particular rain forest has been destroyed and no one has found any of the yellow blooms in any other location. It may have been because of working with a synthetic—perhaps some small error in the formula—that caused the problems. Unfortunately, when he moved from the natural version of the compound to the synthesized one, the animals, while still responding with increased intelligence and skills, eventually went into spasms and died. The pure drug, from the flowers, used on mice, didn't harm them. But it DID accelerate their learning processes. Almost too much. They often found ways to escape their cages. Now this drug, R-456, or Sunshine as Barry named it, seemed to have opposing effects. It appeared to be both a depressant and a stimulant. But when these two elements of the drug got together, a synergistic effect apparently resulted."

"What kind of effect?"

"Synergistic. That's when two things with different effects combine to cause a third effect that's totally different for the first two."

"Oh. Okay. I think I understand."

"Barry was able to isolate the depressant element and found it to be an incredible pain killer and tranquilizer. Actually, it may not stop pain at all, but may make the subject so tranquil he doesn't recognize pain. The stimulant factor is the brain boosting portion of the compound. It was a long time before Barry was able to get Sunshine to a point where he felt it could be FDA tested. Still, they turned him down saying it did not have enough successful animal tests." Boo stopped pacing and looked at Andy. "Are you still with me? I know all this is a bit confusing, but I think if you know the history, you'll understand the rest better."

Andy shook his head. "Yes, I'm with you. Although I'm not sure where all this is leading. What does this have to do with your group?"

"In a minute. First, the rest of the background. Barry felt certain that he'd finally refined the drug to the point where it was harmless. His experience with simians proved highly successful, with no harmful effects on the animals. They lived for years after the experiment, although once taken off the drug, their super intelligence slowly waned. Barry became totally obsessed with testing the drug on humans. So he did something . . . Well, if I said foolish, that would certainly not describe it. He did something disastrous. He tested the drug on himself. Now, Barry's IQ at that time was already in the .25 percentile of the population. With several doses of Sunshine, it rose so far off the scale it was impossible to test."

"That doesn't sound like a disaster to me." Andy found himself leaning forward, his attention completely caught. And he was remembering something. Something he'd heard recently, but he couldn't quite bring it into his conscious mind.

"At that point, the drug far surpassed both his and Mary's expectations. Not only did his cognitive reasoning ability increase, but so did his creative skills. He continued to take the drug, keeping a taped journal of his experiences. After he'd been on it for about two months, he noticed something peculiar. His sense of smell had grown acute. He could separate out and identify all kinds of scents. Much like a dog, or a wild animal. This didn't alarm him, or Mary. He couldn't tell the FDA that he was testing the drug on himself, so he still couldn't get any clinical double blind tests done. At this stage, he could have sold out to a large company and made a modest deal. Let them take on the expense of completing the tests. But the Warrens, Barry and his mother, didn't want that. Mary had something else in mind, besides just helping humanity. That's when they brought me in to help. I studied everything Barry had done and realized he was onto something big. Immense! I helped him refine the drug further, and made plans to go to Mexico, where drug policies are less stringent, and try to get some testing done. It was while we were working together that. . . ." He stopped and looked down at Tyree who had tapped him on the hand. She gave a shake of her head and stood up. Boo nodded. "Well, that's the background. There's more, but first, we want to tell you where you fit in."

"Please," Andy said, getting a bit impatient.

"When Barry began to get ill, Tyree and I persuaded Mary to let us buy into the company. In return, I continued the research."

"It was Boo who finally managed to refine Sunshine to its present, usable form," Tyree said from her place on the fireplace hearth. "Exactly what Mary, and Barry dreamed of. An incredible brain booster, with few side effects."

Tyree's last works echoed through Andy's head. *Brain booster!* Those were the exact words their lawyer had used! Elizabeth had been left the patent on an untested drug that was supposed to be a type of brain booster. He quickly glanced at Boo and back to Tyree. So that was their game! They wanted a share in the patent. Or maybe they already *had* a share of it, unknown to their lawyer. Whatever it was, they had chosen an elaborate method of discussing it with them. And what the hell was all this talk about a club called Sunshine. Did *all* these people have a share in it? Andy felt himself at once cautious, and excited. Perhaps he, or rather Lizzy, had something here of real value. Perhaps they could make money from this Sunshine stuff. Well, he'd wait it out, give Boo his head and let him lead where he wanted. At least now, some of this made sense.

Boo was silent for a minute, gathering his thoughts. He turned and looked into the fire for what seemed to Andy like a long time. Finally, he turned back. "Mary found it necessary to close the company. Barry's illness was so grave that she needed all the money she could raise to have him treated."

"And this illness," Andy said, "is obviously related to the drug he'd tested on himself."

"Not the drug we have today, but an earlier one. Yes. And to date, none of the damage he did to himself has been reversible. He spent months, years, in research programs, hoping other drugs would counteract, or at least control his symptoms." Boo gave an odd shrug. "After Mary died, we continued to try and help him. But . . . lately . . . his problems have escalated. He's getting worse. And his rate of decline is . . . fast."

Tyree got to her feet and put her hand on Boo's shoulder. "So now," she said, "I know you're wondering just where you and Elizabeth come into all of this."

Andy nodded. Here it comes, finally. The big pitch. The gimmick. Whatever it is they have in mind.

Boo sat down in Tyree's place on the fireplace hearth, his long legs crossed in front of him. Tyree raked at her red hair, tossing it first to one side, then to the other. The slight twitch under her eyes increased. Why, Andy wondered, was she so tense?

"The drug we call Sunshine, has been refined into two forms. All of this later work has been done in Mexico. When Mary closed the business, we lost all the money we'd invested. But we had some savings. So we found places in Mexico where the work could be completed for far less than in the States. It was in Mexico that Sunshine had its first tests on human subjects. Both forms of the drug. And I'm glad to say that all of the tests were remarkably successful, with few side effects. And those have been transitory."

"Why," Andy asked. "are there two forms of the drugs? How do they differ?"

"Sunshine I is a much stronger, faster-acting,

more sustained version of the drug, with some very special elements," Tyree answered. "Sunshine II is only about one-tenth the strength, and lacks the extras. The first one may cause some discomfort when first used, but that passes. However, the results are unbelievable. With the second one, no side effects occur. The results, if the drug is used on a daily basis, are quite remarkable, although not nearly as stunning as the other version."

Andy shook his head. He felt himself become more impatient. When the hell were they going to get to the point of all this? It was interesting, certainly. But where did he fit in? Was this the same drug that Elizabeth had inherited from Mary?

Tyree moved away from the fireplace and sat down on the edge of the coffee table in front of Andy. He pressed himself back against the sofa cushion, an involuntary movement. Tyree could be quite intimidating, he realized.

"Okay Andy, here's what you want to know. Here is our reason for telling you this." Tyree smiled at him and gave him the sensation she was reading his mind. But of course, all she was reading was his body language. "Almost all of those who participated in the testing in Mexico—that is, all who were actually given the drug—are in this room."

Startled, Andy looked around at the group of people. Most of them nodded at him, affirming Tyree's words. "Each of them is being given a maintenance dose every day. The result is, they have each developed talents, abilities, that far surpass those of almost any other humans. I, too, am taking the drug, as is Boo. We won't go into the diverse nature of all these talents and abilities right now. Just take my word for it, they exist. Because of this, every member of our Sunshine group has made a great deal of money. Each of us in different ways, using our own special talents."

So, that was it! This so called Sunshine "club" consisted solely of people who were taking an illicit drug. "Wait a minute!" he said in a loud voice. "Your invitation to join this group—that means you . . . you want Elizabeth and me to take this drug, the way all of you are doing."

"No, Andy," Tyree said, her blue eyes blazing, "it means that you, and Elizabeth, *have already taken the drug.*"

Andy jumped visibly in his seat. He tried to connect Tyree's word to some sort of sense. What in the hell was she talking about? Neither Lizzy or he had taken drugs, of any kind. Except for an occasional aspirin. He began to edge forward on the sofa, prepared to get up and make his departure. All this was just a bit too weird for him. And the last thing he wanted was a relationship with a group who used any kind of drugs.

"No, Andy. Please. Hear me out. It's important. To both of us. And to a lot of other people." She reached out in an attempt to keep him from getting up. But he brushed her aside and got to his feet.

"Look, Tyree. I assure you that we have never taken any of these so-called Sunshine drugs. Now, I really have to get home and call the hospital."

Tyree stood up next to him, her tall slender body only a foot away from him. With a deft movement, she reached for her pendant, opened a small compartment on the back of it, dabbed her finger at the contents inside, and snapped it closed. Andy looked at her, puzzled. What was she doing?

"It's important you hear all of what we have to say. Then, you may go, and do whatever you choose." With that, Tyree reached out and ran a sharp fingernail over Andy's cheek. Before he could pull away, she rubbed the flat of her finger into the slight wound. Andy felt as if he'd been hit by some form of paralysis. His entire body went limp. It was all he could do to stand. A floating sensation replaced the paralysis. Tyree took hold of his arms, and gently pressed him down until he was seated on the sofa. He could not control his motions. All he could do was look around at the wonderful orange light from the fireplace and candles. Some part of his mind told him he should be alarmed. Yet no sense of panic overtook him. One Bloody Mary too much? Jesus! It felt good! So damn good.

Tyree sat back down on the edge of the coffee table. "I'm sorry, Andy, to have to do that. But I do need you to hear the rest. Don't worry, what you're feeling is just the result of the pain-killing, or tranquilizing portion, of R269, or an earlier version of Sunshine. It's harmless, and will wear off soon. It's quite remarkable, though, isn't it?

Andy nodded dumbly. Remarkable, yes. Wonderful! The best thing he'd felt since . . . since he and Lizzy had had sex. Better, almost, than an orgasm. Someone should patent that stuff! Stupendous. Fantastic. His mind tried to think of words that could describe it. But none could truly do that, he realized, so he stopped and looked at Tyree. My! What lovely red hair. And those vivid blue eyes. Handsome lady. His head lolled back against the sofa cushion. What was he doing here? He couldn't remember. Something about sunshine. Yes, that was it. Sunshine. "You are my Sunshine, my only Sunshine," he began to sing, slightly out of key, then giggled.

"Andy," Tyree's voice was loud, shaking him out of his reverie. "Listen to me, Andy. I told you that we—our little Sunshine group—have been bad. We did something wrong, but only in the hopes that it would be of benefit to you and Elizabeth. And, of course, to ourselves."

"Yeah. Okay," Andy said, not certain at all what she was talking about.

"We've been giving you increasingly stronger doses of the drug."

"Drug. Use? How?" Andy tried to make sense of it.

"In the casserole dishes I brought over. Only Elizabeth didn't eat as much as she should have. And also, she had much stronger side effects than you. But they would have worn off before long. However, both of you experienced the results to some degree."

"Results?" Andy still felt floaty, but found his thinking processes begin to clear.

"Your increased writing skill. Your accelerated work. The new ideas. All that is a part of Sunshine's effect on you. And Elizabeth's painting. Her new ones. But, because she didn't take enough of the drug, her ability tapered off. However, if she continues to take it, she can achieve a brilliant career. So can you."

For some reason, that struck Andy funny. He let out a cackle of a laugh. "A drug-induced career," he said and laughed again, although reason told him it wasn't funny.

"No, Andy. A drug *enhanced* career. Some amount of talent has to be there to begin with. Nevertheless, this is a most remarkable drug. Take the Zipper sisters as an example."

"No thanks," Andy cracked, still laughing, and not knowing why.

"I mean, take their case history. Twin sisters, both born with a form of retardation that's impossible to treat."

Andy stopped laughing. The Zippers retarded? A bit strange, perhaps, but certainly not retarded.

"Now, with the drug, they are well about the average percentile on any scale."

"Well above," Mable chimed in from across the room. "Somewhere in the 140 range."

"Before the drug, neither of them could even learn to tie their shoes," Tyree said. "Now, they are quite renowned for their design abilities. They've just retired from a design house that has made them a lot of money during the past ten years."

"Ten . . . un . . . ten . . ." Andy tried to get his thoughts connected. "That . . . uh, long?" he finally managed.

"Yes. They were the first subjects we used in our Mexico tests. They were living in a group home in San Diego and the doctor who treated them was a friend of Boo's. Although it was a double-blind test, both sisters just happened to get the drug, not the placebo. With that first set of test subjects, we knew we were on the right track. Every one in the group getting the drug, showed a remarkable change in IQ. Those getting the placebo showed little. Those in the control group showed no change."

"A . . . bout . . . Lizzy and . . . me," Andy tried, but found his tongue didn't respond the way he wanted.

Tyree leaned forward and put her hand on his. Her fingers were warm, almost hot. "You and Lizzy were given some of the drug so you could see for yourselves the incredible accomplishments it would bring about. Poor Elizabeth, it made her ill. But that wasn't the only cause of her problem."

Boo got to his feet. "Umm, Tyree, let's don't get into all of that just yet."

Tyree looked over at him, nodded, and then looked back at Andy. "Yes, of course. First things first."

"Tyree?" Andy said as plainly as possible. "From what I can tell, dis . . . this drug . . . ahhh . . . well, I think that Izzy . . . Lizzy has . . . owns . . . the whatchamacallit."

"Yes. The patent. She does. Mary left it to her. It's the only patent that Warren pharmaceuticals had left, since Mary sold all the others for quick money, to try and help her son."

"So then . . . ah," Andy shook his head again, harder this time, determined to get it together. But he still felt so deliciously comfortable, it was an effort to even stay in the conversation.

"The patent is for the unrefined and untested

form of the drug. But that doesn't matter. She still owns it, and no one can benefit from any of that except her. Not, that is, without some sort of agreement." Tyree got up and began to walk around the room.

"You mean, you want Lizzy to . . . uh . . . sell you some of the whatchmacallit rights?"

"If she's willing."

"And if she's not?"

Tyree gave a short, cryptic laugh. "Then she doesn't. She can sell it to a large company, for pennies in its present state. Or she can raise the millions it will take to have someone else get to the same place Boo has already reached. You have that kind of money available?"

Andy shook his head, no. "No money. No credit."

"Best of all, we make an agreement. Part of the rights to the patent in return for all of the research and test information. That way, it's worth a fortune, for all of us. But only for Sunshine II, not for Sunshine I. The lighter version appears to be more than adequate for almost any use."

"What . . . why not—"

"It was Mary's wish that we reserve Sunshine I for our group exclusively."

"You're going to keep taking it?"

"Yes. And we want you and Elizabeth to join us. Humanitarianism goes just so far. Sunshine II will do the world a great deal of good. But we reserve for ourselves the ability to rise to the status of genius. After all, what kind of world would it be if everyone in it had megabrains? No one would be special. No one would stand out from the crowd." Tyree gave him a narrowed look, her blue eyes deepening. "And of course, we have to be extremely careful about who uses it. We can't risk a new generation Napoleon or Hitler having access to something like this. So the deal would mean our group holds the rights to it. Only our group knows about it. Our security is tight. If anyone should be caught talking about it to outsiders, they would loose their daily supply of the drug. No one wants to chance that. We keep Sunshine I, and give Sunshine II, to the world. This way, everyone benefits, but we benefit the most. After all, we've done the ground work. Taken the risks. The rewards should be equivalent. And just think, you and Elizabeth can enjoy the real fruit of your labors to date, your college educations, training. You will become giants in your field. Not to mention your royalties on Sunshine II. What more could you two ask for?"

Andy squirmed around on the sofa. Did this compute? Or was it some great fantasy? He wasn't in much shape to think rationally. "I don't know, Tyree. I'm not sure what—"

"It's Elizabeth's decision, certainly," Boo said. "But considering it will take her a while to recuperate, we felt that you might help to influence her. And if she decides against it, then we fade away. You do what you want with your patent. We keep our research to ourselves, and the use of the drug exclusively for us. No one can prove we know anything about it." Boo strode to the bar and picked up a clean glass. "Bloody Marys anyone?"

A sibilant sound went through the room, as if everyone had been holding their breath for quite a while and had let it all out at one time. Conversations began to hum. Andy became aware of the storm once again. Heard giant waves pounding on the beach outside. The wind rose, whining at first, whipping great droplets of quick silver rain against the sliding glass door.

"Oh, my goodness!" he heard Sarah Zipper say. "Look who's here!"

Andy turned toward the shutter doors, his equilibrium improved. Dr. Foxhoven stood there pulling off his raincoat. Boo offered him a drink, but he waved it away and strode over to Tyree. Was he a member of their little group also? Of course. It all made sense. That's why Tyree had called him to treat Elizabeth.

"We've got a major problem," he said, his voice more raspy than Andy remembered from the hospital. He leaned forward and whispered something into Tyree's ears.

She stiffened, her face flushed with alarm, then she paled. "My God! No!"

Foxhoven nodded yes, then looked down at the floor, biting his lower lip with his teeth.

"What can we do?" Tyree said. Foxhoven shrugged. "Well then, tell them."

"Foxhoven cleared his throat. The chatter in the room ebbed. Everyone turned toward him. "I'm afraid that . . . Barry has abducted Elizabeth from the hospital. They have no idea where he's taken her, or why."

"Damn him!" Tyree cried. "What in the hell are we going to do now?"

At first, none of it made sense to Andy. Barry? Did they mean Mary's son? Why would he abduct Elizabeth? From what Tyree said, he'd pictured Barry in a hospital or institution, close to death by now from the result of the early experiments of the drug. But, now he saw that Barry was apparently far from that point. Could he be insane? Is that what the drug did to him? He remembered Boo talking about how Barry's sense of smell had been the first clue that something was going wrong with the drug. And weren't unusual smells one of the first indications that something was wrong with the brain. Odors that weren't there? He'd heard of that happening with people who had brain tumors.

"Why would he do this," Andy heard himself say. "Why would he take her away from the hospital. How did he know she was there? You haven't told me everything. God damn it!" He struggled to get to his feet, feeling the effects of whatever Tyree had numbed him with, ebbing away.

Boo came over from the bar and handed him a drink. "Here," he said. "You're going to need this, Believe me. What you're going to hear, is going to shake you up pretty good."

Tyree tried to run a soothing hand over Andy's arm, but he pulled away from her. No more of that stuff she'd scratched him with. He'd be wary from here on. He had to find out what was going on. "One of you tell me what the fuck is going on! What haven't you said?" He emphasized his words by banging the Bloody Mary down on the coffee table.

"Andy," Tyree began. "What we didn't cover yet, was Barry's illness." She looked over at Boo as if pleading with him to help her with the explanation, but Boo only turned and went back to the bar. "Okay then. When Barry tested the drug in its early stages, it did something to his chromosomes. We don't know exactly what happened. The genetists had been working with the drug, and we think that's where it started. But from what we gather, the drug sparked some genes that are not normally used by man. Not needed, at least at this time in his development. The effect of those genes is pretty ugly, at least in the light of our society today."

"Quit fencing, Tyree. Just tell me!" Andy, his legs still a bit wobbly, let himself sink back down on the sofa.

"At first, it wasn't too bad. His sense of smell, as we mentioned, became acute. His physical strength increased. Then he developed a taste for odd foods. He insisted on eating everything raw at that point."

"A lot of people like their food raw," Andy said.

"Not meat, as a rule. Barry developed a ravenous appetite for raw meat and blood. It was terrible. Poor Mary. Barry would come home with blood all over him. He'd devoured a cat, or a dog. Just tore the animal apart, and ate it." Andy felt his stomach lurch. "Good God!"

"He couldn't control it. Nothing helped. Nothing at all. God knows he wanted to be helped. Mary took him to the Mayo, and everywhere else that might do him some good. Some drugs seemed to help . . . for a while. But eventually, his cravings came back, stronger. And they tormented him. He'd try to eat something else. Anything. But he vomited up anything except the fresh meat and blood."

"How grotesque. Couldn't they, like, feed him intravenously or something?" Andy asked.

"Mary kept packets of a powdered blood substitute in the house. They worked for awhile. Then his cravings grew, changed. After Mary died, we all tried to help him. Not only because he needed help, but for selfish reasons too. We thought working with him might help our own research. But it became impossible. He was out of our control. We could do nothing but wait and hope that something would happen to stop him."

"I've never heard of anything so aberrant," Andy turned away, sickened by the story.

Boo's voice echoed from across the room. "It's happened before, similar cases. But from other causes. Unknown causes. The guy in New York who used to stalk people and drink their blood and eat body parts. Or in London some years ago, the guy who invited guests to his mansion, then had them for dinner."

Andy cringed. "Yeah, I've heard stories about such things. But these are psychos. Demented people. Sick in their minds. And they were eating human flesh and blood."

"Yes, but that's . . . that's where it has ended up, with Barry," Tyree said. "His craving has mutated, and seems to now be satisfied only by eating human flesh, and drinking human blood."

Andy turned and stared at Tyree. Was this some

kind of Halloween story meant to scare him? For what reason? To persuade him and Elizabeth into giving them a percentage of the drugs? Christ! With that, Andy decided to get up and leave. He wouldn't listen to any more of this. He'd go home, call the hospital, and if what Foxhoven said was true, that Elizabeth had been abducted, he'd call the police. He'd go out in the storm himself if he had to, to find her. No one barred his way.

He made his way through the room and had just reached the shutter doors when Tyree said, "Andy. You have to know that when we found Elizabeth this morning, she wasn't sick from the drug's side effect. She had been . . . molested by Barry. Why he didn't kill her, as he's done with his other victims, I don't know. We had already turned his name over to the police, with the hope that they would stop him before he hurt any more people. But he evidently found Elizabeth alone in bed, drank some of her blood, and forced her to drink some of his. It caused a roaring infection in Elizabeth. She needs to be in the hospital. If treated, she'll be okay. Fortunately, the Sunshine I we gave her in the casseroles, helped to raise her immune system, among all the other things it does."

Andy looked at Foxhoven for confirmation. The doctor nodded grimly. "She'll be just fine, if we can find her. Even untreated, she'll probably recover. But with Barry. . . ."

"He didn't kill her, perhaps because he felt something for her. I understand they never met, but Mary must have had pictures of her. He probably saw them. After all, he and Elizabeth are cousins.

He may have remembered her. Who knows. But what we do know, is that left alone with her for any length of time, his cravings will return, and no matter what, he'll—"

Andy put his hands over his ears. "No! Don't. I don't want to hear it! I just want to get out there and find her." He started for the door again.

Boo came over to him. "We'll help. We'll do whatever we can. I have some ideas of where he might be. Places he's holed up at times."

"Yes!" said Mable Zipper. "I have some ideas too. We'll all help."

Tyree picked up a small glass bell on the coffee table and rang it. The room grew silent. "Agreed. But we can't all go out and just run around. Let's get some semblance of order here. So we can be effective. In this storm, it's going to be tough." She turned to Foxhoven. "Do the police know about Barry taking her from the hospital?"

"Yes," Foxhoven said. "It was reported immediately. They didn't know who he was, of course. But there's an all-points bulletin on the car he stole from the hospital parking lot."

"Good," Tyree said. "Now, let's get organized. The one thing we do not have is time. We have no idea when Barry's hunger will overwhelm him. We do know that eventually it will!"

Andy turned and surveyed the group. Tyree, with her wild red hair splaying out like a flaming halo, began barking out orders. The rest began to gather their coats, concern etching their faces. Either they were the most concerned group of people he'd ever met, or the most evil. Right at that moment, he couldn't decide which.

"Don't worry, honeybunch," Tyree said, her hand suddenly on his shoulder. "We'll find her."

The flood grew deeper. The calves of Ted's legs roared with pain as he forced his way through the black water toward the end of the peninsula. Silently, he cursed the police car that had shorted out so far from his destination. He had important questions to ask, and he damn well intended to get answers.

The wind blew in off the ocean in a steady howl. Palm trees swayed and bent at an alarming angle, as if at any moment they might snap in half. Parts of the peninsula showed lights, parts were in total darkness. The rain blew crisply across his face in a mass of silver strands, like a metallic curtain.

He turned off Balboa Boulevard and made his way down a side street, then into the alley. The flow of water wasn't as heavy there, and he found the going easier. Lightning flared to the south, and a rumble of thunder rattled down the alley, vibrating trash-can lids and garage doors. He clutched his coat around his neck, trying to stem the flow of rain inside his clothes. The wind screamed around the houses so furiously that Ted struggled to keep his balance.

Suddenly, the alley around him burst into a wild frenzy. Something long and snake-like detached itself from the shadows, and hurtled down toward him with a whipping sound. Flares of blue-white sparks jumped from the end of the black object, crackling like fireworks on the Fourth of July. When Ted realized what it was, he let out a yell, but the din of the storm drowned out the sound. A high-tension wire! It had broken loose from the utility pole. He stood stark still, knee-deep in water. Jesus!

He swung around, looking for a place to leap that was high enough to take him out of the flooding. The only thing he saw was a brick planter that rose just above the water's crest. Too far! He couldn't reach it in time! The wire arched downward, its sparking tip inches from where he stood. The wind convulsed again, caught the treacherous wire, and flung it sideways. It looped over the ragged edge of a wooden fence rail and hung there, precariously. He waited, watched. The wire's tenure on the fence held. He moved again, slowly at first, then faster. He wondered how far and how fast electricity would travel in water if the wire came loose and fell. He'd never out-race it, that was for sure.

Several blocks ahead of him, flashing beacons from police cars parked in the alley behind the Barry Brownstone apartment tinted the floodwater red and blue. His destination was only a few houses from Brownstone's apartment. He would call in an alert for the downed high-tension wire from one of the police radios. Silently, he prayed the wind would ease and the wire would stay in place. He also prayed that no one who lived in the area would venture out to investigate it. All they needed now was for a bunch of people to be electrocuted.

The alley behind the Brownstone apartment was a scramble of yellow tape and uniformed officers wading in murky water. "Get out of the water," Ted shouted against the wind. "Get the hell out of the water! There's a live wire down in the next block!" He waved his arms at the men. One of them responded by plunging toward the wooden steps that led to the apartment. Two of them retreated into one of the police cars.

"Is the power strong enough to reach here?" one of the young men yelled to Ted. "Are we safe in here?"

"I'm not sure," Ted yelled back. He scrambled into an empty cruiser, and picked up the radio.

"This is Bearbower," he growled into the mike. "We've got a hot wire down in the alley between Surf and Shell Streets. Get some Edison crews out here. Better yet, see if they can turn off the power from one of the substations."

"Yes, sir," came a soft female voice. "Between Surf and Shell. Is that the ocean side or bay?"

"Ocean."

"Yes, sir."

"And tell them to hurry. It's hooked on a fence right now, but if it goes into the water, it's going to be deadly."

"Yes, sir. Right away. Oh, detective?

"Yes."

"We got a dispatch in a few minutes ago. Thought you should know about it. They found another one."

"Another what?" Ted wanted to move on. He had to get his answers.

"A . . . body . . . on the peninsula. Young, female. From the sound of the call we got, it matches the MO on your other cases."

"What! Where?" Ted found himself almost screaming into the mike.

"Near the Pavilion. We haven't gotten a car down there yet, with the flooding and all. Maybe you can spare one of your black-and-whites."

"Ah, Christ! Look, if it is the same guy, then we need these cars, in case he's still around. We've got to stop this psycho."

"Okay. I'll see if we have anyone else we can send," she paused. "This has been a hell of a night!"

"Tell me about it!" Ted said, putting the radio mike down. He looked out the open car door at the swirling water. "Shit!" he hissed. "Another body. And here I am playing Russian roulette with that damn wire!" The last thing he wanted to do was stick his feet back into that water. He'd get no warning if the wire had slipped. He could be fried. Or maybe boiled was more like it. But he only had a short distance to go. He had to get his questions answered. He decided to chance it.

He reached out a foot, hesitated, pulled back, then with a thrust plunged it into the water. The dark tide bobbed against his legs like a pillow of ice. So far, so good. To his relief, the wind ebbed slightly. "Stay out of harm's way," he called to the other policemen. "Wait for the Edison crews to say it's safe." No one suggested he, too, should stay where it was safe.

Under the water, the ground felt mushy. Loose sand invaded his shoes. He stumbled slightly on some debris as he made his way cautiously through the shifting, sliding stuff. It seemed to him that he had been stumbling in this nightmare of wind, water, and darkness forever. Above him, the sky lit up like daylight for a second, then faded. Thunder was a good ten seconds in coming. Maybe, he thought, this fucking storm is moving on.

Finally, the huge white house loomed in front of him. The Rattigan residence. From the back, he saw no lights. He didn't give a damn if the occupants were sacked out sound asleep. He moved down the side of the house where the front door was located. Here he found himself pushing against the tide's surge. He heard an enormous roaring of water from the beach. Combers were breaking close by. To Ted, pausing and blinking against the pelting rain, it seemed as if giant waves were pouring out of the black night sky.

He found the front door where a pile of sandbags had been propped against the bottom half to keep out the floodtide. He leaned over and pushed the bell several times, then pounded on the door with his fist. No one answered. Then he pounded again, furiously. Damn it to hell! *They'd better wake up and get their butts down here and answer his questions.* He put his finger against the bell and held it. *Wake up, you ass-holes!* In frustration he banged on the door again, louder this time. Something floated by in the tide. It caught his shoes, lodging itself between his feet. He fished through the water, and pulled it up. Two yellow eyes stared at him. A cat! A fucking dead cat! With a shudder, he flung the sodden animal as far away as he could.

"Shit," he cried. "Double shit!"

He fought for a moment to catch his breath, leaning against the side of the house under the overhang, where the rain didn't penetrate. He wiped away the pools of water from his face, as if wiping away exhaustion. The boyish, freckled-face image of Steve Locke floated in front of his eyes, like some disembodied specter that had risen from the sea, like the dead cat. He squeezed his eyes shut, but the image remained.

With a deep breath, he jumped back three steps from the front door, gathered up every ounce of strength his overstrained body could muster, and kicked the front door open. He smashed it so hard, it flew off the hinges, slammed into the entry hall, and clattered to the floor, just missing a man who stood staring at him, a look of utter astonishment on his face.

"Police," Ted said forcefully, pulling out his sodden ID folder. "I want to speak with Tyree Rattigan." He stepped over the sandbags and into the entry hall.

The man looked at Ted, then at the door lying on the floor of the entry hall, then at the ID in Ted's hand. "Of course," the man said. "But you could have knocked!"

"I did! Tell her that Detective Bearbower is here to see her."

"Yes. I'm Boo Rattigan, Tyree's husband. I'll get her for you." Boo gave Ted a long, unreadable look. Then he looked down at the door again. An odd little smile twisted his lips.

The anger in Ted's voice grew. "I'll have the fucking door replaced."

"Actually, Detective Bearbower, the front door *wasn't locked.* You could have just walked in." He turned and disappeared through a pair of wooden shutter doors.

Ted stood alone in the entry hall, the wind and rain howling in through the opening where the door had once been. "Oh, shit!" he muttered. "That's just great."

Ted felt marooned standing in the Rattigans' hallway, trembling with rage. Boo Rattigan kept him waiting for some time before he came back and politely explained that Tyree would be a short while longer before she could see him.

"She's attending to our guests," Boo said. Then, he promptly picked up the front door from where it lay, and wedged it into the opening so that it kept out most of the storm.

"We've had a houseful tonight, I'm afraid," Boo Rattigan said, frowning.

"Bad night for it," Ted grumbled.

"I assume you're here about the Barry Brownstone thing," Boo said.

"Yes."

"We just heard. The hospital thing. Most of our guests are going out to try and help find this guy."

Ted took in a deep breath. The last thing he needed were a bunch of overly concerned people out trying to catch a murderer. "Listen, we've got some downed wires out there. Just up the way about two blocks. Better leave this to the police." He shifted his feet, suddenly feeling awkward. "Wait, what hospital thing?"

"The woman Barry abducted. Of course, you probably didn't know it was him. But we . . . that is . . . we feel it has the earmarks . . ." Boo stammered and stopped.

"I don't know anything about this. What with the storm, my car shorting out. Shit! What next?"

"You can call in from here, if you like."

"Yes," Ted agreed. His surge of rage had somewhat ebbed, no doubt dissipated by fatigue. His legs ached fiercely from having walked so far in deep water. And then, of course, he'd kicked in the door. That had been an idiotic thing to do. But for some reason, he felt a peculiar sense of satisfaction in having done it. A little chunk of atonement for Locke's death. Not much. But a little. It helped. Still, he wanted to feel the rage again. He didn't want to slip away. He needed it.

The shutter doors to the living room opened, and Tyree Rattigan whispered into the hallway. It seemed to Ted that her feet never touched the floor, her movements so graceful. Her long, flame-red hair flowed attractively around her face. He was struck by the bright blue of her eyes, which held his for a moment before turning to her husband.

"Darling, would you get Detective . . . Bearbower, isn't it? some coffee? He must be chilled to the bone."

"No. Thanks. I have some urgent questions," Ted said.

"You're soaked, Mr. Bearbower. Hot coffee will take away the chill."

Ted ground his teeth together. The last thing he wanted right now was to sit down and have a cup of coffee.

"I'll bring us all some," Boo smiled graciously, and excused himself.

"Fine." Ted gave a curt nod.

"Won't you come into the living room? A few of my guests are still here."

"As you said, I'm soaking wet. I'd better stay right here."

Tyree came over to him, and took his arm. He was surprised at how tall she was. "Nonsense!" she said. "Everyone's wet tonight. You won't hurt a thing. We'll be more comfortable in there." She led him through the shutter doors into the living room. He felt the warmth of the fire from across the room, like the touch of a warm blanket.

He glanced around the living room. Damn! What the hell kind of gathering had this been? Dozens of brightly colored birds flapped their wings in white iron cages. Bowls of flowers everywhere. The place was filled with candles, and stunk with some exotic incense. Only a few couples sat around, talking quietly. In turn, they looked up and greeted him with a smile and a nod but, he could hardly ignore the fact that the smiles were forced.

Tyree led him to the fireplace hearth, and motioned for him to sit down. After that she pulled over a wooden rocking chair padded with blue cushions, and sat down across from him. Wearily, Ted settled himself on the hearth.

"Earlier tonight," Ted began, "we tried to question the man whose name you gave us. The one you suspected was responsible for the recent killings."

"Barry. Yes. Do you know where he is? Have you found him yet?" Tyree leaned forward eagerly.

"I think you should know that this . . . maniac . . . took out four of our best men, sent at least two of them to the hospital. And he . . . my—" At the thought of Locke, most of his earlier rage returned. He stopped, and took in a deep breath. He wanted to explode, but knew he couldn't. He'd get more cooperation if he controlled his burgeoning temper. He looked over at Tyree. She was leaning forward in the rocking chair, her face gone bloodless, her eyes clouded, as if under their marble-blue brightness some obscure horror lurked.

"He killed my partner," Ted finally said, with great difficulty.

She sucked in her breath, sharply. Then, in a quiet voice she said, "Oh, I'm so sorry." She looked away from him for a moment, gathering herself together. "I really am so terribly sorry."

Ted watched the woman as she tried to compose herself. The way she moved, the way she sat back in the chair, stiff-spined, her forehead pinched into two tiny wrinkles, communicated some deep apprehension.

"I told you he'd be unusually strong." She paused. "I. . . . shouldn't have . . . I feel it's my fault."

"They're *all* strong," Ted said, realizing his voice had gone hard. "The really crazed ones. I need some answers from you. Straight ones. I need to know how the hell—"

"Coffee?" Boo appeared with a tray in his hands. Tyree looked grim as he set it down on the hearth next to them. Boo handed him a mug filled with steaming black coffee. "You take anything?"

Ted shook his head, no. "I came here for answers. You called me the other day. You pulled this psycho's name out of a hat and handed it to me. Now, I want to know where the hell you got it. What made you suspect him? How do you and your friends know this man?" He stopped in mid-tirade, inhaled slowly, and went on. "I've learned some alarming things about his background. What's your part in all of this? Right now, you are a party to this whole damn thing. And after tonight, you may very well be an accomplice to murder!"

Tyree looked up, stared at him, unblinking. Silent. Then she lowered her head and rubbed her eyes with her fingers. Boo handed her a mug of coffee. Boo sat down on the floor beside her, cross-legged, his cup in hand.

Ted glanced around the room. The few people who were left, suddenly turned silent. They sat stony-faced, watching him. "Mrs. Rattigan," Ted raised his voice. *My partner was killed tonight by this maniac.* His name was Steven Locke, and he was just a kid." Ted felt his demeanor slip. He cleared his throat. "Just a young man. He was . . . my friend. And this . . . this monster slit his throat, and then . . . he drank most of his blood. It wasn't enough just to kill him. The motherfucker actually sucked the blood out of him." Ted knew he was being deliberately brutal, and it made him feel good. "Now, I want to know what the hell you and your friends have to do with all this. I want to know how you found out about this Barry Brownstone guy. And why you didn't come forward sooner with this information?"

"Where's Barry? Have you heard about the hospital?" she said, not looking at him, her long fingers twining themselves nervously around her coffee cup."

"He took a dive off the Balboa Pier in this storm. Not much chance he survived. What is this about the hospital?"

"Someone abducted our neighbor from Hoag Memorial. We brought her there earlier today. We think it was Barry who took her."

"When was this?"

"Just a short while ago."

"Couldn't be him, then. Look, all I want right now, are some answers to my questions."

"I don't know what I can tell you, at this point."

"Lady, if I have to I'll have your ass hauled into court, along with all your friends," he countered fiercely. "And if you think that's an idle threat, just try me!"

Tyree set her cup down on the tray, and got up from the rocking chair. She paced a small area in front of Ted. Her fingers nervously fondling a medallion that hung on a chain around her neck. She looked down at Boo seated on the floor. He gave her an odd look, as if cautioning her to be careful.

Finally, she stopped pacing, and in a small voice said, "Detective Bearbower." She gave him a humorless smile. "We have to find Barry. We don't have the luxury of time. If we wait too long, he'll kill this woman. The same way he's been killing other people. He may, in fact, have already done it. Find him first, then we'll answer all your questions. I promise."

"You seriously think he could have survived the fall from the pier, the pounding and the heavy seas?"

Tyree's blue eyes burned under amber lashes. She moved away from him, letting her shoulders slump, and peered out the window at the storm. Then, she straightened up, as if some force of will had begun to flow through her. She turned back. Her eyes held him. For a moment the wind lay still outside, the rain only a muted drumming.

"Yes, Detective. I'm certain he survived. And if we don't find him in time, you're going to find something that will make your worst nightmares seem like a day at Disneyland!"

Chapter Nine

The timbers of the old house shook with a surge of wind. Such a realistic dream, Elizabeth thought. Not only did she hear the wind and the staccato beat of the rain, she smelled the dank odor of the rotting sofa where she lay. Or was this more than just a bizarre dream?

She tried moving her hands, but they lay at her sides like chunks of soft clay. She'd had similar dreams before. Dreams where she'd felt helpless, where she'd tried to yell herself awake. She let out a moan, and heard her voice echo around the dampness of the shadowy room. No, not a dream.

"Shhhhh," someone whispered in her ear. Someone held her, rocked her.

"Andy?" she asked, forcing one of her hands to move.

"No."

"But who . . . ?" Her mind kept letting things slip out and float away. She could barely see in the dim light. Tried to remember what had happened. A stench of damp decay surrounded her. The person holding her had strong hands. She tilted her head to look up at him. Then, he smiled and she remembered. The surfer! The one on the beach below her bedroom window. He'd smiled up at her that night. Then all this *had* to be a dream. Only the thought didn't convince her. A small trickle of fear started in the back of her spine. It traveled downward, growing as it went. Had she really been in hospital? Or had that been part of the dream, too?

She closed her eyes, too fatigued to do anything else. The fear continued to grow. "Where am I?" she whispered.

"You can stay with me until you get well."

"What's wrong with me?" She opened her eyes again and tried to make out the outline of the room. Such a strange place. Cement walls. Odd boxes. A flickering candle on the floor not far away.

"It was my fault," he said. "I'm sorry, Elizabeth."

"I want to go home . . . please. Andy will be worried about me." Hot tears sprang to her eyes. She blinked, blinded by the tears.

"I'm sorry. I didn't want to hurt you. Not you. I just. . . ." He stopped talking and rocked her harder, his hands holding her so tightly she could barely breath. "After all, we're cousins, you and I."

"I'll be okay if you just take me home. Andy will take care of me." She let out a sob. "Please take me home."

"I can't," Barry said. "I can't do that. They would find me. I want you to go away with me. Stay with me. I need you."

Elizabeth felt herself shudder. This was no

dream! This was really happening! Bits and pieces of what had happened to her began to undulate through her mind like a distorted puzzle in disarray. She didn't understand why he kept saying they were cousins. She couldn't put all the pieces together but she knew, without a doubt, that she wasn't dreaming. She squinted into the shadows trying to see if there was a door or window in the room. If her strength would just come back, if he let go of her for even a moment, she might be able to get away from him. Find someone to help her.

"Elizabeth," he said, his voice soft. "Such a pretty name." He stopped rocking her and ran his hands over her arms. "So lovely. It's been so long since I've been this close with anyone." He put his head against her shoulder. "My mother loved you too."

"Your mother?" Elizabeth tried to make some sense out of what he was saying. His grip on her tightened. He let out an abject moan. "What's wrong?" she whispered, feeling her throat go dry with fear.

He didn't answer, but moaned again. He ran his lips across her bare skin, and a delicate shiver rippled through her body. What was he doing? Her heart jerked painfully. Then she felt the edge of his teeth press against her shoulder. She tried to pull away, but his arms closed around her like steel bands.

"I . . . I can't breathe, please . . . you're hurting me." She struggled as hard as she could but his grip only tightened. "Too tight!" she wailed. "You're holding me too tight, I can't breathe!"

"The scent of your skin. So delicious." He raised his head finally, his eyes closed. "Can't . . . mustn't. . . ." He loosened his grip on her then. "Did you know that we're cousins?

"You keep saying that. How . . . how can that be?"

"Mary. Mary was my mother. She sent me pictures of you playing on the beach, while I was in boarding school. You were beautiful even then. About twelve I think."

She pulled away from him slightly, drew in a full breath, and scanned the room again for some way out. Only a small window, up high near the ceiling. Stairs. She could just barely make them out. She must be in a basement or cellar. If the door at the top wasn't locked, and she could make a break for it, she might be able to free herself. But was he alone? Or were there others upstairs. She closed her eyes and shook her head. It was all so jumbled. And she felt so weak. Would she be able to run, even if he did let go of her? She doubted it.

"I'm thirsty," she said, hearing how small her voice was. He began to rock her again. "I'm so thirsty. Is there some water? I . . . must have a fever."

"Thirsty." he said. "Yes. I'm thirsty too. I shouldn't be. Not yet. Not this soon." He pressed his teeth against her shoulder again, harder this time. A small pain stabbed at her and she jerked her shoulder back as far as she could.

"Please, could I have some water," she said, her voice almost a sob. If he would leave her for just a few minutes, she didn't care how weak she was, she'd get herself out of there somehow.

He stopped rocking her and looked down. His eyes a dark, icy blue, reflected gold flicks of light from the candle nearby. "Yes. Of course. You must have some water. I'll get you some." He gently lay her back against the rotting wicker sofa. With one hand, he smoothed her hair off her forehead. "Maybe it will go away."

"What will go away?" she asked, a surge of hope rising in her as he let go of her.

"The agony," he said. "Maybe it will subside. I'll go and get you some water. Everything will be okay. It will pass." He stood up, blocking the light from the candle. He loomed above her, a dark figure.

She began to shake. Her cousin? He was crazy! Somehow, she'd been abducted by a crazy man. She couldn't remember how it had happened, but she was sure his intentions were far from benign. She tried moving her legs, but could only manage to shift them an inch or so. Damn it! She had to find the strength to get herself out of there. She'd only get one chance, of that she was certain.

He turned away from her then, picked up an unlit candle from the cement floor, and moved toward the stairs. "Sleep," he said to her. "Rest. I'll be back in a minute." With that, he bounded up the stairs two at a time, opened the door and disappeared.

A sense of tremendous relief poured over her. She pushed the blanket away and forced her legs over the edge of the sofa. Looking down, she realized she had no clothes. She didn't care. She'd get herself out of there even if she had to run naked through the streets. Her bare feet hit the cement floor and a chill, like a river of ice water, flowed through her veins. With the cold, came a renewed sense of strength.

Above her, the storm surged. A blast of wind caught the door at the top of the stairs, whipping it shut. All the beams in the house around her clattered and jangled like the bones of a old skeleton.

Standing in the floodwater in the alley behind Barry Brownstone's apartment, Ted looked at his watch. It was after one in the morning. The storm had made it almost impossible to get an emergency crew to the peninsula. He needed men. Lots of them. And choppers. If what the Rattigan woman had told him was true, they had very little time to find this Brownstone guy, and the woman he'd abducted. Under his breath he said, "Hell and damnation!" His head gave a throb—the beginning of a monstrous headache. He hadn't eaten in God knew how long, and his stomach felt like a meat grinder.

Finding the two of them appeared an impossible task in the storm. The Rattigan's group of neighbors had given him some ideas of where they might be found, but he had little hope that would help. Besides, he had no choppers, and only a handful of men trying to make a sweep of the entire peninsula. A swat team would arrive in a while, but by the time they got here, it might be too late for the Rosemond woman. Standing there, with the storm flailing about him, he felt, for the first time in his life, completely helpless. He abhorred the feeling. He'd become a policeman because it had given him some sense of control over life. But, he realized it was only an illusion. No one had any control over life. Things just happened. Cars had seatbelts and airbags because people wanted to think they could control things. People jogged. Ate healthy food. Stopped smoking. All because they needed that sense of control. But, in the end, none of it mattered. Earthquakes hit. People died. Planes crashed. Drunk drivers slammed through red lights. Kids with guns shot innocent people. Nothing anyone did made an iota of difference.

You've become a cynic, he told himself. He tugged the collar of his suit around his neck. Not that it helped. He was already soaked to the skin. Well, he sure as heck wasn't going to make any difference in this situation if he just stood there. He had the peninsula blocked off. No one could get on or off. He had three men on the ocean side of the peninsula doing a house-to-house search. On the bay side, he only had two. Both of them were moving toward the mainland. Only about ten houses sat on the other side, toward the point. These were his. Even if his efforts made no difference, he knew he had to do what he could. Part of his nature demanded he try to beat the odds. Try to safeguard as many people as he could.

With that in mind, he began to wade through the floodwater, his legs aching from the overexertion they'd already experienced. His pistol, in its leather holster, pressed almost painfully against his side and gave him a sense, however false, of security. In one hand he carried his favorite shotgun, a Mossberg 500 series. It was an older type gun, but one he felt good about. With its 20-inch barrel and its eight-round magazine, he had some power, at least. In his other hand, he held a heavy-duty flashlight. He would have prefered to have some backup, but that wasn't possible because of the storm. But alone or not, if he did manage to find Brownstone, he wouldn't just wound him this time. He'd make sure the bastard went straight to hell.

In the kitchen of the old Victorian house, HE managed to light the candle and set it on the edge of the sink. He could see well enough to search for a container to carry water. He remembered having seen an empty coffee can there during his last visit. It should still be there, unless other people had been through the house during the interim. It took a moment for his eyes to adjust before he spotted it perched on the window sill over the sink. He reached for it and then turned the faucet handle. Nothing! No water. Then it dawned on him. Of course not! What had he been thinking of? The house had been in probate for a year, maybe longer. The utilities would not be on. Damn!

Poor Elizabeth. She needed water. He'd vowed to make her as comfortable as possible. He stood at the sink, the empty coffee can in his hand, trying to shake the terrible sensations he felt rising inside of him. The agony had no reason to be rearing its grotesque head. Not after he'd just fed on the young policeman, as well as the lovely young lady with the bright clown sweater. He should have some control over it. Yet here it was back, and growing—no, burgeoning was more like it. Just the scent of Elizabeth's skin sent an electric thrill through him, tempted him to sink his teeth into the ambrosial flesh. His appitite would not be appeased by a small bite. He would have to have all of her. Every last morsel. He didn't want to destroy her. But he realized that she could not go with him. Would not go with him. So he would pay homage to her lovely body. It would be a feast for him to remember forever. But first, he would see to her needs. Then he would make certain she felt little, if any pain. But he wanted her afraid. Wanted her to know what was happening. To be a part of it. Her fear would give off a scent that excited him more than any other.

Water, he told himself. First, the water. The storm! Of course! He could fill the coffee can quickly in the downpour. Then, after she'd quenched her thirst, he'd begin. He would do it slowly. This was not a thing to be rushed, as he'd done in the past. He'd spend the rest of the night at it. Perhaps even part of the day. And she would be alive for most of it. It was important for her to know how much her body meant to him. How it would sustain him. She would, in essence, become a part of him. Forever.

Outside in the storm, he held the coffee can, heard the rain drumming against it as it filled. Hurry, he told it. Hurry. Got to get back to her. The agony begin to lick at him. Hot, biting licks that made him wince. Just a little longer, he told himself. Then he would go back in and begin an exquisite feast. He was what he was—a gastronome of the old school.

From somewhere in the distance he heard the

clanging of a bell. A ship in the harbor perhaps. Then he laughed harshly, his voice disappearing against the wind, remembering something he'd once read.

That all-softening overpowering knell
The tocsin of the soul—the dinner bell.

Elizabeth managed to crawl toward the window. It was too high for her to reach, but if she could just move one of the boxes a little closer, she could manage it. Her first instinct had been to go up the stairs, but he might be just outside. If she slipped out through the small window, she could disappear into the darkness. That way, she at least had a chance.

The box felt incredibly heavy. Her arms trembled with weakness. It moved far too slow, less than an inch at a time, but at least it moved. A little further. Just a little. Then she would have to crawl up on it and hope she stood tall enough. She also prayed the window could be opened. He'd been gone quite a while now, and she knew that he might return at any second. She gave the box another push. Her foot caught on something and she tripped, feeling her weakened legs splay out from under her. The cement hit her hard, but she felt no pain. She lifted and moved her leg to see if anything were broken. Everything felt okay. She tried to see what had tripped her, but the candlelight barely reached this far corner of the room. With one hand, she felt around the floor, her fingers touching something hard and cold. Picking it up, it felt extremely heavy.

Something long and white. Moving it out toward the light she examined it. A bone! A long, narrow bone. Actually, two bones attached at one end. And below that was a. . . . she let out a gasp! My God! Oh, my God! she screamed to herself. Attached to the bone were more bones. The bones of a hand. A human hand. She dropped it and heard it clatter to the cement floor. As fast as her weak legs would let her, she got to her feet. Looking around the area where she'd tripped on the bone, she saw others. Some of them had what appeared to be mummified skin attached to them, almost as if—The possibility of what had happened to this person suddenly hit her. What leathered skin remained looked as if it had been gnawed on. She came close to screaming, but managed to stop herself. Survive! She had to survive. No one was going to help her, except herself. Her legs moved faster, she pulled herself up onto the carton box which appeared to be filled with old, musty clothing, and stood to her full height. It was a stretch, but she could reach it. Her fingers frantically clawed at the window, trying to discover how it might open.

With a click, she found that it opened from the top, the window held in place by a small chain on either side. The small curtain was rotted and tore away easily. She pulled on the top edge of the window, putting her full weight on it, and the chains snapped, the window dropping down like a trap door. Now, if only she could pull herself up, and then snake through the small opening. She had to! Her life depended on it. He would be back any minute and if she was still there . . . well, she couldn't let herself think about that. With both hands on the windowsill, she began to pull herself upward. If only she'd gone to a gym, the way she should have to keep in shape, developed her muscles. She'd never done even one pull-up on a bar, or lifted a ten-pound weight. How on earth did she think she could pull her own body weight that far? The muscles in her arms began to burn, but she refused to give up. She lifted her leg and tried to get a foothold on the window sill. No! Impossible! She couldn't do it! The burn in her arms became so intense she had to let go, falling to a heap on the top of the box. The odor of musty clothing filled her nose. She couldn't do it! She lay there, her labored breath coming in great sobs. All she could do was lay there and wait. Wait for the crazy man to come back and kill her. Maybe even do worse things than that. The thought of the bones, the remains of what once was a human being, like herself, got her back to her feet. She reached for the windowsill and with a renewed sense of purpose, slowly, painfully, pulled herself toward the open window, and freedom.

At the first house, Ted found the occupants watching a news special on the storm. The electricity was still working on this portion of the peninsula, and for that he was grateful. It made his job much easier. The husband and wife, and two teenage boys led him on a thorough search of the house and garage.

"Would you call your next door neighbor, to the

southwest," he asked them. "Let them know I'm coming. We'll have a SWAT team here in a while, but in the meantime, we're terribly shorthanded due to the storm. And I'd prefer that no one take me for a robber."

The woman shook her head. "No one lives there. The old Victorian is part of some estate. The owner died last fall. And I think the people on the other side are still in the Caribbean."

Vacant! Ted thought. If this Brownstone guy knew either of these houses were vacant, that's where he'd head. Jesus! he wished he had some backup. But the department had every available man on the street now. And, he couldn't wait. If the guy got wind of the search, he'd find a way to slip by them. Maybe hijack one of the many boats from a dock behind the houses. If he went out through the harbor, they'd never find him. He thanked the couple, warned them to be careful, and headed back out into the storm. Standing knee-deep in floodwater on the sidewalk, he purposely kept his flashlight off. He didn't want to announce his arrival, in case the guy was in either of the two houses. Surprise was his best form of attack. He checked his gun. The magazine was fully loaded. The wind howled, an angry animal baying at the night. Lightning flashed, reflecting off the wetness all around him. Seconds later, thunder rumbled, shaking the windows of the houses around him.

He began to walk slowly, each step an effort as he fought the water. His night vision, as a rule extremely good, had been diminished by the frequent flashes of lightning, which burned the night purple

out of his retina. As he approached the Victorian
house, he heard an odd sound over the storm. It
sounded like rain beating on a tin roof. He squinted
through the dimness trying to make out any possible movement. Then suddenly, he saw him—a lone
man, standing in front of the Victorian house, holding something in his hand. Ted lifted his gun, cradling it under his arm, finger on the trigger. Despite
his damp state, he felt a hot sweat broke out all over
his body. This was probably just someone who lived
around here, outside observing the storm. Or, it
could be the suspect. He had to get close enough to
be certain. With his nerves in such a state, he didn't
want to chance wasting an innocent person.

As he approached, the man turned and looked at
him. With all the rain, Ted couldn't make out the
features. But the guy was the right height, and was
wearing all black, like the suspect. Damn it! he said
to himself. Locke, why aren't you here? Why aren't
you backing me up? I need you buddy. Goddamn!
I *need* you! The memory of his dead partner lying on
the hospital gurney sent a surge of adrenaline
through him. His fingers tingled uncomfortably. If
this turned out to be Brownstone, he'd make sure he
was in too many small pieces to even put on a
gurney! The trigger of his gun felt oily against his
finger.

The man set whatever he was holding down on
the porch of the Victorian house. He didn't move
away, but just stood there. As Ted approached him,
the guy grinned at him. As the man's features came
into focus, he realized, without a doubt, that it was
Brownstone. Gotcha! he told himself. Now, if he

could only hold him there until the SWAT team arrived. But if he made a move, then he blow the bastard to hell and back.

"You found me . . . again," Brownstone said, his voice strangely calm.

"Yes," Ted managed, feeling the rage inside him grow. "And I suggest you stand right where you are. We've got a battalion of men on the way."

The man nodded.

"Hands on your head," Ted growled.

"No." He shoved his hands into his pockets.

Ted gave the shotgun a jerk. "Careful," Ted said. "My finger has a mind of its own." He wanted to pump this maniac full of lead right then and there. Just report that the guy had made a break for it, or had pulled a weapon out of his pocket, and he'd had to gun him down. No one would question it. But he couldn't do it. No matter what this fucker had done, something inside Ted refused to blow him away, unless he made a wrong move. It was funny, the way some men could kill without a second thought, while others had some sort of governor attached.

Lightning flashed, so bright this time that for a split-second it blinded Ted. He moved a step closer to the man, wanting to make sure he didn't make a run for it. Thunder rumbled. A gust of wind put him slightly off balance. But Brownstone simply stood there looking at him.

"How long?" Brownstone asked.

"What?"

"How long before your team or whatever, gets here?"

"Any minute," Ted lied, knowing it would be the

better part of a half hour. At that moment, he hoped Brownstone would make a move. Any move. He could shoot then. Without hesitation. Certainly, the guy would do *something* before long. Then it would be over and he could go home and have a hot shower, and get something to eat. But, of course, that was too simple. Things never worked that way. Or maybe this time they would. Who the hell knew? For a second, he felt like a crazed fool, standing knee-deep in floodwater, lightning and thunder all around him. Wind blowing like a hurricane out of Jamaica. His entire body aching like a bad tooth from all the exertion. Worse than a nightmare. He had the urge to just lie down in the black water and let it seep into his lungs, to sleep, to float out to sea, to forget the whole damn thing and join his wife.

The storm quieted for a moment and over it he heard an odd rattling sound, and then a soft groan. He shifted his glance slightly, trying to make out what it could be. He looked back at Brownstone again, but he gave no indication of hearing anything out of the ordinary. The sound came again, louder this time. He scanned the perimeter of the house, but saw nothing. He scanned again. Something at the corner of the house moved—he couldn't make out what. It moved again. A low keening sound came from its direction. He looked back at Brownstone. The guy continued to stare at him, hands in his pockets. If he had a gun in his pocket he was sure taking his sweet time about using it. He knew he could shoot the guy, if he didn't take his hands out and put them on his head the way he'd been ordered. But that was a tight call. He wasn't sure he could blast a man for that. And he wasn't going to stand there and waste energy arguing with him, especially not without some backup. For all he knew, the guy was planning to shoot him through his pocket. But even through the dark, he could tell that the only things in his pockets were his hands.

The sound came again. Ted edged closer the house. "What the hell?" Ted looked down and at the edge of the house, saw the form of a woman. She made a sound, a small animal sound as she struggled to try and reach him, her head just above the floodwater. "Oh my God!" he said aloud, not meaning to. It had to be the woman that Brownstone had abducted from the hospital. "Stay back!" he yelled at her. "Behind the house. I'll get someone here to help you."

"Please!" the woman pleaded.

"Just stay where you are." Ted looked at Brownstone. The guy made no indication that he saw or heard the woman. "Lean against the house. Keep your head up. We'll take care of you." He glanced at the woman to see if she had heard him. To his relief, she pulled herself back to the side of the house. He could see just the faint outline of her as she lay her head back against the boards of the old house.

When he looked back at Brownstone, the guy was gone. Just like that. What the fuck? He scanned the street in both directions, then between the houses. How in the hell could he slip away so fast? Was he some kind of fucking shadow? Jesus! the Gods were mocking him! *Not twice. Ah, Christ! Not twice in the same night!*

His eyes adjusted to the darkness, and just to the right of him he noticed a movement. He swung around to get a better look. Yes! Someone was running through the tidewater toward the ocean side of the houses. Ted took off, sprinting the best he could in deep water. He wondered if his legs would respond, or crumple under him. The first few yards were torture, but then a spike of adrenaline hit him again, and his muscles responded with a surge of energy. The man ahead of him stopped for a moment, and etched himself sharply against the storm. Ted raised his gun, but the man slipped between two houses before he could fire. He moved after him. The rain blew in metallic strands, whipping at his face. The dark form moved slower. Ted slowed his own pace, caught his breath, felt his heartbeat in his ears—a crescendo of percussion—and prayed it would not give out on him. Then his sense of urgency increased his speed. If he could just get within range, he'd take the guy out. No hesitation this time.

With each step, his shoes sucked at the loose sand and the mass of debris carried in the floodtide. Raw, jagged rocks struck at his feet and legs like fangs. He stopped for a moment, sobbing for breath, watching the man ahead of him. Brownstone turned back to look at him. Ted started up once more. So did Brownstone, who reached a corner, hesitated a moment, then turned down the alley behind the oceanfront houses. Shit! Ted thought, if he moves in and out between houses, he could easily lose him. But when Ted turned the corner, he found the guy only a hundred yards ahead. What the fuck was he up to? Ted wondered. Was he playing cat and mouse? Or did he feel omnipotent—certain that no one had the power to stop him? He lifted his gun again, knowing the distance was too great, but wanting to be ready. Brownstone increased his speed.

Ted jogged along the alley, his heartbeat thundering. The muscles in his legs had turned to molten fire, burning so painfully he had to stop and rub at them. It took precious seconds before he could move again. But Brownstone slowed ahead of him, to almost a stroll.

You son-of-a-bitch! What the fuck are you doing? A shudder of fear struck him. He was alone with this maniac. He had eight shots in his gun, but if they all missed, and in this storm and with this guy's agility, that was a definite possibility, then it was hand-to-hand. And the way he'd killed his victims, Ted was certain he had a blade on him. Several blocks ahead, he could see the flashing lights from the police cruisers that were staked out in back of Brownstone's apartment. If only he could alert them. But even if he fired his gun, he doubted they would hear it over the raging storm. If he tried to reach them and use the cruisers, the guy would certainly give them the slip again. No, he was going to stay on this guy's ass until he caught him. He owed Locke that much.

He picked up speed, and pulled himself within a few yards of the guy. The man didn't turn around. Ted moved his gun into position and aimed. Okay, you fucker. That's it. Suddenly, his left foot hit a pile of debris in the surging water. He lost his balance, tried to compensate with his other foot, but his weight pulled him forward. The unexpected motion dislodged the shotgun from his hand. He made a desperate grab for it, and missed. It made only a small impression on the water's surface before disappearing. Unwillingly, he followed the gun, pitching face forward into the black water, letting out a piercing cry as he fell. His bulk propelled him against the ground. Underwater, his nose and mouth ground painfully against sand and rock. It took an extreme effort to push himself into a sitting position. He sat there, up to his chest in water, coughing, gasping for breath, knowing he could not possibly get to his feet. His legs were shot. He rubbed at his bruised face with the sleeve of his coat, clearing his eyes for a moment, fixing his sight on Brownstone who stood only a few yards away, his back turned, not moving. Suddenly, a dreadful crackling noise split the air. He swung his head around, trying to locate the cause of it. It took him a moment, but when he found it, every nerve in his body jangled. The live wire! No one had been there to fix it. Goddamn Edison Company!

"Ah shit!" he roared, suddenly realizing he'd been suckered. Like a sheep! Like a goddamn fucking sheep, he'd followed this guy. And it had been a deadly mistake! Just a little over his head, a cascading sweep of fiery sparks rained down from the loose high-tension wire. The guy had lured him into the alley where the live wire had lost its lease on the fence and was now flailing about like a black viper hissing flames from its mouth. He sat motionless in the swirling water. Fuck the Edison Company! Fuck the police department! He'd called in more than a half hour ago, and they still hadn't turned off the power or sent out someone to fix the damn thing. They hadn't even barricaded the street. Jesus Christ! Right now, all he needed was a slight ebbing of the wind and he'd be cooked!

Brownstone stopped, swiveled around, and gave him an odd look. His icy eyes were lit by bright sparks that danced from the end of the treacherous wire. His mouth was a strange, black smile in a white face.

How the hell had this guy known about the wire? Or was it just a coincidence he'd taken this route? At this point, it really didn't matter. He'd had it. Fear knotted itself in the middle of his gut. He couldn't stand up, no matter how hard he tried. And even if he could, where would he go? Water was everywhere. He felt the floodtide surge, lift him slightly, then release him. The rain eased somewhat. Above him, the wire whipped about, made a crackling sound, shooting out white-hot flares that illuminated the area like phosphorescent fireworks. He was a huge huddle of shivering flesh and icy bones—aching with cold, aching from exertion. Then, to his horror, the wind suddenly calmed. The wire stopped dancing and dropped.

The next moment, Brownstone was standing over him—a dark, evil bird peering down at its prey. He's not even afraid of the fucking high-tension wire! Ted realized. *It's going to cook us both!* He let out a wild laugh.

"We're going together, buddy!" Ted yelled, watching the wire plunge toward the water. "Just you and me, boiled in this soup!"

Suddenly, a pair of iron-hard arms grabbed him around the belly as Brownstone lifted him up. Ted could feel the metal-like muscles in the guy's arms bulging. With a loud roar, he strode toward the edge of the alley, then gave him a tremendous boost. It took him a second to realize that he was airborne, tumbling, clawing at the air with his arms. He let out a yell that echoed back in his own ears. A moment later, he slammed into the top of a small wooden shed, the breath knocked out of him. He made a gagging sound, pulled hard at the air with his lungs, gagged again, and drew in a breath. His hands groped for purchase on the shed, found it, and with pain screaming from every part of his body, managed to straddle the roof. He was battered and bruised, but clear of the floodwater.

He wiped the moisture out of his face, and looked down to where Brownstone stood. The end of the live wire had buried itself deep in the water. The water surrounding the guy turned into a bubbling cauldron. Rays of white light shot out around him like laser beams. It was the most bizarre sight he'd ever seen. He watched with horrified, fascinated eyes as Brownstone let out a high, piercing scream, buckled at the knees, and began sinking into the water. The guy's eyes were open, but all Ted could see were the whites—little rolling marbles of alabaster. Odd little puffs of grizzled smoke curled from the man's face and hair. He smelled the nauseous sweet odor of burning flesh, and felt his stomach retch. He'd wanted the guy dead, but this . . . this wasn't what he'd had in mind. A clean shot, he thought, would have been easier for him to live with. One moment Brownstone was there, raking at empty air with desperate fingers. The next he'd vanished, swallowed by a rush of murky floodwater.

Off to his right, Ted saw a bright flash—a transformer box blowing. The water below him stopped bubbling. The power was apparently now out over the entire peninsula. Barry's electrocution had done what the Edison Company hadn't—turned off the juice. He slumped forward, resting on the top of the shed. He waited, frozen to the small roof by fear and fatigue. For a few minutes he fully expected Brownstone to rise up out of the water like Lazarus rising from the dead. But nothing stirred. The wind calmed. The rain turned to a light shower. When the fear began to recede, he realized something startling. Here he was, safe on the roof of the shed. With tremendous effort, Brownstone had put him there. Had plucked him out of the water a split-second before the wire hit. Had he done it on purpose? Was it possible that someone who had killed so many people, had in the end, *saved* someone's life? With his strength, Brownstone could just as easily have put himself on the shed, and left him there to boil in the water. If he'd done that, the chances were that he would have gotten away, gone somewhere else, and continued his gruesome slaughters. Why had he not done that? He tried to reason it out, but felt so tired, his mind wouldn't function. He'd deal with it later.

From down the alley, he caught the movement of

a police cruiser which had been parked behind Barry's apartment. They'd obviously seen the flare from the wire hitting the water, and the transformer blow. The wind remained calm; the rain dwindled to a fine mist. It was almost as if the storm had dissipated with the killer's death. He glanced up at the sky. Small patches of stars shimmered through tiny breaks in the great hanging cloud overhead. The cloud stretched across the sky like a dark rainbow. He drew in a long breath.

A few minutes later, a black-and-white cruiser pulled alongside him. A young policeman in uniform rolled down the window and said, "We saw a commotion going on down here, sir. What's happening? What the hell are you doing up there . . . sir?"

Ted laid his head down on the roof of the shed and barked a dry laugh. "I didn't want to get my feet wet," he said, then sat up and swung his legs over the side of the shed. "Give me a hand, will you?"

The young man got out and waded through the water toward him. "Good thing you managed to get up there. You'd a been boiled like a lobster when that wire hit."

"Call the other car at the Brownstone place," Ted said, letting the man help him off the shed. "We've got a body here."

"Ahh, yes sir. A body?"

"Just tell 'em, and get 'em here." Fatigue hit Ted with an unbearable pain. "Then you and I have to go to the ocean side of the peninsula and pick up a young woman. ASAP."

They found the woman where Ted had last seen her, propped against the side of the old Victorian house. When she saw him, she lifted her arms toward him, like a young child, and somewhere he found the strength to lean down and take her in his arms, and carry her to the patrol car. Inside, he took the patrolman's jacket and put it around her. She didn't speak, just leaned into him and closed her eyes.

"Now young man," Ted said to the patrolman. "See if you can get us off this fucking peninsula. She needs to get to the hospital, and I'm wet, frozen, and starving to death!"

"Yes, sir!" the patrolman said.

"Fast."

"Yes, sir. It's been quite a night, hasn't it?"

Ted leaned his head back against the seat. He choked back an hysterical laugh. There wasn't an inch of his body that didn't hurt. "You have no idea," he finally mumbled. "No idea at all!"

Ted went home just long enough to get out of his wet clothes and stand in a hot shower for ten minutes. Then he put on a pair of jeans, a T-shirt and some tennis shoes. His muscles screamed so painfully, he couldn't bear the thought of wearing a suit, tie and heavy shoes.

His first inclination had been to find an all-night diner and order everything on the menu. But then he realized, with a certain dismay, that he wasn't the least bit hungry. Not having a roaring appetite, felt foreign to him. He tried to work up enough enthusiasm to stop and pick up a pineapple Danish, or some brioche, but couldn't. Instead, he went into work and spent the early morning hours at his desk typing up his case report. Barry Brownstone had been responsible for the death of one of the Duff girls, the attack on her sister, the man they'd found on the boat, and the woman near the Pavilion on the peninsula. And, in his estimation, he was also involved in seven other unsolved cases in the county, if not more. He didn't even want to think about the out-of-county cases. And, then the worst part of it all—his partner.

The image of Steven Locke's sandy hair and freckled nose haunted him every time he closed his eyes. He wondered if he would ever be able to sleep again. Why the hell hadn't it been *him* instead of a youth like that? With so much ahead of him, so much undone. Ted swallowed a painful knot in the back of his throat. He still had to call Locke's mother in Connecticut, and then help make arrangements for a memorial service. But that would have to wait until he could talk about it. He didn't want to put it in words yet. That made it final.

He slapped the completed report down on his desk. Only, to his mind, it was far from complete. For his own satisfaction, he would talk with the Rattigan woman later in the morning. She had a lot of hard questions to answer. Without her and that odd little group gathered at her house, it might have taken them a long time, if not forever, to discover the killer's identity. But, he needed to know her connection to the guy, how she found out about him, and why she hadn't blown the whistle on him sooner. He wasn't comfortable with the way things had gone, although he should be considering the killer was lying in the morgue. Still, he was used to relying on his investigation. What had happened to all his neat little pile of facts? Two and two used to make four. In this case, things didn't fall into neat little categories. But then, he supposed it was that way with a lot of cases. He just wasn't used to it. Newport now had its own Jeffrey Dahmer—a nefarious distinction. He guessed it really didn't matter how they'd stopped him. The fact that they had, was all that counted.

He sat there a few moments trying not to think about one thing in particular. And, as usual, that one thing keep invading his mind. Why had Barry Brownstone plucked him out of the water and saved his life. Had he intended to kill him? No, that didn't make sense. The guy had actually thrown him a good three feet to the shed. Ted knew it would take incredible strength for anyone to do that, considering his weight. No, the guy had put him on the shed on purpose. An insane killer who had taken numerous other lives without a thought, suddenly did an about-face and not only saved one, but lost his own in the process. He'd seen the live wire. He'd made a superhuman effort to help someone else to safety. It made no sense. His questions had no answers. He'd always believed that a killer remained a killer. This threw him off balance. No one could crawl inside anyone else's brain and know how it felt to be them. A pity that. He shook his head, and felt the beginning of a headache. Well, this one he'd earned!

He picked up the completed report and held it in

his hand. Fuck the Rattigan woman! The whole thing was over and done with. He didn't want to know anything more. He dropped the report off in the Captain's office and headed for home. After he slept, he would sit down and write out his resignation. There was a quaint little cabin in the mountains north of San Diego that he and Sylvia had looked at once, with the idea of retiring there. He'd call some real estate people down there, and see if something like it was on the market. Maybe he'd seriously think about opening a gourmet cafe for the tourists who tramped through that area during apple season. The only thing he wouldn't do was police work. The idea of coping with another Barry Brownstone gave him the green willys. Maybe, up there in the clear air, with the smell of pine trees, he would be able to forget. Maybe the empty space that Sylvia had left, wouldn't ache so much. Maybe Locke's face wouldn't continue to haunt him. Maybe the memory of Barry Brownstone lifting him out of the water would fade away. Maybe.

He took a look at his watch. To his surprise, the damn thing was still running! He'd worn it through all that water and muck and the second hand was clicking away like crazy. He started to laugh, then stopped short. It wasn't funny. Something essential in him had changed, and that felt scary.

Outside, he walked down the steps of the police station, wishing he had even a tinge of appetite for breakfast. If he'd been his usual self, he'd go out and find some really good eggs Benedict, French Roast coffee, and a plate of home fries. Always before, with a meal like that in his stomach, he would have felt like a sovereign.

Below him, down the hill, he caught a glimpse of the bay and the ocean. Already he could see little white dots of sails. It had turned into a beautiful morning after such a fierce storm. The air smelled sweet. He thought about his life, the work he'd done. The people who had died. The night he'd just been through. He took in a deep breath. It was a damn strange world, wasn't it? But then, after all, it was all he had. He'd learn to live with it. Somehow.

Elizabeth slipped up behind Andy as he sat working at his desk, and put her arms around his neck. He responded by giving her a playful little bite on her arm.

"Hungry?" she asked.

"Yes, for you!" He gave her a mock growl, pulled her around onto his lap, and kissed her.

"Ahhh," she sighed. "That's nice. Listen, you've been working all morning, and so have I. Why don't we . . . umm . . . abandon all this, and . . . go to bed?"

"Get some sleep?"

"Sure. We can do that, too." She laughed.

"You seem to be feeling extra good. I'm glad. So much has happened in such a short time, I was afraid it would take you a long time to recover." He touched her cheek. "It's nice to see you so much better, so fast."

"I still miss Judy," she said, the corners of her

mouth turned down. "But she would have been the first to tell us to *get on with it!* You know that."

Andy nodded. "Yes. I can hear her now. She would have been delighted with what we've managed so far."

She leaned over and kissed him, letting her lips linger on his, tasting the wonderful muskiness of his skin. Gently, she explored the inside of his mouth with her tongue—the velvet wetness of it making every inch of her feel deliciously sensitive.

"You're not sorry, are you?" Andy said finally breaking off the kiss. "You do think we made the right decision, don't you?"

"Yes. Of course we did."

"Good. I just wanted to make sure." He slipped his hand under her sweater, found she wasn't wearing a bra. She giggled naughtily. At the feel of her naked warm breast, she heard him take in a sharp, quick breath. "Ah, Jesus!" he moaned. "You feel so damn good!" He ran his finger lightly over the satin of her nipple. It hardened at his touch, and she shivered expectantly. He lifted her sweater, cupped her breast in his hand, and gently sucked on the erect nipple. She let out a moan at the incredible sensation. God, how she wanted him! She wanted him to pull off her sweater and pants, and lay her down on the carpet, spread her legs, and force himself inside her.

She was continually amazed at how sensuous they had become with each other. Such a nice change from the way they'd been just a short while ago. Tyree had told her the drug would do that. And she'd been right in spades! "Come on," she said, hearing her voice go husky with desire. "Let's do it right here. To hell with going to bed!"

Without hesitation, he pulled her sweater off over her head, then deftly undid her pants, stood her up, and peeled them down in one easy motion. Then he slipped off his warm-ups and, instead of taking her on the floor, he made her straddle his lap, sliding her down on his now-erect penis, slowly, teasingly, the pleasure rippling through her body as he entered her.

"Oh, God, Andy!" she cried as she felt him moving hotly inside her. "I didn't dream it could be this exquisite. Don't stop. Please, don't ever stop!"

He laughed softly, and continued moving her up and down in a gentle, sensuous rhythm. She felt him all the way inside her now, and gasped at the ecstasy. "Maybe," she whispered, feeling herself writhing against him, grasping all the pleasurable sensations she could. "Maybe this time. . . ."

"What?" he whispered.

"Ummmm, nothing," she said.

But later, as she felt Andy's seed erupt inside her, she knew. *Knew that this time, without a doubt, their love-making would start a child.* A child, born of their love. But also, a child who would have tremendous advantages. Who would have a remarkable start in life.

Afterward, Andy took her hand as they walked up the stairs to the bedroom to nap. Aunt Mary's Germantown clock struck twelve noon. Elizabeth yawned. She'd completed a lovely painting already this morning, and Andy had managed a remarkable amount of pages of his novel. After they napped, they could work a while longer. Then, it would be a busy evening, as usual.

Tonight the group would meet at Tyree's for Bloody Marys, laced with a generous amount of Sunshine, and some stimulating conversation. She would show them all her latest paintings, and Andy would fill them in on plans for his next novel. Right at that moment though, with a pale November sun reflecting off the ocean, and the great rumbling of surf in her ears, all she wanted to do was climb into Aunt Mary's old Baroque bed and sleep, and dream about all the wonderful things she and Andy would accomplish in the years to come.

Tyree sat in the chair by the window where she could look out on the beach. She gave the Bloody Mary in her hand a stir with a piece of celery. She looked over at Mable and Sarah on the sofa. Mable was busy folding tiny paper birds to use for tonight's get-together. Sarah had her gold-rimmed glasses on the end of her nose, carefully crocheting something in soft, white cotton yarn. Boo stood behind the bar, stirring a pitcher of Marys, humming to himself. She enjoyed having him home more often, now that they'd struck a deal with Andy and Elizabeth. A sweetheart deal. One which benefited everyone.

"She'll make such a wonderful mother," Sarah said.

What's that?" Tyree asked.

"Elizabeth. She'll make a wonderful mother. And

ust think, she'll be the first Sunshine member to
ave a child."

"We're certain, aren't we, that it will be okay?"
Mable said.

Boo stopped stirring and looked up. "Of course
we're certain. We've used Sunshine in our lab experiments with animals over and over. To date, all
of the next generation, as well as all those after that,
ave been influenced in remarkable ways. Nothing
untoward in any of them. And, the offspring never
ave to take the drug. The effects are permanent."

Tyree took a sip of her drink then said, "We
would never consider using it, if we weren't cer-
ain."

Sarah put down her crocheting. "It's just that
. . well, we certainly wouldn't want something
orrible to happen, the way it did with Barry."

"Barry's problem was entirely different."

"Yes," Sarah said. "I suppose it was."

"Well," Tyree said, lifting her glass. "Here's to
Sunshine One, and our little group of mental levia-
hans. And, here's to the future. Who knows what
miracles we can accomplish."

"Yes," Boo said, pouring a Mary for himself.
"Who knows?"

Tyree looked away from them, and out the window where the restless sea pounded against the sand.
She caressed the edge of her glass with her fingertips,
smiling to herself. At that moment, the whole world
seemed luminous, and burgeoning with remarkable
possibilities. Their little group might just put God to
shame, with their accomplishments.

MAKE SURE YOUR DOORS AND
WINDOWS ARE LOCKED!
SPINE-TINGLING SUSPENSE FROM PINNACLE

SILENT WITNESS (677, $4.
by Mary Germano
Katherine Hansen had been with The Information Warehouse
long to stand by and watch it be destroyed by sabotage. At f
there were breaches in security, as well as computer malfuncti
and unexplained power failures. But soon Katherine started rece
ing sinister phone calls, and she realized someone was stalking
willing her to make one fatal mistake. And all Katherine could
was wait. . . .

BLOOD SECRETS (695, $4.
by Dale Ludwig
When orphaned Kirsten Walker turned thirty, she inherited
mother's secret diary—learning the shattering truth about
past. A deranged serial killer has been locked away for years
will soon be free. He knows all of Kirsten's secrets and will fol
her to a house on the storm-tossed cape. Now she is trapped al
with a madman who wants something only Kirsten can give hi

CIRCLE OF FEAR (721, $4.
by Jim Norman
Psychiatrist Sarah Johnson has a new patient, Diana Smith. A
something is very wrong with Diana . . . something Sarah
never seen before. For in the haunted recesses of Diana's tormen
psyche a horrible secret is buried. As compassion turns into ob
sion, Sarah is drawn into Diana's chilling nightmare world. A
now Sarah must fight with every weapon she possesses to save th
both from the deadly danger that is closing in fast!

SUMMER OF FEAR (741, $4.
by Carolyn Haines
Connor Tremaine moves back east to take a dream job as a rid
instructor. Soon she has fallen in love with and marries Clay St
ner, a local politician. Beginning with shocking stories about
first wife's death and culminating with a near-fatal attack
Connor, she realizes that someone most definitely does not w
her in Clay's life. And now, Connor has two things to fear: a
ranged killer, and the fact that her husband's winning charm
mask a most murderous nature . . .

*Available wherever paperbacks are sold, or order direct from
Publisher. Send cover price plus 50¢ per copy for mailing
handling to Penguin USA, P.O. Box 999, c/o Dept. 17M
Bergenfield, NJ 07621. Residents of New York and Tennes
must include sales tax. DO NOT SEND CASH.*